In the Shadow of the Queen

Kim Stokely

Book Layout ©2017 BookDesignTemplates.com
Map by Michael Weir www.patreon.com/levilagann
Book cover design by Bespoke Book Covers
In the Shadow of the Queen/ Kim Stokely. -- 1st ed.
ISBN 978-1720389071

Cast of Major Characters

◊ Historical Figure
* Fictional Character
+ Based on a Historical Figure About Whom Little is Known

◊Salome Alexandra — Queen of Judea 76 B.C. - 67 B.C.

+Anna — Mentioned in Luke 2:36-38.

◊Antipater — Chief counselor to John Hyrcanus. A first generation Jewish convert from Idumaea

◊Aristobulus II— Second son of King Alexander Jannai and Queen Salome Alexandra. Born circa 100 B.C. Died 49 B.C.

*Caleb — Former soldier, now tailor for the Hasmonean nobility

* Daniel— Anna's brother

◊ John Hyrcanus II — Eldest son of King Alexander Jannai and Queen Salome Alexandra. Born circa 100 B.C. Died 30 B.C.

*Judith — Lev's mother

*Lev — Scribe to Antipater

*Malachi — Lev's father and a rabbi with his own school

*Miriam — Anna's mother

+Phanuel — Anna's father. Mentioned in Luke 2:36.

◊ Queen Selene (Cleopatra) — 135/130 -69 B.C. (Monarch of Syria 82—69 B.C.)

◊ Shimeon bar Shetach — Brother and counselor to Queen Salome Alexander

* Ruth — Tamar's daughter

* Tamar — Caleb's sister and a seamstress in the palace

* Tova — Anna's best friend.

*Ziva — Queen Salome's maid

To my sisters
Vicky and Lorraine
Women of faith, prayer warriors,
my confidants and friends

IMPORTANT POLITICAL PARTIES

Maccabees— Meaning hammer, it is the name given to the family of a priest named Mattathias and his five sons because they struck their enemies like hammers. (The name was originally given to Mattathias's son, Judah.) Mattathias led a revolt in 167 B.C. against the Seleucids who ruled Judea. It took two decades to gain their freedom. Mattathias's son, Simon, was the first to assume the roles of King and High Priest.

Hasmoneans— From Mattathias's family name, Asamonaios. The Hasmonean family ruled Judea from approximately 142 B.C. to 63 B.C.

Pharisees— Primarily made up of scribes and the merchant classes. They believed in oral laws and rabbinical traditions as well as the 613 Laws of the Mosaic covenant. They did not believe the High Priest should serve as King. This put them in conflict with the Hasmoneans.

Ptolemaic Dynasty— Egyptian/Greek Empire founded after the death of Alexander the Great. Ptolemy I took the throne circa 305 B.C. The fourteen kings were all named Ptolemy. The seven queens were named Cleopatra.

Sadducees— Primarily made up of the priests and nobles class. They followed the 613 Laws of Mosaic Covenant. Open to assimilating other cultures, especially Greek and Roman ideas and advancements.

Seleucids— Empire founded by Seleucus after the death of Alexander the Great They ruled much of Asia Minor, Syria, Persia, and Babylonia from 312 to 64 B.C.

AUTHOR'S NOTE

I began this story with the idea it would be a short novella. After all, the story of Anna the Prophetess found in the Bible is only four verses long. Then I started researching the time period of her life, roughly 89 B.C. to 4 B.C. The history I uncovered lit my author's imagination and so, here you have not the story of Anna the Prophetess at the Temple, but Anna, the young girl and witness to the reign of the only legitimate queen of Israel. It is a story of courage, love, corruption and ambition. And it is only the beginning.

I read many different books that gave me some, but not all, of the details I needed to write this story. The idea that women were allowed to attend schools under Queen Salome came from Queen Salome: Jerusalem's Warrior Monarch of the First Century B.C.E. by Kenneth Atkinson (*McFarland & Company, Inc., Publishers 2012) Atkinson stated that Shimeon bar Shetach probably spearheaded the program. Because he had been in exile in Egypt, I extrapolated that the Pharisees there would also have been tolerant of educating women.*

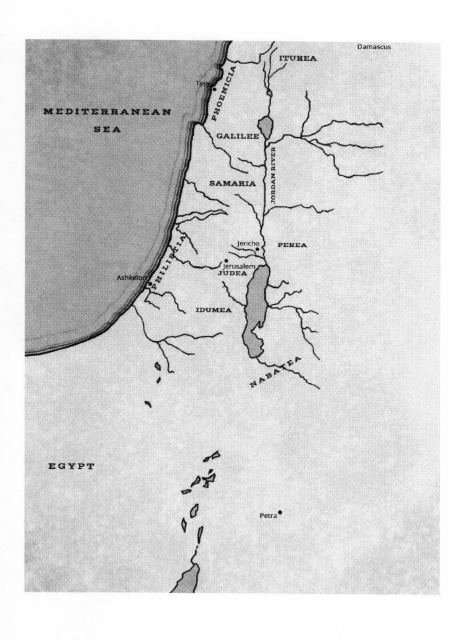

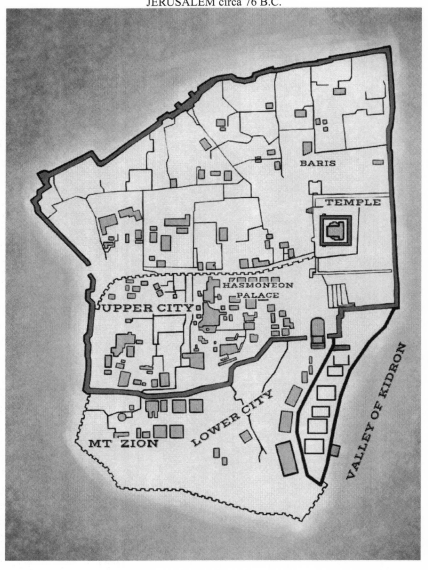

There is a time for everything,
And a season for every activity under heaven.
A time to be born, and a time to die,
A time to plant and a time to uproot,
A time to kill and a time to heal,
A time to tear down and a time to build,
A time to weep and a time to laugh,
A time to mourn and a time to dance...
A time to love and a time to hate,
A time for war and a time for peace.

– Ecclesiastes 3:1-4, 8

BOOK ONE
Circa 76 B.C.

A time to plant and a time to uproot

Chapter 1

Early summer, 76 B.C.

At thirteen, Anna had seen a royal parade before, but never one this grand. The dry, arid wind from the east did little to cool her as she stood in awe, shoulder to shoulder with all of Jerusalem, to watch the procession. Sunlight gleamed off the polished breast plates of the palace guards. The bright light burned her eyes, but she could not turn away. The sound of the horses' hooves clopping on the stone road, the jangling of their bridles, and the cries of those that followed behind, all had her transfixed. All of this because Alexander Jannai, the king and High Priest of Judea, was dead.

The king's body rested on the bier being pulled by six chestnut horses. Soldiers surrounded it as the entourage made its way to the royal tomb. As they marched solemnly by, Anna's mind kept wandering to how this man, who had caused so much pain to so many in the past, would rot away to bone and dust. Then those bones would be placed in a box to rest with those of his fathers. All that power. All that wealth. And what would be left?

Her older brother, Daniel, whispered under his breath as the soldiers passed, "Praise Elohim, the monster is dead."

"Quiet, you fool," their father chastised. "We may yet be in danger."

Anna shivered at the fear she saw in her father's eyes. The king had ordered eight hundred Pharisees, including two of her uncles, crucified. She had only been a baby when it happened, but her parents still wept when they recounted the story.

The wind blew Daniel's dark hair across his face. "They say his wife Salome will be his successor, and she has been far more reasonable to us than her husband."

"She reigns now as a Hasmonean. She will side with the Sadducees," Father argued. His brown eyes flashed. "Just as Alexander did."

"Have faith, Father." Daniel smiled even as a group of paid mourners passed by, wailing and tearing at their clothes. "God has not forgotten us." He reached out to pull Anna to him. "Perhaps Queen Salome will have a heart like our Anna, pure and honest."

She wrapped her arms around her brother's waist, hoping her embrace would show him how much she appreciated his words.

Father placed his hand on her head. "If only I could believe it to be true." He glanced over at Daniel. "Will you come to the house?"

"Malachi will be expecting all his students back tonight."

Anna frowned. "Can you come home for a little while? To see Mother?"

A wave of sadness passed over Daniel's face. "How is she?"

Father put his arm around his shoulder. "Some days good. Some days bad. We take each as a blessing from the Lord."

Anna walked ahead of the men as they wove through the swarming streets of Jerusalem, up the hillside and toward their home near the base of the Temple Mount. The bleached clay and stone of the houses rose around her like a maze, but one she easily navigated. Weaving through the still milling crowds, she thought about what Daniel had said. Salome Alexandra, widow of the last two kings, would be their successor. A woman would rule Judea.

Her heart raced with excitement. She had never known any woman to be more than a wife and mother. Yet Salome would speak and be heard. She would enact laws and edicts that men would follow. The idea was totally foreign even though Anna's father often told her of the powerful women God had used in the past. Deborah, who helped lead an army against the Canaanites, was to be emulated. Athaliah, who had usurped the throne from her grandson, was to be cursed. *What kind of queen will Salome be? And what will it mean for me?*

A haze of dust and dirt, kicked up by the throng of people, settled over the streets as Anna continued to push toward home. She wiped sweat off her forehead and coughed lightly to clear her throat. The world was changing, and first to change would be Jerusalem, the center of their faith. What future would she have here?

"Anna!" Her friend Tova ran up and embraced her. The mantle she wore on her head could not contain the mass of light brown curls that fell down her back. Anna often wished such curls would appear in her hair. "Did you see the king's bier? Was it not magnificent?"

"I saw."

Although shorter than her, Tova was older by half a year. They turned off the main road and down a narrower street bordered on both sides by the smaller, one-story clay houses of the laborers and merchants. She and Tova had lived on this same road all their lives, playing together with sticks and leather balls as some younger children did now, while mothers and grandmothers gathered in their doorways to discuss the funeral procession. Older men stood off to themselves, arguing about the upheaval Alexander's death would cause throughout the land.

Anna would have liked to eavesdrop on those conversations, but Tova continued to prattle. "Did you see the size of the mourning party? Do you think they were all from his family, or did the queen pay for them all?"

"My father says they were paid."

"And the finery on the cart," the shorter girl mused with wonder. "All that gold? It must have cost a fortune!"

Anna agreed. "Money that could better have been spent on refurnishing the temple."

Tova's full lips pouted. "Why must you be so practical? Can you not appreciate the beauty of the spectacle?"

"I am sorry." Anna sighed. "It is the curse of being the daughter and the sister of scribes. It is all my father and Daniel can talk about lately." She pulled her friend closer to her side. "I have learned something else today, something you may not know."

Tova's eyes sparkled. "What is that?"

"Queen Salome plans to rule in her husband's place."

Tova stopped. "But what of her sons?"

"I do not know." Anna shrugged. "Perhaps she feels they are too inexperienced to rule." She pulled her friend along. "Come, I must get home to Mother."

"A queen over Judea . . . ." Tova's face mirrored Anna's thoughts.

"It is an exciting time to be alive, is it not?" *If a woman can rule men, what could Tova and I accomplish in our lifetimes?* Anna stopped in front of her house. "I must tell my mother all about the procession before Father and Daniel get home."

Tova's face lit up. "Daniel is coming?"

"Only for a moment, to see our mother."

Her friend's shoulders sagged.

"He is only concerned with his studies for now. He notices only what is written in a scroll or spoken by his teacher."

"I know." Tova sighed. "Perhaps I should pay someone to draw my likeness on parchment. Maybe then he would realize he should marry me."

Anna laughed as she gave her friend a hug. "I am sorry he cannot see what a prize you are."

Tova's thin arms squeezed her hard. "Tell him you saw me today. Remind him that I exist!"

"I will." Anna pushed open the wooden door to her home. Her eyes struggled to see in the dim light.

"Ahhhhh," her mother wailed from the corner where she lay. "Shut it!"

Anna took one last breath of dusty air before stepping inside and closing the door behind her. She crossed the cool dirt floor and knelt down to where her mother lay in the corner. "Your head still hurts?"

"A knife between my eyes." She whimpered. "Will it never end?"

"Should I go to the well and fetch you some cool water?"

She groaned. "There is no need. It will only be warm by the time you bring it back."

Anna poured her a cup of watered wine and brought it to her pallet. "Here, Mother. Perhaps this will help."

She sat up to sip the drink Anna held to her lips. "Nothing will help."

"Not even the news that Daniel is coming?"

She laid a frail hand on Anna's arm. "Truly?"

"Yes. He found Father and me among the crowd. They should be here any moment."

Mother's cheeks flushed. "Perhaps I feel better after all. I could make us dinner."

"He cannot stay. He is only coming to see you." Anna placed the cup on the floor then stood to grab the comb from the niche in the stone wall. "Let me fix your hair before he arrives."

"Yes, yes." Mother nodded. "I cannot have him seeing me like this."

Anna pulled the ivory-toothed comb gently through her mother's graying wisps. The comb had been a wedding gift from a wealthy aunt, and it was her mother's prized possession. "The funeral bier was something to behold, Mother. Gold and fine linens covered it. There must have been a hundred soldiers on horseback." She spoke softly as she worked, hoping her story would help her mother forget the pain in her head even more than her brother's visit.

Sunlight poured in as her father opened the door. He stepped aside to let Daniel inside. "Look who has come to visit us, Miriam."

Her mother shielded her eyes from the brightness and swatted Anna's hand to make her stop combing. "My son!"

Daniel lowered his tall frame and knelt at her side. "How are you, Mother?"

Anna put the treasured comb back on its shelf then set about making dinner. It would be a light meal, as the priests had called for a fast in honor of the High Priest's death. Though her father refused to mourn the evil man, the markets were closed and any cooking fire might be spotted by the palace guards and reported. In preparation, she had made two loaves of bread the previous day, as well as goat cheese and hummus. They would not be feasting tonight, but they would not be fasting either. She sliced the bread as Daniel talked with their mother, telling her all about his studies with Malachi, one of the chief Pharisees.

"The rabbi has said I am one of his brightest students." Daniel stuck out his chest in exaggerated bravado.

"Of course you are." Her mother beamed, her face showing the first signs of health in several days. "You were always a smart child."

Someone knocked on the door and Anna quickly hid the bread and cheese beneath a cloth in the corner. She sat down in front of it as her father opened the door.

"*Shalom*, Phanuel." A deep, resonate voice spoke in greeting. "Is Daniel here?"

"*Shalom*, Lev." Father stood aside. "Come in. Come in."

Lev, taller than her father, ducked his head as he came through the doorway. Anna tried to keep her eyes downcast, as any modest girl would do, but her gaze strayed up several times. Lev was a beautiful man. Eyes the color of honey. Brown hair, thick with curls. As he was not much older than Daniel's twenty years, his beard was not as full as an older man's, but it framed his strong chin well. She felt heat rush to her cheeks as Lev smiled at her frank stare. She quickly looked to the dirt floor.

"*Shalom*, Anna."

"*Sh-Sh-Shalom*," she answered, humiliated by her stuttering.

"Miriam." Lev stepped toward her mother's pallet. "It is good to see you sitting up. Did the herbs my mother sent help you?"

Miriam nodded. "They were a blessing."

"She will be glad to hear it. I am sure she will make you more." He gestured toward Anna. "Send your daughter to our house sometime this week to pick them up."

Anna tried to hide the smile that threatened to explode across her face.

Phanuel *hrumphed*. "We would not want to be a bother to your family."

Her happiness faded as rapidly as it had appeared. But then Lev spoke again. "Anna is never a bother. And it makes my mother happy to help others."

Daniel leaned forward and kissed his mother on the cheek. "I will pray for your health. As I always do."

The flush of her cheeks paled as Daniel stood. "It was good to see you, my son."

"I will be home again, on the Sabbath."

Lev chuckled, a musical sound that thrilled Anna's ears. "My father is a hard task master. Only the death of the king and the command of God can give us more than an hour away from our studies."

"Send him our best regards," Phanuel said as he opened the door.

"I shall." Anna lifted her eyes in time to see Lev smile at her. "Good night, Anna. I will tell my mother to expect your visit."

Happiness filled her, especially when her voice did not stammer as she answered, "Thank you."

Mother laid down as soon as the door shut behind them. Her father sighed, glancing between the two of them. His gaze rested on Anna. "Do not set your heart on Lev."

Her hands trembled as she picked up the tray of food behind her. "You are both Pharisees."

"His father is one of the finest rabbis at the temple." He stroked his full beard. "I am a mere scribe."

Her mouth went dry.

"I am sorry, Anna. No matter how much attention he gives you, Malachi will not allow his son to marry beneath him."

"Perhaps you think too little of yourself, Father. Too little of Malachi." The tray rattled as she set it down on the table. "And Daniel is certainly in the rabbi's favor."

He placed his hand over hers. "You have many fine qualities. I will find a good husband for you. Soon."

Her eyes filled. She could feel the tears wanting to spill down her cheeks. She turned away to retrieve the wine sack and wooden cups then passed them to her father. He waited until she sat to say the blessing. They ate in silence.

When they were finished, she sliced bread for her mother and mixed it with a little goat's milk to soften it. She sat next to her and lifted her head. "Eat, Mother."

"I am not hungry." She turned her face to the wall.

Anna sighed. "And what if Daniel comes again? Do you not want him to see you well?"

It took a moment, but Miriam shifted herself toward her daughter. Anna placed a morsel on her mother's tongue. Her nose wrinkled, but she dutifully chewed a few times before swallowing. She finished about half her meal before shooing Anna away. Anna cleared the remains of their meal to the courtyard to clean, while Phanuel sat down near his wife. He began to recite a song of David. The words soothed Anna's aching heart like a balm. Under her breath, she sang the words her father spoke, "The Lord is my strength and my shield; my heart trusts in Him, and He helps me."

Later, as she lay awake on her pallet, staring at the ceiling, Anna prayed, "El-Shaddai, please. Give me the desire of my heart. Soften Malachi's heart toward me. Let me be betrothed to Lev." For she knew, in her soul, she would never love anyone the way she loved the rabbi's son.

Chapter 2

One Week Later

Anna marveled at how quickly Jerusalem had settled back into the normal chaos of daily life after the death of the king. Merchants crammed their stalls with their wares. Colorful awnings shaded them from the summer heat. Farmers brought their produce from the fields outside the city to sell there, too. They called to Anna as she passed, trying to entice her to buy lentils, spices, fish, linens or jewelry. She did not give in to the temptation to look at what they offered; her family could not afford such luxuries.

A shepherd guided several lambs through the narrow streets and up to the Temple Mount. Anna reached out to pet one of the animals as it trotted past, her heart heavy. The animals were on their way to the Temple to be inspected. Those unmarred would be kept in pens and sold to pilgrims needing to make a sacrifice to Adonai. Lambs deemed unacceptable would be slaughtered and sold for food. Either way, they would not be going back to the fields outside of the city.

She turned her attention back to the market, hoping the colors and smells would lighten her spirits. Her father promised he would find her a good husband, but she feared it would be one of her cousins from the north, where her father's tribe of Asher lived. He had been the first and only member of his family to leave the coastal village where he had grown up. He owed his good fortune to a rabbi named Reuben bar Ezra. The rabbi heard her father, then just fourteen years old, discussing the law with the elders at the town gate. Reuben had been so impressed with her father's bright mind, he had asked her grandparents' permission to take him to Jerusalem and make him his disciple. And so it was that Father travelled away from his tribe to settle in the land of Judah.

I want to stay here . . . with Lev as my husband. Especially now, when all around she could sense the changes coming to the city. Queen Salome already sought peace with the Pharisees who had survived her husband's slaughter some twenty years ago. Although her father feared Salome would revert her favor back to the Sadducees, to whom most of her husband's family had been loyal, the queen seemed to desire peace between the two factions. Anna longed to stay and watch how the queen ruled and brought peace to the land. She did not want to miss one moment of the excitement. And she could not imagine marrying anyone but Lev.

All these thoughts swirled in her mind as she made her way up to Rabbi Malachi's house. Her mother's head still pounded and only the herbs Lev's mother brewed gave her any comfort. Anna planned her visit strategically. Too early in the morning, and she would be bothering the family as they prepared for the day. Too late in the morning, and the rabbi and his students would be on the Temple Mount, debating points of law with other rabbis. Too late in the day, and she would interrupt the preparations for supper. Early afternoon, however, when the sun was high and heat pounded down on the bleached ground, then the rabbi was known to allow his students to find shade to rest. And Lev, the rabbi's son, might leave the school room, cross the courtyard, and find refreshment in his father's kitchen . . . or perhaps visit his mother.

Anna turned the corner to Malachi's house. Sunlight danced off the white limestone. Two servants leaving with baskets scurried down the street, probably heading toward the market to get dried fish or some spice for the evening meal. As her family expected no company, Anna would not be stopping for such luxuries on her way home. She had already set a pot of lentils to simmer over the fire. That and a loaf of fresh bread would be their meal tonight, as usual.

She paused at the entrance to Malachi's courtyard. Slate tiles lined the open area to her right. Two stone benches sat there, shaded by a date tree. Noa, the cook's young daughter, skipped out from the house and headed toward the garden planted off to left, stopping when she caught sight of her.

"Anna!" The girl's round cheeks lifted in a smile. "Lev said you would come this week."

"And here I am." Anna gave her a quick bow, as if she were royalty. Even a servant deserved respect. "I am not interrupting anything, am I?"

"Mother sent me to pick garlic bulbs and onions for the dinner tonight." Noa gestured to the plants nearby. "But I will let the Mistress know you are here."

"Thank you."

"The Mistress has herbs ready for you," the petite girl ran back toward the house. "Follow me!"

Anna quickened her steps to keep pace with Noa. Once   inside, she struggled to adjust to the dim light after the bright sunshine of the courtyard. The air inside was cooler as well.

Noa took a few steps down the hall, then stopped in the threshold of a room. "Mistress?"

"What is it?" A gentle voice answered from behind the wall.

The girl curtsied. "Anna, daughter of Phanuel, is here to see you."

"Send her in. Send her in."

Noa scooted out of her way so Anna could enter the large room. A testimony to Malachi's status as a man of wealth, this formal sitting room was the finest Anna had ever seen. Plush wool rugs of brown and red covered the wood floor. An upholstered couch sat in the middle of the room with two chairs   facing it. Anna had heard that the priests of the temple had even more ornate homes, but the extravagance of having a room where nothing was done but sitting and talking was impressive enough to her.

Lev's mother, Judith, sat on one of the carved wooden chairs. Her light brown hair had been woven into an elaborate braid around her head, resembling a crown, and she exuded an air of self-confidence Anna found intimidating.

"Welcome." The beautifully draped sleeves of Judith's cream linen tunic flowed gently as she waved toward Anna. "I was hoping you might come by today as my husband's best robe needs mending, and none of my servants have your gift of embroidery." Her eyes, the same dark honey color as Lev's, studied Anna's face. "Can you spare an hour to help repair it?"

Anna's fingers trembled as she straightened the sash around her simple blue tunic. "Of course. It is the least I can do."

"Please." Judith gestured her ringed fingers toward the chair opposite her. "Make yourself comfortable." She clapped her hands as Anna sat, then ordered a servant boy to fetch wine. She pushed a basket at her feet toward Anna. "I kept this with me, on the chance that you would come by today. I would not let my maid touch it."

Anna pulled out the heavy robe of red wool. Embroidered squares of gold and maroon thread embellished the trim of the coat. As she admired the weaver's craft, she noticed a hole in one of the elbows. Examining the garment further, she found several tears along the bottom hem and sleeves, fraying the intricate embroidered design.

"Do you think you can repair it?" Judith asked.

Anna nodded. "Although I believe it will take me more than an hour."

"Can your mother spare you for the afternoon? I could send Noa to your home to tell her where you are."

"She was sleeping when I left. I am sure she will not need me any time soon." Anna tried not to let her excitement show. The longer she stayed in Malachi's house, the more opportunities she would have to see Lev. The servant boy returned with a jar of wine and promptly poured Judith and her a cup. Anna took the silver goblet with some hesitation.

"Is something wrong?" Judith asked.

"No, my lady." She hoped her embarrassment did not show, but she had never drank from anything more than a wine sack or wooden cup.

Judith set her cup on a table beside her. "You will find what you need in the basket."

Anna knelt on the floor and spread the robe out before her. "It's a beautiful garment."

Tiny lines creased Judith's eyes as she smiled. "Malachi wore it at his niece's wedding. That is when it was torn." She pointed to the bottom of the robe. "But it is the fraying of the border I that concerns me. Can you match the pattern?"

"I will try."

Anna worked with red thread first, repairing the tear in the arm. A pit formed in her stomach. "Are you going to be attending another wedding soon?" *Please, do not let it be Lev's. Please, Lord.*

Judith chuckled. "No. Queen Salome has asked to speak to Malachi and some of the other rabbis. I believe she wants to bring peace to the temple. Stop this fighting between the priests and the scribes."

Anna's heart slowed, relieved at the news, and she put all her focus into the work at hand. This garment was to be worn before the queen. It had to be perfect.

Before she had become ill, Anna's mother had taught her how to use thread to decorate cloth with beautiful designs. Anna soon surpassed her mother in her skill with the needle. Her nimble fingers wove intricate patterns that became well-known at the market. She was proud of having provided enough money from her skill to secure Daniel a place with Rabbi Malachi. She knew her father kept some of her profits in a chest for her dowry as well.

It had been a year or so since her mother began suffering from the headaches and fatigue that left her weak and almost bedridden. Anna had too many household chores to accomplish now and little time for needlework. She reveled in the feel of the needle at her fingertips and the intense focus her mind put into the task. She made her stitches small and wove them into the weave of the fabric so that they were nearly invisible. Judith watched, silently sipping her wine.

Once Anna finished the repair on the elbow, she again flattened the garment on the floor to better examine the tears along the hem. Most of them were in the gold threads as they were so delicate. She knelt over them as she carefully sewed new thread among the old, matching the pattern perfectly.

"Mother," Lev's voice rang from the hallway.

Anna jumped at the sound and snapped the shimmering thread.

Lev bent to kiss Judith's cheek. "Putting a guest to work? How could you?"

"Thankfully, Anna agreed to help. She has the finest needlework in Jerusalem."

Anna's cheeks warmed at Judith's compliments and Lev's frank perusal.

"Your brother's tunic is the envy of all my father's students." He winked. "Perhaps one day, you will make one for me?"

Judith put her hand on his arm. "You are embarrassing her. Go and ask Reba for some refreshment."

He bowed to them both before leaving the room.

Anna struggled to take a breath.

"You will have to excuse my son," Judith spoke quietly. "He spends so much time with his father, studying the law, he forgets how to properly address a young maiden."

Anna wiped her palms on her tunic, not wanting to dull the gold thread with the sweat from her fingers. She glanced up, hoping Judith's face might tell whether she was upset that Lev had been so forward as to ask her to make him a garment; or that the request suggested he might be interested in her. Judith's expression revealed nothing. Anna carefully rethreaded the needle and went back to work.

Several hours later, she finished. She flexed her fingers and stretched her back, trying to loosen the tension in her muscles before standing. Judith had long since left her to attend to household matters. Anna put the remaining thread in the basket then lifted the robe to inspect her work.

"Beautiful."

Anna gasped as she turned to the doorway. Lev stood, his light brown eyes admiring . . . what? Her or the robe?

He approached slowly. "I did not mean to frighten you."

"Y-y-you did not. I did not realize anyone was there."

His hand brushed Anna's as he drew the robe closer to himself. She shivered at the touch.

"Are you cold?"

She shook her head. She had no breath for words.

He draped the robe over his arms, but his attention was on her. "Why do you tremble?"

Anna's voice came out as a whisper. "My muscles are tired from the work."

"Truly?"

She could only nod.

"What are you looking at?" Malachi's booming voice echoed off the stone walls. Although not a short man, his stature seemed smaller because of his massive girth. Like a well-fed bull, barrel-chested with a stomach to match. He strode into the room, instantly filling the space both in size and energy.

Lev backed away. "Daniel's sister has repaired your robe, Father. Come, take a look."

Malachi's gaze ranged swiftly between his son and Anna, his annoyance evident in the crease of his brow. "Let me see."

Lev held the garment out for his father's examination. Malachi turned over the sleeve. He frowned, then turned over the other one. He put them side by side. His gaze finally lifted to Anna. "The unknowing eye would never see the repair." He lifted one brow. "You have done well."

"Thank you."

He glanced toward Lev. "See if Judith has the herbs ready. We do not want Anna's family to worry for her safety."

"I have them here." Little Noa flitted into the room with a cloth bag in her hand.

Malachi took the bag and passed it to Anna. "Good day."

She heard the dismissal in his voice and bowed her head. "Good--"

"It is late, Father," Lev interrupted. "I should accompany her."

Malachi glared. "There is much daylight left, if she does not tarry."

"Good day." Anna hurried to the entrance before Malachi made his dislike of her even more apparent. She ran down the hill toward home, hoping to arrive before her father.

She was not so fortunate.

Her father sat on the floor, eating a bowl of lentils. He frowned when she entered. "Where have you been?"

Anna held out the small bag of herbs. "To fetch the medicine from Judith."

"You said you would go in the early afternoon. What took you so long?"

"Judith begged me to repair the rabbi's best robe." She carefully poured the herbs into a clay jar. "I felt obligated as she has never taken payment for the medicine she gives us."

Her father *hrumphed*, the wrinkles in his face seeming to dig deeper into his cheek as he watched her.

She took a small handful of the herbs and wrapped them in a piece of linen then set the bundle in a pot of water to boil. "I want to make sure to have a cup ready for Mother when she wakes."

Her father tore off a piece of bread. With it, he wiped his bowl clean. "I have decided to take a trip. After the Sabbath."

A knot formed in Anna's stomach as she poured a ladle of soup into her own bowl. "Where will you go?"

"To my Uncle Ilan. In Tyre."

The knot tightened. She could not bring herself to ask why he would take such a long journey. One that would take him to his family in Asher. "Are you taking Daniel with you?"

"He cannot afford to leave his studies for so long." He tore off another piece of bread. "No. There is a caravan heading north with goods to trade. I will journey with them."

Anna peered over to where her mother lay sleeping.

"You will remain here to care for Miriam." His gaze grew cold. "You must stay by her side while I am gone. No leaving for hours at a time. No matter what the cause. Do you understand?"

"Yes, Father." She forced herself to eat. The lentils, though perfectly seasoned, tasted like dead leaves in her mouth. She lifted the pot off the flame when the water began to boil, but still, she would not ask her father the purpose of his trip.

Silence hung over the house like the heavy gray clouds of spring—a torrent of rain held inside, waiting to burst.

It was not until Anna had cleaned the dishes, helped her mother drink the tea, and then unrolled a wool blanket to prepare her pallet for sleep that her father spoke to her again.

He coughed quietly as he stood up from his evening prayers. "I know you dream of a life with Lev, but I know Malachi. He is proud. Powerful. He wants his son to help him gain an even greater position

within Jerusalem. He will use his wealth to marry Lev into position."
Phanuel clasped his hands together as if still in prayer. "I will find a
husband for you from my uncle's people. You will have a home of
your own soon enough."

"Away from here?"

He did not meet her gaze. "A wife must leave her home and cleave
to her husband. It is the way of the Lord."

Her throat felt as if she tried to swallow a rock. "When?"

He undid his belt, revealing the long, cream-colored linen tunic
beneath his robe. He slipped off his outer garment and folded it with
precision before laying it on the ground by his wife. "I go to see about
a betrothal. If there is a man worthy of you in my uncle's family, we
will travel together before the fall rains to make the contract binding."

Anna's eyes stung, her vision blurring as she blinked back her
tears.

"The marriage may not take place for another year. Maybe two."
He glanced down at his wife. "We must see what the Lord wills for
your mother before we make plans."

The flames in the silver candlestick flickered as Lev pushed away
his empty plate and sat back in his chair. He waved the wine steward
over from across the room to refill his goblet.

His mother sat opposite him at the long wooden table.   Judith's
eyes were bright with curiosity. "Are you staying in tonight, my son?"

He drained most of his drink. "No. I plan on going back to the
school to study."

Malachi snorted. "With all the studying you claim to do, I would
expect you to be more advanced in your learning."

Lev finished the rest of his wine. "I do the best I can, Father."

Malachi belched. "You could do much better, if you would only
stop . . . ." He waved his hand in front of him, as if trying to conjure
the right word from the air. "I do not understand where your mind is."
His brows knit together. "Unless it is on things you wish to keep
secret."

Lev looked toward his mother, hoping she would put an end to his
father's accusations, as usual.

Instead, Malachi coughed into his fist. "Perhaps Lev and I should speak alone."

Judith motioned to a servant waiting in the corner. "Nama, I wish to retire. Please bring tea to my rooms." She turned to her son and husband. "I pray you be civil with each other." She lowered her voice. "Remember the servants are listening." She strode out of the room, leaving an emptiness behind her.

Malachi hunched himself over the table, his soft whisper accusing, "I can guess where you go at night. More, your mother believes that you have been visiting the adulteress. If you do not care for my reputation, surely you want to spare her heartache."

Lev's skin prickled, but he did not flinch. "Did you say something to her? Before speaking with me?"

His father's cheeks reddened. "The servants gossip."

Lev rested his forearms on the table. "And that is all it is. Gossip."

"You deny it, then?" Malachi's chin quivered. "If the reports are false, then tell me where it is you go at night."

"I go to study, Father."

Malachi's fist pounded the table. "Do not lie to me! It is a sin to dishonor me in such a fashion."

Lev watched his father's outburst with mild amusement. He still respected Malachi, but he no longer thought his father the final authority in all matters. Especially when his father's notorious temper got the best of him.

"You mock me!" Malachi continued to rant. "I see it by the scorn on your face."

Lev sighed. "I do not mock. I only wait for you to calm yourself."

The older man's cheeks shook with hostility, but he said nothing.

"I do not study with your other students, that much is true. But neither do I visit the prostitutes."

Malachi stilled himself, his voice cold as stone. "Then where do you go?"

Lev took a deep breath. "I have ingratiated myself to the Idumaean governor, Antipater."

His father sneered. "Why would you converse with that swine? Little better than a Gentile."

"He is a strong political ally." He leaned forward. "And he is a brilliant man, Father. Cunning."

"A pig pretending to be a Jew," Malachi spat. "Do not trust him to speak the truth."

Lev's blood pounded in his ears as he tried not to raise his voice. "Antipater's family converted to our faith after Jannai's father conquered their land. Antipater was raised as a Jew."

"But has he studied with a rabbi? Offered a sacrifice for his sins? Does he truly know the one true God?"

"He knows enough to make himself indispensable to John Hyrcanus. That's enough for me."

"John?" His father dropped back in his chair. "The queen's son?"

Lev nodded. "His father was one of John's counselors. Antipater has taken over that role." He grinned as he stretched out his legs. "Queen Salome is set to make John Hyrcanus the High Priest." He clasped his hands together as he relaxed into his seat. "And when that happens, I shall be in position to become Antipater's personal scribe."

"You?" Malachi's smile mirrored Lev's own. "You are sure of this, my son?"

"As certain as one can be. Antipater has come to value my opinion on the Law. I have been a guest at his home. Dined with him and his family."

"Why did not you speak of this before? Why did you let us believe the rumors of your behavior?"

"I was not sure which would be the worse sin in your eyes, if I were a fornicator or a collaborator."

Malachi scratched his chin, letting his fingers run down his long beard. "I still do not like, or trust, the Idumaean. Then again, it is always wise to know one's enemies." He nodded. "Keep your head about you, my son. Do not be taken in by flattery. And keep me informed about what is said. Together, we may play them to our best advantage."

"Of course, Father," Lev couched his lie behind smile.

Chapter 3

Twelve days later

Anna fought against the despair that tried to swallow her within the four walls of her home. As a kind of peace offering, her father bought her cloth from the market to embroider. She was glad to have work to keep her mind busy with something other than the sound of her mother's labored breathing, or the bitterness that tried to seep into her heart.

Being the daughter of a scribe, she had been raised on the word of God. Phanuel recited psalms every night after dinner throughout her childhood. He had spent hours discussing the law with Daniel while she helped their mother prepare the dinner or embroider a garment. In her earliest memories, she knelt on the bench at the table, mashing chickpeas for hummus, and listened. Always she listened. She had known it would be the only way she could learn the ways of Adonai since she could not attend school herself.

Her mother had said that years ago, the Temple Mount was not divided. Women had been allowed to worship with the men. That was another of Alexander Jannai's edicts after a riot broke out at the Feast of Tabernacles. Acting as High Priest, Jannai had dared to pour the wine offering at his feet, rather than on the altar. Miriam had been only a child, barely weaned, but she claimed to remember the people throwing citrons at him in their anger. The large yellow fruits pelted the High Priest and king until he was forced to leave the altar. He soon had a wall   erected so only the priests and men could see the sacrifices. As if the women alone had been to blame for the uproar.

Her father had left a week ago. During the long afternoons and evenings, while Phanuel traveled to find her a husband, Anna fought against hopelessness while she sewed and meditated on the scriptures she had heard her father speak throughout her life. She thought about the stories of the patriarchs: Jacob, the deceiver who became Israel, the father of the twelve tribes; his son, Joseph, sold into slavery but raised to glory because of his faithfulness. All throughout their history, Adonai had chosen the poor, the flawed, to serve Him. Even women could be used for His purpose. Rahab, Deborah, Ruth; these were women Anna had heard about from her father's stories. Perhaps she herself could serve the Lord, even far from His holy city.

Lost in these thoughts, she jumped when someone rapped against the door. They knocked again as she stood and stretched out the stiffness in her limbs.

"I am coming!" Sure it was only Tova, Anna paused to set down her embroidery and check on her mother. Miriam still slept, oblivious to the sudden noise. Anna opened the door, surprised to see little Noa preparing to knock again. "What is wrong?"

Noa panted as if she had run the entire way between their houses. "A servant comes!" She pointed down the street. "From the queen! I was instructed to bring her to you."

Anna peered out of the doorway. An older woman strode toward them. "What does she want with me?"

"Queen Salome commented on the fine embroidery on my master's robe. She demanded to know who had such skill with a needle." The little girl stopped to catch her breath. "She sent a servant to inquire of my mistress when he claimed ignorance of your name." Noa glanced to make sure the queen's servant was still a distance away. "My mistress was very angry," she whispered furtively, "to know the master did not reveal your name immediately to the queen."

Anna ran her hands over her wrinkled tunic. She pulled the sash around her waist to tighten it so it hung properly. With a quick movement, she straightened the scarf around her head.

The queen's servant huffed up to Noa's side. Her stern gaze stole little from the woman's beauty. Her dark brown eyes flashed with the intensity of a spring storm. Her graying hair hung in beautiful ringlets under her headdress. "Are you the one called Anna? The seamstress and daughter of Phanuel?"

Anna's voice caught at the woman's obvious confidence and authority; she could only nod.

"My name is Ziva. First servant to Queen Salome Alexander. She wishes to meet with you to discuss your employment within her household."

Anna's knees weakened. She leaned against the doorjamb to keep her balance. "What?"

Ziva's dark eyes flashed with annoyance. "You are not deaf, are you?"

Anna shook her head.

"Then you understand what Queen Salome commands. Do not expect her, or anyone within the palace, to repeat commands that are comprehensible to even the most ignorant of minds."

"But . . . but . . . ." Anna fought against the near panic conspiring to leave her a babbling idiot. She forced herself to speak clearly. "My mother is ill. My father has commanded I remain with her throughout the day."

The woman huffed. "Where is your father now?"

"He is away on a journey." Anna counted the days he had been gone. "I look for his arrival by the next new moon."

"Very well. I will tell my mistress." Ziva started to go, but stopped herself as her gaze fell behind Anna. "May I see it?"

Anna followed Ziva's stare, then scrabbled to retrieve the scarf she had been embroidering. She held it out to the woman who took it with reverence and held it up to see the pattern fully. Her eyes seemed to survey each stitch. "May I take this to my mistress? So she might judge the quality of your work?"

"Of course."

Again Ziva turned to go but paused. She untied a leather pouch from her sash. "An artist should be paid."

"It is only a sample of my work." Anna stepped back. "I could not accept payment for something unfinished."

The woman's harsh veneer cracked as her lips rose to offer Anna a smile. "Consider it a payment in advance of future work." She thrust the pouch into Anna's hand. "I have served the queen for many years. I know she will be pleased to give you a position within her home."

Noa's eyes grew round. "A position in the palace!"

"Come, child," the queen's servant called. "Guide me back through these streets. They twist and turn so, I will never find my way."

Noa waved goodbye as she trotted off. Anna watched them for a moment before her mother groaned from her pallet.

"Shut the door. The light hurts my eyes."

Anna took one last look down the road. Noa and the woman still walked together. It had not been a dream. The pouch in her hand confirmed it. She shut the door and crossed to her mother. "Can I get you something?"

Miriam wiped a hand across her brow. "Some of Judith's tea, if there is any left."

Anna placed the bag of coins in her sewing basket before settling herself to making the tea. She had been careful with the herbs she had been given, so there would be enough to last her mother for several weeks. She reused the bag of herbs brewed that morning, adding a pinch of fresh leaves before setting it over a small brazier to warm.

Her mother moaned. "Who was at the door?"

Anna hesitated. Would the news of her possible advancement please her mother, or would it bring her more worry?

"Who were you talking to?"

Anna knelt by Miriam's bed and stroked her mother's hair, hoping the gesture would bring her some comfort. Miriam's eyelids fluttered as she tried to focus on her daughter's face. "Was I dreaming?"

"Noa came to the door with a message from Judith."

"Ah." Miriam smiled. "Did you thank her for the herbs?"

Anna's fingers continued to caress her mother's forehead. "Yes."

Her mother sighed under her soothing ministrations. When the water boiled, Anna rose slowly so as not to disturb her, then took the cup from the flame to let the tea cool.

Her eyes were drawn to the leather pouch atop her sewing. She glanced to see if her mother lay awake, but Miriam's eyes were closed. Anna sat down and loosened the string that held the bag closed. She pulled out five silver coins. More than she had ever seen in her life at one time. Each bore the inscription of the former king. His name, Alexander Jannai, bordered each in raised letters. Anna shivered. Was it a sin to be excited by the prospect of working for Queen Salome? The king had been no true follower of Adonai, but what of his wife?

Miriam stirred and Anna slipped the coins back into their pouch then stuffed it under the linen in her basket. With a ladle, she scooped out a cupful of tea. "Are you ready for your medicine?"

Miriam struggled to push herself up. Anna knelt and slid her arms around her mother, sad to feel her shoulder blades pressing against her hands like pieces of slate. She placed a pillow behind Miriam's back so she could rest against the wall. Once settled, Anna lifted the tea to her mother's lips.

Miriam's eyes studied Anna. "You are a good daughter."

"And you are a good mother."

Miriam's trembling hand reached over to touch Anna's cheek. "You are too young to play nursemaid to me."

Anna sat back. For the first time in weeks, her mother's eyes were alert. "I love you. Of course I should take care of you."

"No," Miriam whispered hoarsely, as if she spoke through pebbles. "Now you are young. You should have the chance to live your life."

"I am living it. Here. With you."

"I heard it all." Miriam coughed to clear her throat. "I know your father wants you away from Jerusalem. But you are like me." She clutched Anna's wrist. "The city lives in your blood. You will never be happy away from its life. The temple and the markets. The Festivals." Miriam's bony fingers dug into Anna's skin. "You will go to the palace. You must."

"Father will never allow it."

Her mother's chuckle turned into a cough. She sipped the tea Anna offered before speaking again. "I will tell him he must let you go. It is my last wish."

"Do not say that. With the money I earn, we could pay for a physician to come heal you."

Miriam waved her hand as if swatting away Anna's words. "When I was young, I dreamed as you do. I wanted to marry a merchant's son. Travel with him to distant lands until we had children. Then I would raise our sons here, in the shadow of the temple. I hoped my skill as a seamstress would move him to notice me, but . . . he fancied my friend Elizabeth more." Her eyes grew distant, as if she could see the memory before her. "As Phanuel had no family here, his master came to talk to my parents on his behalf." Miriam again focused on Anna. "Your father is a good man. Kind. But he does not understand how a woman's heart can yearn, can cry out, for passion. He loves his words, his writings . . . I craved to live life. You do, too."

She sank back against the pillow, as if by talking so long she had spent all the air in her body.

"Mother?"

Miriam breathed in deeply, but her eyes remained closed. "I will talk to your father when he comes home. You will have your chance to live."

Early the following morning, Anna shouldered the heavy clay jar by the door and set off for the well in the square. She eyed the narrow streets, hoping to spy Tova's tell-tale walk and wayward curls, but her friend did not appear.

As she waited for her turn to draw water, Avigail, an old friend of her mother's, approached her.

Avigail brushed a faded brown lock of hair back under her scarf. "There is talk you had a visitor yesterday."

Anna shrugged, wanting to tell Tova first of her news, not this gossip.

"I heard the same story," another woman, Dasah was her name, also stepped toward Anna. "I heard money was exchanged." One eyebrow rose. "It made us wonder what the daughter of Phanuel the scribe had to sell . . . while he was away."

Several other woman drew closer as Dasah continued, "Where did your father go in such a hurry? I hope there is no trouble." The eager hunger behind her eyes contradicted the expression of compassion she tried to wear as a mask.

"There is no trouble." Anna took a step closer toward the well.

"Thank the Lord." Avigail followed her. "With your mother so ill, we could not help but be concerned."

Anna stifled a sharp retort. When the headaches first began plaguing her mother, her friends rallied their support. But it had been several months since any had visited. Anna chewed on her bottom lip to keep from chastising the older woman. The others waited expectantly. "My mother is fine, thank you."

The women circled like vultures. Dasah pressed close. "Who was your visitor, then?" She paused as if worried about Anna. "Was it a creditor? Perhaps, if Phanuel owes money, I could ask my husband to loan—"

"My father owes no one money," Anna spoke harshly. "The visitor had only an opportunity to present to my father, and as Phanuel is not in Jerusalem, you all will have to wait to discover if he will accept this gift or decline it."

Avigail huffed. Dasah's eyebrow rose again. The rest clucked with disappointment.

Anna did not care. She did not want to speak of her good fortune to these loose-tongued women. Not until she had told all to Tova. Even then, she would hesitate telling anyone else lest Phanuel deny her this opportunity. She could not bear to live under their judgmental gazes. She spied Tova making her way into the line waiting to draw water and left her position to stand by her friend.

Tova yawned. "You never beat me to the well. What could possibly have stirred you this morning?"

"You have not heard?"

The heaviness of sleep slipped from her friend's face. "Heard what?"

The other women craned their necks, trying to listen. Anna hardened her lips together.

Tova lowered the jar from her shoulder. "What has happened?"

Anna ducked her head down so she could whisper, "I will tell you later. When we walk home."

Tova frowned, but said nothing more.

The two friends drew their water then set off up the hill. Tova glanced around as they turned away from the square. "Tell me now! There is no one to hear."

Anna relayed the previous day's events, including the conversation with her mother. "But I am afraid Father will not let me go."

"Would he defy the queen?"

"What if he has already made a contract for my betrothal? Would not the law demand I fulfill it?"

"Perhaps he has sought an agreement for now, not a legal contract. Then he would have no excuse but to let you serve at the palace." Tova's eyes danced with excitement. "Think of it!"

Anna could not let herself get caught up in her friend's fantasy. "Even if I go to the palace, I will be a servant." They approached the door to her house. "All I will do is sew, nothing more."

"But maybe one of the princes would see you? Or a priest?" Tova shifted her water jug to her other shoulder. "Perhaps now Malachi will see you are worthy to be a wife for Lev."

Anna's heart jumped at the thought but she quickly stilled it. "Malachi would not even speak my name to the queen. I am sure my serving in the palace would not elevate me enough in his eyes."

Tova lingered outside Anna's house. "You have forgotten what it is to dream, my friend. Sometimes it is all we have."

"No, we have the life with which God blessed us. That is enough. If I yearn for more, am I not spitting on all He has already given me?"

"Do you think David did not daydream about being in battle while he tended his father's sheep? And those dreams gave him the confidence to stand up to Goliath."

Anna chuckled. "I think God gave him the strength he needed."

Tova stamped her foot, causing some of the water in her jug to slosh onto the street. "But David had to believe he could succeed. God gives us His strength only after we believe we must attempt something. You must believe that this is possible. That God may call you to the palace for a reason, not only to be a servant."

Her friend's strong words filled her with hope. With passion. "Do you really think so?"

"Pray. Ask God to lead the way to your destiny."

Anna nodded. "Would you do something for me?"

"Of course."

"The trek for water is the only outing my father allows me while he is away. The queen's servant gave me coins. Would you take two to the market today?"

"For what purpose?"

A smile lifted Anna's lips. "I have an idea to make myself indispensable to the queen."

Chapter 4

The following day

Miriam rallied her strength the following morning to sit up and knead the dough for their Sabbath dinner. Anna's mouth watered at the thought of the warm, buttery *challah* bread melting on her tongue later that evening. Her mother had a gift for baking. Although Anna would copy her preparations exactly, her bread never came out as moist, or her cakes as flaky, as Miriam's. By late afternoon, the heavenly smell of the baking loaf filled the house while Anna stirred a fresh batch of lentils over the flame.

"You keep looking toward the door." Miriam watched her from her pallet while she sipped some of Judith's tea. "Your father is not due home for two more Sabbaths. And you were never so anxious for Daniel's coming. Who are you waiting for?"

Anna added a pinch of pepper to the pot. "I asked Tova to buy me something from the market. I had hoped she would bring it before Sabbath."

Miriam's fingers trembled as she put down her tea. "And what is it she brings?"

Anna wiped her hands on a cloth tied to her sash. "I thought to work on a belt for Queen Salome. As a gift." She sighed. "If Father even allows me to go to the palace."

"He will." Miriam pulled a blanket over her thin legs. "But you may not work on it over the Sabbath, so why worry about Tova's arrival?"

Anna turned back to watch the soup bubbling lazily. "I wanted to study the fabric. It may seem foolish, but I wanted to pray over it to see if Adonai might give me a vision for what I should sew."

"You are not foolish." Miriam glanced toward the fading sunlight coming through the cracks in the door. "But I fear you may have to pray for His wisdom without the cloth. It looks as if the sun has nearly set."

Anna followed her mother's gaze. "I suppose—"

The door flew open, causing her to jump back.

"*Shalom*, Mother." Daniel bowed his head toward Miriam before hurrying over to Anna. He pulled her into a tight   embrace.

"Is something wrong?" She fought to breathe within his strong arms. Although Daniel's presence for the Sabbath was expected, his show of affection was very unusual.

His laugh reverberated through her body. "Wrong? No!" He pushed away so he could look at her. "Lev told me of the queen's offer."

"But how did . . .?" *Did Malachi tell him?*

Daniel beamed down at her. "How does he know half the things he does?" He hugged her again before letting her go, his gaze sweeping the room. "Where is Father?"

Anna hurried over to their mother as Miriam strove to lift herself up. "Father has gone to Tyre."

Daniel knelt down to help.

Miriam grasped his arms. "It is good to see you. Quickly, Anna, light the candle before the sun sets."

Anna turned to where she had put the Sabbath candle and hurried to the cooking fire to light it before placing the long, white taper on its stand on the table. Her eyes caught the fading sunlight from the doorway as she grabbed three bowls and filled them with lentil soup. Lastly, she set her mother's Challah loaf down.

Daniel helped Miriam to the stool at the head of the table. She pulled the thin shawl around her shoulders so it covered her head. "Shut the door."

Anna shut it as the last pink rays of the sun set streaked across the gray sky. She sat on the bench beside her brother.

Miriam sighed deeply. "Adonai, please forgive my weakness, that I cannot stand to say Your blessing, but know, in my heart, I honor You." She circled her arms over the flame of the candle three times, then covered her eyes. "Blessed are You, Adonai, King of the universe, Who has sanctified us with His commandments and commanded us to kindle the light of the Holy Shabbat. Thank You for the blessing of my son's visit this Sabbath day. And be with Phanuel as he travels. Keep him well and bring him safely back to us." She lowered her arms and gazed at her children. "*Shalom.*"

Anna and Daniel responded together, "*Shalom.*"

Daniel ripped off pieces of bread then passed one each to his mother and sister. He groaned with pleasure as he chewed a mouthful. "I have missed this." He turned his focus back to Anna. "So, tell me exactly what happened."

Anna explained all about Ziva's visit and the queen's offer of work. Daniel's excitement lifted her spirit and filled her with hope.

He pulled the loaf of *challah* closer. "Why did Father go to Tyre?"

Anna did not want to talk about her possible marriage. Sabbath was a time to rest. To pray. Not to let her thoughts spin in impossible circles like leaves caught in the wind.

"He went to find a husband for your sister." Miriam pushed away her barely touched bowl.

Daniel frowned. "Do you need to lie back down?"

Miriam nodded. "Forgive me."

"Sorry I was late tonight." Daniel helped her to her pallet.

His mother patted his cheek. "We will talk tomorrow. Go. Eat."

Anna shoved her own bowl away as Daniel sat on the bench next to her. "How are your studies going?"

Daniel swallowed a mouthful of lentils. "Fine. Why is Father looking for a husband for you in Tyre when there are eligible men here in Jerusalem?"

She dropped her gaze to the table and clasped her hands in her lap.

"Anna?"

She fought back the tears threatening to fall. "I do not know."

He lifted her chin. "You have never lied to me before. Why do you start now?"

"It is Lev." She forced herself to keep her voice level. "Father fears I have grown too fond of him."

Her brother groaned. "You, too? Every girl has fallen in love with him."

"I never said I loved him."

"You would not be the first." Daniel grinned as he mopped up the last of the lentils in his bowl with a piece of bread. He leaned close to Anna's ear. "Would it please you to know Lev was excited about the queen's interest in you? That he told me to congratulate you?"

She would never admit to her brother how her heart danced at his words. "Why would he think of me?"

"Who knows, Sister? Perhaps he cares for you as much as you do him."

Later, as Anna lay in the dark listening to her mother's labored breathing and her brother's heavy snores, she pondered Daniel's news. Did Lev care for her? Was there a chance they could be wed?

She stared up at the ceiling. "Adonai, please, bring my father safely home, but let his journey come to nothing. Do not send me from Your holy city. Do not send me far from Lev."

Candles blazed in the house of Malachi, lit by one of the gentile slaves Lev's father bought specifically for that purpose—to cook, clean, and light candles on the Sabbath since the children of Israel were forbidden to do any kind of work. The same slave had set several logs to burn in the hearth and a faint haze of smoke hung in the air.

Lev stretched his arms above his head, trying to loosen the knot in his shoulders. He had been leaning over one of his father's scrolls since supper ended and now his muscles ached. His mother had long ago retired to her rooms. His father had left the dinner table before her but Lev did not know where he had gone. He would not have left the house, as even traveling fifty feet from their dwelling was considered work.

Lev sighed as he stood, frustrated at the laws that made him prisoner for one day out of every week. He understood the law: God wanted His people to rest. But the Pharisees had changed the definition of "rest." It was not enough to refrain from one's vocation. No. One could not even strike a flint to make a fire, as they considered that work. For Lev, the constant reading, the inability to walk outside other than to go to the temple for worship, the nothingness of the hours—it made him frenetic. He would much rather be with Antipater, the older man who had taken Lev under his wing, discussing the political intrigues roiling in Jerusalem.

Lev picked up the silver goblet of wine a slave had left for him earlier and sat in a chair facing the fireplace. He stared into the orange flames dancing before him as he contemplated the latest gossip he had heard from Antipater. As the governor of Idumaea and an intimate to the princes, he was privy to the secret political decisions in the court.

Queen Salome would make her oldest son, John Hyrcanus, High Priest by the end of the month. She also planned on naming him her heir, passing the mantle of rule to him upon her death. As she was already nearing her seventh decade, the possibility of her death coming within the next few years loomed.

Antipater was happy with the queen's plans. He felt certain John would keep him on as his chief counselor. He confided to Lev, "Although we must ingratiate ourselves to both princes, we must ultimate align ourselves with John. He is weak-willed and easily controlled. And I plan on being the one who will control him."

Lev had his doubts. Not about John, but about his younger brother, Aristobulus. Where John was happy to study the Law and surround himself with priests and scribes, Aristobulus was far more volatile. Lev suspected he had eyes on the throne. With the Pharisees and Sadducees still vying for power, Aristobulus need only back whomever his brother did not in order to raise his own army and stage a revolt.

"Why am I not surprised to see you daydreaming?"

Lev lifted his head at his father's voice. "I am meditating on the scripture I read."

Malachi lowered himself into the chair next to him. His substantial girth spread out like bread rising in the oven. His corpulent face radiated displeasure at something.

"What have I done now, Father?"

"This afternoon you overstepped your position as my son, confronting me over the situation with Daniel."

Lev shook his head. "I do not understand your hatred of his family. You admit he is your finest pupil. Why not honor Phanuel for raising him to love the Law as you do?"

Malachi wagged a finger at his son. "Do not mention that man's name again. Not in this house."

"What has he done? That you hate him so much?"

"It is none of your concern. Obey me in this."

Lev sipped his wine. "But why do you hold Daniel's sister in such obvious contempt as well? She can have done nothing to you."

His father leaned back into his chair and scratched his beard. "She herself is innocent, but not worthy of your attentions."

"Surely her new position in the palace has lifted her in your sight?"

"A seamstress?" Malachi laughed harshly. "She will be little more than a slave."

"She will be an intimate to the queen. That, in itself, is a worthy asset for a man who wishes to move within the palace. Gain a foothold in the government. Do you not realize that gossip from inside the queen's court is more highly valued than gold?"

Lev watched his father and the familiar coldness in his eyes.

"You can gain your desired information from her brother. I am sure she will tell him anything he asks." Malachi said. "But you must not encourage her. I will never stoop to speak to that man on your behalf."

"But I—"

"No!" Malachi pounded his fist on the arm of the chair. "I have seen the way you look at her."

Lev forced a smile. "I look at many women that way. I find them fascinating."

"But it is different with her. Why?" He threw his arms up in exasperation. "There are more beautiful women around every corner of the city."

Lev's chest ached thinking of Anna. Of her dark hair, thick and straight, and the way the sunlight danced in its golden highlights. At least, it had when she had been younger. Before custom dictated she keep her head covered when out in public. Her eyes, too, bright. Brown in some light, but sometimes, if she were excited, flashes of emerald sparkled in them.

"Get your mind off her." Malachi's voice was ice. "It is a match I will never allow."

As the sun set the following evening, Tova came to the door. "Anna! I brought your cloth. I am sorry I could not bring it to you yesterday. Mother was in a mood and my little sisters would not stop fighting. I had to take them—" Her cheeks reddened when she caught sight of Anna's brother. "Daniel! I-I-I did not know you were here."

Seemingly oblivious to Tova's infatuation, Daniel smiled broadly. "*Shalom*, Tova. How are you?"

Anna followed the line of her friend's gaze and noted it rested directly on her brother's lips. She gestured for Tova to come in. "Would you like to sit for a moment?"

Her friend nodded, nearly collapsing on a stool by the table.

"Do you need a cup of water?"

Again, Tova nodded. Her eyes remained glued on Daniel, as if memorizing his face. He sat, bowed over one of the few scrolls Phanuel had saved the money to buy.

He glanced up again. "Your family is well?"

"Yes." She nodded, a spastic movement which caused some of her curls to escape her mantle. "Very well. Thank you for asking. And you? Your family? Are they well?"

He chuckled. "I am well." He glanced toward his sister. "Anna? Are you well?"

"Always, brother." She gave her friend a cup of water. "Mother? How are you today?"

Miriam was sitting up on her pallet, her back supported by the wall. "I am well today, thank Adonai."

Tova lifted her hands to hide the bright red blush of her cheeks. When she did, the cloth she carried waved like a flag, bringing even more attention to her embarrassment.

Anna came to her rescue by stepping to Tova's side, blocking her from Daniel's view. "Is that my cloth?"

Hidden for the moment, Tova let her shoulders droop. She took a deep breath and sat up straight before answering, "Yes. It is made from Egyptian flax. Just as you asked." With a nod of her head, she indicated Anna should move out of the way.

Anna held the linen stretched across her arms. "It is beautiful. As soft and light as a whisper." She crossed to her mother. "Feel it."

Miriam caressed the fabric. "Worthy of our queen. What pattern will you make?"

"I am not sure." She turned back to Tova. "Were you able to get the thread I asked for?"

Tova pulled a skein of silver thread the size of a hen's egg from a pouch at her waist. "I tried to talk the merchant down in price, but he would not budge. This is all I could get."

Anna placed the items carefully into her sewing basket. "It will be an accent to the design. Enough to catch the light and call attention to the one who wears it."

Tova folded her hands on the table, then pulled them apart to straighten her plain brown tunic. She folded her hands again. Her eyes pleaded for Anna's help as Daniel went back to reading the scroll.

Unused to having to force conversation in her house, Anna struggled to think of something to say. She sat down on the stool next to her friend. "Daniel decided to sleep here again tonight."

Tova glanced at Daniel, but he remained engrossed in his scroll. Her brows furrowed for a moment before her face lit up. "How long will you be able to stay?"

"Daniel," Anna called when he did not answer.

He lifted his head. "Hmm?"

"How long did Malachi say you could stay with us?"

He stretched his long arms over his head. "Only until the morrow. He expects me back for instruction as always."

Tova studied him as he scratched the stubble on his chin. "I wish you could stay longer." Her cheeks blazed red again. "For your sister.

And mother. While Phanuel is gone." She jumped to her feet. "I should go. *Shalom*."

Anna rushed to follow her to the door. "I will walk with her. It is a lovely evening. I could use some air."

Tova raced outside then turned to drop her forehead against the wall. "How could I be so foolish around your brother? What can he think of me?"

Anna wrapped her arm around her friend's shoulders. "It was not that bad. Honestly."

Tova's eyes peered up at her. "Lying is a sin."

"Come." Anna gave her a squeeze. "You must not brood about it. I am sure Daniel did not notice anything. He was probably thinking only about the Scriptures he read."

Tova lifted her head from the wall. "Really?"

"He is just like Father. When he is reading, he sees and hears nothing. Come."

They strolled hand-in-hand down the middle of the narrow street. "I have thought of so many ways to capture his attention, but I was not prepared to see him. You should have told me he was staying later than usual."

"I did not know!" Anna playfully yanked as if to let go of Tova's hand, but her friend would not let go. "Besides, it was the Sabbath. I should break God's law to let you know? I should risk His punishment for the sake of your love of my brother?"

"Yes!" Tova smiled.

"What a friend you are!" The two girls put their heads together as they giggled.

"What do you see that amuses you?" Daniel trotted up behind them.

Tova and Anna laughed harder. Anna dropped her hand and shifted so Daniel could walk between them. "Nothing, Brother."

"Mother thought it best I accompany you, now that it is dark. To keep you safe."

Anna knew Tova was disappointed he had not thought to come on his own. "We can take care of ourselves. We are not children anymore."

"All the more reason I should come." He glanced between the girls, his eyes lingering a moment on Tova, as if noticing her for the first time that evening. Silver moonlight danced across her face. When she stumbled, he reached over to catch her arm before she fell.

Tova looked up at him, her eyes bright. "Thank you,   Daniel."

"Did you hurt yourself?"

"No." Her lips turned up softly at the corners. "I only took a misstep on the uneven ground."

Anna watched her friend with envy. She had never been so clever around Lev. Tova's calm proved she had pretended to fall. If she had really tripped, she would have been mortified at her clumsiness. Instead, she gazed at Daniel while he still held her arm. His demeanor changed as well. In this short moment, he finally saw Tova as not only Anna's friend, but as a young woman.

Daniel suddenly let go of Tova, as if her touch burned him. He placed his arms awkwardly at his sides.

Tova smiled. "Will you stay home longer next Sabbath?"

"I-I-I am not sure." His shoulders tensed, though his eyes were drawn back to Tova's face. "Malachi is a hard task master. Perhaps, with my Father gone, he will let me . . . ."

"That would be wonderful." Tova flashed him a quick smile. "For your mother and Anna."

The three walked in silence until they reached Tova's house. After saying their goodbyes, Anna and Daniel turned back down the street. A woman stood in her threshold, sweeping out the dirt from her house. Several couples took advantage of the warm night to stretch their legs after the Sabbath. A group of children ran back and forth across the narrow street, shrieking with laughter.

Daniel kicked at a pebble. It bounced several feet in front of them. "Tova . . . is she your age?"

Anna warmed at the thought of her brother finally taking interest in her friend. "She is a little older. She was born the spring before me."

He nodded absently then turned his gaze toward the sky.

Anna looked up too. The stars shone bright in the night, like a great river of diamonds.

She nudged Daniel with her shoulder. "If Father seeks a husband for me, I think Tova's father will seek her betrothal soon, if he has not already."

He sighed heavily. "We are poor, Anna. What would I have to offer a bride?"

"You are a student of one of the finest rabbis in Jerusalem." Her voice grew sharp. "You may have your own school one day."

He let out a pathetic laugh. "I will be lucky to work as our father does. Writing out legal documents for the illiterate."

"Our father provides well for us. We eat. We have a roof over our heads. Clothes and blankets—"

"I know that, but—"

"I know you want more. I do, too. But if this is all Adonai gives you, at least know that it will be enough for Tova."

Daniel studied her. "What has she told you?"

"I will not betray her trust. But be at peace. I know if you convinced our father and hers of the match, Tova would not be disappointed."

Daniel slipped his arm around Anna's so they walked side-by-side. "And what of you? Will you be happy if Father finds you a husband in Tyre?"

"What do you think?"

He pulled her close. "I cannot envision you anywhere but here. You love this city."

"I do." She rested her head on her brother's shoulder. She thought about the choices laid before her. To marry and move to Tyre or to work as a servant in the palace. "I would rather remain a maid than leave Jerusalem."

Daniel stopped them. "Do not tempt Adonai with such thoughts. It is your duty to marry and bear children."

"But to leave everything I know. Everyone I love. To live among strangers?"

He stepped away from her. "It is the way of Adonai. Your husband's family would become yours."

"But what of the market?" She knew her argument sounded petty, but she still voiced her fear. "To never again smell the spices from the Syrian traders, or touch the linens from Egypt?"

"Tyre is a port city. There will be traders there as well."

"But what if this man I am to marry does not live in the port? What if he lives up in the mountains somewhere? What if he is cruel? If he beats me?"

Daniel took hold of her shoulders. "You know our father will seek out a kind man for you. A man worthy of you."

The fears she had wrestled with over the past week spilled out of her. "But to never again hear the *shofar* calling me to worship? Or the songs of the priests? To never smell the incense lifting up our prayers to Adonai?" Her chest ached. "I cannot bear to live so far away from the temple."

He shook her gently. "You must not say such things. You know what the Law demands."

"Yes! Of course I do." She lowered her voice as she spied several doors opening and faces peering out at them. "But I know our God is merciful. He is El-Roi, the God who sees me. And as long as I have breath, I will pray that He will see my distress and allow me to stay in His holy city."

Chapter 5

Two Weeks Later

"Phanuel." Miriam sat up to embrace her husband when he knelt by her pallet. A small cloud of dust rose from his robe as she patted his back. Anna noted the mud caked on his sandals. She hurried to pour a bowl of water from the cistern in the courtyard so she could wash his feet. Although not clean enough to cook with, the collected rainwater meant she did not have to run to the well for such a task as this. Her trembling hands made the water slosh over the rim as she carried it back into the house.

"It is good to be home." Phanuel sat on the floor next to his wife. "The journey was harder than when I was a boy." He leaned back on his hands. "You look well, Miriam. Perhaps my absence is good for your health?"

Her eyes danced. "It is your returning home that has made me better."

Phanuel kissed her cheek.

Anna placed the bowl down by the table. "Come, Father."

He groaned as he stood, and when he lowered himself to the stool Anna set for him, his body popped and creaked. She knew his journey had been long and difficult but, as she lifted his right foot and placed it in the bowl, she again prayed that his mission had been unsuccessful. With a washcloth, she gently scrubbed off the sand and caked dirt. Once clean, she rubbed olive oil on the chaffed skin to help it heal. She did the same for the other foot. All the while, neither she nor her parents spoke.

When she finished, she took the bowl of water to the courtyard and poured it out on the small garden of herbs planted in the corner. She glanced up at the swath of evening stars visible overhead. She whispered before she went back inside, "Let me stay here in Jerusalem. I beg of you."

Phanuel watched her re-enter the house. "You have not asked whether I was successful in my journey."

She dried the bowl then set it on a wooden shelf, unable to meet his gaze. "I know you will tell me when you are ready."

"My Uncle Ilan has a grandson. A shipbuilder." He paused as if to see if Anna would speak. "I met him. He is a fine young man. We could travel before the winter rains come to make the betrothal official."

Anna pressed her hands against the wall as her heart sank to her stomach. All her prayers had been in vain.

"Did you sign a contract with him?" Miriam called from her bed.

Phanuel dragged his gaze from Anna to look at his wife. "We shook hands on the arrangement. I gave him my word."

Miriam groaned. "An honor contract . . . still, it is not as binding as one written and sealed."

His face grew dark. "If I should break it, my word will mean nothing."

"Tell him your news, Anna."

The lines in her father's face deepened as his brows furrowed. "What news?"

Anna glanced toward her mother, drawing strength from her nod of approval. "While you were gone, I had an offer from the queen."

He blinked, as if he could not understand her words. "An offer?"

"She has seen my skill with the needle and wishes me to work for her in the palace." Anna licked her lips. "She asked to speak with you upon your return to Jerusalem."

Embers in the cooking fire crackled, filling the silence in the small house.

Phanuel watched as a log crumbled in the heat, sending sparks into the air. "Did she command I go to the palace?"

Anna shook her head.

Her father let out a long, gravelly sigh. "Perhaps we will journey to Tyre earlier than I anticipated. If the betrothal ceremony were completed—"

"You would defy the queen?" Miriam pushed herself so she sat up straighter. "Anna has a gift, Phanuel. She surpassed my skill at such a young age. Imagine what she could create given the kind of material and thread she would find in the palace."

Phanuel waved a dismissive hand. "To have her serve a monarchy that embraces everything our God has told us to avoid? I must protect my daughter from such a thing."

"But Queen Salome is returning to the old ways, Father." Anna struggled not to raise her voice. "Daniel says she has already sent letters to the Pharisees who sought refuge in Egypt during the king's reign. She is calling them back to Israel."

"To kill them, most likely."

"No, to give them more power in the courts. Positions within the Sanhedrin. Daniel says—"

"When have you seen, Daniel?" Her father's cheeks reddened. "You have not been to his school, have you?"

Her heart raced at his anger. "He visited here. For the Sabbaths."

Phanuel rested his arms against the table. Slowly, he lowered his head into hands. After a few moments he spoke again, his voice barely above a whisper. "I wish to protect you, Anna, from the hardships of this world. The vanity in the palace will only lead to pain and disappointment." He kept his head down. "I will go to the market tomorrow and see if I can find another caravan traveling to Tyre."

Anna folded her arms across her stomach, desperate to keep her emotions inside. All her life she had listened to her father rail against the monarchy. She knew he desired to keep her safe. But her fear of living so far away from her family, with a man she did not know, was greater than her fear of whatever blasphemies may exist in the palace.

"Phanuel, please—" Miriam held a hand toward her husband. "Let us pray about it together."

"My mind is clear on this. We will speak no more of it." He let out a long sigh, like a desert wind. "I am tired now. Turn out the lamps, Anna." He stripped off his outer robe and lowered himself down into the alcove next to his wife.

Anna snuffed out the lamps. She unrolled her reed mat and spread out her wool blanket but knew sleep would be a long time coming. She sat on her pallet in the corner, drawing her knees up to her chin while she stared at the fading flames in the hearth across the room. The hope she had of staying in Jerusalem died like the embers in the hearth. Once burning bright, they now lay cold and black in the ashes.

"I will talk to Tova's family tomorrow to see if she may care for Miriam." Phanuel spoke in a whisper as his wife slept the following afternoon. "I have found a caravan leaving for Tyre in a week."

Anna nodded, afraid her voice would betray her if she spoke. Her emotions were scattered and unfocused. One moment she longed to crumple to the floor and cry until her tears dried up. The next she wanted to rail at the stars and demand God change her father's heart.

Phanuel seemed to understand her mood. "He is a good man, your kinsman. His name is Menahem."

Anna continued to stir the lentil soup she was making again for dinner. *Always we have lentils. Never fish. Or lamb. Always lentils.*

"He is not much older than Daniel," her father continued. "A strong man. With a fine trade. He looks forward to meeting you."

I wish I felt the same. The gentle boiling of the soup   mesmerized her. The bubbling liquid seeming to mimic how volatile and distressed her soul felt as her life was dictated by others. Phanuel. Menahem. One man she loved and honored. One man she did not even know.

"I hope you come to trust me in this matter." Her father stood by her side. "I want only to make you happy. To keep you safe."

Again, she could not speak. She closed her eyes and breathed deeply.

Phanuel gathered his stylus and parchment together. "I will return at sunset. I may as well see if anyone has work for me to do with what remains of the day." He opened the door, taking a step back when met by a woman and a soldier. Anna recognized the woman as the Queen's servant.

Ziva spoke first. "You are Phanuel, I presume?"

"Who asks for me?"

"I am Ziva," She bowed her head to him. "A servant to Queen Salome Alexandra. She asks to speak with you regarding your daughter, Anna."

He drew himself up. "She cannot serve in the palace."

Ziva's brows rose in surprise. "You would deny your queen without even a meeting?"

Phanuel clutched the parchment to his chest, his harsh countenance cracking under Ziva's scrutiny.

"I hope you will not make me return to Queen Salome, the ruler of all Israel, and tell her that Phanuel, a scribe, turned away her direct request. One she did not have to make."

His eyes shifted between Ziva and the guard. "I meant no disrespect."

Ziva stood several inches shorter than Phanuel, but her voice and stature carried an authority that made her appear much taller. "I cannot believe you would be foolish enough to consider being called a traitor when all she asks is to speak with you. To deny the queen could be considered treason."

Anna grieved to see her father so uncertain. In all her life, even when she did not agree with his decisions, she had known one thing: he believed he was in the right. It gave him his strength. Now this woman had stripped him of that confidence.

"Go to the palace, Phanuel." Miriam sat up on her pallet. "Trust Adonai. If this is not the right choice for our daughter, He will make a way out."

He gave her a short nod then drew in a deep breath before stepping over the threshold.

"She desires to meet your daughter, as well." Ziva peered into the house. She smiled when she caught sight of Anna in the shadows. "Come, child. Come meet your queen."

Anna's heart beat so fast she feared it would burst from her chest. "Father?"

He lifted his head in her direction. Defeat etched in his face. "We must obey."

Anna ran to her sewing basket to retrieve the belt she had completed while her father travelled. She folded it carefully, then wrapped it within another piece of fabric so the dust on the streets did not sully her gift.

Phanuel glanced toward Miriam. "Are you well enough? Can we leave you alone?"

"Go." She clasped her hands together as if in prayer. "We will trust in the Lord."

With that, Phanuel turned to wait with Ziva and her escort for Anna.

She knelt to give her mother a kiss. "What should I do? If she asks me to serve her?"

Miriam cupped her cheeks. "Pray for wisdom, my little Anna. You know in your heart what you desire. Pray now that the Lord will make a way." Her eyes took on a glassy appearance. "Perhaps, like the blessed Esther, you have been chosen for such a time as this." She kissed Anna's cheek. "Hurry now. Do not forget, I love you."

"I love you, too, Mother." Anna swallowed the hard rock of emotion in her throat. She had dreamed of this moment for weeks, but now that it had come, she feared it.

"Anna!" Phanuel called from the street.

She glanced around the room where she had lived her entire life. Taking a deep breath, she stepped outside.

Chapter 6

The Same Day

Ziva bowed as she walked through the threshold of the throne room. "Your Majesty, I present to you Phanuel, a scribe of the tribe of Asher, and his daughter, Anna."

Anna and her father were ushered in by a duo of armed guards. As Anna took a timid step forward, her sandal scraped against the stone beneath her feet. She had never seen marble as beautiful. The temple may be made of similar stone, but years and weather had dulled and yellowed the rock. Here, the marble was pure white with streaks of grey and black swirling through it like clouds on a windy day. The walls were made of the same stone and glistened in the light of the torches surrounding the room. Great columns shouldered the massive roof some thirty feet above her head. It took every ounce of courage to pull her gaze from the magnificence of the room to look to the far end. A tall man, dressed in the robes of a Pharisee, stood at the bottom of the dais. Sitting on her throne was the queen.

Queen Salome Alexandra could not be called beautiful, not in a traditional sense. Anna decided the best word to describe the queen's features was handsome. She had the high forehead and wide nose more common in a man. Her brown eyes looked keen and aware of everything around her. Studying. Observing. Forming instant judgements about the two subjects standing before her.

Queen Salome sat upon a dais of the same white marble that made up the floor. Seven steps led up to her throne, an immense chair that appeared to be made of solid gold. A silver crown circled her head, nearly blending with her glorious silver-gray hair, which was coiled in an elaborate braid. Her cream colored gown, edged with gold thread, shimmered as she leaned forward when they approached. A robe of deep indigo flowed over her shoulders and down to her feet, where it pooled on the floor like water.

Anna reached over to clutch her father's hand and felt him squeeze her fingers in return. She willed herself not to faint.

The queen smiled down on them. "Ah, I have been waiting for your return, Phanuel. Was your journey successful?"

He bowed his head. "Yes, Your Majesty."

"That is a blessing." Her voice was deep, much lower than most older women's. Rich and full, almost like the priests' when they chanted their praises to God. "And may I ask the purpose of your trip? A scribe does not usually travel so far from his home."

Phanuel took a deep breath before looking up. "I went to find a suitable husband for my daughter. She is to be betrothed."

"Indeed? But Anna did not go with you. The betrothal ceremony has not yet taken place. Am I correct?"

Her father clasped his hands together, signaling he was thinking how best to answer. "An agreement was made between myself and her cousin."

The queen maintained a serene appearance, but Anna sensed the tension emanating between both her and her father. "Did the agreement include where they would live, should they marry?"

A deep crease formed along the bridge of her father's nose. Anna had seen it before when he studied a particularly hard piece of scripture.

Salome played with the large emerald ring on her finger. "What were the terms of your agreement, Phanuel?"

"That I would bring Anna to him before the rains begin for the betrothal ceremony. She would return within the following eighteen months for the wedding."

"We will send for the man. Perhaps he would be willing to live here, in Jerusalem. If not, we will ask him to forgo the betrothal. Neither of you would lose honor if you both conceded to end the agreement." Her smile returned. "We have need of your daughter, Phanuel. She has a gift that would be an asset, not only to myself, but to the Temple as well."

His eyes narrowed. "The Temple? I do not understand."

"No?" Salome waved toward the gentleman standing along the nearest column. "This is my brother, Shimeon bar Shetach. Explain your thoughts regarding Anna's talents."

The tall man strode forward, his black silk robes reflecting the torch flames that hung along the stone walls and lit the immense hall. His thick gray beard hung down to his substantial stomach. Anna's knees shook at his appearance, but he smiled kindly at her before nodding to her father.

"Phanuel, it was I who first noticed the fine stitch work on Rabbi Malachi's robe. Although the initial design was not your daughter's, it was obvious she could copy the master's design. Such a keen eye and steady hand would indeed bless the priests in the Temple. Their robes must be replaced as they get stained from the sacrifices. And of course, the ephod of the High Priest must be made to exact specifications."

Her father's eyes widened. "You want her to sew for the High Priest?"

"If you would allow it, yes." Shimeon nodded toward the dais. "Of course, the queen would also employ her to sew for her, as well, on occasion."

"I am not the ruler my husband was, God grant him rest." Queen Salome's sight focused inward. "I long to restore order to Israel and order to our faith. The Pharisees will again be allowed to teach their beliefs freely, without fear of retribution. I will reestablish the proper observances of the Feasts of the Lord." She turned her attention to Phanuel. "I promise you, your daughter would be well looked after in my household. And you, as her father, would rise to a greater position within the ranks of the Pharisees. My brother would see to that."

Shimeon folded his hands together, resting them on top of his stomach. "Indeed. If you would care to show me some of your work, I could see where your talents would be best suited."

Phanuel closed his eyes. His lips moved almost imperceptibly, but Anna knew he prayed for Adonai to speak to him. To guide him.

Shimeon raised an eyebrow toward the queen. She turned her focus to Anna. "How old are you, child?"

Anna forced herself to speak loudly and with a steady voice. "I will have seen fourteen years when the rains come."

"We do not wish to force our will on you. Would you be willing to forgo this betrothal to serve us?"

Anna's spirit leapt with joy. She struggled to appear faithful to her father without letting her voice betray her happiness at the thought of remaining in Jerusalem. "I wish to obey my father's will in all things . . . but if Adonai allows it, I would be honored to serve you, and Him, in whatever way He deems possible."

The corner of the queen's mouth rose. "A diplomatic answer. Very good." Her focused gaze danced to Shimeon. "It is not often we see one so young able to curb their own desires for those of their elders, is it?"

"Alas, no."

Salome again addressed Anna. "What is that you hold, child?"

Anna's hands shook as she unwrapped the gift she had made. She held the belt toward Shimeon. "I made this for the queen. A small token to show my gratitude for this opportunity."

"Bring it to us, Brother."

Shimeon carried the cloth up the dais. He bowed his head as he passed it to the queen.

Salome unfolded the linen with a sigh of approval. She laid it across her legs to study the design. Her fingers traced the intricate pattern of leaves and vines Anna had sewn throughout the fabric.

Shimeon bent over to see it better. "Exquisite. I have never seen such fine work from one so young." He glanced at the queen. "If she is half as talented with the loom as with the needle, she could weave the curtain for the Holy of Holies. It would be the most splendid addition to the temple in many years."

Salome inclined her head. "It would be a blessing to be able to give such a gift to Adonai . . . ."

Anna's chest tightened so that she could barely take in a breath. *To work on the curtain for the Holy of Holies . . . could there be a higher honor for any woman?*

Phanuel stood tall at her side, eyes now open, his shoulders back. "If Menahem is willing to move here or forgo our agreement, then I will allow Anna to work as a seamstress. I entrust her future to you, and to Adonai."

Anna gasped, her heart leaping within her chest. *There is still hope!*

"Then we will send for him immediately." Shimeon clapped his hands. "For we hate to have even one more day pass until your daughter can use her talents to honor our God."

Queen Salome lifted the belt off her legs and passed it to him, but her focus remained on Phanuel. "Perhaps you will allow Anna to stay with us until this Menahem can arrive? It would please us greatly to have her work on the High Priest's new ephod until the final decision is made regarding her fate."

Anna's father turned to her. A mixture of pride and fear fought behind his eyes. He held out his hands to her, grasping hers tightly when she placed them in his. "You have always been obedient to me and to the Lord. I command you to remain true to all I have taught you in my house." His voice cracked. "You are a maid of honor and virtue. Do not forgo who you are for any fleeting offer or kindness. Do you understand me?"

She knew her father spoke of Lev. With her new position in the palace, it was possible Malachi would change his mind about her. But she had been promised to Menahem. Any indiscretion on her part and not only would her betrothal be void, but possibly her life.

"Do you understand?"

"Yes, Father. I understand. I promise, I will not betray your trust in me."

Lev sat with his father's other students on one of several wooden benches in the school. Located across the courtyard from their house, the building was made of limestone blocks and lit by oil lamps. He stared at one of the dancing flames as he shifted on the bench. His back ached from hunching over to read the scroll on his lap. He should have been studying a passage in Solomon's Proverbs, but he thought instead about Antipater. His mentor had hinted they might dine again at the palace tonight. Lev enjoyed this new development in his relationship with the older man. The Idumaean trusted Lev to be discreet and often asked him to act as a scribe as Antipater counselled John Hyrcanus. Sometimes, if John were busy elsewhere, Antipater would seek out Aristobulus's company. Although seemingly more than his brother, Aristobulus could be counted on to have the latest news regarding the political machinations in other countries such as Egypt, Nabatea, and Syria.

"Congratulations, Daniel." Although a heavy man, Malachi seemed to glide into the library where his students sat bent over scrolls. Lev's mind turned over the reasons his father would have to congratulate his friend.

Daniel looked up. "Have you heard news of my sister?"

The rabbi slapped a hand on the young man's shoulder. "As of yesterday, she is settled in the palace. She is already working on a new ephod for John Hyrcanus. His mother wants him properly attired when he officially becomes High Priest."

A murmur ran throughout the room as the other students congratulated Daniel. For such an honor to fall on his family was a blessing indeed.

Although his father appeared to celebrate Daniel's good fortune, Lev could feel an undercurrent of malice radiating from him. There must be more to this news than Malachi revealed. His father looked toward Lev as he spoke again. "And Anna has been betrothed."

Lev's heart went cold.

"To whom?" Daniel asked.

Malachi continued to watch his son, his face full of happiness. "I do not know the man's name, only that he is a shipbuilder from Tyre." He turned to Daniel. "I congratulate you, again. But now," he pointed to the scroll on Daniel's lap. "It is time to get back to work."

The young men let out sighs or groans depending on their dedication to their studies.

Lev let out neither. He stared at the parchment in front of him while the letters jumbled mindlessly in his head. Anna betrothed. To another man. Some other will take her in his arms and lie with her.

Sweat beaded along his forehead and in his palms. Will this man appreciate her gentle laugh? Will his touch elicit the same trembling when he brushed her hand? His blood pounded in his ears. Pain throbbed behind his eyes.

He placed his fingertips on his temples and rubbed, trying to get control of his anger. Malachi enjoyed causing him this pain. It made Lev despise him all the more. He was tired of his father's juvenile displays of power. Malachi longed to be considered a great teacher, and by most he was. But Lev knew the truth. Malachi's knowledge of scripture was sophomoric at best. He could retain the words on the page, but to understand them? To extract the heart of the words? That escaped him.

Lev barely participated in the class's discussion of Solomon's description of wisdom. He longed to plead his case to Anna's father. Custom dictated that betrothals were worked out between fathers, but this was a new era. A woman ruled Israel. Why should a man not fight to marry the woman he desired?

The day passed in a blur as Lev continued to imagine how he could approach Anna's father. At last, Malachi dismissed his students. He placed a hand on Lev's shoulder. "I heard it is a binding contract. One that cannot be broken."

Lev flinched at his father's touch.

"Do not humiliate me, or yourself, by your actions. She is another's wife."

"What ails you tonight?" Aristobulus, the queen's younger son, lifted his goblet of wine as he perused Lev. A few years older than Lev, the prince's smile was cheerful and kind. His eyes twinkled with lighthearted mirth. He turned to the distinguished-looking gentleman at his side. "Antipater, what is the matter with your young friend?"

The older man stroked his thick, black beard. "I do not know, my prince. He seems rather melancholy tonight, does he not?" He strode over to Lev then peered into his goblet. "He is already out of wine. Perhaps that is it?"

Lev did not respond until Antipater took the cup from his hand. "I was not finished with that."

"I believe you were." Antipater tipped the vessel upside down. Not a drop poured out.

Lev shook his head. "I am not much company tonight."

"And why is that?" Aristobulus asked as he signaled to a servant in the corner. The young slave took his cue and brought a jar of wine to refill the empty cup. "What has distracted you today? Perhaps a particularly hard scripture?" The prince held out his own cup to be refilled, swallowing several mouthfuls before speaking again. "I am sure my illustrious brother could enlighten you." He let out a snort of disdain.

Antipater watched the younger prince with a keen eye, but did not try to defend John Hyrcanus. Instead he grinned at Lev, his smile bright against his dark brown skin. "Although an intelligent student, my friend seldom meditates on the Law once he is done with school." A tall man, it took him a moment to lower himself to Lev's side on the couch. He glanced toward Aristobulus. "I think our younger friend is in love."

Lev slouched back against the couch. He did not want to admit his weakness to the prince nor his counselor, but he had wanted to return to his father's house even less.

Antipater put his arm around Lev's shoulders. "What is her name?" He winked toward the prince. "Perhaps we can have her brought to you, if she is a woman of loose morals."

Lev stiffened under his friend's touch. "She is an honorable maiden. A true daughter of Israel."

"I apologize." The older man placed his free hand over his heart. "I did not mean to offend you. Only tease you out of your melancholy."

Lev stood and paced the room. "I did not know how deeply I cared for her until she was promised to another man."

Aristobulus sighed. "Is that not always the way? Once you learn you cannot obtain something, it becomes an obsession. Maybe I could help." He ran a hand through his thick, curly hair. "Being the queen's son does have a few advantages."

Lev shook his head. "My father holds some grudge against the girl's father."

"Family can get in the way of one's plans." The prince scratched his chin. He kept his beard cropped close to his face in the Greek fashion. "But, if you do not hold their affection too dear, you may be able to manipulate things to your advantage."

"Who is she?" Antipater stretched his long legs out in front of him.

"Anna, daughter of Phanuel the scribe." Lev paused in his pacing. "The queen has settled her into the palace as a seamstress. Even now, she is working on the new ephod for your brother's confirmation as High Priest."

"Lucky girl, to receive such an honor." Aristobulus sniffed. He studied Lev. "What would it be worth to you, if I were able to intercede on your behalf with my mother?"

"Your Highness, I would not presume—"

"You presume nothing." He sipped his wine. "I am offering my help, but should I ask for yours at a later date, would you give it? A favor for a favor?"

Lev glanced at Antipater. He knew his mentor preferred John Hyrcanus to be the next ruler of Israel, but that did not mean his brother would not be a worthy ally.

The prince set down his goblet. "Well?"

"I would be glad to help my prince in any way he desires, barring treason to the throne."

"Heaven forbid any of us ever contemplate that." Aristobulus grinned as he stood. "I am tired now. You are welcome to enjoy more of my mother's wine if it pleases you."

Both Lev and Antipater bowed, but it was Lev's mentor who answered, "Although grateful for the offer, there would be no pleasure without your company."

"You do not have to pretend. I know you would have preferred to spend the evening with my brother, though for the life of me, I cannot imagine why." He chuckled softly. "John will be busy with the priests until the dedication ceremony. I am afraid you are stuck with my company until then."

"We desire to serve you both, my lord." Antipater bowed again.

"I am sure you do." Aristobulus strode out of the room.

Antipater waited a moment after the prince had disappeared before turning his back on Lev. "Come."

"You are angry with me for saying I would return the favor."

Antipater was silent down the long hallway until they were outside, in the courtyard. "It is never a wise idea to indebt yourself to man who has that much power."

"What could I ever do for him politically? I am nothing."

They strode from the palace courtyard and made their way onto the narrower streets until they reached Antipater's house. He paused outside his gate.

"Perhaps I was wrong about you." He looked down at Lev. "I thought you were ambitious. That you desired more from your life than teaching at your father's school."

Lev drew himself up. "You know I do."

"Do you think I desire to be the princes' lackey for the rest of my life?" He spoke in a harsh whisper, but his anger still came through. "Although we must keep both princes within our favor, Aristobulus is not Salome's heir."

"I understand."

"Do you?" Antipater swung open the gate. The metal hinges squeaked in protest. "Then act like it in the future."

The gate clanged shut, leaving Lev in the street. *I understand better than you, old man. I do not plan on putting my future solely on the shoulders of John Hyrcanus. He is too weak to carry the responsibility of the crown on his own.*

Lev surveyed the street. This area of the city, where the rabbis, priests, and wealthier merchants lived, was dark and quiet. A few lights flickered in the nearby homes, probably old men studying the scriptures. If he returned to his father's house tonight, that would be his fate also.

Instead, Lev walked down the hill, away from the palace and the Temple Mount. There he knew he would find someone to share a drink . . . and maybe her bed . . . for the night. The only thing that might help take his mind off losing Anna.

Chapter 7

The Following Day

Anna sat on a stool near an open window. She preferred working in natural light rather than in a room lit by oil lamps and torches. She laid her hands on the ephod spread out on the table. This garment would cover the High Priest's deep blue tunic as a kind of apron. Another seamstress had started the work, but the queen had not been pleased. From a distance, the squares of red and blue that decorated the shoulders of the ephod looked well enough. Upon closer inspection however,   Anna could see where the embroiderer had left tiny gaps between her stitches. Anna set out to fill in those slivers then add her own squares to the pattern. After that, the entire ephod must be bordered with gold thread. It was an immense amount of work. And she had only three weeks to finish it.

She carefully pulled the dark blue thread through the eye of the bronze needle, all the while praying silently, *Adonai, I ask that You guide my fingers and my eyes. Help me create a garment worthy of Your High Priest. Let the sacrifice of my time, and the talent You have given me, be acceptable to You.*

Piercing the linen with the needle, she began. It was her second day to work on the ephod, and the thrill of it had not left her even though her back ached from yesterday's hunching over the garment from sunup to sundown. She prayed over each stitch, asking Adonai to help Israel, by blessing its political leader, Queen Salome, and its future religious leader, John Hyrcanus.

She paused at noon when a young slave girl brought a tray with bread and cheese. The girl did not speak, but placed a small jug on the table as well before bowing out through the doorway.

"Thank you," Anna called as she stood. Her muscles protested as she stretched and reached an arm toward the ceiling, enjoying the sensation of tension being released from her shoulders. She reached the other arm up.

"That is an interesting dance."

She let out a startled gasp. A man stood in the threshold. She guessed him to be of around thirty years, although it was hard to judge because he kept his beard shaved close to his face, unlike most of the men she knew who let their beards grow with age. He was of high rank, as his linen tunic and robe were pristine with no tears or fraying of the edges. The color also indicated wealth; few people could afford the deep indigo dyes that came from the northern countries. She hoped to one day learn the process of creating that color. She knew it involved using shells collected from the ocean, but she had never seen one, never mind the ocean.

She bowed. "You caught me unaware, I am afraid. I was merely allowing my muscles to ease before I began to work again."

The man took a step inside the room. "May I see it?"

His deep hazel eyes stared intently at her, causing her stomach to knot. "I am not sure the queen wants anyone to see it before the ceremony."

With only his short beard to cover his face, she could easily see the dimples in his cheeks when he smiled. "I am sure my mother would not mind me taking a peek at it beforehand."

Anna's face grew warm and she knew she blushed. "I am so sorry, my lord." She dropped into a deep curtsey. "I-I-I did not recognize you."

"Why should you? We have not yet been introduced." He reached his hand out to help her up. "My name is Aristobulus. It is quite a mouthful, is it not?" He laughed softly. "My friends call me Ari."

His hand felt smooth. And warm. "Your Highness."

He lifted her chin so she had to look him in the face. "If I had to guess, your name is Anna, yes?"

She had trouble finding her voice, so she nodded instead.

He perused her with his eyes, not in a leering way, but as if he were absorbing every detail of her. She could not fathom why. Could the queen have sent him to investigate her work? To make sure it met with her standards? She shivered at his scrutiny.

"I have only just begun." She stepped away, allowing him a clear view of the table. "I hope it meets with your approval."

"It is not mine you need, little Anna, but my brother's and my mother's." He bent over the ephod, his face softening as he looked at it. "Already I can see how exquisite your stitches are compared to the woman's who started it." He lifted his gaze to her. "Perhaps it is your youth. Your eyes are strong. Keen. And your fingers much more nimble."

Her cheeks warmed again at his compliments. "I pray it will be a garment worthy of your brother."

He let out a snort of air. "Never fear that, Anna. It is my brother that should worry about being worthy to wear something so fine." He seemed to smile at her embarrassment. "I will leave you to your work."

She curtsied again as he walked toward the door. He paused in the threshold. "I think I know a friend of yours."

She could not help the small giggle that escaped her throat. "I doubt very much that any of my friends know you, Your Highness."

"Ari," he reminded her. "Please, call me Ari. And my friend's name is Lev. His father is Malachi, a rabbi."

The room seemed to tilt. Anna reached her hand out to the table for support.

The prince watched her. "Are you unwell? Are you faint?"

She centered her thoughts before she answered, "I am well. Only tired from my work this morning."

Ari walked back to the table and poured her a cup of   watered wine. "Of course. Drink now. Regain your strength."

Her hands trembled as she took the cup. She had to concentrate to bring the wine to her lips without spilling any. "Thank you."

"He asked about you last night." The prince's eyes never left her face. "Our friend, Lev. He wanted to know about your betrothal. Has a contract been signed?"

"No." Anna's voice quivered. She struggled to keep her thoughts on the prince instead of wondering why Lev had spoken about her betrothal to him. "Your mother has sent for the man . . . my kinsman . . . Menahem . . . to ask if he would be willing to live in Jerusalem so that I may continue my work."

"So he does not live here?" He sounded intrigued. "Where is he from, this Menahem?"

"Tyre. He works as a shipbuilder." She took another sip of wine.

Ari grinned. "There is not much call for a shipbuilder in Jerusalem. Did my mother say what she would do if Menahem did not wish to relocate?"

Anna could not comprehend the prince's curiosity, but would not dare to question him about it. "She hoped he would agree to void his verbal contract with my father."

"Hmm." Ari nodded. "Interesting." His voice was kind, not belittling. His countenance that of a concerned older brother. He waited to speak until Anna turned her face up toward him. "And how would you feel about that? What is it you desire most, our little seamstress?"

"I pray continually that the Lord would allow me to stay in Jerusalem."

"Well, then." The prince refilled her goblet. "As I know it would also make our mutual friend very happy, I will endeavor to do all I can to make it so." He put the jug down and took her hands in his. "It was a pleasure to meet you, Anna. I am sure I will be seeing you again as you continue to work here in the palace."

When he left, Anna lowered herself onto the stool and tried to catch her breath. She did not know what made her heart race more: the fact that she had spoken with the prince, or his news that Lev had spoken so intimately about her. As she felt her lips dance upward into a smile, she knew her answer.

Maybe Tova had been correct. Now that she served in the palace, perhaps Malachi would give his permission for her and Lev to marry. A giddiness rose up from her toes, as if she were filled with feathers that that would allow her to fly. She hopped off the stool and ran to the open window. She wanted to shout her joy to the hills around her, but covered her mouth with her hands instead. She would not risk censure from anyone passing by exclaiming her love to the world. *Oh, that I might be Lev's wife and stay here, in David's city!*

The sky over Jerusalem shone a brilliant blue with barely a cloud to mar its pristine beauty. The city bustled below her at its normal, chaotic pace. In the distance, a flock of doves rose up from the Temple courtyard as a priest guided a man through the gate that barred women from the altar. The man led a young lamb behind him as an offering.

Sorrow dampened Anna's happiness as she backed away. She had never gotten used to the Lord's demand that blood must be shed in order to cleanse His people of their sins. She was glad she was too far away to hear the animal's bleating. She cried every Passover when her father led the lamb they had kept in the house to slaughter. Although the Feast was a time of celebration for God's deliverance, she could never enjoy the meal knowing that the lamb she ate had given its life for her.

She refused to dwell on sad thoughts today. Instead, she ate her lunch of bread and cheese then set herself to her task. All the while, she thanked God for the new hope He had given her. So intent was she on her work that she did not lift her eyes from the garment until someone coughed. She was surprised to see the sun had set below the hills, oil lamps had been lit in the room while she sewed, and the queen's counselor stood in the doorway.

"I will take the ephod back to the priests now." Shimeon came to her side. "Unless you wish to continue working through the night?"

Anna rubbed the back of her neck. Now that she had been disturbed, she felt every kink and knot in her muscles. "I had better stop until the morning."

Shimeon gazed down at the table, the flames of the lamps reflecting in his eyes. He bent to examine her work closer. "Our Lord's providence never ceases to amaze me." He straightened himself up. "I had only just told our queen that a new embroiderer would have to be found to complete the High Priest's ephod, when the following day she met a man with an exquisite robe." He smiled warmly at her. "That man led us to you." He folded the ephod with care. "Truly, you were sent by God to finish this task."

Anna bowed. "I am thankful to serve Him."

He glanced toward a tray of uneaten food. "Perhaps you should eat first before you go to rest."

"I never heard the servant come in." Her stomach rumbled as she caught the scent of lemon and fresh bread. "I am famished now."

Shimeon held up the ephod. "I will bring this at first light, as I did this morning."

"And I will be waiting for you." She bowed her head. Once he left the room, she went to the tray of food and quickly tore off a mouthful of bread, hoping it would quiet the gurgling in her belly. A piece of fish also lay on the plate. She used more bread to bring the meat to her mouth. Although now cold, the fish still melted on her tongue. Seasoned with lemon, onion, and garlic, she reveled in its intense flavor. Fish had been served for special feast days or when guests visited their house when she was young. Lamb was served on Passover, of course, but other than that, her daily fare had been lentil or barley soup, cheese, and occasionally a stew with goat meat. The food at the palace seemed to be an endless bounty of bread made with fine wheat flour, not the course barley flour she was used to eating, fruits of all kinds, and always for dinner, there was meat or fish.

She sighed contentedly as she finished her plate of food, unfamiliar with the sensation of her stomach being full. She snuffed out all but one of the oil lamps, planning to use it to light her way through the dark hallways. The slave girl who had brought her food for lunch sat on the floor outside of the room.

Anna smiled at the girl who appeared to be only a year or so younger than her. "I am sorry you had to bring me a tray   today. I will try to finish tomorrow in time to eat with the   other servants."

The girl's eyes widened. "The mistress says you are not to be disturbed. I am to bring you whatever you need, whenever you need it." She struggled to stand, her muscles obviously stiff from having sat for so long. She held out her hands for the tray Anna carried. "I wait to serve you alone."

Anna passed it to her, stunned at the revelation. She followed as the girl scurried down the hall. "You have no other work in the palace?"

"Not until after the ephod is done. Until then, I am yours."

The oil lamp cast their shadows against the wall. "What is your name?"

"I am Esther." The girl disappeared around a corner.

Anna caught up with her. "How long have you served in the palace?"

"Only a few months. I was given to King Jannai as payment for my father's debts."

"How old are you?"

"Twelve." Even in the dim light, Esther's sad expression could clearly be seen.

"Perhaps the Queen will release you during *shmita*." Anna hoped Salome would heed the Law that ordered all debts cancelled every seventh year.

"Perhaps. Do you hope to be freed then, too?"

"I am not a bondservant." Guilt tried to creep into her thoughts, but she pushed it away. She was not to blame for Esther's position.

"You are fortunate, then." Esther stopped in front of an entryway. "This is the way to the kitchen. Hagar does not like anyone in it she does not know. Will you wait for me? I do not have a lamp to light my way."

Once the tray had been returned, Anna and Esther continued to the women's quarters. Exhausted from her work, Anna gratefully lay her head on the hard pillow in the room she shared with about a dozen other women. Yesterday, her first night in the palace, she had laid awake, missing the familiar sounds of her home. Tonight, she fell asleep quickly, with Lev's face being her last coherent thought.

Lev groaned as he rolled onto his back. His head pounded like a mason cleaving stone. He struggled to open his eyes then cursed as the morning light accelerated the throbbing.

"Drink this."

The pungent smell of cheap wine forced the bile in his stomach to surge. He turned his head away from the offending liquid and swallowed back the acid in his throat.

"Unless you want to pay for more time, you must leave."

Lev blinked as he sat up. Random memories slipped into his mind as he grabbed the wine from the whore who knelt beside him. After leaving Antipater, he had gone to a friend's house, a former student of his father's. There had been a party. And wine. Good wine. Not like the swill he swallowed now to wash the sour taste of bile from his mouth.

"Do you need more?"

He shook his head. Her face, which had seemed so beautiful last night, was haggard and lined. Streaks of kohl smeared the weathered skin under her eyes.

She motioned with a nod of her head. "Your clothes are there. If you are not out when I return, you will pay another coin."

He fought the urge to slap her for her insolence, and instead drained the cup. He tossed it to the corner. The whore glared at him as she drew a faded, torn curtain across the doorway. Glancing down, he saw he was naked. He drew the bed cover around his waist then stood, his stomach recoiling at its sudden change of elevation. He waited until the floor stopped rolling before shuffling to the corner and retrieving his clothes. He held on to the wall for balance as he slipped on his tunic and then his robe. His fingers could not work the leather strap of his girdle so he threw the belt over his shoulder. The money pouch attached to it felt much lighter than it had last night, and he wondered if he had spent that many coins on wine and the whore, or had she filched some while he slept? Either way, he had no desire to give her any more so he made his way out of the alcove.

The woman eyed him over her shoulder as she squatted by her hearth. "Visit me anytime, my lord."

He snorted. He would find one a little younger the next time he needed a distraction. He brought his hand to his forehead to block the sun as he opened the door. The deserted streets of last night now teemed with life. The air was still cool, signaling he had time to stop home and change his clothes before heading to his father's school. His coat smelled of wine and a whore's perfume for the second *or is it the third* time this week.

Lev shambled up the hill, cursing himself with each step. Trying to forget his frustrations with a harlot was one thing. Drinking to excess was another. He could not show such a fault to Antipater. The Idumaean was fastidious in his appearance and his behavior. He would not approve of Lev's drunkenness and lack of discretion. His mentor never seemed surprised by any crises or problem. He controlled his emotions, a skill Lev needed to emulate if he wanted to succeed in the same political arena.

Antipater had not sent for him since their disagreement, but surely their breach was not permanent. Lev had worked too hard to make himself indispensable to the future High Priest's counselor to see all his work come to nothing. Although the Idumaean was politically astute, the nuances of Jewish Law still evaded him, and that made Lev a valuable asset. Others might have more knowledge, but few were willing to serve Antipater because of his lack of Jewish blood. By the Law, circumcision made Antipater a Jew, but his blood-line only went back to his father. He was not a child of Abraham. His family had not crossed the Red Sea with Moses or destroyed the walls of Jericho with Joshua. Two generations did not make a Jew. Only hundreds of years of suffering could do that.

Lev cringed as the gate to his father's house shrieked when he swung it open. He hoped no one else heard the iron's protestations. He ducked his head inside the entryway, grateful to find it empty. He wanted to go to the kitchen where he knew he would find a crust of bread to settle his sour stomach, but his first priority was to change his clothes. He tread softly toward his room.

"Where have you been?"

Malachi's thundering voice seared Lev's brain like a lightning bolt. He shuddered and grabbed his head.

"Have you nothing to say?"

Lev cleared the phlegm from his throat. "I spent the night with Antipater. We were with Prince Aristobulus until late in the evening. I thought it best not to—"

Malachi's jowls reddened. "You dare lie to me? In my home?"

The pain in Lev's head beat against his temples. He did not have the energy for subterfuge this morning. He lowered his voice to keep his mother from hearing, "I went to visit Saul."

His father's brow furrowed. "The boy from Gad?"

Lev nodded.

Malachi stepped closer and sniffed. "I can smell a whore's perfume."

Anger caused Lev's already upset stomach to churn faster. How else did his father expect him to forget Anna's betrothal? "I was discreet. Do not worry."

"Go. Wash. Change your robe. That Gentile you are so fond of sent a messenger for you this morning. I told him you were running an errand for me."

"Antipater is a Jew. Circumcised into the covenant as you and I are." He waved his hand to dismiss the argument. "What was the message?"

"If you can be at his house by the third hour, he wants to hire you as a scribe for the week." Malachi's eyes darkened with intensity. "I will allow it, since I verified what you have said is true. He is the High Priest's first counselor."

Lev fought his growing irritation. He had not sought his father's blessing when he began cultivating his friendship with Antipater. What made Malachi think he would seek approval now?

"Make yourself presentable." He wagged his finger in Lev's face. "And do not embarrass this family by your behavior. I expect you to keep me informed of all you learn."

Lev watched his father walk away. Malachi would have to rely on someone else to keep him informed.

Chapter 8

Two Weeks Later

As the ceremony to anoint John Hyrcanus as High Priest approached, Anna found herself working later in the evenings. She told Esther not to bother bringing her anything warm to eat, as she often did not stop sewing until the food turned as cold as stone.

She had finished the intricate pattern of red and blue squares on the ephod. Now she worked meticulously to outline each one with gold thread. She had less than a week to finish the garment and worried it might not be enough time. Callouses hardened the tips of her fingers. Her shoulders had a permanent stiffness to them. The only part of her body not affected by the long hours were her eyes. It was as if God granted her the sight of a falcon when she sewed. She could see each individual stitch clearly, no matter what hour of the day or night.

"Anna!"

The sudden intrusion caused her to sit up quickly, sending a shock of pain through her neck and back. She rubbed at the muscles, trying to ease the spasm. "I am not to be disturbed."

Esther stood in the doorway. "I am sorry, but the queen has requested to see you."

Anna grimaced as she stood. "Did she say why?"

"No. I was told only that it was important, and that you should come immediately." She gestured to a guard standing in the hallway. "You are to follow him."

Anna continued to try and work out the knots in her muscles. "Then you must watch over the ephod. Do not let anyone touch it."

Esther nodded.

Anna followed the guard through the winding hallways until he stopped outside of the throne room. Another guard opened the door and ushered her inside. At the other end of the cavernous room stood her father, her brother, and the queen's counselor, Shimeon. The queen's throne sat empty. The three men turned as Anna approached, but it was Daniel, his expression grave, who ran to take her hand.

Her heart fluttered with fear. "Is it Mother?"

"No. She is the same." Daniel gave her a weak smile. "She wanted to come, but she had another of her headaches."

"Does she need me home? To care for her?"

Daniel led her up to the older men. "We have hired Tova to care for her. Do not worry."

Phanuel drew her into an embrace. "How have you been?" He held her at arm's length. "You look thinner. Tired."

"I am well. Please," her voice quivered with fear. "I was told the queen wanted to see me. What has happened?"

"It is Menahem."

It took her a moment to place the name, so focused had she been the past two weeks on her task. "What about him?"

Phanuel's brow furrowed. He turned toward Shimeon. The queen's brother folded his hands as if he meant to pray. "As discussed, the queen sent soldiers to Tyre to escort him to   Jerusalem to discuss the terms your betrothal."

"Is he here?" Anna glanced between the three men. Again her heart fluttered wildly with anxiety. "Does he demand I leave with him now?"

"No, child." Shimeon's brown eyes watched her with concern. "While they travelled here, Menahem was killed."

Her knees trembled. "Dead?"

Phanuel's voice cracked, "Yes."

Anna stood stunned. "How?"

"Thieves," Shimeon explained. "They killed Menahem and two others. A third barely escaped to tell us what happened."

"You are pale." Her father led her over to sit on the stone steps leading up to the dais. "I knew you would be upset, though the match was not of your choosing."

She crossed her arms over her chest, trying to hold back her apprehension.

Shimeon stroked his beard. "If you need time to grieve—"

"There is no time." Anna rocked on the stairs. "I must finish the ephod."

"You look exhausted." Phanuel sat beside her. "You must rest."

"Take time to deal with this turn of events." Daniel stood in front of them. "Come home."

"No. I will not leave the work to someone else. Not at this most intricate stage." She rose to face her brother. "God will give me the strength I need to finish the work. Then I will grieve."

"Give her leave, sir," Phanuel spoke to Shimeon. "Look at her. She is exhausted. She must rest."

The counselor's brows furrowed. "Perhaps your father is right."

Pain radiated down her back as she forced her shoulders to straighten, but she did not cry out. "I promise you, if I believed the garment would be compromised in any way, I would stop my work. I am well, if a little tired. I pray you give me leave to continue."

Shimeon nodded. "Very well."

She gave him a small bow. "Thank you."

"I do not give you leave," Phanuel's voice was firm. "Anyone can see you are not well. Is it worth your health to keep this pace?"

"It is only for a few more days, Father." Anna tried to give him a convincing smile. "This may be the most important work of my life." She took his hands in hers. "God will give me the strength I need."

His anger turned to worry. "Your mother once had your strength. I do not want you to lose it as she has."

"Only five more days and the ephod must be complete. Then I will take my rest. I promise you."

"How can I be sure?"

Shimeon stepped forward. "Once John is installed as High Priest, we will send Anna home to you so she can recuperate under your care. Would that be agreeable?"

Her father's grip tightened. "Are you sure you want to continue?"

"I am certain." She raised herself on her toes and kissed his cheek.

He returned the gesture. "I will pray for your strength."

Anna kissed her brother goodbye then walked back through the maze of hallways to her sewing room. Esther sat in the doorway. She stood as Anna approached.

"Is everything well?"

Anna stared at the ephod as she spoke. "The man I was to marry is dead."

The slave girl gasped.

Anna returned to the table and her work. She shivered as she picked up her needle. Something nagged at the back of her mind, but she could not grasp hold of it. Something about Aristobulus, but as her needle poked through the fabric, the thought slipped away. Menahem. Aristobulus. Her father. Shimeon. Nothing mattered now except the ephod. Once it was   finished, perhaps then she could concentrate on her life again.

Chapter 9

One Week Later

Lev stood next to Malachi in the temple courtyard. His father's other students, including Daniel, surrounded them, as did most of the Pharisees, scribes, rabbis, and Sadducees in Israel. All had come to see the installation of John Hyrcanus II as their High Priest. Next to Queen Salome, he would be the most powerful person in Israel. Lev smiled inwardly. Actually Shimeon bar Shetach was probably the second most powerful person, followed closely by Antipater. Lev had worked hard over the past week to assure his mentor of his worth, working as a scribe whenever the Idumaean had need of him. Lev hoped now that John was High Priest, and Antipater his most trusted advisor, he might be given a permanent position in Antipater's household.

Lev shifted his feet. He had been standing with the others since daybreak. The sun now stood about midway through the sky. A choir of white robed priests stood on the steps opposite the temple. Their deep voices sang psalms of praise that echoed off the stone columns. Several other priests, also dressed in white linen robes, brought more coals for the fire under the altar. He squinted as he watched them, their garments so pristine they glowed in the sunlight.

Shimeon spoke to the assembly, "This is what the Lord has commanded to be done." He brought John forward, clad only in a loin cloth

Lev hid his snort of disgust with a cough. Clothed, John did not strike an imposing figure. Practically naked, the man looked absurd. Unlike Aristobulus, John had not served in the army. His lack of muscle and slightly round belly were evidence of a life of leisure. Shimeon washed the prince's arms, head and chest with water then put a blue tunic on him and tied an embroidered sash around his waist.

Until now, Lev felt little interest in the ceremony. But then Shimeon held out his arms. Two priests paraded in front of the crowd. Between them was the ephod Anna had made. A low murmur of approval rose from the spectators. Several Pharisees called out praises to God as it passed by them. The priests carried the garment up the steps to Shimeon, who then put the ephod on John. He also fastened it with a decorative waistband. Lev marveled at Anna's craftsmanship. Even from this distance, he surmised that no High Priest had ever been so adorned. An elaborate breastplate was placed over the ephod, its twelve gemstones flashing as they caught the sun. A priest poured oil from a jar into Shimeon's hands. He poured the oil on John's head to consecrate him.

Several more hours passed as the ceremonies continued. The High Priest placed his hands on all the necessary sacrifices for his ordination. Two loaves of unleavened bread, a bull, and two rams were offered to the Lord. Blood spilled into the trough under the altar. The priests mixed the ram's blood with oil, which Shimeon then rubbed on John's right ear lobe, his right thumb, and finally his right toe. The ritual had been ordered by God back when Aaron, the brother of the prophet Moses, was consecrated as Israel's first High Priest. But, like much of what God demanded, He gave no explanation. Malachi taught the blood showed man's fragility, that death hovered closely over all, even God's chosen people. Daniel said his father believed it to be a symbol of how the High Priest must seek righteous in words, in actions, and in life. Words are heard, the hands act out man's will, and the feet direct a man's path through life. Lev did not know who was right, and as the hours crept on, he cared little for the truth.

Finally, the crowd cheered as the priestly choir struck up a hymn of praise, signaling the end of the ceremony. Lev's knees ached when Shimeon at last dismissed them.

"It is a day for celebrating." Malachi clapped Daniel and Lev on their backs. "There will be no studying today."

The young men cheered at the news. They dispersed into groups of two and three as they left the temple courtyard. Lev noticed Daniel remained behind.

"I would have thought you would be running home to see your new love. What is her name?"

Daniel pushed his friend's shoulder playfully. "You know her name is Tova. And I would indeed be going home if I could, but I must wait for my father."

"Why is that?"

Daniel grinned. "We have been asked to attend one of the queen's banquets to celebrate this day."

Lev tried not to show his surprise, but knew his friend probably saw it on his face. "That is indeed an honor."

"It is because of Anna."

"As well your sister should be rewarded. Her work was remarkable."

Daniel's smile faded. "Indeed, she has been working so hard, Father and I feared for her health. Especially after she received the news about Menahem."

"What news?"

Now it was Daniel who looked surprised. "Your father did not tell you? I am sure he has heard."

"I have been working in the house of Antipater, writing letters for his household."

"I wondered where you had been."

They walked together through the courtyard. "Last night was my first at home in some time."

Daniel put his arm around his friend. "Anna's betrothed was killed by bandits as he travelled here to speak with the queen."

Lev stopped. "Truly?"

"A terrible tragedy, though I never met him. He was still my kinsmen."

Conflicting emotions ran through Lev's mind. When Aristobulus had offered his help preventing Anna's marriage, he had thought it would be through bribery, never murder. Perhaps it was a coincidence? "Have they caught the demons who did it?"

"They still roam free." Daniel waved as he caught sight of his father at the other end of the courtyard. "It weighs heavily on Phanuel's head."

"He could not have prevented it."

Daniel turned as Phanuel approached so that he faced Lev and stood between the two. "Now may be your last opportunity, my friend." He placed a hand on Lev's shoulder. "If your feelings for my sister are the same as they have been in the past, do not wait to seek my father's blessing for the match."

"You know I would marry her this day if my father would allow it."

Daniel frowned. "Even he cannot think my sister unsuitable after she has found such favor with the queen."

"Lev," Phanuel interrupted their discussion. "I hope you are well."

"I am, sir."

Daniel gave his friend a knowing smile. "Will we see you at the palace tonight? I would think your family was invited."

"Indeed. My parents and I will be there."

"*Shalom*, my friend." Daniel turned away.

"Peace to you, also." Lev said the words, but received no peace from them. He made his way in a daze to his father's house. He needed to change out of the robes he wore, now heavy with sweat and dust, and into more ornamental robes to dine at the palace. A servant met him as he entered the home. The older man had been a fixture in Malachi's house for as long as Lev could remember.

"Come, Master. I have water prepared. You must wash yourself before you put on your new clothes."

"Do not fret. The queen will not run out of food this early in the day." As the servant cleansed Lev's feet, the worry that had pressed down on him washed away as well. However it had come to pass, Anna was a free woman again. She would be at the palace this evening. He had to find a way to see her. Talk with her. Make her his own.

Lev could barely hear his own thoughts over the sounds of the flutes, lyres and timbrels the musicians played throughout the banquet. He picked at the delicacies set before him, roasted lamb and savory goat stew. Pomegranates, dates and nuts. Loaves of bread made with fine wheat flour. For once, the opulence mattered little to him, his mind consumed with finding Anna.

In the end, a few denarii in the palm of one of the queen's servants bought him news of her whereabouts. Several more coins and he was told when she left the women's banquet room. Lev excused himself to his father, claiming Antipater needed his services. "I may not be home tonight."

Lev felt Malachi's eyes watch him as he followed the servant to the hallway. The boy hurried down several more before pointing to a courtyard. "She will pass through here on the way to the servants' quarters."

Lev stepped outside. The sun had long since set, but torches lit the garden in a warm glow. Two women took no notice of him as they walked the stone pathway. He slipped into an alcove just as Anna appeared in an opposite doorway.

"Anna," Lev whispered as she walked across the courtyard. She lifted her head at the sound, as if to determine from where it came, but did not look in his direction. He called her name again as she started to move away.

This time, she turned and saw him in the shadows. Her eyes narrowed. "Lev?"

He motioned for her to come to him.

She surveyed the courtyard before crossing to the threshold where he stood. As soon as she was near enough, he took her hand. She gasped as he drew her into the dim alcove.

With his free hand, he cupped her face. Her eyes widened, but she did not run from him. He took a deep breath, reveling in the musky scent of her skin mixed with a light tang of citrus. His head spun. "I have been looking for you."

"Why?" Worry crept into her eyes. And fear.

"I heard about Menahem."

She stiffened.

Standing this close to her, he could barely think coherently. "It was the Lord's will, Anna."

Her warm breath danced across his cheek. "I do not believe the Lord desires any of us to die."

"But He has opened the way for us to be together." He smiled as she caught her breath. He drew her even closer so that their bodies almost touched. "I love you, Anna."

Her bright smile was like a kiss. "I never truly believed you could love me."

He dared to press his body against hers, reveling in how she trembled beneath his touch. He bent his mouth to hers, but she turned away. A moan escaped him. "Please, Anna. I have longed for this day."

"We are not married." She squirmed out from under him. "We are not even betrothed. We cannot do this."

Lev's muscles were as taut as the string of a bow. He pulled her back to him. "Do not deny what you feel."

She was unyielding. "I will, until you talk to my father."

His hand caressed her back. "Why? When we have admitted our love?"

Again she pushed him away. "The Law says it is a sin for us both, but should either of our fathers deny the match, I will be the one to pay with my life." She stepped out into the pale light of the courtyard. "I am no whore."

"No one would dare say that of you." Lev followed her. If they were discreet, she would face no serious repercussions. "Please."

She stared at him then as if seeing him for the first time. "You would risk my life to satisfy your desire?"

"No." His voice sounded petulant to his own ears. "Of course not."

"You know that I would be your wife as soon as we could perform the ceremony." A small crease of worry appeared   between her eyes. "But Malachi has never favored me. I am not convinced he will ever let you marry me."

Lev ran his hand through his hair, wishing it was hers he touched. "We do not need his permission. Only Phanuel's."

"You would defy your father?"

"I am no longer under his authority." At least he hoped to soon be out of Malachi's house for good. "I live with Antipater. I work for him. It will not be long until I have enough saved to buy a home of my own."

"Then go to my father. Obtain his permission and we will be married."

"One kiss, Anna, please." He reached for her hand, but she pulled away.

She surveyed the courtyard, her gaze furtive. Although she kept her voice low, it carried her anger. "What has happened to you? Any number of eyes could be watching us. Even your father's."

"I told you, I am no longer under his authority."

"But I am. If he should see us, his testimony would be enough to convict me of fornication. Do you want to see me flogged?"

He stepped back. "Of course not."

"Then go to my father. Speak to him." Her glare pierced him. "Until then, do not come to me again, Lev. It is too dangerous here."

Her feet padded softly against the stone path as she ran from him. The blue mantle fell from her head, revealing a long, brown braid of hair down her back. She clutched at the linen and drew it up again. Lev groaned as he pictured undoing that braid and watching her hair spill over his shoulders.

"She is right."

Lev spun around. Malachi stood in the alcove across from him. His father crept out of the shadows. "If she ever lets you touch her, I will bring her before the Sanhedrin. The court will not be lenient to a fornicator."

Lev's fingers curled into fists at his side.

Malachi's grin was like a serpent's. "Salome may have ideas of giving women more equality under the law, but in this matter, men will rule. We all want the virgin on our wedding night, though we are more than willing to sleep with the whore outside our home." Malachi opened his arms wide. "And this is how we know God is a man. Because He makes it so easy for us to take advantage of the weaker sex, and so hard for the woman to prove her innocence." He placed his hands on Lev's shoulders. "Are you willing to risk her life? My spies and I will be watching."

"You hired spies?"

"Who do you think informed me of your little tryst?"

Lev fought to keep his fury at bay.

Malachi studied him. "Are you willing to give up all your ambitions for her?"

Lev's teeth ground together. He could barely loosen his jaw enough to speak. "I love her."

A scoffing laugh escaped Malachi's throat. "You *want* her. Any fool can see you pant after her like a dog." He dodged his son's punch and gripped Lev's wrist firmly in the air.

Lev grunted in surprise at his father's quick reflexes. He had not thought the heavy man still fast and strong.

Malachi brought his round face directly in front of his son's. "I have told you, the daughter of Phanuel will never be my daughter under the law. She will never breed my grandsons." Malachi's cheeks reddened. "I have already spoken to many of the priests. They know my will in this. None will marry you. You will have to leave Jerusalem if you persist in this folly."

Lev's resolve weakened under his father's pronouncement. He voluntarily lowered his arm. "What are you saying?"

"To marry her, you will have to leave Antipater's service, the temple, everything here that you truly love." The serpent's smile returned to Malachi's lips. "Do you love her more than you love your ambitions? If so, go now." His father lifted his hands then brushed them together, as if wiping off dust. "I will denounce you as my son and you will lose everything you have worked so hard to attain." He clapped Lev's arm. "If you are ready to achieve all you desire, then come home with me tonight. We can discuss a suitable wife for you. We will make it a short betrothal so you can take her to your bed and put the scribe's daughter from your mind."

Lev shook his head. "Why do you hate him so? If I understood—"

"You need only to obey me in this matter. What say you?"

The air left his lungs. "You would do this? Ruin everything I have worked for?"

"Is she worth it? Do you love her more than you love power? Wealth?" He slapped Lev's chin lightly. "Wake out of this childish dream of yours. If you come home tonight, I will know you have accepted my proposal. But if you are not at my house by morning, I will assume you have chosen the girl and I will destroy you. It is your choice."

As Malachi strode away, Lev stumbled to a bench in the alcove. He rested his forehead in his hands, hoping to push back the pounding pain in his head. He loved Anna. Since the first day Daniel introduced her to him, he had desired no other woman as his wife.

But was she enough to satisfy him? How long would it be until he grew to resent that she had cost him everything? All he had dreamed? Would they turn into his parents? Cold strangers who no longer shared their lives together, never mind a bed? For the first time in many months, Lev turned his face to the sky and lifted a prayer to the Lord.

Anna hurried through the dimly lit halls, trying to match her pace to the pounding of her heart. Tears of confusion and fear welled in her eyes. She paused before crossing the courtyard to the palace gate where Daniel would be waiting to walk her home. She could not face anyone. Especially not her brother.

Adonai, help me. She thought she knew Lev, but she had never seen the hunger in his eyes before. For a moment, she had feared he would force her to kiss him. Something she had dreamed of for so long, but not like that. Not pushed up against the stone walls of the courtyard like a harlot on the street.

Is that what love is like? She had no real experience with men. Had only heard her parents' quiet coupling in their small house. She did not think it would be so . . . violent. She had dreamed of Lev for so long, but those dreams had been soft and comforting. She had seen him protecting her from bandits or embracing her when he came home at night. Never had she envisioned he would hurt her. But tonight she had sensed his frustration and the desire that fueled it. It was like a madness. *Was his passion love?* She had thought it would be different.

Anna took another moment to quiet her breathing. *Perhaps I misunderstood.*

Of course. That must be it. She was young yet and not familiar with the ways of men. He was still Lev, the man she had set her heart on since the day she first saw him outside of his father's school, laughing with Daniel. His voice like music as he joked with his friend. If he could convince Malachi of her worth, then she was sure he would curb his desire until they were properly wed, as the Law instructed.

She straightened her mantle, praying her face would not betray her emotions, and took one last deep breath before setting off to find Daniel.

Her brother smiled when he saw her. "It is about time. I would think you would be ready to return home for a rest." He put his arm around her neck as he used to when they were younger, dragging her down the street. "Of course, why would you be in a hurry to leave the comforts of the palace and have to converse with us peasants again?"

"Comforts? I sleep in a room with ten other women. The older ones snore and the younger ones giggle through the night." She shoved him away, his teasing giving her a way to expel what remained of her emotions. "That is when I left my task at all. The past two nights I have slept in the corner for an hour or two so my eyes could rest, no more."

Daniel slid his arm around the crook in her elbow. "And your work was magnificent. You should have heard the priests and Sadducees exclaim when they saw it. Even the Pharisees approved, though they do not agree about who should wear it."

Anna playfully blocked her ears. "No more politics. I am tired of all you men fighting about who should be High Priest and who should not."

"And who included you, a mere child, in their discussions?" He poked her side as he teased.

She swatted his hand away. "I may have been secluded in my work, but the window and door were kept open throughout the day. You would be amazed at the intrigues in the palace that are discussed openly when they think no one is listening." Her countenance turned serious. "I have learned in only a month to trust no one, not even to speak my thoughts aloud. Always someone listens. Someone watches."

"I am sorry for you."

"It will be good to be home. If only for a short time. I've missed you all."

"If you are called again to the palace, perhaps you will not be so lonely."

"Why is that?" Her heart quickened, thinking he may have talked to Lev.

"Shimeon has brought Father into the palace as a household scribe. He helps to keep the kitchen and stable inventories. Maybe you will be able to see him."

They continued to their house. Anna sensed there was more her brother longed to tell her. She tugged on his hand. "What is it? You have a smirk on your face. That can only mean you are hiding something from me." She tugged again. "You never could keep a secret."

"I cannot tell you. Not yet, but soon. I promise."

No amount of goading could coax the secret from him before they reached their house. The only hint he would give her was that if she hurried, she would find out sooner. With that, she let go of his hand and raced down the hill toward her father's house, darting between random neighbors who strolled the streets.

Daniel passed her as they neared their final turn. He dashed around the corner, disappearing before she made it to their road. She slowed down to catch her breath as she approached the door.

Daniel flung it open and stepped inside. Tova stood next to him, a bright grin on her face. They held hands. Anna squealed with joy. "Is it official?" Anna embraced her friend. "When did it happen?"

"Just last night. Phanuel and Daniel walked me home and asked my father for his blessing."

Daniel waited until the women parted before adding, "We did not want to wait. Life is too short. Too unpredictable."

A chill ran through Anna. She knew he spoke of Menahem's death. Tova hugged her again. "Your time will come soon. I know it."

Her father sat on the floor by her mother. He gestured for Anna to sit by them. "I have been telling Miriam of the ceremony today, and of your masterpiece." His eyes shone with pride. "All who saw it said you must have been blessed by God's Spirit to create such beauty."

Her cheeks warmed at his compliments. "I know the Lord gave me the strength to complete it."

Her mother reached out to her. "You look exhausted."

"I am," Anna admitted.

Tova beamed at Daniel. "I should be returning to my own family."

"I will walk you home." Daniel glanced over his shoulder. "I'll be back shortly."

A wave of melancholy washed over Anna at the sight of them walking through the doorway, hand-in-hand. Would Lev ever defy his father and come ask Phanuel for her hand in marriage?

"You seem distracted, Daughter," her father's voice interrupted her thoughts. "What worries you?"

"So many changes are happening quickly. I feel as though I cannot take a breath or my life will be over."

Her father held her gaze. "Surely our days are numbered. That is why we must be careful to appreciate each one that Adonai graciously gives to us." A sadness filled his eyes. "And know that every choice you make now will ripple through your life like a pebble thrown into a well." He placed his hand over hers. "Rest now. Pray over the coming days. Decide then whether you will go back to the palace or no."

Anna bowed her head, her father's words taking root in her heart. She felt as though she stood at a crossroads, the path she chose would decide the course of her life. If Lev managed to secure his father's blessing, she felt certain Phanuel would give his to their union, knowing Anna's love for him. But now that she had begun this new life in the palace, one that offered her a chance to use her talents for God, did she want to give it up, if whomever she married asked her to?

Chapter 10

One Week Later

The goblet shook in the young woman's hands as she brought it to her lips. An indigo mantle covered her head, but Lev caught a glimpse of the dark brown hair that hid underneath. Her eyes almost matched her hair in color. Rich, warm, brown . . . and clearly terrified.

Lev fought back a snort of disdain. Anna would not have looked at him with such fear. Her face would have been filled with joy. Her eyes, he was sure, would have shone with desire. The same passion that stirred in him even now as he thought of her.

Malachi took the wine from the girl and passed it to Lev. "Drink it, my son."

His father had invited all his students to attend the ceremony. They stood around the room in a tight semi-circle with Lev and . . . Sarai, her name was Sarai . . . in the center. The young men all grinned as if this was a joyous occasion. Lev drained the goblet, wishing, as he gave it to his father, that it had contained more alcohol.

Malachi lifted it above his head. "As you have both drunk from the same cup, you have sealed this betrothal. Sarai, you are Lev's wife. Remain true to him and only him all the days of your life." Malachi's gaze turned to his son. "And you, Lev, must remain faithful to her."

Lev despised the look of triumph on his father's face. He reviled himself for giving in to Malachi's demands. Most painful of all was the look of betrayal he caught as Daniel watched the betrothal ceremony from the farthest corner of the room. As the other young men called out "*mazel tov*," Daniel kept silent.

Sarai remained docile as her father maneuvered her closer to Lev. Benjamin bar Judah was a Pharisee newly returned from exile in Egypt, where he had amassed a great deal of wealth. Malachi had explained the financial and political benefits a marriage with Sarai would give to Lev and the family. Benjamin's status allowed his father further access to Jerusalem's elite. For Lev, the benefit was moot. His footing into the higher echelons derived from his position with Antipater. But that position could only be held by marrying Sarai and staying in Malachi's good graces.

Lev looked at the girl one more time before dismissing her. If his father thought this timid thing would make him forget Anna, he was sorely mistaken. But at least, as a servant of Antipater, he could stay in the counselor's home more often than not. He would lie with his wife enough to give her a son. Maybe two. But then work would be his excuse to stay far from home.

He suffered through the congratulations of his father's sycophants before managing to find his way to where Daniel stood next to a bookcase. His friend would not look at him. Did not speak to him. Lev watched his future bride from a distance as her father and Malachi drank to their betrothal.

A hole opened in his soul. A great chasm of emptiness. His arms broke out in gooseflesh.

"How could you?" Daniel seethed. "How could you deceive my sister so?"

Lev kept his gaze on the center of the room, not wanting to see how his friend now despised him. "You do not understand."

"Explain it to me, then."

Lev knew their hushed conversation would not be heard over the celebrating. "I love your sister. I always will."

"A strange way to show it, marrying another woman."

"My father denied his blessing. He told me he would disown me if I dared to go against him. We would have been forced to leave the city. Start our lives as destitute strangers in another part of Israel." He dared to glance at his friend. "I would not do that to your sister."

"You did not choose this wife to protect my sister. You made this choice for yourself. Because you could not give up your dreams of power." Daniel turned to face him full on. "I hope your wealth will keep you warm. I hope it buys you the happiness you think it will."

Lev took hold of his arm. "I need to see her. To explain why—"

Daniel ripped himself from Lev's grasp. "Never come near my sister again. The pain your betrayal will cause her will never be healed. Do not keep sticking the knife into her heart."

Daniel stormed from the room. Malachi paused in his conversation to look at Lev. The same chill as before filled his soul. He had made his choice. Now he must live with the consequences.

Anna woke before sunrise after the Sabbath. In truth, she had not slept. She had wept throughout the night, as silently as she could, so as not to wake her family. She suspected they heard her anyway, but they did not comment or try to comfort her. They let her grieve the news Daniel brought home of Lev's betrothal. She clung to the knowledge that she would not have to suffer the loss without anything to take the place of her disappointment. She had a future in the palace. A life there, separate from Lev and all she had once hoped for.

The queen had allowed Anna a week to rest once she finished the ephod. But now she would return to her work and try to find satisfaction in using her talent for Salome and for Adonai.

Anna's head pounded as she stood. She would drink her own cup of herbal tea this morning in hopes it would ease the pain for her as it did for her mother. She caught her breath as she spied her mother sitting at the table. Miriam put a finger to her lips then motioned for Anna to come sit by her on the bench.

Anna sat down. "What are you doing up so early?"

Her mother lowered her head. "I should have told you long ago, when I first suspected your feelings for Malachi's son. I should have told you then to close your heart."

"You know why he hates me?"

"He does not hate you, my precious child," Miriam whispered fiercely. "He hates Phanuel. He hated my father, too, God rest his soul." Miriam ran her hand through Anna's hair. "Malachi once loved me . . . as Lev loved you. But my father refused his suit. He thought Phanuel the better man."

Anna tried to read her mother's eyes in the dim morning light. "Malachi loved you?"

"He thought he did."

For a moment, Anna could see past the wrinkles and gray hair to the young woman her mother had been. Round, dark eyes not clouded with pain. Light brown hair, full of the same curls as her own. She imagined a younger Malachi, asking for her hand, and facing her father's rejection. "All this pain . . . is because of Malachi's pride?"

"He never forgave my father for refusing his request. Nor Phanuel for gaining what he felt should be his." Her fingers still played with the strands of her daughter's hair. "I am sorry I never told you. I had hoped Malachi would eventually let go of his need for vengeance. I did not want your feelings for him to be tainted if he did."

"Why did you send Daniel to him? Knowing how Malachi felt?"

"I believe he tarnished Phanuel in the other rabbis' eyes. They would not consider your brother. Malachi hoped he could turn Daniel away from his family. All his hatred, it will cost him in the end."

"I do not see how." Anna fought back the tears pooling in her eyes. "He has succeeded at everything else he wanted. He has money. Influence in the temple. And a bride for Lev that is not me."

"I know Adonai will punish him for his pride. For what he has done in revenge to this family." Miriam wiped am escaped tear from Anna's cheek. "Already I see God's hand righting the past."

"How do you mean?"

"After my father refused him, Malachi set about to ruin Phanuel. He spread rumors of his incompetence and loose tongue. Your father is a brilliant man, and humble." A soft smile spread across her face as she glanced toward the corner where Phanuel slept "He never opened his mouth against Malachi. He prayed his reputation and work would be enough to combat the lies."

"But it was not."

"But the Lord knows all, and He honors those who are faithful. Can you not see how your gifts are part of His plan? Now, because of you, Phanuel has become a scribe in the palace, a far more prestigious position than Malachi's. I am sure your father's new-found success only aggravated Malachi's obsession to deny his son your love."

"Lev did not love me."

"Anyone with eyes could see how much he cared for you."

"But not enough to fight for me." Anna traced the woodgrain in the tabletop. "It is a small consolation to learn how little he thought of me before we were wed."

Daniel stirred in the corner. The two women quieted.

Anna whispered, "Is there anything I can do for you before I return to the palace?"

"I am well. Your father and Tova take good care of me."

Daniel yawned loudly as he sat up and stretched his arms over his head. After a moment, he shuffled over to the table. He looked at Anna, his face a mask of concern. "Did you sleep at all?"

"A little," she lied. "What time must you go back to your studies?"

"I am not going back to school."

Anna gasped as her mother asked, "What are you saying?"

Phanuel groaned in the corner.

"I will not study under that man anymore. For the past six years, I have listened to him belittle Father. No more."

"Do not do anything rash, my son." Phanuel's voice rose from behind them. "Calm your temper and think rationally."

"I am." His hands gestured wildly through the air, matching the way his hair stuck out at all angles. "Before Anna's position in the palace, I was forced to put up with Malachi's petty digs at our family because I knew he was one of the most influential Pharisees." He grinned toward his sister. "But while we dined at the palace, I had three rabbis ask if I would be their scribe. I am ready to be out from under Malachi's influence and earn money for my family."

Phanuel propped a hand along the wall to help pull himself up. "Very well. But before you rush off, let us discuss whom you should serve."

"Of course." Daniel sat at the table across from Anna and their mother. "And you, little sister, what will you do now?"

"I will prepare our breakfast." She walked to the shelf by the hearth and took down the leftover cheese and bread Tova had made the previous day.

The others watched in silence as she set out the simple meal. Phanuel blessed the food when she placed it on the table.

"I will seek another husband for you," Phanuel said, breaking off a piece of bread. "One here in Jerusalem."

Anna lowered her head. "Please, Father, do not hurry to find me someone."

"Why not?" He spoke around the mouthful of bread he chewed. "You are of age."

"Only just." She lifted her eyes to him. "There is so much I can learn from the other women in the palace. Shimeon promised he would take me to the weavers to see if I can learn the loom." She tried not to sound desperate, rather more sure of herself and assertive. "If I were betrothed and planning a wedding, I could not take the time to learn these things, or do the work I feel the Lord has called me to do."

"But to remain unmarried . . . ."

"I did not say I never wanted to marry, just not now. Let me grieve what might have been with Lev. Even with Menahem. Let me learn all I can so that I might be considered a woman of worth, able to contribute to her husband's household."

Daniel chuckled. "You have proven that already."

"Indeed." Phanuel nodded. "For now, I will agree not to seek your betrothal. I will pray Adonai will bring you a good man. A man worthy of you, one who will heal your heart."

"You are at my gate early this morning." Antipater gazed through the bars at Lev. "I would have thought you would be planning your wedding."

"It is my father's wedding, not mine."

His mentor opened the gate. "So your bride is not the woman you spoke of?"

"I never met the girl before in my life." Lev pressed on, "I have chosen a life like yours over one with family."

The gate clanged shut behind them as they strolled through Antipater's courtyard toward the house. "What do you mean by 'a life like mine'?"

"One of politics. I want to serve you in any capacity you choose for me. Scribe, confidant, messenger—it matters not to me. Only that I am allowed to be a part of what you do."

"You would do all that I asked, without question?"

"Without question."

Outside the courtyard walls, the city was coming to life. Neighbors called greetings to each other. Animals bleated in the distance.

"You would be faithful to my cause only?" Antipater's gaze was a knife, desiring to slice open Lev's mind. "Not your   father's, or even your own?"

Lev swallowed the last of the spit in his mouth. "Yes."

Antipater slipped his arm around Lev's shoulders and drew him toward the house. "Welcome, my son. Together, we will create a new order for Jerusalem. For Israel. For the world."

Chapter 11

The Same Morning

Anna and her father trudged up the hill toward the Temple Mount. They parted company as her father went to take an inventory of the palace stables in his new capacity as a royal scribe. Anna entered the palace gates, unsure of where she should go, now that the ephod was complete.

"Anna!" The queen's servant, Ziva, stood under an arched threshold across the courtyard. "This way."

Although tired from her sleepless nights, Anna's nerves jangled. She wondered what the queen would assign her next.

Ziva smiled as Anna approached. "You need not look so worried. The work will be much simpler than the High Priest's ephod." They passed under the archway into a wide stone hall. "This is the easiest route to sewing rooms. Salome felt you might need some less taxing work for a time. She thought your father would approve of you helping the women who make the robes for the priests."

The queen's servant walked quickly. "Unlike you, the seamstresses are wives or daughters of priests. As such, they are paid by the temple treasury and will go to their homes at night." Ziva glanced over at Anna. "As Queen Salome is paying your wage, you will continue to sleep in the servant's quarters, but may return home for the Sabbath, as you did before."

Anna nodded as they stepped out into a small garden courtyard. A slight breeze rustled through the leaves of the five   almond trees that grew beside the slate-stone path, one in the middle, the others at each corner. She turned her attention back to Ziva.

"The priests' robes must be replaced if they rip or become too stained with the blood of the sacrifices. It is a never-ending task." Ziva strode across the courtyard, through a doorway, then turned left down a hallway lit only by un-shuttered   windows in the stone wall. Loud voices and laughter drifted from a room up ahead.

Ziva paused in the room's threshold. "Ladies . . . ." The women fell silent. Anna felt the blush of embarrassment heat her cheeks as Ziva unceremoniously pushed her into the room. "This is Anna, Queen Salome's appointed seamstress and embroiderer. The queen asks that you show her how to make the priests' tunics until she again has need of her."

The introduction done, Ziva left. Anna stood, wondering what to do next. Four women stared back at her from their positions around a large wooden table in the center of the room. Sunlight from two large windows provided light, although Anna noticed several unlit oil lamps along the walls. Shelves held bolts of white linen. On a narrow table beneath them lay scraps of material and metal scissors.

A broad-shouldered woman stood up. Brown hair streaked with gray peeked out from her mantle. "You will not learn anything if you just stand there." She grabbed a bolt of linen and thrust it in Anna's arms then nodded toward a younger woman at the end of the table. "Mary will show you the pattern. They must all be made the same, but in varying sizes." She placed a wrinkled hand on her chest. "My name is Tamar. Do not bother me unless you have a question Mary cannot answer."

"Do not mind her." Mary came to Anna's side. "She acts hard and gruff, but she is as sweet as a honey cake."

"More like horseradish!" said a round-faced woman as she stabbed some linen with her needle and pulled her thread through.

The others laughed loudly.

"Here," Mary said. Although Anna guessed her to be more than twenty years old, Mary's small stature made her appear younger. "Watch me." The slender seamstress laid out the fabric and cut it using a muslin template as a guide. The pattern seemed simple enough, with only six pieces. She put them aside and spread out more fabric. "You try."

Anna copied her teacher exactly and soon had her own garment to sew. She and Mary sat next to each other as they stitched, but they did not talk. Anna waited for Mary to say something, but she seemed lost in another world. In contrast, the older servants joked and laughed about their husbands and their children. Anna was glad her companion remained silent. She did not want to speak of Lev or Menahem ever again.

Over the next five weeks, Anna came to know the women nearly as well as she knew her own family. Mary, whose husband had died of sickness two years before; Bilah, the round-faced woman with a sharp wit; Rachel, soft-spoken but with a joyful laugh; and finally Tamar, whose husband had been chosen to go into the Holy of Holies last year to burn the incense, an honor she could not stop speaking about. These women did most of the sewing, weaving, dying, and mending of the priests' garments.

The work was much easier than the embroidery Anna had done for the High Priest's ephod and although she enjoyed the women's company, she missed the intricacies of fine needlework. It was a relief when she was ordered to create a new garment for John Hyrcanus.

As it would not be proper for Anna to take the High Priest's measurements, a tailor was instructed to work with her. Together they would create a new robe for the prince to wear at the upcoming Fall Festivals.

Anna tapped her fingers against the table as she waited for the tailor to take her into the High Priest's presence. She had never met any of the tailors, even though they worked along the same hallway as the seamstresses in the palace.

Mary folded the linen tunic she had been working on throughout the day. "Impatient?"

Anna stilled her tapping. "And nervous. I do not like speaking with royalty. I am always afraid I will say the wrong thing."

Bilah put her needle and thread away in a basket. "Do not worry, little Anna. The nobility are no different than you or I. They still pass wind and sit on the pot to pass the other things we do."

Anna's cheeks warmed at the woman's blatant honesty.

"Look at her blush!" Bilah pointed to the others. "She still has not gotten used to my mouth."

Rachel threw a scrap of linen at her. "None of us have, we are only better at ignoring your terrible language."

Tamar approached Anna. "Did the queen say who would be helping you with your task?"

"She said his name was Caleb."

A smile pulled at the older woman's lips. "I am glad for him."

"You know him?"

"He is my younger brother." A sadness swept over Tamar's features. "It has been hard for him—"

A sudden rapping on the threshold startled the women. A man stood in the doorway. He grinned when he caught sight of Tamar.

"Sister!" A ribbon of tenderness flowed through his rich voice. "I would have thought you would be home by now, taking care of that oaf—I mean, your husband."

Tamar put her hands on her hips. "Just because you men might quit before sunset, do not think we women do." She winked at him. "Anna, this is Caleb. Caleb, this is my friend, Anna." Her eyes narrowed as she gave him a stern look. "Do not work my friend too hard, Brother. She needs her rest to do *my* work tomorrow!"

Caleb's laughter filled the room. The lines around his green eyes deepened as he smiled, but they did not make him appear older. A few white hairs streaked his otherwise dark hair and full beard. He gestured to Anna. "Come. If we hurry now to the prince's rooms, I may yet get to go to my own home tonight." As he walked from the door, Anna noticed he favored his right leg. "Bring an oil lamp with you," he called over his shoulder, "in case we have to wait for him."

Anna took the lamp Rachel thrust into her hands, and she hurried to follow him down the hall. Even with his limp, he moved quickly. He paused to let her catch up then directed her outside to cross one of the many palace courtyards. "I have found this is the fastest way."

The sun sat below the walls, leaving behind an orange and purple sky to herald the end of the day. Caleb took a stone path around a fountain and through a flower garden, now laying fallow. He stood several inches taller than Anna, so his eyes seemed to close when he looked down at her. "Tamar told me you did the work on the High Priest's ephod."

"Yes."

Again his face softened as he smiled. "It is no wonder he wants you to work on a new robe. You are very talented."

His voice warmed her. Like an ember on a cold night. "Thank you."

"It would be best to let me speak directly to the prince, unless he speaks to you first. If you have any questions, pose them to me and I will ask them of John." Caleb shrugged. "Some of the priests are more cautious than others when they have to deal with women. Before his appointment, John was never concerned." He stepped through an alcove leading to another entrance to the palace. "He may have changed since taking the title."

Relieved not to have to speak to the prince, Anna answered, "I will do as you say."

They wound through the many hallways and climbed a staircase. A guard let them through the doorway.

John Hyrcanus looked unimposing to Anna as he reclined against pillows made of gold and maroon fabric. Several other men occupied the room as well and Anna felt her muscles tremble. She desperately prayed she would not make a fool of herself among such an important figure as the High Priest.

John looked up from the low couch. "Who are you?" Recognition sparked behind his eyes. "Ah yes, the tailor and the young seamstress." He waved them over. "I am entertaining tonight, so be quick about your work."

Caleb and Anna bowed. The tailor limped forward. "It will take no time at all, Your Highness." From his sleeve he drew forth a thick, wound cord. "Will you please stand for me?"

A sharp intake of breath caught Anna's attention. She turned to the corner of the room and recognized Aristobulus. A dark skinned, older man stood next to him. Her heart caught when she recognized the third man on the end of the couch.

Lev.

She tore her eyes from his and instead studied how Caleb measured the prince. He held the thread with one hand, then pulled it out until it reached the floor or the prince's wrist. When he found what he wanted, he marked the thread. She assumed he had a different mark for each measurement. Her stomach turned with pity when she noticed that Caleb's left hand was deformed. The last two fingers were fused together and looked like a gnarled stick. Even with only four fingers and a limp, Caleb moved deftly around the prince, taking measurements.

"Anna!" Aristobulus called to her from across the room. "It is you, is it not?"

Anna willed herself not to faint. As she could not ignore the prince, she summoned her courage to look at him. "Yes, my lord."

He strode into the middle of the room. "What an unexpected pleasure to see you again." He gestured to a pitcher sitting at a nearby table. "Would you care for some wine?"

She kept her eyes focused on the floor, not wanting to see Lev's face. "No, thank you."

"So formal?" His words slurred a little around the edges. "I thought we were friends, you and I?"

Anna did not know what to say. She and the prince had only spoken once before, but she could not contradict him, could she?

"Remember? I told you to call me Ari, and you told me about your betrothal."

"You will have to excuse my brother." John lifted his arms to his side so Caleb could measure them fingertip to fingertip. "He has already had too much to drink tonight."

Caleb glanced between the princes and Anna, but then turned his attention back to his work.

"Nonsense." Aristobulus shook his head. "Anna knows I am her friend. And she knows someone else here, do you not? Lev, come here and say hello."

Anna stiffened, but would not turn her gaze to the man who had betrayed her.

Aristobulus wobbled unsteadily on his feet. "Did you not tell me you and Lev were friends?"

Anna summoned enough bravery to not only answer, but look at the prince as she did. "Lev was my brother's friend, my lord. Not mine."

Lev's eyes flashed as he pressed his lips together.

"No?" The prince scratched his chin. "What about you, Lev? Were you not Anna's friend?"

"I still am."

Aristobulus lifted his arms in an exaggerated shrug. "I am a learned man, but this is a perplexing puzzle. He is her friend, but she claims no friendship with him . . . ."

Although it still pained Anna to see Lev, weeks had passed since his betrayal, and she would not allow herself to be swept away by his words. "Perhaps, because my brother once felt a kinship with Lev, I did, too. But that kinship has been broken for some time now. It would not be proper for me to remind him of any . . . relationship we may have shared, as he is a married man."

"Come now, little Anna. I insist you shake hands." The prince strode over to her and grabbed her forearm. "I will broker peace between you two. Come."

Anna gasped as he led her across the room to Lev. She tried to pull away, but the prince gripped her tight. Lev took hold of her hands.

"There, is that not better?" Aristobulus placed his mouth next to Anna's ear. "We are all gentlemen here. His wife need never know."

Anna yanked her hand from Lev's and stepped back. "Forgive me, my lord. But I feel you forget yourself."

The prince's eyes turned dark and hawkish. "Have I? My sincerest apologies."

"Leave the girl alone, Ari," John called. "Go out to the balcony while I finish here. I need to discuss my thoughts for the design on my new robe."

"Very well." Aristobulus waved to the servant in the corner. "Bring the wine out to us."

Anna shuddered as Aristobulus, the other man, and Lev—with a long glance over his shoulder, left. She tried to quiet her nerves by taking a deep breath, but still she shivered.

Anna flinched when Caleb asked, "Are you unwell?"

"I am fine." She choked back the lump in her throat before turning to face the High Priest. "What do you have in mind for the design?"

He described elaborate borders of geometric shapes and waved his hand. "Draw them for me."

Anna bowed. "Forgive me, but I do not have pens or parchment. I have never used them."

The High Priest glowered. "Then why did my mother send you to me? What good are you?"

Caleb bowed. "Anna and I will work together. We will, of course, return with the sketches for your approval."

"Whatever it takes. But I want the drawings by next week and the new robe by the Feast of the Tabernacles. Understood?"

"Yes, my lord," Caleb said as he bowed again. The two of them walked backwards toward the door.

Once out in the hall, Anna turned and placed both hands against the wall, hoping some of the rock's solidness would transfer to her body. Her chest shook as she breathed in, forcing herself not to fall apart. After a few moments, the powerful wave of panic left her and she was able to turn around. "Thank you."

Caleb's expression was only one of concern, not pity. "For what?"

"For your help . . . with Aristobulus . . . and your offer to help sketch my designs for the High Priest."

He smiled then. It eased her pain even more. "It will be my honor to work with you." He glanced at the small shelf where she had placed their lamp. "Now, would you mind holding that while I see you to your rooms? You would not like the way the light sways when I carry it with my gait."

They walked in comfortable silence back to the servants' quarters. Caleb did not continue down the last hallway. "My home is outside the palace, in the city."

"Do you want the lamp?" The flame's glow gave his skin a youthful, peachy color.

A sadness filled his eyes. "I am fine."

She felt awkward and embarrassed under his stare, as if he might judge her for what happened with Aristobulus. She knew if they were to work together, she could not let those emotions take hold. "Where should we meet? To work on the sketches?"

He pulled his gaze from hers. "I will come to the sewing room tomorrow. It is more proper that I should be in a room full of women, than you should be in a room full of men."

"Goodnight then."

"Shalom, Anna."

He turned before she could wish him peace as well.

Lev wanted nothing more than to run after Anna and force her to look at him. To speak to him. How could she act like she had never had feelings for him? He had seen her passion. Felt the heat from her body when he had touched her. He knew she had loved him. How could she act like those feelings were in the past?

"Drink, my friend." Aristobulus passed him a goblet of wine. "It will make you feel better."

He downed the contents in four long gulps.

"Perhaps you are not feeling well?" Antipater eyed him from across the balcony where he sat on a marble bench. "Should you go home?"

"Nonsense!" The prince patted Lev's shoulder. "He will be fine. He is only surprised at the girl's response to him, no? Did you think she would run to your arms in a room full of men?"

"Of course not." He slammed the goblet down the railing. He wanted to fill it again, but abstained, knowing Antipater would not approve.

"No. You said yourself, she is a virtuous girl. But now, what do you think she will do tonight?"

Lev wiped his mouth with the back of his hand. "I cannot even imagine."

Aristobulus frowned. "I thought you had more imagination than this." He walked over to Antipater. "You, Counselor, what do you think our little seamstress will be doing tonight?"

At first the older man seemed unwilling to play the prince's game. Then he leaned against the bench and stroked his chin. "She will be thinking about Lev. About whatever moments they may have had together in the past. How seeing him again makes her remember why she loved him."

Ari clapped his hands. "Exactly! Very good." He whirled around to face Lev. "Our little seamstress will be dreaming of you in her bed tonight. I know where she sleeps." He gestured to the servant to refill Lev's wine. "Should I send someone for her? I could have her brought to my rooms."

Lev's muscles coiled with tension, like a twig ready to snap.

Ari's eyes widened. "I meant to bring her for you. I would certainly never betray a friend." He threw his arm around Lev's shoulder. "I have done much so that you could have her, I was surprised when you did not seize the opportunity to take her for your wife when her betrothed was so tragically killed."

Lev's head spun. Seeing Anna again, and all the wine he had drunk. He stumbled away from the prince. "I wanted to . . . but my father made it impossible."

"A pity." The prince watched him. "But my offer still stands. Anytime you want her brought to you, all you need do is ask me."

Another servant stepped outside. "The High Priest commands you return now."

Ari rolled his eyes. "Does he?"

Antipater stood. "It is our pleasure to serve him. Come, Lev. It is time we get to work tonight."

"May I have another moment?" Lev asked.

"Of course," the prince answered. He pushed Antipater inside. "Let the boy clear his mind of the girl or he will be of no use to anyone."

Lev grabbed the stone railing. His work had kept his mind from dwelling on Anna, but now that he had seen her . . . there had to be a way he could cross her path again.

Chapter 12

The Following Day

"What did you think of my brother?" Tamar asked the following morning as she spread a piece of linen on the table.

"He seems a very knowledgeable tailor."

Tamar smoothed the fabric with harsh, hard strokes. "He served Alexander Jannai for almost twenty years."

Anna looked at the garment she worked on. "How—"

"How did he hurt his leg?" Tamar's hands slapped the table with a sharp crack. "Or is it his fingers that bother you?"

The other women went silent around them. Anna's nerves, already frayed from thinking about Lev all night, tingled with frustration. "It is just . . . he seems so nice . . . I only wondered, was he born . . . ."

"Disfigured?" Tamar's voice snapped in the air.

"Why do you speak to me like this? I only want to know so that I may better understand him. We are going to be working together for the next several weeks."

Tamar's face softened. "Our father did not have enough money to send both Caleb and our older brother to school. Caleb chose to serve in the army. It was in a battle with the Idumaeans that he was burned by flaming oil." She sighed heavily. "He never wanted to fight. He only wanted enough money to be able to become a priest. But now, with his wounds, he is forbidden to serve in the Temple." Tamar resumed her sewing. "He was able to apprentice himself to a tailor who looked past his limitations. And he has excelled."

"He seems a very kind man," Anna said.

"He is. The very best of men."

Anna continued to work on the tunic until Caleb arrived in the afternoon. He carried with him chalk and slate. The ladies in the room gave them space along the table to sit together to work.

"I thought it best to start with this." Caleb pointed to the slate. "I can get an idea for your design and then you can tell me the colors you envision. We can make the sketches once we've narrowed down ideas."

Anna rubbed her hands over her face. She had not thought about the High Priest's robe since leaving his room. Now she prayed God would clear her mind so she could think of a design—anything—to tell Caleb.

He remained quiet as she sat with her head bowed. The other women gossiped around them. Anna's mind stayed blank. She lifted her eyes to him. "I am sorry. I have nothing today."

Caleb passed her the slate and chalk. "Come with me, child."

He favored his right leg as he led her to another of the palace's gardens, this one blooming with early lilies of Sharon and sycamore blossoms. Caleb placed his hand on a stone bench, using it to help lower himself to the ground. "Come here."

Anna knelt by his side.

He cupped a lily in his rough hands. "What shapes do you see?"

She warmed at his enthusiasm. "The petals are like fans."

"What more?"

She bent over to examine the plant. "Some are heart-shaped. And the leaves are ragged. Like they have been torn."

Caleb laid his hand on a marble stone along the garden's path. "Now this. What can you see in here?"

"I see clouds of gray in a white sky. Long and wispy." She caught Caleb's excitement. "And there are flecks of stone, like diamonds sparkling."

He paused a moment before he spoke, "I knew you were like me."

Anna sat up, confused. "How do you mean?"

"You cannot be inspired within the walls of the palace. It is God, and His creation, that lights your imagination."

She surveyed the garden and all its splendor and knew he spoke the truth. Here she could sense Adonai's presence everywhere. In the shape of the sycamore leaves, the vivid blue of the sky and the way the water in the nearby fountain danced in the sun. Her spirit lightened as her senses feasted on the beauty around her.

"Are you ready to try again?" Caleb asked as he struggled to pull himself up onto the bench. He groaned as he sat down then patted the stone next to him. "Bring the slate. See what God inspires you to create now."

Anna closed her eyes as she lowered herself to the hard seat. "What about leaves, like the sycamore tree? I could use silver and green thread, like how the tree looks when the wind blows before a storm."

"Excellent." Caleb said as she drew a simple outline. "Go on."

They worked together until the sun sat on the palace roof. The air chilled when a cold breeze blew through the courtyard. Caleb looked at the forms they had sketched. "This is a good start. I will put these ideas on parchment tomorrow and bring them for your approval." He passed her the slate and chalk. "Hold these for a moment."

Anna stood, her heart breaking at Caleb's grimace as he stretched out his legs in an effort to stand.

She held out her hand.

At first he seemed angry at her silent offer of help, but then he sighed, took her hand, and used it to balance himself so he could get up.

"Thank you, child."

"I need to thank you. You are a good teacher."

He smiled then. "I will walk you back to my sister."

"I can find my way."

"Of course."

As Anna passed him the slate and chalk she sensed the older man was upset about something. She did not know what she had done to anger him. "I look forward to seeing you tomorrow."

"*Shalom*, my child."

"*Shalom*, Caleb." She felt his gaze on her as she made her way through the courtyard and into the palace. She paused to look out one of the hallway windows. Caleb stood under the sycamore with his eyes closed. A shadow moved in an alcove behind him. Anna squinted to see clearer. Her heart fluttered when she caught sight of Lev staring at her.

Now that Anna had seen Lev spying on her from the shadows, she felt his eyes on her constantly. She refused to look for him, knowing it would only encourage him further. The only time she could put him from her mind was when she worked with Caleb.

The gentle man had a quick wit that often made her laugh. She loved to watch his hands, even the one with the flaw. His touch was light but purposeful. Graceful. When he pushed ink and parchment to her, she sketched out her designs. She used his chalks to color in the patterns, while Caleb taught her how to blend the colors together to make new ones. For a week, they spent every afternoon together, and for those few hours of the day, Anna was at peace.

But when the sun set and she and Mary walked through the dimly lit halls to the servants' quarters, Anna knew Lev observed her. His presence, like a shadow, trailed her wherever she went. She slept little.

She had once thought she would never stop loving him, but God had, in His mercy, granted her the gift of this new position to fill the void left in her heart. Her work with Caleb excited her in ways she had never thought possible. She learned new things every day, and with each new idea, her mind hungered for more.

Once the final sketches were made, she and Caleb were invited again to the High Priest's rooms. This time, he was alone.

Caleb lay four drawings out on the floor as John stood above them. The High Priest studied each for several minutes before settling on the second in the series; a deep purple robe with an intricate pattern of vines along the neck and the sleeves. Silver and green leaves decorated each vine. "This is the one." He snatched it up. "But I want the gold border that one has." He pointed to the picture on the end. "Can it be done?"

Caleb and Anna looked at the sketches together. The tailor's eyes questioned her. *Can it be done? In just seven weeks?*

She shook her head as she glanced at the prince's first choice. The fabric for this robe would have to be dyed purple, an intensive process that took several weeks. The intricate embroidery would take her more weeks to finish. To add the gold border the prince desired, it would take another month, unless she had help or worked through the nights again.

She saw Caleb swallow as he turned to the prince. "It may not be ready in time, my lord." The High Priest listened as the tailor explained exactly what Anna had thought on the matter, as if he had read her mind. "She would need help, my lord."

"Then you help her. I know you sewed some of my father's robes. Surely you can do the border while she does the more intricate work." John looked between the two of them. "I will reward you both handsomely for your efforts."

Although he spoke harshly, he seemed nervous. Anna realized the High Priest did not wear his new position easily. She studied the sketches again. *He needs this robe. It will be his costume when he appears during the Feasts.*

She touched Caleb's arm and gave him a quick nod. He dipped his head toward John. "Very well, my lord."

"Good." The prince lifted his shoulders, sure his forcefulness had won the argument.

They left him gazing contentedly at the sketches. Once they were well away from the prince's room, Caleb asked, "What changed your mind?"

"The border will be simple, but time consuming. I can show you how to do the stitches so they lay side-by-side. If you work on that while I complete the original design, we should be able to finish it on time."

"There is some other reason, I can tell."

"Could you not see how he needs this? I do not think he has much confidence in himself. He believes the robe will make him look the part of High Priest and future ruler of Israel. If he looks the part, it will be easier for him to act the role."

Caleb smiled. "You are a very compassionate young girl. It is not a common trait these days."

Even though his praise warmed her, it piqued her that he kept referring to her as a child or young girl. She was old enough to be betrothed. Within a year or two, she may very well have her own household to run.

"Did I offend you?" Caleb asked. "I only meant that many your age no longer take the time to read others as you do and take into account their feelings."

She shook off her discontent. "You could not offend me. You do not have the heart for it."

"I hope you feel that way when we've finished this task. I fear it will tax both of us by the end."

"I was surprised you agreed it could be done at all in the time we have."

Caleb chuckled. "I would have told the prince it could be done even without your nod of approval."

They reached the courtyard where the sun still shone overhead. Leaves from the sycamore tree danced like raindrops on the wind as they floated down to the ground. Anna stopped under the tree. "But why? If he did not allow me to have help, the robe would never get done!"

"Because I know something you do not, child."

His teasing manner softened the ire she felt at being called a child again. "What is that?"

"I was certain he would pick the purple robe." Caleb smirked. "I ordered the wool to be dyed last week. We should have it within a few days."

Anna's mouth dropped open. "You fiend! Then why did you tell him first it could not be done?"

"I have worked for these Hasmoneans for years. They will not pay you what you are worth unless they think they are getting more than what they asked for."

She grinned. "Caleb, I look forward to learning more while we work together. You have much knowledge."

His broad smile at her compliment faded as he gazed at her. He reached over to brush a leaf from her shoulder. "Who says I will tell a child my secrets?"

She put her hands on her hips and raised an eyebrow in what she hoped was a haughty manner. Two could play this game. "I can be very persuasive, old man."

He blinked, as if surprised and hurt by her insult about his age. But then he must have seen the humor behind her comment. He sniffed. "We will see, little girl. We will see."

Chapter 13

Six Weeks Later

Anna barely noticed the late summer days passing by as she and Caleb worked on the High Priest's robe. Always the tailor joined her in the women's sewing room by late morning. The two of them worked on opposite sides of the long, narrow table that allowed them both easy access to the fabric. As they both insisted on using natural light as much as possible, they had the table set lengthwise in the room so they could sit near the window. Tamar often brought her sewing by her brother so she could tell him the news about her family or tease him with some memory from the past.

Every afternoon before the Sabbath, Daniel or Phanuel waited at the palace gate to walk her back to her childhood home. She spent the next day resting with her family and listening to her father and Daniel discuss the scriptures. The greatest blessing, however, was her mother's improved health. Although still weak and plagued by headaches, the medicines they could now afford meant the pain no longer lasted for days on end.

Tova arrived at the door when the Sabbath sun set and the two girls spent an hour talking and laughing as they had before their lives changed so drastically. Anna appreciated that Daniel shared his betrothed with her for this short time before he escorted Tova back to her home. In the morning, Daniel and Phanuel walked Anna up the hill to the palace, usually leaving her at the gate while they went to the temple to watch the morning sacrifice. She had settled into the rhythm of this life, so that when the weather grew colder and the month of *Tishri* drew near, she fell into a kind of melancholy, knowing that life would soon change again.

"What is wrong, little Anna?" Caleb asked one gray afternoon. "You have been quiet lately."

She strained her eyes to see the silver thread she sewed against the flickering shadows from the oil lamps. "The robe is almost finished."

Caleb straightened his back. It cracked loudly. "And for that, I am eternally grateful. I am not sure my muscles can take much more of this bending."

Anna kept her focus on her sewing. *And what of our time together?* She would miss seeing him daily. His gentle manner and instruction had become as much a part of her life as Bilah's rude talk and Mary's quiet companionship.

Caleb glanced at Tamar, who sat at the far end of the table. "Do you know what ails our young seamstress?"

His sister frowned. "Who can say? Perhaps it is the turn in the weather?"

"I did not think she was the fragile sort who withers in the winter like a flower left in the cold." The lamp's flame heightened the twinkle in his eyes. "I thought she came from heartier stock than that."

Since he looked forward to the completion of their work, Anna refused to admit she would miss him. She stabbed the wool and, for the first time since they began, cut herself. The sharp needle sliced at the tip of her finger and she drew her hand away with a hiss, praying nothing spilled on the robe. She stood and brought the wound to her lips to suck the blood. Her mouth filled with the metallic tang of it.

Caleb stretched himself over the fabric. He sighed before speaking. "Not a drop on your work." The lines in his forehead deepened. "How badly did you hurt yourself?"

"It is only a prick."

He came to her side. "Let me see."

She let him take her hand, surprised that his trembled. She realized it was the first time they had held hands since she helped him stand in the garden almost two months earlier.

"It is not deep." He wiped a drop of blood with his thumb. For a moment it seemed he would bring her finger to his own mouth, but then he let her hand go. "Tamar, do you have a spare bit of cloth to wrap it with?"

Anna became aware of the unusual silence that had fallen over the room as everyone watched them. Tamar broke the spell. "Quite right. We cannot have her bleeding all over the prince's robe, can we?"

Nervous laughter spread through the women. Bilah strode over with a small strip of cloth. "At least it is not the other kind of blood. Then you would have to start the whole thing over again."

Anna blushed as the other women shrieked at Bilah's crudeness. Caleb waved his arm. "Do you mind?" He shuffled to the door. "I will return when you find your decorum again."

"Then do not hurry back," Bilah called after him. "I have held my peace for months. Now that I've spoken my mind again, I may not be able to stop."

Tamar took the bandage from her friend. "Please, try."

The women all seemed to need a moment to relax with Caleb out of the room. Tamar wrapped Anna's fingers while the others joked in the manner they had before a man entered their sanctuary.

Anna looked up, surprised to find Tamar staring at her with concern.

"What is it?" Anna whispered.

"Be careful."

Anna examined her finger. "I will pay more attention to my work."

Tamar snorted softly. She glanced toward the door her brother had just passed through. "See that you do."

Lev often patrolled the hallways of the palace in the late afternoons, hoping to catch sight of Anna as she headed to the servants' quarters. Since seeing her that evening, nearly two months ago, he made this activity a nightly routine. As long as Antipater had no immediate need for him, Lev excused himself and found his way to the sewing room. In the warmer weather, he had stood outside in the courtyard, listening for the sound of her voice. Sometimes, he caught a soft murmur as she spoke to the crippled tailor. But sometimes . . . sometimes her laughter rang out loud and strong. The sound both thrilled and pained him. He was glad she was happy but he ached to be the one to make her so.

With the colder weather, he often waited in one of the darker hallways for her, lingering until she passed his hiding place to follow several paces behind her. He suspected she knew he was there, but she never acknowledged him. Never turned around.

If his father's men still spied on him, he did not know, and he did not care. He and Anna had not been alone together since the day of the High Priest's installation. His father could not find fault with him, except to complain that he spent little time with Sarai, his betrothed. One night a month Malachi insisted Lev come and have dinner with the girl, but that was their only interaction. And each encounter only made him more certain that he would never love her. He could barely tolerate her presence. She appeared as content as he to keep their wedding something to plan for the distant future.

Antipater kept his young scribe busy—writing letters, learning the inside secrets about the Hasmoneans, and generally proving his worth to John Hyrcanus. Antipater was ever at the High Priest's side, while Lev stood nearby, wax tablet and stylus in hand, to write down whatever they deemed necessary.

Lev had been crossing the courtyard when Anna pricked her finger. The sudden movement in the window caught his eye and he stopped to watch her. His blood heated when the tailor took her hand. He knew he should not be jealous of the cripple. The old man could barely walk, but still, he had touched her and she had not flinched. She looked the man in the face, something she had not been able to do for him when last they met.

Lev's chest tightened when Anna moved away from the window. He hurried to the hallway that led to the sewing room, hoping she might leave now that she had been hurt. Instead, the tailor limped out.

He frowned when he saw Lev, as if trying to place where he had seen him before. His displeasure did not lessen when recognition sparked in his eyes. "Is there something you need?"

Here was the same hostility and protectiveness toward Anna Lev had felt from Daniel.

"Do you want something sewn or mended?" The cripple pointed away from the women's room. "The tailors are down this way."

"I do not need a tailor."

The older man drew himself up to his full height, an inch taller than Lev. "Leave this area." His gaze was hard as iron. "There is nothing for you here."

Lev knew he could best this man, no matter his size, but he did not want to cause a scene that would reflect badly on him, or Antipater. He bowed slightly. "Please. I only wish to catch glimpse of her again. Have you never been in love?"

The tailor braced a hand against the wall. "You have a wife to love. Leave Anna alone."

Lev's nerves sparked in rage. The audacity of this man, this crippled thing, to act like his equal.

The tailor did not back down. Instead, he matched Lev's anger with his own, his dark eyes flashed with contempt. "Stay away from her."

Lev let out a sharp laugh. "I am the scribe to the High Priest's most trusted counselor. What are you?"

To the man's credit, he did not waver in his stance. "I fought in King Jannai's army before you were weaned, boy." He spit the insult out in disdain. "I have served this family for almost twenty years. Anna has my protection, as well as that of the queen and the High Priest. One word from me and they will have you thrown into the streets, no matter who you benefactor is."

Lev stared into the man's eyes. The threat was true. John Hyrcanus was too weak to go against his mother's wishes. If Salome wanted Lev gone, then gone he would be. He took a step backward, his palms up. "You are wrong about me, sir. I mean the girl no harm."

"Then leave her be." The tailor glowered. "Marry your wife. Raise your family. Let Anna go so that she may find a husband worthy of her."

The man's words struck Lev as deeply as the blade of a sword. It was hard enough to imagine his own life without her. He did not think he could survive knowing she lay with another man.

Chapter 14

Anna again received accolades when John Hyrcanus wore his new robe for the Feasts of Trumpets and Tabernacles. He let the other priests officiate over the sacrifices and only made appearances to offer prayers. He wore his full regalia, including the ephod, for the Feast of Atonement, or *Yom Kippur*, as that was a time when he alone, as High Priest, could offer the sacrifices.

The winter months came in hard and fast. Although the constant rain was a blessing, a precursor of good harvests, Anna found the gray, cold days depressing. She enjoyed her time with the women in the sewing room, but while they talked about their lives, her mind often wandered. Though she longed to one day marry and have a family, she also dreaded the real possibility that her husband would not allow her to work. She hoped her father would find her a man who appreciated her gift, for she knew it was a talent God had given her. *Maybe my husband and I could work together? What a joy that would be.*

She found herself in such a daydream one afternoon in the month of *Adar*.

Bilah rapped her knuckles on the table. "Wake up, Anna."

Anna blushed to see everyone staring at her. "I am sorry. My thoughts were elsewhere."

The large woman snorted. "Obviously."

"Leave her be," Tamar said. "It is getting late. Are you almost finished?"

Anna nodded as she sewed the rest of a sleeve together then tied off the thread.

"Well, what do we have here?" Bilah asked as a young man stepped into the room. "Would you like me to make you a new tunic? All you need do is slip off the old one so I can measure you."

The servant's cheeks pinked. "I-I-I—"

Bilah approached him. "You-you-you cannot live without me? Is that it? Well, I am sorry to say you are a little too late, my boy. I am a respectable married woman. You shall be forced to live alone."

The servant ignored her. His gaze swept over the others in the room. "I have come for the seamstress, Anna."

"I am she." Anna crossed to the door.

"My master, the prince, wishes to commission you. Follow me."

"Summoned to make yet another robe?" Tamar folded a tunic. "He certainly likes your and Caleb's work, does he not?"

"I am honored." Anna felt her stomach flutter. After several months with nothing to sew but simple linen garments for the priests, she looked forward to more challenging work. But more than that, she and Caleb would soon be sewing together again. Her eyes swept over the hallway before she stepped out. "Should we wait for Caleb, the tailor?"

"My master sent for him earlier. He is already on his way."

The young man wove through the hallways, seemingly unaware the courtyard offered them quicker access to the prince, or perhaps unwilling to walk outside in the winter air. Anna wondered why Caleb had not asked for her to accompany him, but supposed the High Priest did not want a woman present again while he was measured. Her heart skipped a beat when they did not turn toward John Hyrcanus's rooms, but down another hallway.

"Where are we going?"

They young man glanced over his shoulder, his expression one of surprise. "To my master's rooms."

"But who is your master?"

"Prince Aristobulus."

Anna stopped. "I thought it was the High Priest who desired a new robe."

"No, his brother is my master." He approached a guard at the end of the hall, giving the man her name.

The guard opened the door. "The one named Anna is here."

"Excellent!" Aristobulus exclaimed. "Show her in."

Fear enveloped her, weighing her down so her feet moved as if in mud. Her heart pounded within her chest. As an unmarried woman, she should not be alone with him. But could she deny the order of a prince? Perhaps Caleb was already with him. Or a female servant to act as a chaperone.

She took a hesitant step across the threshold. Her stomach dropped when she caught sight of who else was inside.

Lev.

He reclined on a low couch in the center of the room. The prince stood to his side. Torch light flickered and glistened off the walls. Their warmth seemed oppressive after the damp cold of the hallway.

Anna looked for Caleb. He was not there. She was alone with the prince and Lev. "I was told the tailor was called."

Aristobulus open his arms wide. "Is that any way to greet your prince? All business without a proper greeting? Come, I will show you how the Greeks welcome their guests." He gestured for her to approach him. "Closer, my little seamstress."

She forced herself to step within a few feet of him. He closed the distance with one long stride, grabbed hold of her shoulders. She froze as he kissed her, first on one cheek, then the other.

"Oh, my dear." He placed his hand on his chest as if trying to stem his laughter. "You look shocked. Such an innocent! It is so refreshing to see." He collapsed on the couch next to Lev. "The people surrounding me have become so jaded. I forget that such purity even exists anymore."

Anna jumped when the door behind her shut. Closing her, an unmarried woman, inside with two men. If anyone told her father, it would bring shame on his name. *But dare I risk disobeying the prince?*

Aristobulus looked at her with amusement. He motioned to the chair opposite him. "Sit down. On my honor, I will not embarrass you further."

She took a hesitant step toward the chair.

From the moment Anna stepped into the room, Lev's eyes never left her. He recognized her fear when she realized the cripple and the High Priest were not here to protect her. He could see the faint, panicky pulse of blood in her neck. He had known she would react this way, had told Aristobulus not to play with her in this manner, but the prince had convinced him otherwise.

Now Lev was glad he had agreed.

Her terror excited him. To know his presence could evoke such a response in a person filled him with power.

She let out an unconscious cry when Ari kissed her cheeks. Lev wanted to push the prince aside so he could try to elicit the same sound. But he held himself still, even as he watched her tremble.

She lowered herself to the chair in front of him, but still would not lift her eyes.

"Please," she murmured, her voice like the soft coo of a dove after the rain. "It is not proper for me to be here without Caleb."

It took a moment for Lev to realize she spoke of the cripple. Jealousy took seed in his gut at the way the other man's name fell so effortlessly from her lips.

The prince dismissed her concerns with a wave. "He is on his way, but moves so slow with that limp of his." He turned to Lev. "A shame, really. No woman will take him as he is. Disfigured and lame."

Anna's hands balled into fists on her lap. Lev wondered at her response then decided it must be compassion for the older man.

Ari rested his elbows on his knees and leaned forward. "I will not keep you longer than necessary. After seeing your work on my brother's robe, I wanted to commission you to design one for me."

Her head remained bowed, but she gave a slight nod. "I would be honored, my lord."

"Good, good."

Anna flinched when the prince stood quickly.

"Do you want to take the necessary measurements?"

She raised her head, her brown eyes wide. "I cannot!"

"Of course you can."

"But it is not proper, my lord. I cannot touch a man not my husband."

Ari stared down at her. "The old ways are dying, Anna. My mother sits on the throne of Israel, the only woman allowed to do so in the history of our people." He reached over and slid the mantle from her head so the light blue cloth, symbol of her virginity, rested on her shoulders. "The old laws are being rewritten as well."

She grabbed the edge of the cloth and started to pull it back in place.

"Leave it," the prince barked.

The fabric shook in her hand, hovering in the air. She did not cover her head, nor did she lower it. Her breath came in rapid pants, as if she had run a great distance. Lev reveled silently in the energy of the moment.

"You dare deny me?" Ari took her by the wrist. "Let it go, or I will tell everyone you came here willingly. Of your own accord. To seduce me."

She whimpered, but held steadfastly to the cloth.

Lev's chest tightened as the prince's fingers squeezed her wrist, digging into her soft skin.

"Let it go, now," Ari said. "And I will not touch you anymore tonight."

Anna dropped the cloth.

"Things will be much simpler if you only do as I say."

Lev could not take his eyes from the wisps of hair freed from the mantle that danced around her forehead.

Ari released her. "Now, you will take the necessary measurements for the garment."

Anna stared at the floor. "I do not know how."

"You have watched the tailor. I know you know what to do."

Her voice came out dull and soft, as if she spoke in her sleep. "I do not have the proper tool."

The prince strode over to a writing desk in the corner of the room while Anna continued to focus on the rug at her feet. Lev ached to reach out and undo her braid. He longed to watch her brown hair spill over her shoulders but he did not want to share the experience with the prince.

Ari returned with a ball of corded thread in his hand. "Here you are. I bought this for you. It is about time you had one of your own."

A tear dropped to the carpet.

"Do not refuse my gift, little seamstress."

She whispered something Lev could not make out.

"What was that?" the prince asked.

"Why are you doing this?" Her voice cracked.

"Because I want a special garment made, and you are the finest seamstress in Israel." He thrust the cord out to her again. "Now stand and take the measurements."

She let out a low moan as she rose to her feet. One arm clutched at her stomach as if trying to suppress vomit. With the other, she reached out and took the measuring cord from Ari's hand. They stood for a moment facing each other, neither moving. Finally Anna said, "Please lift your arms."

The prince placed his hand under her chin. "The robe is not for me."

Her brows furrowed in confusion.

Ari pushed her cheek with one finger, turning her face to Lev. "I want you make a robe for my friend. For his wedding."

Lev's own heart froze. The prince had not mentioned this part of his plan before now. The idea both angered and excited him. He hated to be reminded of his wedding, especially with Anna so near to him. And yet, she would have to touch him to take his measurements. He smiled as Ari stepped aside so he could take his place in front of her.

"Go ahead, my little seamstress," the prince ordered. "Do what you must."

Tears streamed down her face. She would not raise her eyes to look at Lev. "Please turn around."

Lev did as he was told.

"Lift your arms." When he did, she placed a quaking hand against his wrist. She stretched the cord out and took a step until she could reach his other wrist. "I need something to mark with, my lord."

"Of course." Ari took his time crossing to his desk.

"I promise you. . ." Lev looked over his shoulder. "I did not know this was his plan."

She kept her gaze toward the ground. She did not look at him. Did not speak to him.

Ari returned and handed her a piece of kohl. She grabbed it quickly then marked the cord.

The prince glanced at Lev. "Turn around."

Lev obeyed. The thrill that Anna's fear had caused cooled in his chest. Anna's pale face was now splotched with a crimson blush. The sparkle in her eyes had been snuffed out. Instead, the deep brown pools seemed still. Dead. But then he took a breath, and his passion stirred again. Citrus and honey. He wondered whether the scent came from her hair or her skin. He longed to draw her close and discover its origin.

Anna flinched when Ari bent to whisper in her ear, "Finish the rest of the measurements."

The door swung open behind them. Anna ducked away from Lev and the prince. Her arms folded across her stomach.

"Get out!" Ari's eyes flashed with rabid anger. "I told you I was not to be disturbed."

"It is me, brother." John Hyrcanus stepped into the room. "There seems to have been some kind of confusion." His brow arched as he took in the scene. "The tailor came to my room saying he had been ordered to make a new robe for the prince."

The crippled man lurched through the doorway. He eyed Lev, his face a mask of contempt.

John gestured to the odd trio in the center of the room. "It appears the seamstress has already begun the work."

"I told him I did not know how but he-he-he . . . ." Anna crumpled to her knees with a soft groan.

Lev reached for her but the tailor stopped him. "You have done enough. Leave her."

"The robe was to be a wedding gift for my friend." Ari pointed toward Lev.

"I will finish the work." Caleb pulled his own measuring cord from a pouch on his belt. With swift strokes and violent pushes, he maneuvered Lev and took his measurements as Anna knelt, trembling.

Ari yawned. "Come, Brother. Have a drink with us." He clapped his hands. A servant scurried in from the adjoining room with a jug. "Who else wants something?"

The tailor finished his work. "I think it best I accompany the girl back to the servants' quarters. Your mother asked to see her in the morning and she needs to get her rest."

Ari shrugged. "We will have to discuss colors and design when she is feeling more herself."

The tailor grunted as he helped Anna to her feet. Her legs trembled so violently she had to lean on the crippled man just to stand.

Lev's stomach turned at the sight of her misery. No matter how much he longed to be with her, he would not put Anna through such an ordeal again. "I trust her judgment. Whatever she chooses for my robe will be fine."

Lev and the princes watched in silence as the two servants walked unsteadily to the door.

Once they turned the corner and were away from the prying eyes of the guards, Anna stumbled. Caleb caught her before she fell. She clung to his robe and cried, her whole body quivering with fear. "I told him it was not proper. I could not do what he asked."

"Shhh," Caleb's warm breath caressed her face as he pulled her mantle up to cover her hair. "It is over now."

Anna's emotions churned within her. She longed for his protection, but knew it was every bit as forbidden as the prince's attention. With a strangled sob, she pushed him away. "He said you were coming. I looked for you." She staggered down the hall, needing to put as much distance as she could between herself and Aristobulus. "I asked for you. He said you were coming."

"He never summoned me. It was by chance I met Tamar on my way home. She told me where you were." Caleb followed a few feet behind her. "I realized it had to be Aristobulus, but knew, if my fears were correct, I would need the authority of the High Priest to get inside his room."

Anna tried to gain her balance before starting down the stairs. They seemed to sway before her. "What am I to do? I cannot stay here, but if I leave, my father will want to know why." Her breath hitched, an awkward hiccup of a sound as she caught her balance against the wall.

The weight of what had happened crushed the air from her lungs so that her words rushed out, "Oh Caleb . . . what am I to do? I am ruined."

"You did no wrong, my love. Do not fear."

Her vision darkened and her legs gave way beneath her. For a moment she felt as though she fell down a deep well, but then Caleb was there, speaking gentle words she could not understand. She burrowed herself against his chest, longing to find a way to disappear. His woolen tunic scratched her cheek as she slipped into unconsciousness.

Chapter 15

"What made you return home last night?" Malachi watched his son as one of the servants brought him a plate of bread and cheese.

Lev waved the servant away. "I want nothing." *I deserve nothing.*

Malachi scratched his long beard. "From me, or from the servant?"

"Both."

His father stuffed a large piece of bread in his mouth, followed by a substantial piece of cheese. After chewing for a moment, he washed it down a mouthful of milk. "What has happened? Have you argued with that half-Jew master you serve?"

Lev rubbed his face with his hands. Why had he bothered to come here rather than to his bed at Antipater's house? He had not thought clearly about anything since Anna fled with the cripple last night. He had never seen anything as pathetic as the sight of her trying to lean on the tailor for support. The two of them . . . barely able to walk together without falling to the ground.

And Aristobulus? What was it about him that had made his suggestion sound good? Bringing Anna to his rooms on the pretense of having a new robe made . . . Lev agreed to the plan only so that he might see her again. That she might have to look at him.

Even though she kept her eyes from him, her fear was at first intoxicating. Like a fine wine that stirs one's passion. Now, in the morning's light, remembering he had used her like that sickened him. He loathed himself. How could he have found pleasure in hurting her?

"Have you offended him in some way? Has he thrown you from his house?"

Malachi's questions interrupted Lev's thoughts. "No, Father."

"Then why are you here?"

To remember who I was before I knew the princes. Before I knew how power corrupts a person. Lev stood but rested his fists on the table. "I thought to see Mother this morning. I have missed her."

Malachi snorted a laugh. "Lie if you must." He finished the last bite of food. "We expect you this Sabbath for dinner with Sarai. Do you remember her? The woman you are betrothed to marry?"

"I remember."

His father brushed bread crumbs from his beard. "You could make a little more effort to know her. Her father is concerned at your lack of progress in getting your own home."

"I thought she would reside here, with you and Mother."

"Why would we want her? She is your wife."

The servants scurried to the corners as Lev paced the room, feeling caged. "My work with Antipater often goes late into the night. It is easier if I keep a room at his house."

Malachi stood to block his way. "Give the girl a home to run. Servants to order. That will keep her father happy." He held up his hand when Lev started to protest. "I do not care how often you visit the house, just give it to her. Then give her a child. That will keep her happy."

"Yes, Father."

Malachi nodded briskly. "I am glad you are seeing reason." He rinsed his hands in a bowl of water left on a table by the door. "I will see you on the Sabbath. Good day."

Lev stood still as his father left the room. The servants watched him from their shadowed corners, waiting to jump if he demanded something from them. Instead, he growled with frustration and strode down the hallway to his mother's sitting room.

The room was empty, the lamps still unlit, but the dim light from the hall was enough for him. He paused in the threshold, a wave of melancholy washing over him. His earliest memories were of sitting in this room at his mother's feet. He must have been only three years old. Too young to have been worth his father's time, but Judith had always wanted his company.

He reclined on the couch, shielding his eyes with the crook of his arm, wanting only a place to be quiet, to try and wrestle with his thoughts. If only he had a way of making sure Anna was well. That whatever her state last night, rest had restored her.

Noa scurried in with a lighted wick. She gasped when she spied him. "I am sorry, Master. Your mother is eating her breakfast now and I thought to ready the room for her."

"You may." He watched the girl as she hurried about the room. She moved silently, like a mouse. If he had not seen her every day of her life, known her since she was a baby, he probably would not notice her at all. A thought pricked his mind like a thousand tiny pins. "Noa?"

She stopped in the doorway. "Yes, Master."

He swung his legs around so he could sit up. "I have something I would like you to do for me."

"Of course."

"But it must be done in secret. You must tell no one. Not my mother. Nor yours."

Her tiny features scrunched in confusion. "Is it something wrong? Will I get in trouble?"

"Not wrong. Just secret. Something for me alone." He smiled warmly. "I will pay you well for your trouble."

"Pay me?" Her eyes lit up with excitement. "I have never had money of my own."

"Come here, and I will tell you what I need."

Something was wrong.

The stiff woolen blanket that normally warmed her body at night was gone, replaced by a softer one. The familiar smell of home eased some of the fear in her belly.

Until she remembered the night before. The prince touching her. Kissing her cheeks. Forcing her to put her hands on Lev. She groaned in despair. What would her father say if he were to find out? A true maid of Israel should not be alone with a man, to say nothing of touching him. She sat up as nausea overtook her, but the shock of seeing Tova pushed down the bile in her throat. "What are you doing here?"

"You are home, Anna. Your mother asked me to come help take care of you." Her friend lifted a cup of water to her cracked lips. "Drink this. You must be thirsty."

Anna's fingers brushed against Tova's as she took the cup. Physical proof that she no longer dreamt but had returned to the safety of her father's house. Her mother sat nearby, worry etched in her face. Anna longed to tell her everything, but feared the consequences. "How did I get here?"

Her mother groaned as she rose. "A man from the palace brought you."

Anna's muscles quivered, sending water sloshing. "What man?"

Tova took the cup before Anna dropped it. "The tailor you told us about. He carried you all the way from the palace, though I do not know how he managed with his bad leg."

"Caleb?" Anna pulled the blanket up to her shoulders.

"Do you remember anything that happened?"

Anna closed her eyes. She could see everything clearly.

"He said you must have collapsed in the sewing room after everyone had left for the night. He had heard of other servants falling ill, too." Miriam shooed Tova away so she could sit by her daughter. "It was only God's providence that made him look into the room before he set off for his home."

Anna blinked, her mind whirling with the story Caleb had told.

"He said he tried to revive you," Tova continued the story. "But you never woke. He thought you would be more at peace with your parents, so he carried you here. Do you remember any of it?"

Anna shook her head. *Bless you, Caleb. Bless you.* Now there was a reason for her to be home. She shivered with relief.

Her mother's eyes searched her face, as if she suspected more to the story than what the tailor had told them. Miriam's bony fingers brushed the hair from Anna's forehead. "How do you feel now?"

"Tired."

"Lie down and rest until your father comes home."

Her mother continued to stroke her hair as Anna pretended to rest. "Sleep, my child. Sleep and be well."

Anna gasped.

"What is it?" Miriam's fingers stopped. "Are you going to be ill?"

"I thought I was," Anna lied, "but it passed." She rolled to face the wall. In truth, her mother's words made her recall something else from last night. Something far less frightening, but worrisome nonetheless. She remembered Caleb's arms around her, his words as he tried to comfort her. *"You did no wrong, my love."*

He loved her. She was certain she had heard the words correctly, even in her pain. He loved her.

She tried not to think of Lev or the prince and instead she thought of Caleb. Kind, gentle, strong Caleb, who smelled of chalk and wool. Whose smile warmed her heart and whose laughter thrilled her ears. Something deeper and more honest than the excited, passionate emotion she had once experienced with Lev. Dreams of Lev and the future they might have together once consumed her, but they had been replaced over time with more comforting thoughts of the tailor. Whenever she heard a new story from one of her friends, or learned a new stitch from Mary, she found herself wishing Caleb were beside her so she could share the moment. In his absence, she had felt unanchored. Adrift on a restless sea.

Anna hugged her arms close to her chest. Her conflicting emotions threatened to tear her apart. She wanted to laugh with joy, but the humiliation of the prince's behavior tempered her excitement. She pushed away the memory and forced herself to think only one thing. Caleb loved her, and she knew, without a doubt, that she had come to love the tailor.

"I heard a rumor that you came home last night." Lev's mother peered at him from over her cup. She lounged on the couch he had occupied earlier. "I did not presume you would still be here. To what do I owe this unexpected visit?"

"A fit of melancholy, I suppose." Lev shifted a pillow on the chair opposite her so he could sit down.

She blew on her drink. A wisp of steam scattered on her breath. "I know you do not miss Malachi. Could it be me?"

He grinned. "Always."

"You lie well. Like your father." She studied him as she sipped her tea. "What is it that troubles you? You have come home for some counsel, but I cannot offer advice if I do not know the problem."

He lowered his head. He did not want to admit his behavior to his own mother, but she was the only person, besides Antipater, whose opinion he valued. She had keen insight, and he could always trust her to tell him the truth. "Have you ever found yourself behaving in a way you knew was wrong?"

Her brows rose as she lowered her cup. "Have you broken any laws?"

"Of the state? No." He could feel deep creases forming on his forehead as he thought hard about what he wanted to say. "Morally, yes. Spiritually . . . probably."

"Does it have to do with Anna?"

He lifted his gaze. "How did you know?"

She chuckled softly. "Your father is a stubborn fool. I knew you would not forget the girl so easily." She scowled at him. "What have you done?"

"I cannot seem to let her go. When I am not busy with my work, I am thinking of her."

"Thinking of her would not cause you this distress." Her frown deepened. "Have you hurt her?"

"Not physically." His guilt stirred him to stand so he would not have to see his mother's face. "Although I am tempted. When I am near her, I am consumed by her."

The cup clinked harshly on the table as Judith set it down. "And what reason would you have to be near her? She is a seamstress for the palace. Surely she does not frequent the home of Antipater to do his sewing?"

He heard her irritation. Understood it. But did not know how to admit all he had done.

She sighed. "You are more like your father than I realized. I knew he had taught you the art of manipulation and the desire for power. I did not know you had inherited his obsessive traits as well."

Lev sat at the edge of the couch. "Was he with you?"

"Obsessive?" She laughed darkly. "Not with me. With Phanuel. Surely you can see how his irrational hatred of Anna's father is like your love of her."

"Irrational?" He meant to argue with her, but then realized she was right. His love for Anna bordered on irrational. Unexplainable. Obsessive. "What do I do?"

"That depends." She placed her hand on his knee. "What have you already done?"

He closed his eyes. "I stood by and did nothing while the prince shamed her last night. He broke her spirit."

"Did he . . . did he force himself on her?"

"No. But I think he would have had we not been interrupted."

She exhaled. "Who knows of this?"

"Myself and the princes. The servants." Lev's stomach roiled. "And a tailor."

"The servants will not speak of it. What of the princes?"

"I doubt the High Priest understood all his brother had in mind for the girl. I know I did not."

Judith took up her cup. "This tailor. Where do his loyalties lie? With the princes or himself?"

He thought about his encounter with the cripple outside of the sewing room. "Neither. They lie with Anna."

She sipped her tea. "Then you need not worry. The princes will respect your silence on the matter. Anna will certainly never speak of it and neither will this tailor."

"But how do I stop thinking of her?"

"Find yourself another passion. Whether it be your work with Antipater or perhaps your future with Sarai, fill your mind with something far removed from Anna."

"I will try." He sat back down.

"When you find yourself thinking of her, think of your father instead. Do you want your sons to find you as distant and cold as you do Malachi?"

The idea sickened Lev. He found himself desperate to get away from the thought. "Excuse me," he pushed himself up and staggered outside.

Beyond the courtyard walls, the business of Jerusalem could be heard. The frigid air of winter tried to clear his mind of its negativity. He circled the garden a few times, hoping to find relief. To find something to stop him from becoming a man like his father.

He turned as the gate opened. Noa hurried inside, changing direction when she spotted him. She crossed to where he stood, far from the house under the fig tree.

"She is no longer in the palace."

He reached out and grabbed hold of a limb. "Where is she?"

"There were different rumors. But the one I heard most was that she fell ill last night. That the . . . the tailor . . . he carried her to her father's house. She lies there still."

"Did they say what is wrong with her?"

Noa shook her head. "One said sickness, another exhaustion." She wiped her nose with the back of her hand. "I heard a woman tell another that she fell into a trance rather than . . . ."

"What?" Lev stood up straight. "Rather than what?"

She seemed to be trying to recall words she did not understand. "Than let the prince take her." Noa frowned. "But she did not say where the prince wanted to take her."

Lev's heart thundered in his chest. He took several denarii from his coin purse and handed them to the little girl. "You have done well, Noa. Remember, tell no one, and perhaps I will use you again for my errands."

A wide grin spread across her face. "No one saw me, Master. I swear it. I can go anywhere in the palace. I can learn anything you want."

Chapter 16

Two Days Later

Anna rested within the comfort and peace of her father's home. Phanuel feared she may have caught the plague from some visitor to the palace. When no boils or sores appeared, he concluded she must have been worked too hard.

Her mother knew the fatigue came from some emotional turmoil. She asked questions about the other seamstresses and the men with whom Anna had contact. She asked about Lev. Daniel also asked about him, too, when he came home at night. Anna said little, claiming exhaustion before pretending to sleep.

The nights lasted far too long. She knew no one had followed her to her father's house, but she could not erase the fear that someone, maybe even the prince or one of his guards, hid in the corners, waiting for her to wake long enough so they might torture her again.

The afternoon of her third day home, Ziva arrived to announce Queen Salome requested her presence at the palace the following morning. "When you arrive, have a guard bring you to the queen's sitting room."

After another sleepless night, Anna prepared to return to work. She and her father walked in silence up the hill toward the palace. He embraced her before leaving her at the gate. "I still do not think you are well."

She tried to give him strong smile. "I am well enough. I will see you soon on the Sabbath."

Anna took her time crossing the palace's large courtyard. Although the days with her parents had helped her mind, her heart still beat fast at the thought of returning to work. What would she do if she saw Aristobulus or Lev again? What would they do? She wiped the sweat from her palms onto her dove gray tunic as her stomach twisted itself into a knot. She would not be sick, she had not eaten enough to be ill, but she had to pause for a moment to find the courage to resume her life.

Anna had not entered the palace through the front gates since the day she had come with her father, almost six months earlier. As she climbed the stairs, she said a prayer that God would still her heart. That He would help her to face whatever consequence her encounter with Aristobulus would bring.

She told one of the guards she was to meet with the queen and followed him down a long hallway. Ziva approached from the opposite direction.

"Come, child. You are not in trouble." The older woman's assurance calmed her anxiety for a moment, until Ziva led Anna into one of the queen's private rooms. "Wait here. She will be with you in a moment." Ziva directed her to a richly upholstered chair. "Do you want anything to drink?"

Anna shook her head. She sat on the edge of the chair, afraid that dust from her clothes might dirty the bright turquoise fabric. Mosaic tiles on the floor created a geometric pattern of circles. Heavy burgundy curtains lined the walls, keeping the palace insulated from the cool winter air. Torches provided light and a small fire pit in the center of the room provided warmth.

Queen Salome entered from a hidden door in the wall opposite Anna. "I hope you are feeling better after your rest." Two servants followed behind her. One shut the door. The other came to stand behind the queen.

Anna jumped to her feet and bowed. "Yes, Your Majesty. Thank you."

"Sit, sit." Salome swept her arm gracefully in front of her. "I want us to talk intimately today. No formality."

Anna dropped onto the chair, her legs too weak to hold her up. It was obvious by the intense focus of her gaze that the queen knew about what had happened the other night. Someone had told her. *Aristobulus? A servant?* Anna found herself staring at one of the mosaic tiles in the floor. Square and green. Slightly smaller than the ones around it. She dared not look at the queen lest the woman see her shame.

"Please do not be frightened. You are in no danger." Salome let out a soft breath of disgust. "At least not from me."

Anna could not find words to speak.

"I would like you to tell me what you remember from the other night."

"I do not know what you mean."

The queen sat on the couch opposite Anna. Although her cream tunic and blue robe were not ornately decorated, Anna could tell they were made of fine silks and linen. "Your father is a Pharisee, is he not?"

Anna nodded.

"A scribe too, if I remember correctly."

"Yes."

"I am certain then, that you were fortunate enough to be taught the commandments of Moses, were you not?"

A chill settled into Anna's bones, although the fire kept the room warm. "Yes."

"Repeat them to me, please."

Anna pictured her father as he taught Daniel the laws of God. "You shall not have any gods before Me. Do not make idols or worship them. You must not take the name of the Lord in vain. Observe the Sabbath day and keep it holy. Honor your father and your mother. Do not murder. Do not commit adultery. Do not steal. Do not give false testimony against your—"

Queen Salome lifted her hand. "Stop there." She narrowed her eyes, as if trying to read Anna's mind. "Do you understand what that means? Not to give false testimony?"

"You must tell the truth about what you know. What you have seen. You must not lie when giving testimony."

"You must not lie. Do you understand that means even about events that concern you?"

Anna shivered under the queen's inquiry. Her tongue seemed to grow in size, making it impossible for her to speak.

Salome stood. "You must tell the truth, even if it reflects badly on yourself, or on someone else. To lie would be to break God's law. Do you understand?"

Anna could barely push her breath out to make a sound, "Yes."

The queen waved her hand. "Leave us." Her two servants left the room through the same hidden door they had used to enter. "I have heard several different accounts of what happened the night you fell ill." She shrugged. "Most, I can dismiss as gossip. The others, I must contemplate. I want to hear the truth from you, Anna. I demand it as your queen."

Tears slipped down Anna's cheeks. Humiliation and fear, the same emotions that hounded her while she stood in front of Aristobulus, now warred within her as she sat under his mother's scrutiny.

Salome placed her hand on Anna's head. "You have nothing to be afraid of if you tell me the truth. Did you go to the rooms of my son, Aristobulus?"

Anna nodded.

"For what purpose?"

"A messenger came to the sewing room late in the afternoon to say the prince requested a new robe." She raised her head. "I thought the High Priest wanted another robe. I swear to you, I did not know it was Aristobulus."

"Why should that matter to you? Have you been to John's room unaccompanied as well?"

"No!" Anna lifted her head higher. "But he is a kinder man. And the High Priest. I would not have gone with the servant if I had known he came from Aristobulus."

"What did the servant tell you?"

"He said Caleb, the tailor, was already with his master." Anna wiped her cheeks. "But he lied. They all lied."

"Who else do you accuse?" Salome walked behind Anna's chair. "I want the truth."

Anna folded her arms across her chest to try to stop her shivering. "The prince told me Caleb had been sent for, that he was on his way."

"Did he not arrive after a time?"

"But Caleb told me he had never been sent for. It was only by chance he found out where I had gone."

Salome placed her hand along the back of Anna's chair. "There is no chance. Only God's providence. What transpired while you were with my son?"

Anna related all the prince had said and done.

"This Lev, he is a servant of Antipater, the Idumaean." The Queen circled the chair as she spoke. "What is your relationship to him?"

Anna stiffened. "For my part, I have none with him, Your Majesty."

The queen snickered. "An interesting answer. What does it mean?"

"My brother studied under Lev's father. For many years I had hoped we might marry." Anna focused on the mosaic at her feet. "His father refused to give his blessing and now Lev is betrothed to another. I have kept my distance. I do not speak to him, but . . . ."

"Go on."

"He follows me in the halls. He has tried several times to speak to me alone, but I refuse him." She looked up, desperate that the queen believe her. "I swear to you, I have never encouraged him."

"Do you think this Lev asked my son to have you make his wedding garment?" The queen's keen eyes rested on Anna's face.

"Lev claimed he did not know."

"Do you believe him?" Salome's voice was hard.

Anna lowered her head into her hands. "I do not know. I only know I told your son it was not right. A maid should not touch a man not her husband. But he insisted. Please, I did not know what to do. He is your son. The prince of all Israel. What he commanded was wrong, I knew it, but he is still a prince." Her voice rose in pitch as her fear grew. "I did not know what to do. If Caleb had not come. . . ."

"Yes, yes." Salome sat on the couch. "The tailor. You and he have given similar versions of the events."

Anna wondered whether the queen had called Caleb in to question him or whether he had come to her of his own volition. She dared not ask.

"My advisors all ask me why I have chosen John Hyrcanus as my heir." The queen seemed to be talking to herself. "This is why. Because John is good and kind at heart. Empathetic. While Ari is . . . Ari is like his father. Hot-blooded. Hot-tempered." She sat straight and faced Anna. "I should bring my son in front of the Sanhedrin for trial."

Anna gasped. She would have to stand before a roomful of men and admit she had been a fool. She had gone to the prince's room alone.

"Do not fear, my child." Salome stood to pace the room. "Even though I would desire them to punish my son for his indiscretions, I know they would prefer to punish you for being young and trusting and a woman. It would be your word against my son's, and they will never convict another man of lusting after a girl because they have all been guilty of it."

Anna let her breath out slowly, trying to still the panic in her chest.

"One day, I hope all our voices shall be heard. That even if a woman does not wear a crown, she would still be treated with respect. Did you know that God created us to be man's helpmate? His life saver? And yet, most forget God's intent and choose instead to keep their wives as chattel." Salome sighed. "The tailor had an interesting idea, one that I approve of, if you are willing."

"Caleb?"

"He believes you are the most talented embroiderer he has ever known. I have certainly not seen your equal in quite some time." She resumed pacing until she came to face Anna again. "There is still much you could learn, but I fear my palace is not safe for you, at least at this time." She raised Anna's chin. "You are young yet, and may not want to take what I am going to offer you, but I ask you to consider it. Pray about it."

"What is it?"

"After the Sabbath, I travel to Egypt. I would take you with me. If you are willing, I would leave you with friends of my brother. Upstanding Pharisees with daughters your age, no sons. I would pay for them to keep you and teach you the art of the loom and working Egyptian flax."

Anna's mind spun with the news. Leave Jerusalem? "For how long?" She shook her head, trying to speak coherently. "How long would it take to learn such things?"

"You are a quick study, but to become proficient? I would say at least two years. Perhaps three. And, in Egypt, you could attend school. Be instructed by a rabbi. Learn the word of God." The queen's long fingers caressed Anna's cheek as if she were a small child. "By the time you returned to us, you would be a woman. One, I believe, who will have learned to thrive on her own. No longer afraid to speak her mind or stand up for what she knows is right in the Lord's eyes." Salome smiled down at her. "I long for all women to have the luxuries I have been afforded as the daughter of Setah Bar Yossei and the wife of Alexander Jannai. I want all children, not only the rich, not only the sons, to be taught the word of God. If you take this opportunity, you would come back to this holy city a different person than you are now. Are you willing, Anna?"

She had never wanted to leave Jerusalem, but she had never been offered an opportunity such as this. To follow the queen to Egypt. To learn not only a trade, but the word of God. "I am willing, if my father allows it."

"Good. I will talk with him this afternoon and you will know our answer."

Chapter 17

Five Days Later

Lev sat across the table from Sarai. He forced himself to smile at her. She gave him a surprised look in return, then something bordering on fear crossed her face. Was this the first time he had offered her anything but his frustration? The debacle with Anna and Aristobulus had given him that much at least. A small amount of pity for the girl who would be his wife. She appeared too timid and shy to eat a bite of food without the approval of her father. Peering discreetly at her while he sipped his wine, he could not help but think the only way he would ever be able to bed the girl would be to force himself on her.

As images of Anna slipped into his mind, Lev tried to push them away. His mother had been correct: if anything would cure him of his obsession, it was the truth that his behavior resembled that of his father. He loathed the thought he could be anything like Malachi. To prevent more thoughts of Anna, Lev reviewed the latest letter he had written in his mind. It had been for the High Priest. A formal letter of greeting to Cleopatra Ptolemy, ruler of Egypt. He laughed to himself. With Salome running Israel, Cleopatra in Egypt, and Selene ruling the Seleucid Empire, soon the whole world would be run by women.

"What do you find amusing, Lev?" his future father-in-law, Benjamin, asked.

"The state of the world, sir." He swallowed some wine. "It is interesting to consider all the plans Queen Salome would like to achieve while on the throne." He took another sip. "What will be the role of men if we continue to let women rule?"

"It does not make me smile," Malachi said. "I heard a rumor she is already planning to change the laws of divorce to favor women. It will make it more difficult for a man if he wishes to put an unfaithful wife aside."

Lev could not help but notice his mother's grimace. "You think the queen is right, Mother?"

Judith flashed a look of anger at Malachi before a smile softened her face. "I have known women to be set aside for simply being too old. It is right they should have protection under the law." She nodded toward Malachi. "I am thankful to have a husband who would never consider such an option."

"She is a progressive thinker, our queen." Benjamin brought a forkful of fish to his mouth. "But, I think time will prove her to be an exceptional ruler."

Malachi picked at something caught in his teeth. "It may not be a long rule. She is already nearing her seventh decade. And who knows how this latest trip to Egypt will affect her health?"

"You sound as if you hope her to fall ill, husband," Judith murmured. "I know that is not your wish."

"Of course not. But it is prudent to be thinking ahead." He made a sharp squeaking noise as he sucked air through his teeth. "You have met the princes, Lev. Do you think she was wise to make John Hyrcanus her heir?" He mopped the juices on his plate up with bread. "He does not impress me as High Priest. Too dependent on the council of your mentor. A Jew of some lineage should have John's ear, not—"

"We are boring our guest, Malachi." Judith shifted her gaze to Sarai, who sat hunched over the table, as if fearing someone might take her plate before she finished eating.

Sarai shifted so she sat upright in her chair after her father whispered something in her ear. She cleared her throat. "The fish is quite good."

Benjamin let out a long sigh, reminiscent of a groan. Judith and Malachi exchanged amused glances. Lev thought of Anna for the hundredth time that day. He forced back several yawns as they ate the rest of the meal while discussing the weather and their hope for a good grain season. After the meal, Judith and Sarai retired to the sitting room while the men went to Malachi's library.

Benjamin patted Lev on the back. "I know my daughter is not the most brilliant of conversationalists, but she has been taught the Law. She knows her place in a marriage."

"Does she have anything she enjoys doing?" Lev asked. "Any skills or hobbies to keep her occupied?"

Benjamin stroked his beard. "Her mother died so young, she was not able to teach Sarai much in the ways of sewing and needlework. But she knows how to manage a household."

Malachi snapped his fingers. "Which reminds me, have you heard who will attend the queen on her journey to Egypt?"

Lev thought his father spoke to Benjamin and so was surprised to realize the question had been directed to him. "My duties to Antipater do not often mix with Salome's. I have no idea who travels with her."

Malachi's gaze darted to Benjamin's before he turned his full attention on his son. Lev took it as a warning to remember they had a guest. "Your friend Daniel's sister, the seamstress."

Lev felt as if the floor had dropped from below him. "Anna?"

"I am surprised Daniel did not tell you, but then again, you probably do not see him much anymore." Malachi poured goblets of undiluted wine. He passed one to his guest before giving another to Lev. "The rumor is she will be staying there for some time."

"What does that mean?"

"She will be gone for two years. Probably more." He grinned wickedly down at his son. "Perhaps it is a good thing her betrothed was killed. What man would want to wait that long for his bride?"

"Speaking of which." Benjamin leaned forward. "Should we not be picking the date for your wedding?"

Lev fought to swallow the bile in his throat. It burned, but not as much as his hatred for Malachi. His father's pleasure at dispensing this news galled him. He stared into his cup of wine. Anna was going to Egypt. It might be years before he saw her again. He may as well get on with his life. He had only to get a son by Sarai. That would be his only investment in this marriage and the plans his father had forced on him. Have a son. Then be done with her. "Why not in the month of *Ab*?"

Malachi blinked. "This year?"

Lev shrugged. "Why not? It will be a year since our betrothal. I think that would be perfect."

Benjamin grinned. "Sarai will be pleased."

Lev thought of the timid girl across from him at the table and doubted the news would make her happy at all.

A gray sliver of twilight slipped in through the doorway. A late winter rain threatened to soak the ground one more time. It only added to the sadness of having to say goodbye. Anna placed the tied bundle that contained her clothes on the table.

"Be safe." Miriam's wiry arms wrapped her in a tight embrace.

"I will." Anna tried not to cry, knowing if she did, she might weep all the way to Egypt. "I love you." She longed to tighten her hold, but her mother's bones felt frail under her grasp. As if the slightest pressure would snap them. A heaviness settled in Anna's heart. Would her mother still be here when she returned? Anna took a deep breath, committing her mother's scent to memory. Lavender and chamomile from the herbs she drank for her headaches. The faint aroma of flour and honey, from the years of baking. Anna vowed to hold onto them like a precious perfume.

Miriam let her go and pushed her toward Phanuel. He carried Anna's bundle as the two of them walked to the palace gate. She was to sleep with Ziva and the queen's other servants the night before they left for Egypt, so she would be ready to go as soon as the caravan set off for the port city of Ashkelon in the morning.

"*Abba*," Anna's voice cracked as she stepped in front of him.

His eyes widened, filling with tears at her use of the endearing word for *father*. He took a stuttering breath through his nose but kept his mouth shut in a hard line, surveying her face before he finally reached out to hold it between his hands. "You know what God expects of you."

"Yes."

"You will conduct yourself with honor."

"Yes, Father."

He put his hands on her shoulders. "You have been a blessing to your mother and me. A light in our lives." He drew her into his embrace. "I will pray every morning when I wake, and every night before I sleep, for your safe return to us."

The tears she had struggled to hold in flowed freely. "I will pray for you, too."

With a final squeeze, he let her go. "Go, now. Before my heart breaks and I change my mind."

Anna took one last look at her father then hurried through the gate into the palace courtyard. She glanced over her shoulder before entering the servants' door. Phanuel lifted his right arm toward Anna. She could see his lips moving and knew he said a blessing over her. She prayed silently for Adonai to protect her family, then stepped inside the palace.

She spent a sleepless night in Ziva's room. When dawn came the following morning, Anna told the older woman she wanted to say goodbye to her fellow seamstresses, but she would return before the queen broke her fast. In truth, she met Tamar in the courtyard as the sun crested the horizon.

Anna had searched for Caleb at various times throughout the week to no avail. He appeared to have vanished. She could get no answer from any of the tailors in the workroom. The thought of leaving without seeing him again cut through her like a blade. Finally, she had begged Tamar to take her to his house so she could speak with him before she left.

"He will hate me for doing this." Tamar pulled her cloak tighter around her shoulders as they made their way into the city, still gray with dawn.

"Why?" Anna tried to make out her friend's expression. "I do not understand why he has hidden himself from me." *Unless he blames me for what happened?*

"All I know is he has been secretive for the past week." Tamar turned down a narrow street. At the third house, she stopped and pounded the door. "And he's been in a foul temper."

Anna's heart beat as fast and hard as Tamar's knocking. This would be her first time to see him since that night. She could not leave for Egypt without knowing for certain how he felt about her.

"Caleb!" Tamar knocked again. "It is me, you fool. Open up."

Anna could hear something scraping against the door, probably a lock of some kind, before it swung open.

The tailor stood puffy eyed in the threshold. "What is it? Is something wrong with one of the children?"

"No, they are well."

"Then why are you here?"

Anna stepped around Tamar. "She brought me."

With the haze of sleep still hanging over him, Caleb looked on her as if he were still dreaming. His voice came out husky. "Anna?"

"It is me."

"Why have you come?" His eyes cleared as he scanned the street. "You should not be here."

"Then let us in, you fool," Tamar said. "So no one sees us out here at such a time."

He backed into his house to give them room to enter. Anna took in the surroundings quickly. A square table with one stool. Embers glowing in the fireplace toward the back of the room. A pallet next to it, the blankets rumpled and worn. Simple. Clean. Honest. Like the man who stood before her.

His face grew hard. "You should be with the queen. You leave today."

Anna brought her gaze back to him. "I do."

His mouth twitched, as if he struggled to find words to say. "Why have you come?"

"I must know, before I go . . . ." Now that she stood before him, her courage dwindled.

Deep creases lined his forehead. "Know what, my child?"

She drew herself up. "Why do you call me that? Is it to remind yourself that I am young, or to try to make me see you as old?"

"You *are* young."

"I know that, you need not remind me of it every time you see me."

"Anna . . . ." He let out a choking cough.

"Do you blame me for what happened with the prince?" Anna ignored Tamar's gasp behind her. She prayed her friend would be loyal to her brother and keep quiet about what was said in his house. "Is that why you have refused to see me?"

"Of course not." Caleb's face bore the marks of frustration and doubt.

"Then why? Why have you not come to see me? Why have you hidden from me?"

His shoulders stooped slightly as he reached out to balance himself on the table. "You could not possibly understand."

"Is it that you fear I do not love you, Caleb?"

He flinched. "I am a foolish old man, but even I have feelings."

Tamar yanked Anna's shoulder to turn her around. "How dare you do this to him! How dare you hurt my brother this way. He is a good man. He—"

"I know he is." Anna pulled away. "I know he is good and kind and gentle. He is the best man I have ever met."

Tamar's hand flew to her mouth. "Oh."

Anna turned to Caleb. "I need to know. Did you advise the queen to send me to Egypt to keep me away from Lev and the prince, or do you send me away from you?"

He waited a moment, as if deciding whether he should tell her the truth. He took a deep breath. "Both."

"Why do you want me to leave you?"

"Because, child." He shook his head.

"Because you love me? Because you think I cannot possibly love you in return?"

His voice was choked with emotion. "Yes."

"But I do love you, Caleb. I have loved you for some time now."

His green eyes filled with tears. "Do not mock me. I am twenty year's your elder. And you are worth so much more than the humble life I can offer you. Your father knows this."

She reached up to cup his face with her hands. "You are the strongest man I know. And the gentlest. When I am with you, I am safe. I am happy. I love you."

He looked at her as if he thought he still dreamed. "Truly?"

"Yes."

He lowered his mouth to hers, pulling away the moment their lips touched. "You are real."

She nodded. "Yes."

He looked at Tamar. "I am not still sleeping?"

"No, you fool. You are awake."

He stumbled back from Anna. "Forgive me. I swore I must still be in a dream."

She smiled. "I am glad you did. Now I will dream of this moment when I am in Egypt."

"You are going, then?"

"I must. But when I return, I hope you will not see me as a child anymore. I hope I will be a woman whom you would be proud to make your wife."

BOOK TWO

Circa 71 B.C.-70 B.C.

A time to weep and a time to laugh,
A time to mourn and a time to dance

Chapter 18

Spring, 71 B.C.

Wind billowed the ivory-colored sail of the ship. Anna marveled how men of such different skin tones, sizes and tongues still managed to speak the common language of sailors and maneuver the massive boat across the sea. She ran to the front of the ship so that she might be the first to glimpse the coastline of her homeland. The bow cut through the green water, sending salty spray onto her skin.

A barrel-chested man shouted from above her, "I see land!"

Anna turned her gaze to the horizon, straining to make out a shadow of land in the vastness of the green water and the bright blue sky. When it did appear, her heart soared. She was home.

But even as her spirits lifted, her stomach churned with worry. She had grown much over these past four years in Egypt. Changed. Would Caleb be pleased when he saw her? Or was his love only for the young girl she had been before she left?

It took another full day until they docked in Ashkelon. Anna let the sick and desperate stumble off the boat before she took her turn on the wooden walkway.

"Anna! Anna bat Phanuel!"

She turned at the call and spied Ziva waving from the end of the pier.

"Ziva!" Anna ran to the plump, older woman. "I did not think the queen would send you to meet me."

"Welcome home, child." Ziva kissed her cheek.

Anna reveled in the woman's embrace. They had become close friends while she lived in Egypt. Ziva and Queen Salome had visited several times during her stay. "It is good to be back."

Ziva pushed her to arm's length. "But look at you. You are no longer a child, are you? I have to look up to you! How tall have you grown?"

"I believe I may be as tall as my brother now. I cannot wait to see."

"And dark skinned, like one of the Ethiopians!"

Anna swatted her friend. "This is from the trip on the water. I could not bear to be below the decks."

Ziva grinned. "It becomes you. You have grown into a beautiful woman." Her eyes narrowed. "Now, have you studied to become a smart one, too?"

"I am brilliant, I tell you. Simply brilliant. Only the queen can be smarter than me." With that, she broke down in laughter.

"Not so grown up after all, I see!"

Anna glanced down the pier to where sailors unloaded the ship's cargo. "What do I do with the gifts I have brought for the queen?"

Ziva pointed toward several soldiers. "The queen's guards will take them." She took Anna's arm and pulled her along the pier. "There is much to tell you, but we have all night to talk. Salome arranged for us to stay for the night so that we may start for Jerusalem in the morning." She stopped when they reached the end of the quay and tugged Anna close to her side. "Had we not had a letter from the queen, I doubt we would have found a room to stay."

"What has drawn so many here?" They turned the corner and Anna saw the cause. Men scurried about a massive wooden structure set in what appeared to be the city's central market. "What are they building?"

"Not building, dismantling," Ziva answered, her voice hushed. "Remember Shimeon bar Shetach, the queen's brother and chief advisor?" She hurried on when Anna nodded, "He ordered eighty witches to be hung. It took them two days to kill them all. The last hung until this morning."

Anna shivered. To let the bodies hang overnight was to curse their souls. Her eyes were drawn to the gallows, then to the crowds around them. "These people came to watch?"

"Not since the days of Samuel has there been such a purge of those who practice necromancy. I suppose it was quite a spectacle."

Anna's stomach had not caused her a moment's discomfort while on the ship. Now she felt as green as those that had been sick below the deck. "I could never watch such a horror. All that death."

"They claimed they wanted to honor Adonai, but I am sure many of them only came for the drama." Ziva led her down another street, away from the gallows.

Anna had not encountered such violence in Egypt—or perhaps she had merely been more sheltered from it. She shivered in revulsion, but then realized something more caused her to tremble. Something stirred in the air of her homeland. She had not felt it as a child, but now that she returned, it seeped under her skin. An expectancy. The sudden quiet before a storm, when people shut up their homes and even birds silenced their songs. An undercurrent of hostility, as if the very ground itself demanded the sacrifice of blood.

Arms and elbows jostled Anna out of her thoughts. *Or had it been more than thoughts?*

"Are you unwell? Ziva asked. "Or do your legs still feel as if you are at sea?"

"Just tired," Anna lied. She knew she could not explain what she felt to Ziva, as she barely understood it herself. But she had found, in the past year especially, that the more she studied God's Law, the more she had moments like this. Moments where her mind and soul seemed to be searching for an answer just out of reach. "Is it much farther?"

"We are nearly there. We will stay with Rabbi Ezra tonight. Tomorrow morning, we will make our way to Jerusalem with Shimeon and the queen's soldiers to guard our way." They turned a corner and started down a less populated street. "A cup of wine and something to eat. That will freshen you up."

"I am sure you are right." Though Anna knew whatever troubled her would not disappear with food. It was something that only prayer would help to clarify. They wound down several more streets before Ziva approached the wooden door of one of the homes that lined their way. A round-faced woman opened it wide.

"Welcome back, Ziva." The woman smiled broadly. "I see your friend arrived safely." She moved aside. "You must be Anna. I am Martha, Rabbi Ezra's wife. Come in, come in."

Anna stepped into a wide hallway. Although not as grand as Malachi's house, it was certainly larger than it appeared from the street. Martha guided her guests out to a courtyard shaded by a date tree. "I will not pepper you with questions about your journey yet." She gestured to a set of stairs. "Ziva can show you to your room. Settle in and rest the afternoon. We will talk at dinner."

True to her word, Martha stuffed Anna and Ziva full with a dinner of fish, couscous and dates; all the while chattering like a magpie, barely letting either of them get a word in to respond to her constant questions. Rabbi Ezra, a distinguished gentleman with a long, gray beard and sorrowful eyes, sat silent throughout the meal.

The following morning, Martha provided them with bread and goat cheese to break their fast. She tried to give them food for their journey as well, but Ziva assured her that the queen had supplied them with plenty of provisions for the two day trek. Anna had only just fastened her veil when someone pounded on the rabbi's door.

Martha returned a moment later. "The queen's guards have arrived to escort you to Jerusalem."

A contingent of twenty-four foot soldiers waited on each end of the small street. Shimeon bar Shetach sat tall and imposing atop a donkey. Four other donkeys carried what looked like supplies, while three more held the crates and bags Anna recognized as her gifts for Queen Salome.

Shimeon nodded toward them. His deep voice broke the odd quiet of the morning. "Welcome home, Anna. The queen is looking forward to having you back in her service."

The soldiers cleared a path so they could walk within their protection. Once the women were ready, they closed up the hole in their ranks. A soldier from the rear called out a command and they began to move as one down the road. The rhythmic pounding of their sandaled feet against the packed dirt sounded like heavy rain on the roof of her old home. Anna glanced toward Shimeon. The Pharisee's eyes focused straight ahead, his face settled into a mask of determination.

Anna stepped closer to Ziva and whispered, "What is going on?"

"The families of those executed have sworn vengeance. It may be Shimeon fears some kind of retaliation before we leave the city."

Anna's skinned prickled as they came within sight of the city gate. A mob of people stood on either side.

Cries of "There he is!" echoed off the nearby buildings as the crowd glimpsed Shimeon riding toward them. "Murderer," shouted several young women. "Pharisee scum!" yelled others.

The foot soldiers closed in around Shimeon, Anna, and Ziva. Those nearest to them raised their spears in the air, creating a defensive fence. Those on the perimeter pointed their spears outward to keep the protesters from getting near. As they drew closer, some threw citrons at the man sitting on the donkey. One managed to fly through the soldiers' spears and hit Shimeon on the leg. The old man did not flinch. As far as Anna could see, he did not even look toward the villain who had thrown the fruit. Instead, Shimeon remained tall and proud as they moved through the gate. The protesters followed them for several miles, hurling both insults and more citrons as they made their way across the Jezreel Valley. Finally, as the sun rose higher on the horizon and the day grew hotter, the remaining crowd turned back toward Ashkelon.

No one spoke. At first, Anna tried to concentrate on the scenery and judge how far from Jerusalem they might be. Then her mind wandered back to thoughts about the witches and those that defended them.

They travelled throughout the day with only one stop to let the soldiers and animals drink from a well. Anna's back ached by the time they stopped for the night. Ahead lay the hill country of Ephraim they would climb tomorrow.

Shimeon's rich baritone voice finished the blessing over the food. His brown eyes reflected the flames of the cooking fires set around them. Although his face was deeply wrinkled, he exuded the energy of a young man. "So, Anna, how did you find Egypt?"

Anna's hands shook as she took the piece of bread Ziva passed to her. Shimeon had not spoken to anyone throughout the day, except to bark out orders. "Exciting . . . exhausting . . . and hot."

The Pharisee's laugh resounded through the camp. "Indeed. I found it hotter than Judea as well."

Anna took a portion of dried fish. "You have been to Egypt, my lord?"

"We fled to Egypt like Jacob and his sons after the king executed my fellow Pharisees." He lifted a hand toward heaven. "Praise Adonai, the queen does not share his love of the Sadducees." He lifted a mouthful of fish but left it hovering while he spoke. "I also heard that you were the beneficiary of Salome's progressive thoughts on learning." He eyed Anna over his food. "What kind of things did the rabbis teach you?"

Anna shared how the teacher had his students memorize a passage and then broke them into smaller groups to discuss it and how it related to other verses in God's word.

Her host nodded as he brushed crumbs from his long, graying beard. "And what was your favorite passage?"

She paused for a moment, considering the many she had learned over the years. "I am fond of the songs of David. Especially those which tell of God's provision over us." The strange apprehension which had come over her in the street swept through her again. "My lord, I have a passage which troubles me. It came to me while I waited for sleep and I wonder if you might instruct me?"

The rabbi belched softly. "What is your question?"

"Moses said we were to expect a prophet like him to arise in Israel. Has that prophet already come? Or should we expect another?"

Shimeon raised an eyebrow. "This is what you think on before you sleep? Heady thoughts for one so young." He scratched his temple. "Did you draw any conclusions?"

Around her, the air stilled. The donkeys, which had been braying to each other, stopped to eat the oats the soldiers fed them. In the silence, Anna prayed for wisdom. "At first, I thought the words may have been about Samuel or Elijah, but now I believe they refer to someone else."

"And why do you think this?"

Her food lay untouched in front of her. The questions in her mind burned fiercer than the hunger in her stomach. "Moses said that God would put His words in the prophet's mouth. The prophets that have already come, they spoke *for* God, but their words were their own. Does that make sense?"

"And the one Moses spoke about? How will he be different?"

She looked away from the old man's scrutiny. Ziva sat beside her, eating her meal, seemingly lost in her own thoughts. The soldiers sat off a ways, their conversations muffled by distance. Anna gathered her courage and turned back to Shimeon. "I believe God will actually put His words into the prophet's mouth. That they will be united in thought, so that the coming teacher will actually speak God's words."

Shimeon's mouth frowned in concentration. "United in thought? How?"

Anna shook her head. "I do not know, my lord. But Adonai's ways are so much higher than ours. Somehow, they will be of one mind."

"Interesting." He stared into the flames. "Many believe the teacher Moses spoke of is the same about whom Isaiah prophesied."

"The ruler on whose shoulders the government will stand?"

"The Messiah," Shimeon whispered.

"Then you do not believe he has come yet. You still wait for him?"

"Yes." The old man's eyes seemed to seek some answer from the fire. His deep voice resonated through the night, though he did not speak loudly. "I wait. He has yet to come, this wonderful counselor God has promised us. But I do not think we will have to wait much longer."

Anna pondered this for a moment before she found herself asking, "Do you sense it, too?"

He looked up as if she had woken him from sleep. "Hmm?" He blinked. "Sense what?"

Her courage fled. How could she confess her feelings to this man? The queen's own advisor? "Nothing, my lord." She picked up her plate. "I am famished."

Ziva yawned. "I can barely keep my eyes open. Hurry and eat so we can go to the tent together."

Anna complied, finishing her meal quickly so she could leave before Shimeon asked her any more questions. She lay awake on her pallet of woolen blankets, listening to the breeze rustling in the palm trees outside of their tent. Rolling onto her back, she stared into the darkness above her. *Help me, Adonai, to understand your ways. Help me not to be afraid of what is to come.* She tossed to her side. *And please, please let Caleb still love me, as much as I still love him.*

Chapter 19

The sky turned brilliant pink as the sun dipped behind Jerusalem the following afternoon.

"I had forgotten how beautiful it is," Anna whispered under her breath. "Look at it sitting on the hills like a pearl."

Ziva raised an eyebrow. "Have you become a poet now? It is still the same crowded, smelly, dirty city it has always been."

"It is God's jewel. His masterpiece. You will see, Ziva. He has great things in store for His holy city."

"Now you are a prophet, too?" She lifted her hands in exaggerated exasperation. "What next? A scribe?"

A twinge of resentment tugged at Anna's heart as she walked up the hills toward her home. "No. The Rabbi Chaim taught me much, but he would not teach any girl to write or read. All scripture was read to us to discuss."

"Why is that, do you think?"

"Because in those things, there is power. The ability to put your thoughts down for eternity for anyone to read them." She winked at her friend. "Can you imagine what we women would do with power like that?"

Grief washed over her as they climbed the hills to Jerusalem. Her beloved mother was dead. Almost a year ago, a messenger had read the letter to her, written in Phanuel's hand, which bore the heavy news. Miriam had slipped into a kind of sleep for several days, and then passed into Sheol while surrounded by Phanuel, Daniel, Tova, and their baby, Isaac. Tears of guilt welled in Anna's eyes. They often came unexpectedly. She should have been at her mother's side. She should have held her hand as she left this world.

Anna studied the buildings coming into view. She tried to recall her childhood home, but could not picture the house without her mother in it. Her time in Egypt had made many things cloudy, lost in a kind of fog as they were crowded out by new experiences and sights. But one image did not fade from her mind.

Caleb.

She had had no way of communicating with him over the past three years. No way of telling him how she thought of him every night when she could finally stop sewing or studying or weaving. For those few moments before sleep took her, she called his face to mind and remembered, as she had promised him, the touch of his lips on hers.

Many of the Pharisees who taught her classes had sons who expressed their desire to know her better. Probably because, unlike most of the women her age, she did not show any interest in them. "There is nothing so beguiling," Rabbi Chaim once told her, "as the woman who does not want a husband."

She did want a husband, only the man she loved lived in Jerusalem. But, now that she was older, would Caleb still feel the same about her? Or was it her youth he had been drawn to?

"We are almost there." Ziva smiled knowingly at her. "Do not fret."

They passed through the city gates a short time later under the watchful eyes of the guards and merchants who stood nearby.

As their caravan ambled up the hill, Ziva gestured toward the neighborhood where Anna had grown up. "The queen has given you permission to spend the week with your family before returning to the palace." She pulled Anna aside. "Go. See your father. Grieve your mother." She gestured toward the donkey carrying Anna's belongings. "Take your bags with you."

Anna's excited fingers fumbled to untie her saddlebag. "Thank the queen for me."

Ziva pushed her aside to loosen the knots herself. "You can tell her next week." She eyed the three donkeys behind her, laden with other boxes and satchels. "What of this?"

"It is all for the queen. All that I have made for her while in Egypt."

Ziva chuckled. "She will be delighted, I am sure. What woman does not like presents?"

"That reminds me!" Anna exclaimed as she slipped her saddlebag over her shoulder. "I made you something as well." She looked over the animals until she found the bag she wanted. Instead of trying to get it off, she simply opened the pouch and pulled out a mantle of russet brown. She hurried back to Ziva. "I dyed it myself. I thought the color would bring out the gold in your eyes." She held it up to her friend's face. "And it does!"

Ziva's face glowed. "It is exquisite. Too good for such as me to wear."

"For a celebration, then. For the *Shavout* festival. Everyone wears their finest then."

The older woman nodded, her eyes bright with excitement. "Yes! For that, I will wear it proudly." She hugged Anna tightly. "Now go to your family." She pointed to one of the guards who had escorted them from Ashkelon. "Bring her trunk. See that she arrives safely home."

Anna waited until Ziva had set off again before walking the final mile to her father's house. The street seemed smaller to her. Narrow and confined. She wondered how the buildings had ever overwhelmed her. Several people stopped to stare, but none called her name, and she was too tired now to speak to them. She wanted only to see her family again.

She could not bring herself to walk into her father's house without knocking first. The door swung open to reveal her friend Tova. A pudgy, round-faced baby rested on her hip. Tova's mouth dropped open and she squealed as if she had stepped on a pin. The baby's lips quivered as his eyes widened with fear.

"Anna!" The girls embraced as Tova's son wailed. He quieted as soon as Tova bounced him a few times. "We did not expect you home so soon." She glanced at the soldier still standing in the doorway.

Anna coaxed him inside to place her belongings down. "Thank you for your help." The man gave her a quick nod before leaving. "I have been gone so long, but now that I am here, Egypt seems like a dream."

Tova's gaze kept sweeping over Anna. "You look so different." She kissed her baby's cheek. "Isaac, this is your Aunt Anna. She is a very talented woman."

Anna's nephew gummed his fingers and drooled in greeting.

"He is perfect." Anna caressed the silky skin of his arm.

"Daniel and I think so. And Grandfather." Tova nuzzled his neck. "Do we not? You are spoiled with love."

"Tell me all the news. I have missed you all so much." Anna sat down on the bench by the table. "How is my father?"

Tova set Isaac down on the floor with a piece of bread to gum while she sat to talk to Anna. "The baby has helped him with his grief. He already felt your loss, even though he knew you would return, and then Miriam died." She reached over to cover Anna's hand with her own. "She was not in any pain. She had the most peaceful smile on her face."

"Thank the Lord for that." Anna's voice caught in her throat. A tight ball of sadness lodged there and she struggled to swallow. "The house seems smaller without her."

They talked while Tova prepared dinner. When Daniel and Phanuel arrived home, Anna wept with joy as she embraced them.

"You have grown so much in four years." Phanuel's eyes shone with tears as they sat down at the table and Tova served them all a bowl of stew.

Anna breathed in deeply. The scent of garlic and rosemary settled in her soul. The aroma so familiar. Her mother must have taught Tova how to prepare food the way Daniel and Phanuel preferred. She lowered her head as her father said the blessing, but could not close her eyes, as was her usual custom when she prayed.

Instead, she surveyed the faces of her family and took note of the differences. Tova had changed little, her hair still a wild mane of curls that sought to break free of her braid. Daniel's beard now covered not only his chin, but grew full and thick down his neck. A few wrinkles now lined the corners of his eyes and mouth. Anna's gaze turned to her father. Gray streaked his black hair and beard. His face had thinned, the bones of his cheeks more pronounced than she remembered them. She dipped her head as he said, "Amen," so he would not catch her staring at him.

Phanuel took a piece of bread and passed the loaf to Daniel. "Did Tova tell you? Your brother is working for Rabbi Bartholomew. A learned man. Very respected."

Daniel spoke about his work with the rabbi while Anna took a few mouthfuls of stew. She felt her father's eyes on her, as if he did not believe she had truly come home.

"And you, *Abba.*" She smiled at him. "How have you been?"

He took a moment to swallow before speaking. "I am well. My work keeps me busy. And now you are home, my heart can again rest."

"I hope you did not worry all the time I was away." Her stomach tightened at the thought.

"I prayed every day to Adonai that He would keep you safe." He father sniffed, as if forcing back tears. "And He has." He leaned forward. "Were you happy there? Did they treat you well?"

"I missed you all," Anna folded her hands on the table. "But I was treated very well."

"Good." He nodded. "Good."

A heaviness had set over the room. Anna fought against the guilt she felt at the pain her absence had caused him. She struggled to lighten the mood. "Wait until you see what I made for you."

"I thought the things you made would go to Salome?" Her father's brow furrowed. "Was she not paying for your keep?"

"But every time I learned something new, I had to practice, did I not?" Anna grinned. "And I could not give the queen anything less than perfection." She spoke in a loud whisper, as if telling a great secret. "Although some of the things I kept behind were pretty close." She clapped her hands. "I cannot wait any longer." She swung her legs to the back of the bench so she could stand without upsetting anything on the table.

Daniel chuckled. "She may look older, but she still acts like my little sister."

Anna stuck her tongue out at him. "Just for that, I will give you your gifts last." She presented Tova with a beautiful gown of deep green with leaves and flowers decorating the yolk and hem. "I wove and dyed the linen myself, and added the embroidery over time."

Tova marveled at the garment when Anna placed it in her arms. "It is the most beautiful thing I have ever seen."

"And this is a veil made of Egyptian gauze. It is amazing how fine they can get their flax." As Anna passed it to her, the fabric caught the air like a ship's sail.

There was a robe each for Phanuel, Daniel, and even little Isaac, for when he was weaned. "I also made these for you." She gave her father and brother each a prayer shawl with the traditional white and blue stripes and long tassels on the ends. "The teachers had us practice making these when we were first learning how to use the loom. The other girls had to give everything they made to be sold, but because Queen Salome was my benefactor, I was allowed to keep these."

"If this is what you call your beginning work, I can only imagine what you brought for the queen." Phanuel's fingertips ran lightly over his new robe. "I have not seen finer on any of the Pharisees in the temple."

"I am glad you like it."

As he spread the new garments over his lap, his eyes searched her face. "I did not expect you to stay away so long."

"I know." She sat at his feet and rested her head on his knee. "I had planned to come home last year, I missed you all so much." She sat up straight. "But then Cleopatra herself requested I embroider two special gowns for her. After all that Queen Salome had done for me, I knew she would want me to do this for her ally." She looked deeply into her father's eyes. "And I did not know mother was so ill."

"It happened too fast to send a letter."

Tova picked Isaac up when he began to fuss. "It is late for him to be awake."

Phanuel yawned. "It is late for all of us. But it is wonderful to be a family again." His gaze turned inward. "Your mother would have been proud."

Anna kissed his cheek. "Thank you, Father. For allowing me to go."

He waited until Tova and Daniel had moved away before he spoke again. "It was not my choice. I told the queen I would not give my permission. Then she said it was not safe for you to stay." He paused to stare into her eyes. "Do you think you will be safe now? If you return to her palace?"

She knew she had accomplished what Queen Salome had desired for her. She had matured into a young woman no longer afraid of speaking her mind. She had refused the advances of several men in Egypt. She had spoken not as an equal, but with confidence to Cleopatra and those in her inner circle. Anna felt sure that she could hold her own against Aristobulus and Lev, if she ever needed to again. More importantly, she knew she must return to the palace so that she might work again with Caleb. "Yes, Father. I will be safe."

Chapter 20

One Week Later

"There is much to be done today," Antipater waved toward a servant who crossed to the table to pour him more *doough*. The curdled yogurt was a favorite drink of the High Priest's counselor. "John needs to be instructed on the situation in Damascus. Queen Selene and King Aretas are set to battle for the city. And, I fear, the Romans may have designs on this area soon."

Lev finished the last of the cheese on his plate. "The Romans have designs on most of the world."

"You are right about that. Familiarize yourself with their current leaders, political and military. Find merchants who have travelled through Damascus recently. I want a better sense of what is going on than what John receives in official dispatches." He drained his cup, setting it down with a heavy hand. "We need to have eyes everywhere in this matter before it erupts."

Lev nodded. "Should I set out for the market first thing?"

"Report back to me by the noon hour." Antipater brushed his hands down his tunic as he stood. "And I hear your wife is again with child?"

"Yes."

Antipater scrutinized him. "I will pray the Lord blesses you with a son."

Lev sighed. As he had suspected, Sarai proved to be fearful of the marriage bed. An unpleasant experience for them both. At least she had demonstrated herself fertile, becoming pregnant soon after their wedding night. He had not had to sleep with her past those first weeks of marriage until his daughter was weaned. He thanked the Lord for that. Fortunately, he found that his work with Antipater satisfied his need for power, and on the occasion when he desired something more . . . base, he paid well for the bed of a discreet prostitute. The arrangement seemed to suit both he and his wife. Sarai was a decent woman. She kept a clean and orderly house. But she did not satisfy him physically. He needed a passionate lover, and Sarai shivered at his touch, even when he tried to be gentle. If only she would bear him a son, they could dispense with the need to ever sleep together again.

Lev followed Antipater out into the streets of Jerusalem, but turned down the hill toward the main marketplace while his mentor climbed upward toward the palace. Lev maneuvered through the bustling crowds. Some heading up toward the temple to work or pray. Others, like him, heading toward the market or perhaps one of the city gates.

A flash of color, in contrast to the browns and dark blues most of Jerusalem seemed to wear, caught his eye. A woman wore a tunic in a ruby color, not the garish red of a prostitute, but of a fine wine. Its rich hue contrasted beautifully against the cream gown with thin brown stripes she wore beneath it. Her mantle was made in the same pattern as the tunic. The cloth had fallen forward and hid her face. He was not the only one to be transfixed by the woman's appearance. Many around him followed her with their eyes, or whispered to their companions about her.

Lev turned his attention to her companions. "Daniel?" He had not seen his friend since his betrothal to Sarai. "Is that you?" He bowed his head toward his friend's father. "Phanuel. It is good to see you again."

Daniel sneered. "Amazing."

"What is?"

"Anna is back for less than a week and you have managed to sniff her out like a dog in heat."

"Quiet, Daniel," his father hissed.

"What are you . . ." He turned his attention to the woman standing between them. Taller than he remembered, her back straight with confidence. "Anna?"

"*Shalom.*" Her voice was deeper. Confident. Her eyes were bright with a new fire. She did not lower them to the ground as she had in the past, but held his gaze.

"You are back?"

Her light chuckle was dismissive. "It would seem so." After a slight nod to her companions she continued, "The queen is expecting me. Please excuse us."

With that, she strode away from him, Daniel and her father at her side. He did not know how long he stared after her, only coming back to himself when a merchant leading a donkey bumped into him.

The man muttered as he passed, "Get out of the street if you want to nap, you fool."

Lev's mind reeled with the vision of Anna, and he tried to remember where he had been heading.

The market. He was to go to the market to get information. He looked back over his shoulder to try to catch another glimpse of her, but she had already vanished up the hill. He smiled to himself. She must be returning to the palace and her work for the queen. He would seek her out there as he had before.

Guilt tried to seep its way into his thoughts but he pushed it aside. He convinced himself he was no longer obsessed with her, what he felt was simple curiosity. She had been gone for years. It was natural to want to see her and tell her of his life. To find out about hers.

Lost in thought, he was surprised to find his feet had led him, not to the marketplace, but to his father's house. He paused outside the gate, wondering what had led him there, when he saw Noa in the courtyard, picking a citron from the tree.

"Noa," he called. "I have a job for you."

Daniel continued to fume as they walked toward the palace. "I do not understand how the Lord works." He hit his thighs with his fists.

"I have not spoken to the man in years, successfully avoided him at the temple and the streets, and today he appears in front of us?"

"Do not fret so, Brother." Anna rubbed his shoulder. "Perhaps it was a test for me. One that I passed."

Phanuel grunted. "You are sure?"

"I am." The encounter had lightened her heart. "Whatever hold I allowed him to have on me in the past is gone. I am free."

"Then Adonai has answered all my prayers."

At the palace courtyard, Anna hugged her brother. "My schedule will likely be much as it was before, and I will be able to come home for the Sabbath." She embraced her father next. "If not, I will send a messenger."

Phanuel held her tight. "Now that I have seen you again, it will seem a lifetime until the Sabbath. Send me word that you are safe. Please."

"I will." His worry constricted her throat. Her voice cracked as she forced herself to speak. "As Joshua told us many times in the scriptures, we must be strong and courageous. We have nothing to fear if we are following the Lord."

With a final squeeze, Phanuel let her go.

Ziva welcomed her outside of the queen's wing, holding her at arm's length. "Let me see if you slept at all your first night back in Jerusalem."

"I slept as soundly as when I was a babe." Anna grinned. "Although I missed the rocking of the boat and the brisk salt air. I should have been a sailor."

"Queen Salome sent you to learn the art of the loom and the needle," Ziva chided, "not to learn the ways of the sea."

Anna followed her friend down a long hallway to the private sitting room where she had met with the queen after the debacle with Aristobulus. The heavy maroon curtains that kept warmth inside during the harsh winter months had been tied back with thick, gold cords. Sunbeams danced through the narrow windows, illuminating the room with soft morning light.

"I will tell the queen you have arrived." Ziva bowed out of the doorway, leaving Anna alone.

She marveled at how calm her nerves were now. She had spent the last few years in and out of the palace of Cleopatra of Egypt and had learned how to converse with royalty. Although opulent, with its grand mosaics and marble floors, the Hasmonean palace of Queen Salome paled in comparison to the Ptolemaic palace of Cleopatra. Anna chuckled under her breath. She could never keep straight the names within the Egyptian court. It seemed everyone within the royal palace was named Cleopatra or Ptolemy.

"You look as if Egypt agreed with you, child."

The queen's voice broke Anna from her memory. She stood and bowed, her heart swelling to see Salome wearing one of the robes she had sent to the palace with Ziva. The deep violet of the material complemented the queen's silver hair. The gold embroidery shimmered in the sunlight. "I can never repay you, Your Majesty, for the great gift you gave me in sending me there."

Salome still moved with grace and authority, but the past four years had aged her about the eyes. "I think the crates of linens, veils, and robes more than repays any debt." She spread her arms wide. "Let me look at you."

Anna straightened her shoulders and lifted her chin.

The queen raised one brow. "More assured, I see. No longer afraid to meet my eye. I like that." A shadow darkened her face. "But that confidence may be a detriment."

"I hope you do not think me proud, Your Majesty. I only wished to show you how I've grown."

Salome motioned for Anna to take a seat. "Oh, I see how you have grown." Her gaze fixed on Anna's face. "You say you are not proud?"

"No."

"But you should be. Your work is exquisite."

Anna nodded with satisfaction, remembering how she used to be embarrassed by such compliments. "I am pleased you like my gifts, but to boast in my work would be a sin. I have been well-taught by others of great skill, and I consider any talent I have to be a gift from God. It is in Him only that I will boast."

The queen sat down. "A very wise answer. I am glad to hear the reports from your teachers were not exaggerated for my benefit." She rested her arm on the chair and stroked its fabric with her fingertips.

"When I said before that your confidence may by a detriment, I meant that such self-assurance can easily besot a man."

Anna frowned. "I am not sure I understand what you mean."

The queen's fingers stopped their tracing. "No?"

"I thought most men did not approve of educating women."

"They do not." Salome leaned back in her chair. "But they are intrigued by a woman who does not need them. Those women are like a wild animal they desire to capture as a prize." She brushed a tendril of silver hair from her face. "What will you do if someone in my court, perhaps one of the princes, makes advances toward you again?"

Anna took a deep breath. "I am no longer a child. I will not be so naive as to enter any man's chamber unaccompanied again." She returned the queen's direct gaze. "And I am no longer too meek to risk the displeasure of any man, whether he be royalty or no, by calling on God to empower me with the strength to fight against any such advances."

"I am glad to hear it." Salome flicked her hand as if waving off a fly. "Aristobulus's wife, Helena, is now living with us. And their children. But do not think that makes you safe from him. He is still arrogant and self-absorbed. And Helena loves her position in the palace too much to nag him about remaining true to her alone."

It surprised Anna that the thought of Aristobulus no longer filled her with anxiety. Instead, she chose to remain calm and think about the problem rationally. "I will be careful to be accompanied whenever I attend to her or the prince."

"Again, a wise answer." The queen sighed. "You need not worry about him for long. He has asked to represent Israel's concerns in Damascus. That should keep him occupied for some time." Her stare turned inward and Anna remained silent. Finally, she blinked and turned her attention back to Anna. "I would have you perform another duty for me, if you were willing."

Her mind raced. *What else could Salome want of me?* She dreaded the thought that she might have to leave Jerusalem again. "Of course."

The queen's smile, which had remained hidden throughout their interview, returned, reaching her eyes. The years of care seemed to melt away. "My brother, Shimeon, has finished building a school. It will be open at the end of the month. Would you be willing to spare an afternoon a week to instruct the students on what you have learned in Egypt?"

Anna felt her brow crease with confusion. "But will you have enough Egyptian flax for me to teach them how to weave?"

Salome let out a sharp laugh. "Not your skills as a seamstress! I would like you to discuss what the rabbis taught you Egypt."

"I am not a teacher, Your Majesty." Anna struggled to comprehend the queen's command. "Will there not be rabbis to instruct the students?"

Salome's mouth hardened into a line as she twisted the massive emerald ring on her finger. "The rabbis here lack the . . . tolerance of those in Egypt. They have agreed to teach all the children God's law and the stories of our people. But they will not discuss passages with females, only the boys." The queen's eyes darkened. "How can anyone learn if they cannot ask questions? If they cannot discuss the finer points? You will do that for the girls. Eventually the other women I sent to Egypt will join you."

Fear spread up from Anna's toes. A tingling sensation as if her body were being pricked by a thousand tiny needles. "But, I am still a student myself."

"Nonsense." Salome waved her hand again. "Any good rabbi would tell you the same thing."

"But I—"

The queen slapped the arms of the chair as she stood. "Enough. Shimeon has already confided to me that he deems you capable."

Anna's knees trembled as she rose. "Yes, Your Majesty."

"My anger is not with you. It is with all those who have opposed this school since I set my mind to building it." Salome crossed to Anna and lifted her chin. "Of course I would have loved to have a more seasoned rabbi discuss God's law with the girls. All but Shimeon refuse, and he is much too busy as my counselor to take the time." Resignation softened her voice as she returned to her chair and sat. "I prayed that God would fill you with knowledge and wisdom while in Egypt."

Upon leaving the queen, Anna stopped, trying to remember the way back to the sewing room. She used the familiar central courtyard as a marker with which to navigate the maze of hallways.

Mary was the first to embrace her. "We suspected you would be returning soon. They cleared out the storeroom next door and brought in a new loom." Her old friends joined in welcoming her home.

Tamar, Bilah, and Mary still spent their days there, but two new women had come. Tamar introduced the younger one to Anna. "This is Dina"

"She prattles constantly. We try to ignore her," Bilah whispered. "It does not matter, she continues speaking to the air." She pointed to a much older woman. "This is Naomi. She is the opposite of that one. If you can get her to speak, you will have accomplished something as miraculous as Moses and the Red Sea."

Tamar took her hand. "Let me show you the new loom." She let out a frustrated sigh when the others followed them into the converted storeroom.

"You are not the only weaver," Bilah clucked as she looked at the machine. "Naomi can run this thing as well."

Anna turned toward the older woman. "I will be grateful to learn from you then, as my skills are so new."

Naomi's mouth curved into a slight smile.

"Did you see that?" Bilah shouted. "It is only the second smile we have seen from her in the year she has been with us."

"Stop teasing and get back to work." Tamar shooed the others toward the hall but kept hold of Anna's hand. When they were alone, she pulled her close. "My brother . . . where does your heart stand with him?"

"I have thought of none but him while I was in Egypt. How is he?"

"When the new loom was set up last month, we began to anticipate your arrival. He has become taciturn since."

Anna tightened her grip on Tamar's fingers. "Why? Does he fear I have forgotten him? Or does he no longer care for me?"

"I do not know. He speaks to no one. He has been working from his home the past few weeks."

"I must see him."

Tamar embraced her as footsteps echoed in the hall. "I will see what I can do."

Chapter 21

Two Days Later

"There is not much to tell, Master," Noa said as she stood before Lev. "She is still a seamstress but now she also weaves. There is a loom set up for her next to the sewing workroom."

Seeking information about Anna's return to the palace, Lev had hired Noa to spy for him. Still waif-like and small, even though nearly twelve years old, he often used her to gather secrets from those that served the queen and her family. No one suspected a child of spying.

"Does this workroom have a door?"

Noa seemed to picture the room in her mind before answering. "The sewing room does not. The one with the loom does."

"Do any of the tailors work with her?"

"No, Master."

"Have you seen a cripple in the halls? A tall man with a limp?"

She shook her head. "I have seen no men in the halls but the occasional guard that walks through. Usually at the noon hour and again on the sixth watch."

"Does she live within the palace or with her father still?"

"I asked at the well, and she has not been home since her first day back, so she must stay in the palace. But one of the women said she will probably come home for the Sabbath as that was her habit before."

Lev slipped a silver coin into her palm. "You have done well."

"Thank you."

He debated with himself as he walked back into the palace. Was it worth attempting to see Anna while she worked? Or would it be better to try and catch her in the streets on the way home to Phanuel's house for the Sabbath? It had been two days since he had glimpsed her and he was unsure if he could wait another for the Sabbath. He decided to risk walking through the servants' hallways that afternoon.

Lev crossed quickly past the entrance to the sewing room, but did not see Anna inside. The door to the next room was closed. He heard voices from within and so continued down the hall. He had only a few more minutes before he must meet with John Hyrcanus and Antipater. Tension left his shoulders as the door squeaked open behind him. An older woman exited, then turned into the sewing room without catching sight of him. He took a breath and walked back toward the now open weaving room.

Anna sat on a stool, wiping her eyes as he stepped inside. She jumped to her feet when he shut the door. He stepped toward her even as she backed away. "Please, do not be afraid. I only wish to speak to you."

When her back pressed against the wall, she held out her hand to stop him. "Open the door."

"What?"

"Open the door and stand in the corner, and I will let you speak. Take one step closer, and I will shout for my friends in the next room. They will alert the guards."

Lev bristled, but did as she asked. "I only wanted to tell you how sorry I am for everything. All that I did, or rather, did not do, for you." She stood straight and tall, her eyes not wavering from his face. This was not the same girl he had known. She was a woman now. Still beautiful, but not so naïve. "I should have defied my father and gone to Phanuel for your hand." He risked taking a step toward her. "I should have protected you from Aristobulus, but I swear to you, I did not know the extent of his plan."

"Come no closer." She had removed her mantle as she worked. Her hair lay in a braid across her shoulder. The maroon color of her tunic brought out the green of her eyes. Especially when she chuckled.

"Why do you laugh?"

"I am reminded of the story of Joseph and his brothers. What you and Aristobulus meant for evil, God turned to good."

Lev bristled. "How so?"

"Your actions led the queen to send me to Egypt. Fear of Aristobulus gave me the courage to leave my home, my family. I learned more than I ever dreamed possible."

Her fervent response stirred his blood, but the coldness behind her eyes stopped him from closing the space between them and taking her into his arms.

"I am no longer bound to you by some unseen thread. You hold no control over me." She folded her hands together. "I forgive you for everything. To hold onto my anger would only give you power over me. I will never give that to you again."

"Anna, please—"

"Leave me now." She returned to the loom. "I want nothing more to do with you."

He stood frozen as her delicate fingers caressed the threads as he once hoped she would touch him. His voice came out as a strangled whisper, "Anna . . . ."

She did not look at him but continued with her work. "Leave or I will scream. What will the queen say if she learns you were here?"

Once in the hallway, Lev turned and watched her. He had accomplished so much in the past four years, becoming well established among those in power in Jerusalem. But as he took his leave of Anna, he knew no good had come to him from letting her go.

Anna felt Lev's eyes on her as she worked the loom. It was not until she heard his footsteps recede down the hall that she rested her hand against the wood and sighed with relief. She had anticipated Lev would seek her out as he had done before, and she had questioned what her response would be. She thanked God for the words he had given her to say and the confidence with which she said them. She needed no further proof: she was not the child who left Jerusalem four years earlier.

Anna lost herself in the rhythm of the loom, her body rocking as she wove the spindle through the thread, then lowered the bar to set the warp in place. Her mind dwelt, not on Lev, but on the strange dread she had felt since coming home. She wondered if any of the rabbis at the new school might concede to talk with her about it, this overwhelming urgency sparking through the air like lightning. Her awareness of it grew the more she meditated on what she had learned in Egypt. Isaiah's prophecy of the suffering servant, in particular. *Led as a lamb to slaughter . . . an offering for our sin.* She had confessed to God that she loathed his command to sacrifice for atonement. To kill an innocent animal, so that its blood might cover her guilt, seemed cruel. But she had always taken solace that He never demanded the blood of a human being as did the gods of the Canaanites, Amalekites, and other nations. But Isaiah seemed to be predicting that this servant would indeed be sacrificed. *Crushed . . . despised . . . his life a sin offering . . . .*

"Mistress?"

Anna gasped in surprise at the interruption but kept hold of her spindle. A young woman stood in the doorway. After a moment, she recognized her face. "Esther?"

The servant smiled. "You remember me?"

She was taller now, her body rounder and less childish. Anna crossed to her. "Of course. How have you been?"

Esther's smile faded. "I am well enough."

Although Anna wondered at the flash of sorrow in the girl's eyes, she sensed her reluctance to talk about it. "What do you need of me?"

"My mistress, Helena, the wife of Aristobulus, wishes you to come to her."

"When?"

Esther continued to keep her focus on the floor. "Now."

"It seems God is set on testing me today," Anna thought aloud. "Do you know if the prince is with her?"

The young woman shuddered before she answered, "He is not with her presently, but he sometimes visits in the late afternoon."

Anna would seek reinforcements before she walked into this lion's den. "I must ask another to accompany me. Come."

She led Esther to the sewing room where Bilah and Dina worked side-by-side at one of the tables. Tamar and Naomi folded linen while Mary cut another piece of cloth. "Tamar, could you spare an hour?"

Her friend lifted an eyebrow. "Is something wrong?"

"No, only I am called to the presence of Helena, and I do not wish to go alone."

"The prince's wife?" Bilah exclaimed. "Of course she wants you to make her a new garment after she has seen what you made for the queen. It is about time she sought a seamstress from Jerusalem, instead of always buying from Jericho or Damascus." She turned to Tamar. "I will go if you do not want to. I have always wanted to see the private rooms of the nobility."

Tamar's eyes sparkled with excitement. "So have I." She passed the linen in her hands to Naomi. "Wait until I tell the children tonight."

Esther led them through the hallways and up the stairs to her mistress. Anna noticed how Tamar looked around in wonder, her eyes widening as the architecture took on the more spectacular decorations of royalty. Precisely cut marble replaced the roughhewn rocks of the servants' quarters. Columns supported the higher ceilings.

Esther stopped outside a large entryway. "Mistress? Anna the seamstress is here."

Even Anna, who had been in the palace of the Ptolemys in Egypt, marveled at the luxury around her. The walls, painted a vivid red, stood in stark contrast to the bright white of the marble floor. A pool of blue water rippled in the center of the room as a gentle breeze from an open window blew across its surface. A young man sitting in the corner played a five-stringed lyre inlaid with gold.

"Welcome, Anna." A woman with dark brown hair rose from where she lounged on an ornate couch. Her ivory-colored silk gown flowed down her body like cream. "I have heard much about your talents."

Anna bowed her head. "I am honored, my lady."

Helena gave Tamar only a dismissive glance before focusing her attention to Anna. "I would like you to make me a new robe for this year's *Sukkot* festival." Tamar remained by the doorway as the princess motioned for Anna to come nearer. "I would like it made of wool, for warmth, but I want it soft," she ran her fingers over her silk gown. "Like this. Is it possible?"

"Yes, my lady. I can weave a fabric like that."

They discussed the robe's design before Helena stood to allow Anna to take her measurements. The princess yawned as Anna finished. "I need to rest. Can you have it done before the month of *Elul*? So that I might have time to make alterations before *Tishri*?"

Anna bristled. Not one to be boastful, she still resented that Helena thought she might not make the gown to her exact specifications. She held her tongue, answering instead, "Of course."

"Good." Helena snapped her fingers and the musician abruptly stopped strumming his lyre. She strode from the room without another word or glance. Esther followed silently behind her.

Anna waited until the princess was out of sight before turning to Tamar. "I suppose that means we can leave?"

Tamar rolled her eyes. "I do not know why you needed my help. The woman did not even look at me."

"If nothing else, I will need your help finding our way back to the sewing room."

Her friend laughed. "As if I remember which way to go?"

Aristobulus brushed past Tamar as he entered the room. Anna had not seen him since that fateful night four years ago. He had not aged, except to grow a little broader in the chest. Perhaps a little fuller in his face. But his features were still handsome, with brown eyes the color of burnt honey and a strong nose. He still bore a definite Greek influence in his bearing and his dress. He glanced at Tamar. "I was told my wife was here."

Tamar blushed as she bowed. "She just left, my lord."

He perused her. "I have not seen you before." He groaned as he sighed. "Has she hired yet another servant? What possible use can she have for you?"

"No, my lord." Tamar did not lift her eyes. "The queen employs me as a seamstress for the temple."

"The temple?" He snorted. "Then why are you here? Surely my wife does not want to become a priestess?"

"No." Tamar looked toward Anna. "She requested the talents of my friend."

Anna prayed silently as she felt Aristobulus's attention turn to her. He stepped further in the room.

"And who might you be?"

"I am Anna, my lord. We have met before."

The prince paused as if struggling to remember her. "The little seamstress? Back from exile in Egypt? Not so little anymore." He chuckled lightly. "But still too timid to meet my gaze."

Anna lifted her face. "I only lower my eyes out of respect for your position. And I was not sent to Egypt in exile."

Aristobulus surveyed her appearance. The corner of his mouth lifted into a grin. "My, my . . . how you have grown."

She held his stare a moment longer before speaking again. "If you will excuse us, we must return to our duties for the queen."

He waved his hand at Tamar. "You may go, but you . . . ." He stroked his beard. "Perhaps we could talk about a new robe you could design for me?"

"No, my lord."

His dark eyes flashed. "You defy your prince?"

"If you wish me to stay, then Tamar must also be allowed to stay. Otherwise, you ask me to betray the commands of my father and the queen, and that I will not do."

"My mother has ordered you not to be in my presence?"

Anna's heart pounded within in her chest but she drew courage from the knowledge that she spoke the truth. "The queen expects me to follow the rules of modesty as I will be her representative at her new school. As an unmarried woman, I cannot be alone in the presence of a man."

The prince walked toward her but did not speak. Anna continued to look him in the eye, even as her knees trembled. He stopped only a foot from her. So close, she could hear him breathe. Could smell the faint scent of garlic and the subtle musk of his sweat.

He reached his hand out toward her face, but stopped, his fingers hovering near her cheek. He brought them closer as he traced down her neck, still without touching her skin. "You have grown up in many ways, seamstress. But I do not have time to discuss the finer points of law and decorum with you now. Perhaps another day." With that, he marched past her to the exit his wife had taken minutes ago.

Anna forced herself to breathe once the prince left the room, but she did not move until Tamar commented, "Now I understand why you asked me to come."

"This has been a day for confronting former fears." Anna joined her friend in the threshold. "Shall we attempt to find our way back?"

"We may as well try."

"We will find the way together." As they started down the hallway, she leaned her head toward Tamar's. "Now that we are alone, tell me, have you seen Caleb? Spoken to him?"

"No. He did not answer his door when I knocked."

Anna took Tamar's arm. "You must see him. I must know if his feelings for me are still the same."

"Of course they are. But he is afraid."

"Of what?"

Tamar stopped. "That he is unworthy of you. That any love you have for him will grow cold when you see how little he can offer you. How scarred he is."

"He told you this? When?"

"Soon after you left for Egypt. I know it is why he avoids you."

Anna drew Tamar down the hall. "Then assure him I do not seek wealth or youth in a husband. I desire someone I can respect. Someone who will share his thoughts with me. Not treat me as an object to own, but as a person to love."

Tamar paused on the stairs down to the servants' wing. "Are you certain? Although I love him, he is not a young man."

"But he is the man I love. Surely, that would be better than a few more years as the wife of a husband I may never grow to love or respect."

Tamar sighed. "I will try again, my friend, to talk with my stubborn mule of a brother."

Chapter 22

The Following Week

Antipater paced the length of his library, so agitated that each step pounded against the slate floor. "Is the queen blind? Is she deaf? She has been warned about Aristobulus over and over again." He hit his thighs with fists as he walked. "He has already taken the fortresses in the south for the Sadducees."

Lev surveyed the map spread out on a wooden table in the center of the room. "He has her convinced he is only offering them refuge from the vindictive Pharisees, not building an army."

Antipater turned sharply. "To send him to Damascus is foolhardy at best. Too many battle for the city. King Aretas has lost it to Queen Selene. But the Ituraean, Ptolemy, now claims it as well. If we are lucky, perhaps Ptolemy will think Ari is another rival for the city and kill him."

"At worst . . ." Lev smoothed his hands over the map. "At worst, he will form an alliance with Ptolemy."

"Do you know the troops the Ituraean could give the prince?" Antipater waved his arms in disgust. "Thousands. Perhaps tens of thousands. This is a disaster."

"What can we do?"

Antipater circled the room, his dark skin glistening with sweat. After his third pass, he stopped. "You will join him there. I will have John sign an order demanding you be given full privileges. Aristobulus will have to allow you in to any meeting he has with Selene."

"He will only ignore it."

"Not if it bears the royal seal." Antipater began to pace again, only slower, more methodically. "Salome has been giving John more and more power, wanting him to get used to his role as future king. I can convince him to ask for the seal for this purpose." He whirled to face Lev. "Ari left only yesterday. If you make preparations now, you could leave tonight."

Lev shook his head. "Tonight begins the Sabbath. I cannot leave for another full day."

"Damn these stupid laws." Antipater growled in frustration. "Make the preparations this afternoon. Go to the market for supplies. I will arrange for you to have soldiers for protection on the journey."

A screech broke through the air. "Give it back, Phasael! It is mine!"

Mocking laughter answered the cry, followed by the scuffling of approaching footsteps.

"Mine!"

Antipater looked toward the open doorway. "It seems my sons are at it again." He gave Lev a conciliatory smile. "Perhaps you have been lucky to have a girl instead of boys. Is she not easier to control?"

Lev would never consider Sarai's inability to produce a son as *lucky*. It only meant he had to continue to lie with the woman until she proved herself honorable by producing him an heir. He hoped the child she now carried was male so he could be done with her. A sudden jolt to his back pulled him from his thoughts as Antipater's two eldest children barreled into him.

Phasael, already tall at six years of age, held a wooden sword above his head. Three-year-old Herod did not reach his brother's shoulder. He jumped up and down at his brother's side in an attempt to yank the sword from Phasael's grasp.

"What manner of insult is this?" roared Antipater. "You would interrupt me in my study while I am working? Have you no respect for your father?"

Both boys immediately fell still, as if struck by a spell of immobility. Herod's brown eyes grew wide and glistened with tears.

"Sorry, Father." Phasael spoke with the assurance of the oldest child. "We did not know you were still at home."

Herod's lip trembled as he echoed, "Sorry."

Antipater's own eyes twinkled with suppressed mirth but he kept his voice harsh. "And what do you say to my guest?"

Phasael passed the wooden sword to his brother. "We are sorry for interrupting your conversation, Lev."

Herod clutched the weapon to his chest. "Sorry."

Antipater's lips curled up into a grin. He took hold of both boys' shoulders. "Leave us now. Phasael, I am sure your tutor waits for you." He shifted them toward the door. "Perhaps, if you behave yourselves this morning, I will take you to the stables today to see the horses."

Herod's round face beamed up at his father. "Oh, please! I promise to be good."

"Only if you behave." Antipater pushed them gently into the hallway. "Now go." He watched them for a moment before stepping back into the library. "So different already, those two. Phasael is so impulsive. Passionate. Good qualities if he can learn to temper them with patience." He seemed to look past Lev, as if seeing the future. "And Herod . . . he is so smart and yet . . . I fear he is too tender. His emotions may prove to be his failing."

Lev said nothing, unable to comment on either child as he knew so little about them. But he thought of his own daughter, Tirzah, and how she too, even at her young age of three, already demonstrated her stubborn temperament.

Antipater clapped his hands together. "I will talk to John about arranging protection for your travels. You should make the necessary preparations to leave after the Sabbath."

"At once, my lord." Lev gave his mentor a slight bow. "Is there anything else you need from me today?"

Antipater waved him away. "I will see you tomorrow evening when we can discuss your trip in detail."

Lev made his way through the main hallway then out into the courtyard. Late spring rains had left behind soggy ground and he grimaced as his sandaled feet squelched in the mud. In the streets, the markets teemed with life as farmers brought in the latest barley crop to sell. He pushed his way through those waiting with their baskets to buy some to take home.

An older man dug his hands into a basket at his stall, then let the golden heads of grain sift down through his fingers. "Even better than last year's! Look at the size!"

"Thanks be to Adonai!" answered another man.

A third added, "And praise to our queen!"

Although the harvest seemed plentiful, Lev doubted that Queen Salome had anything to do with it. One thing his work with Antipater had taught him, the nobility were no different than ordinary men, they had only manipulated themselves into positions of authority. With hard work and good luck, any man could attain such power, and he was well on his way to achieving it for himself.

After ordering supplies of water skins, grain, and dried meat from the market, Lev headed to the house he shared with Sarai to inform her of his journey. A servant greeted him at the door.

"Your wife is in the courtyard, my lord," the man said as he bowed. "Your mother is visiting as well."

Lev ran a hand through his hair. He had not seen his mother in several months. Visiting her meant seeing Malachi, something he loathed. But he did regret not spending time with Judith, whom he still considered one of the wisest people he knew.

Sarai and his mother appeared to be deep in discussion as he stepped out into the courtyard. His wife's wide eyes expressed how few were his visits home. "Is anything wrong?" She stood to greet him. "I did not expect you."

For his mother's benefit, he kissed Sarai on the cheek. "I did not think I needed to send a messenger to my own house." He softened his rebuke with a smile, as if he joked, but knew from the tenseness of her muscles, his wife understood she had angered him.

Sarai lowered her eyes. "I . . . am glad you are here." Her hands went to her rounded belly, as if protecting it.

Lev left her to cross to where his mother sat in the shade. He leaned down to embrace her. "It is wonderful to see you."

Judith kissed his cheeks. She raised an eyebrow as she looked at him. "It is about time you came home on one of my visits."

Her subtle reprimand irked him, but he smiled graciously. "Being scribe to a man of Antipater's station keeps me busy." He sat next to her on the marble bench then glanced toward his wife standing awkwardly in the fading sunlight. "Perhaps you should tell Abigail that I will eat here tonight."

Sarai's head bobbed in assent before she scurried into the house.

Lev pinched the bridge of his nose, hoping it would ward off the headache he felt creeping up behind his eyes.

"You are too hard on the girl," his mother muttered.

"Do I beat her? Do I starve her?" His anger boiled in his stomach like a pot of lentil soup. "Does she not have fine clothes to wear?"

"A woman needs to know she is loved, my son. She needs to feel wanted."

He stood to pace around the date tree. "I tried to be that man for her, but she is frightened of her own shadow. She does not want me near her."

"It is not her fault that she is not Anna."

"You do not need to remind me of that." He grabbed hold of a tree branch, as if it could calm the war of emotions inside of him. "She is back, you know. Anna. From Egypt."

Judith's brows lifted. She studied her son. "You have seen her?"

He nodded.

"Spoken to her?"

Lev pushed himself from the branch with a huff. "I only wanted to apologize for my behavior before she left."

His mother stood, her eyes not leaving his face. "She rebuked you . . . as well she should."

He closed his thoughts off, assuming a mask of calmness refined from years in Antipater's service. "There was no rebuke."

Judith's lips curved up into a half-smile. "She would have been good for you, that girl, had Malachi not been so hard-headed. She would have challenged you more. Pushed you more. Not to crave power, like you do now . . . but to be a better man."

Lev barked a laugh. "Why thank you, Mother, for telling me I disappoint you."

"It is not disappointment, only concern." Her eyes took on a faraway look as she shook her head. "I only wish Mattias had not died. Perhaps you would have been happier with less."

The memory of his beloved older brother took the breath from Lev's lungs. He had worshipped Mattias, six years older and full of bold, reckless confidence. The fever that struck him down left a cold emptiness in the household and forced Lev to take on the role of firstborn son. A position his father never believed he could fulfill as successfully as Mattias would have.

Judith reached out and cupped his face. "I do worry for you."

For a moment, he let himself accept her caress and push down the memories of his brother. "Why?"

"Because you have been the one consolation of my life. And if your heart does not soften toward Sarai and your life here, I fear it will take you far from me."

"You must be a prophet, Mother, for just today I was given the task of journeying to Damascus."

She dropped her hands. "For what purpose?"

"To keep an eye on Aristobulus. The queen is sending him into the fray between Ptolemy the Ituraean and Queen Selene of the Seleucids. My master does not trust the prince."

"Does anyone?"

"The Sadducees. He is their hero. Their savior." Lev paced away. "Should he decide to rebel against his mother, they will raise him a great army."

"Would he do that? Commit treason for the throne?"

"My desire for power is nothing compared to that man's hunger for it. He is insatiable. Like a dying man in the desert, thirsting for a drop of water."

Judith touched his shoulder. "Be careful. Do not trade one obsession for another."

He frowned as he turned to her, but did not speak.

Her eyes conveyed her concern. "You lost Anna, choose now to pray for guidance from Adonai, not from Antipater. Only God's will can give you peace, my son. Man's desires only lead to destruction."

Relieved to leave the palace for the Sabbath, Anna waited for Daniel and her father to walk her home. All her prayers regarding Caleb had gone unanswered. He successfully avoided her, Tamar, and anyone else that might urge him to meet with her. Anna allowed herself the freedom of watching the various people passing by from her position just inside the palace gate. Priests and Pharisees, scribes and merchants, all made their way down from the Temple Mount to their homes in the city. The Sabbath was indeed a blessing. A time to let go of the stress of the week and renew oneself in God.

When she saw her father among the throng, she left the safety of the courtyard to make her way toward him. She noticed Daniel a few paces behind, walking beside a tall, gangly young man.

Her brother waved excitedly. "Anna! Come meet our friend, Eli."

The steady stream of people did not allow her to properly stop and embrace her father or brother. She could only nod as they set off together down the hill.

Daniel slapped his friend on his shoulder. "Eli works as a scribe for the Sanhedrin. He is well respected."

The young man stood almost a full head taller than her brother. She peered up at him. "Have you been a scribe long?"

"For several years. I have my own house now."

Anna's nerves jangled at her brother's obvious attempt to introduce her to a possible marriage candidate.

"His father is a scribe as well." Phanuel added with a nod toward Anna. "They are of the tribe of Benjamin. From a long line of scribes."

Anna did not answer, afraid of what she would say if she did.

As they continued to their homes, Eli and Daniel talked about a case brought before the court earlier in the week. Anna was grateful when their neighborhood came into view. She said a polite goodbye to

Eli as she turned down their street with Phanuel. Daniel stayed behind to whisper to his friend before jogging up to join them.

"What did you think of him?" he asked.

"Who?"

He nudged her arm. "Have your years in Egypt made you a snob?" She stiffened. "No."

"Then why so cold?" Irritation marred his normally gentle voice. "You are home now and well beyond the age of a betrothal."

"You sound as if I should be desperate for a husband." Her voice matched his in pitch and tenor. "I am not."

"And why is that?" Daniel asked. "Did the Egyptians fill your head with strange ideas?"

"Enough of this," Phanuel barked. "You are calling attention to yourselves. We will discuss this at home."

Anna fought the urge to run like a child down the road to her house. Daniel seethed beside her. He started into her the moment they closed the door.

"Do you think you are too fine for a scribe now that you are favored of the queen? How long until she finds another pet to pamper?"

"How dare you! I have worked hard for everything I have received from her. Nothing was given to me out of pity."

"Your brother did not mean to criticize." Phanuel glared at them both. "But now that you have returned, it is time I seek a suitable husband for you." He gestured for them to sit down as Tova looked over from where she sat playing with Isaac. "I have been approached by several men interested in you. If you could tell me what kind of man you would consider for your husband, I could judge them better for you."

Anna could not sit. She knew her family had every right to seek a proper marriage for her, but she would not be settled to it until she had spoken with Caleb. "Please, Father. I have only just come home. Can I not have some time to enjoy my family again? To readjust to life here, in Jerusalem?"

Tova stood to ladle stew into clay bowls. "I, for one, am glad to have Anna's company, if only on the Sabbath."

Daniel threw his cloak in the corner of the room before sitting next to his father. "And you would still have that. We are only talking of making a betrothal. You would not marry for some time."

Tova glanced apologetically at Anna as she set the bowls down on the table. Anna knew her friend would not go against her husband to defend her further. Tova placed Isaac in Daniel's lap. "Come, sister. Let us light the Sabbath candles."

Anna took her place next to Tova and they recited the prayer they had learned from their mothers, "Blessed are you, Adonai, King of the universe, who has sanctified us with His commandments, and commanded us to kindle the light of the Holy Shabbat."

Daniel and Phanuel answered in unison, "Amen."

Anna sat opposite her brother. "I have learned so many new things while I was away and Queen Salome already has me teaching another how to weave the flax I brought back from Egypt."

Daniel spoke with a mouthful of stew. "I told Eli of your work in the palace, and he would allow you continue."

"Would he?" Anna glared at her brother. "And what if I do not care a fig for what your friend Eli would let me do?"

A heavy silence fell over the room. Phanuel dropped the piece of bread he held. It plopped into the stew. "And what of your father? Do you care a fig for what I want you to do?"

Her anger left her. "Yes, Father."

"And what if I want you to marry Eli? He is a fine man. A scribe of good renown. One who understands your position in the palace. Would you do as I ask?"

A sudden ache took hold of Anna's heart. She could not catch a breath. Her life with Caleb had been all she had dreamed about while in Egypt. It had motivated her to learn everything she could about weaving, about embroidery, about God's word. All because she knew she would share her knowledge with Caleb while they worked side-by-side. And now . . . now it would be taken away.

"Well?" Daniel's voice was ripe with accusation. "Has your learning made you too grand to answer our father?"

Anna fought back tears. "I am bound by God's word to honor my father in all things. Whatever he commands, I will do."

Daniel grinned. "Good. I will talk to Eli after the Sabbath."

"You will do no such thing," Phanuel turned his attention to his son. "I told you, I have had others inquire after Anna. I will consider all their petitions before agreeing to a betrothal." He ripped off another piece of bread. "And Anna has not said what kind of man she would prefer."

Daniel scoffed. "A girl does not understand what makes a good husband."

Tova let out a laugh, but stifled more with a bite of stew.

Daniel glared at his wife. "You disagree?"

Tova took some time swallowing, as if giving herself a moment to compose her answer. "Anna knows that I set my hopes on having you for my husband long before you even noticed me. You were not the first man to ask for a betrothal. I, like Anna, asked my father to wait. I prayed that Adonai would lift your eyes from your studies long enough to notice me, and He did."

"But Anna has not set her heart on anyone," Daniel argued. "While Father and I have kept our eyes open, looking for—"

"Enough now," Phanuel interrupted. "We will talk more of this tomorrow, after everyone has rested."

The family finished their meal in silence. After dinner, Phanuel read aloud to Daniel and the two wrestled with a passage from the prophet Elijah. Isaac kept Tova and Anna entertained as he tried out new syllables and yelled them over and over again.

Once the candles burned low, they prepared for bed. Tova and Daniel now slept in the alcove Anna's parents once used, Isaac snuggled between them. Phanuel slept by the hearth, so the embers heated his aging bones through the night. Anna took her old pallet in the corner by the door. She spent the night tossing and turning, praying for some way to speak to Caleb. Both she and Tamar had been unsuccessful . . . but perhaps, if he thought the queen desired to speak with him. Maybe then he would at least return to the palace at an hour when Anna could arrange to meet him.

"What is the matter?" Ziva stood in the threshold of the weaving room. "Is everything not up to your standards?"

Anna hurried to close the door behind her friend. "It is all perfect. More than I ever could have expected."

Ziva pushed a graying strand of hair away from her eyes. "Then why did you ask for me? The queen was worried something was wrong."

"I needed to talk to a friend." Anna wrung her hands. "I did not know who else I could trust."

The older woman's face grew hard. "With what?"

"Please, is there any way you could send for Caleb? The tailor?"

"One of the princes has not sent for you again, has he?" She seemed to want to pace, but the small room would not allow her to take more than a few steps in any direction. "Salome will be furious."

"No." Anna reached toward her. She explained in detail what had happened before she left for Egypt. "But now, Caleb has disappeared. His sister says he will not open his door when she knocks. He comes by the palace at strange hours to pick up or drop off his work."

Ziva crossed her arms. "You called me here to play matchmaker between you and the tailor? What do you think I can do for you?"

"I know it is imprudent, but could you go to him? Pretend the queen has sent for him?"

"And then what?" Her hands moved to her hips. "What am I supposed to do with him?"

Anna sank onto a stool. "Why am I so foolish? Why do I always give my heart where it is unwanted?"

Ziva knelt by her side. "It is not foolish to want love. We all crave it."

"But why does it hurt so much? I thought he loved me. But he must not. He must have loved the young girl I was and does not want me now."

Ziva stroked Anna's hair as her mother had to comfort her. "I am sure that is not it."

"Then what? Why does Caleb stay away?"

"Perhaps he fears you met someone younger in Egypt who now holds your heart."

"But if he will not see me, how can I convince him otherwise?"

Ziva let out a long sigh. "In my long life I know only two things for sure."

"What is that?" Anna leaned against her friend's shoulder.

"God is good and men are fools."

Anna laughed sharply even as her tears fell. "Amen to that."

Ziva patted Anna's knee then used it to brace herself as she stood. "Let me think on it. Perhaps I can unravel this puzzle."

Anna wiped the tears from her cheeks. "Thank you. And I will endeavor to focus on my work and nothing else."

Ziva looked skeptical. "I wish you luck with that."

Chapter 23

Two Weeks Later

Aristobulus sneered at the document in his hand. "So John sent you here to spy on me?" He tossed the papyrus aside as if it might contaminate him. "At least he had the decency to announce his intentions to my face, instead of hiring some random mercenary to report back to him." He stared at Lev with barely concealed contempt. "Why you align yourself with my brother is beyond my understanding. He is a loathsome creature. Not a leader."

It had been years since Lev had spent any time with the prince without Antipater present. He had kept his distance since the night Ari had brought Anna to his room to play with her like a trapped mouse. Now he stood in the prince's private sitting room in Queen Selene's palace.

Torchlight illuminated the sparsely decorated chamber. Parchments, maps, and dishes covered a rectangular table. He knew he treaded on shifting sand, but, as he was alone with the prince, decided to speak the truth. "It is Antipater who sides with your brother, Your Highness."

Ari reclined on the one opulent piece of furniture in the room, a plush maroon couch adorned with several silk pillows. He took a long sip from the goblet of wine he held, all the while watching Lev from over its rim. "Betrayal from the ranks, Lev bar Malachi? Are you really so self-serving?"

"Not self-serving." Lev longed for a drink to ease his parched throat, but the prince offered him no hospitality. To ask would admit weakness. "I only like to keep my options open. Weigh the choices in front of me before I make a decision."

The prince smirked. "An opportunist, then, not unlike myself."

Lev bowed slightly. "I can only hope to be as wise man as you."

"Ha!" Ari stood. "What would your master say if he knew of your betrayal?"

Although a chill ran down his spine, Lev forced himself not to shudder. "My service is beyond reproach, my lord. Antipater has sent me so I might keep him informed on the situation here in Damascus, which I will do with skill. But if I can be of use to you . . . without betraying his cause . . . what would be the harm?"

The prince's gaze turned hot. "I am too tired to unravel this puzzle and decide what use to make of you." He set down his goblet. "Tomorrow morning I meet with Queen Selene."

"I am also to attend."

Ari lifted a brow. "You've already announced your presence to my mother's toadies? Your idea or hers?"

"Your mother does not know I am here, my lord. As a representative of the High Priest, I sent word of my arrival to Queen Selene."

"Did you?" The prince's lips rose in a half-smile. "And did your announcement bear my mother's royal seal?" He gestured to the abandoned letter on the table. "As that one did?"

"Of course."

"So Selene assumes my mother sent you, when you and I both know you come in Antipater's interests."

Lev matched the prince's stare but concentrated on thoughts of the long trip to Damascus and how hot and cracked his feet were from the dry air, hoping to keep Ari from reading anything else in his face. A charged silence filled the room.

Aristobulus stepped even closer, until they stood no more than a foot apart. "You are like me in many ways. A full-blooded son of Abraham who understands that the world is larger than Israel. The time has come for us to embrace the future, look beyond the Promised Land, and seek alliances with those in the world who can help us achieve greatness. For ourselves and our people." He paused at Lev's silence. "Will you allow me to see what you write to Antipater?"

"What will you give me in return?"

The prince's eyes locked on Lev's. "Your life."

Lev did not flinch. "You will not kill me."

Ari's face reddened. "You dare to tell me what I will and will not do?"

"You are no fool. To kill me would only temporarily solve your problem. Antipater would find someone else to replace me. Someone you do not know as well. Someone who is not your friend."

The prince continued to glare at him. "I do not trust you, Lev bar Malachi, but I do admire your ambition." He turned away. "Leave me now. I suppose we will see each other tomorrow when we meet with Selene."

Lev bowed but said nothing more as he left the room. Outside the prince's door sat two servants, a wrinkled older man and a youth, no more than thirteen or fourteen years. A guard stood at either end of the hallway. Lev took the measure of both servants and decided to trust the boy over the old man.

"You, come here."

The servant jumped to his feet. "Yes, my lord."

Lev fiddled with the leather pouch at his belt. "Where could a man of means find . . . companionship for the evening?" He spoke loudly enough for the guards to hear him.

The boy's gaze fell on Lev's pouch. "Hadil, just off the main square. If she is already committed for the evening, she will direct you to another."

"And how do I find the main square?" Lev fingered the coins so their metallic clinking could be heard. When the boy finished giving directions, Lev pulled out a silver coin. He pressed it into the servant's hand while whispering, "I am staying in a room in the next hallway. Come find me there should the prince leave the palace and I will give you two more." Then louder, "Thank you, boy. I hope Hadil is as fine a companion as you say." Lev strode past the guard at the end of the hall and returned to his room to wait.

He greeted the two soldiers he had left outside his door. "I have bribed a servant boy to tell me if Aristobulus leaves the palace. Wake me if he should come. Make sure to tell your replacements."

The guards nodded as Lev passed them to enter his room. Sparsely furnished with only a table, chair, and a pallet of straw in the corner with a warm blanket. It was enough for Lev. A clean place to sleep and a cup of whatever the jug left on the table held. He poured the liquid into a wooden mug, glad to find the queen had sent him wine. He sipped, pleased she had sent him good wine and not diluted it as most did for "messengers." He supposed Queen Salome's seal had made Selene disposed to treat him with a little more respect. He downed the first cup and poured himself another.

Sighing deeply, Lev stripped off his cloak and outer tunic then sank to the one wooden chair to take off his sandals.

"My lord?" called one of his guards.

Too tired to stand, Lev answered, "What is it?"

"A servant brings bread. Should we let her in?"

Lev's stomach growled. "Yes."

A woman entered. Although a cloth covered her head, he spied thick brown ringlets of hair flowing underneath. She placed a loaf of bread on the table before turning to bow toward him. Her round, hazel eyes lifted to his face.

"My mistress asks if there is anything else you might need."

Lev sighed again. If his muscles did not ache so much from the long journey here, he would have considered taking this woman to bed. But he needed rest to keep his wits about him. "No. Leave me."

She smiled, he sensed in relief, before bowing to leave the room. He snatched the loaf from the plate and tore off a hunk. He shoved it in his mouth as he ripped off another piece. Although Antipater had seen him well provided for the week-long journey, the harsh terrain had exhausted him. It had been many years since he had travelled so far, and he was not as young as he had been then.

He made short work of his meager meal before collapsing onto the straw pallet. Lacking the warmth of a hearth, he wrapped his cloak around himself then drew up the woolen blanket Selene had provided for him. He supposed he should be grateful for her generosity. At least he had a room to himself. His guards would take turns sleeping in the army quarters located just outside the palace.

Sometime later, a persistent series of taps woke him out of dreamless sleep. He roused himself from the floor, his muscles fighting against him. Another knock, this one a little louder than the others, pulled him toward the door. He cracked it open and blinked at the light from the torch lit hallway. "What is it?"

The young servant he had spoken to earlier stood between his guards. "Prince Aristobulus left his rooms."

Lev stifled a yawn, forcing himself to focus on the boy's words. "Do you know where he's going?"

"Had it been to the whorehouse, I would not have come, my lord. But he received a message from Ptolemy."

Instantly awake, Lev swung open the door. "How can you be sure it was from him?"

"I recognized the soldier's uniform. Aristobulus left with him only a few minutes later."

Lev found his money pouch and drew out two silver coins. He held them in his palm as he crossed back to the boy. "Do you know where Ptolemy stays?"

The servant's eager eyes stayed glued on his reward. "Yes, my lord. Outside the walls of Damascus. But he is heavily guarded."

He slipped the coins into the boy's hand. "You have done well. Do any soldiers guard the hallway to Aristobulus's room?"

"No." His closed a fist around the money. "They left with him."

"And the old man?"

"Gone for the night."

"Good. What time is it?" Lev scratched his head.

"Just past the second watch, my lord."

"Make yourself scarce for half an hour, and I will leave you another denarii outside the prince's door. Understood?"

The young man grinned. "Yes, my lord." With that, the servant ran down the hallway.

Lev turned his attention to his two guards standing nearby. "If anyone else comes to the door, tell them you are under strict orders not to disturb me." He grabbed his tunic from the floor and slipped it over his head. "I will return shortly."

Walking quickly to Aristobulus's room, Lev's bare feet made no sound on the stone floor. He carried no torch, so the moment he left his lit hallway, he had to wait for his eyes to adjust to the blackness of the next until he reached the hall to the prince's room. A torch remained burning near the door. He paused outside, his mind devising some excuse should a guard be inside. Pushing the door open, his shoulders relaxed.

An oil lamp on the table flickered, but the room was empty. He closed the door behind him and made his way to the table strewn letters, maps, and papers. His own orders from John Hyrcanus lay on top. Next to it, another missive with a broken wax seal Lev did not recognize. He held the paper closer to the lamp.

To Aristobulus, a prince of Israel,

I am glad to learn of your desire to broker an alliance between our two countries. My one demand is Damascus. If you believe you can aid me in my quest to secure this jewel of a city, my guards will escort you to my tent so that we may discuss the terms face to face.

Ptolemy, King of Ituraea

Lev slipped the letter inside his tunic and continued to rifle through the papers. He found no other sealed documents, but one other letter caught his eye because of the signature, *Zacharias bar Judah*, one of the high ranking Sadducees now in exile because of Queen Salome's support of the Pharisees. Whether she wanted to admit it or not, Salome's allegiance to those scholars who believed in following not only God's written Law, but the teachings of the rabbis, threatened to undermine the stability of her kingdom. Aristobulus courted the favor of the Sadducees, who followed only the Law of Moses. The fact that they came from Israel's wealthier citizens and nobility meant they could well finance Aristobulus should he decide to make a play for his mother's throne.

Afraid to stay longer in the prince's private rooms, Lev hid this letter as well in his tunic. Having them might put his life in danger, but they might also guarantee the prince's favor should he choose to ransom them at a later date. He weighed it worth the risk to take them.

Lev arrived outside the queen's throne room at the appointed hour but was not allowed inside. He paced the mosaic floors. The turquoise, magenta, and saffron colored tiles shimmered in the sunlight streaming in from windows high along the wall. His hand wandered again to the belt he wore under his tunic. Secured underneath were the two letters he had taken from Aristobulus's room. Lev had passed by the prince's quarters before making his way here, and learned from the guard that Ari had not returned the previous night. He breathed a sigh of relief as his fingers crinkled the parchment strapped to his waist. He had spent a sleepless night wondering how to proceed and still did not know the best course of action. Should he send the letters directly to Antipater to show Ari's treachery? Or would the letters gain Lev and his family safety should Ari wrest the throne from his brother?

The sounds of footsteps pounding down the hall pulled Lev from his puzzle. Aristobulus ran around the corner then pulled to a stop at the sight of him. The prince took a moment to brush off his tunic and straighten his cloak. "Selene has not called us in yet?"

"Obviously."

Ari's eyes flashed with anger, but he quickly turned the look to one of mirth. "I guess I enjoyed the queen's wine and the hospitality of one of her maids a little too much last night. It was difficult to wake up this morning."

Lev smiled, as if in agreement. "Lucky you. I fell asleep within moments of leaving you. Much needed rest after the journey."

The large, gold-plated doors to the throne room swung open and a guard requested them to follow. The ceiling soared at least fifty feet above his head. The gold columns shimmered at his side. A far more opulent display than the Hasmonean palace in Jerusalem. At the far end of the hall, the queen sat on her golden throne atop a dais.

Aristobulus bowed to her. "Your Majesty."

Queen Selene wore her hair in an intricate braid wound around her head, cradling her gold crown. She was younger than Israel's queen, Lev thought, but not by many years. Her flowing robes cascaded around her throne. She eyed him with a vague smile on her lips. Lev could not read the meaning behind it. "Welcome, gentlemen. What are your petitions?"

Ari straightened his back. "I have come to offer Israel's help."

"And how will Queen Salome help us?" Selene spoke Aramaic in clipped, nasal tones, like a chattering, angry bird. "Will she fight with us, against our enemies?"

"Who would dare to come against one so beautiful?"

Lev heard the condescension in the prince's voice. The queen frowned. Did she understand Ari thought her nothing more than a figurehead? She rose from her throne. "Do not think . . . because I lack a man's outer form . . . I am weak and foolish." She seemed to be translating her words into Aramaic. "I have risen . . . to this position . . . because I have fought better men than you to secure it." She glared at Aristobulus. "We know Ptolemy plots to take this city from us. We know it is only a matter of time until Tigranes, the Armenian, moves his army to my country." Her words flowed easier, as if her anger helped her speak. "If Salome wishes to keep Israel safe, she would be wise to send her troops to fight with mine against these villains."

Ari lowered his head. "I meant no dishonor."

Her mouth rose in a sneer. "Yes, you did."

The prince straightened his shoulders. "Israel is ready to send ten thousand troops should you have need of them."

Selene's face softened. "Tell Salome we have need. Ptolemy camps outside our walls like an adder waiting to strike. He says he comes in peace . . . but we think he lies." She lowered herself to her throne. "Does Salome have a . . . a price . . . for her assistance?"

"Only your aid in the future, should Israel need your help."

The queen nodded. "Of course." She glanced toward Lev. "And you, Salome's messenger, have you anything to add from my sister-queen?"

Lev felt Ari bristle as she turned her attention toward him. He hurried to answer before the prince could reveal the truth. "Your Majesty, although Salome's seal did adorn our message, it is on behalf of her heir and the High Priest that I come. John Hyrcanus desires you to know that he too, will abide by any agreement you make with his mother, Queen Salome."

"So you came on his behalf?"

Ari made a sound. It could have been a cough, but it sounded like a laugh.

Selene turned her attention back to him. "You have . . . thoughts . . . in this matter?"

The prince shrugged. "My brother is not smart enough on his own to make decisions like this. It is his *counselor*," Ari practically spat the word. "Antipater is the one who rules over my brother and tells him what to do. My brother is his puppet."

"Excuse me, Your Majesty," Lev interjected. "But as much as Aristobulus hates the idea, his mother has chosen John Hyrcanus as her successor. He is the one who will honor his mother's treaties with you."

Selene shook her head. "Brothers already in battle for their mother's throne . . . while she yet lives? I will make offerings to my gods that Salome reigns for many more years . . . I do not wish to be caught in your squabble for her position."

"John Hyrcanus is her chosen successor." Lev did not glance at the prince. "Although his brother is a most capable leader in his own right."

"My concern now is for myself and the people of Syria. Ptolemy must not be allowed to take our lands or this city." She waved a hand. "I do not care which of you returns to Israel with our request for aid, only that you do it quickly."

Ari's stare burned toward him. "Send the messenger back to his masters."

Lev bowed. "Of course. I will return once my men have rested and gathered supplies for our journey."

Queen Selene dismissed them with another wave of her hand. Ari sped out of the throne room as if pursued, while Lev took his time leaving.

He had no desire to go back to his solitary room, so instead sought the way to an outer courtyard and then into the city itself. The exotic smells and sounds that hung in the air soon entranced him. Garlic, cumin, and rosemary mixed with an unfamiliar floral scent. Near the center of the market, a man played a strange wooden flute, or was it a horn? The music that came from it was harsher than flutes Lev had heard in the past, yet the instrument was able to carry a melody unlike the trumpets at the temple.

A woman danced as the man played. She undulated and spun, her bright red costume flowing around her like wings. A veil hid her nose and mouth, but her eyes were uncovered. Gray, the color of the sea in a storm. Sunlight sparkled off the gold sequins on her headdress, casting rainbows on the crowd gathered around her. Men stood transfixed as she thrust her hips and her ample chest heaved in exertion.

A man groaned beside him. "I wonder what a night with her would cost."

Lev's blood stirred. He had never witnessed such a display of raw sensuality in a public gathering place. "I am sure she would be worth every last coin." The man chuckled in agreement.

An old woman pushed her way between them. She reached out her arm, brown and cracked liked old leather, and touched Lev's elbow. "I know where you can find a woman like her." Her smile revealed her lack of teeth. Her voice held the same clipped tones of the queen's. "If you have money to buy her."

The dancing figure held Lev's attention. "I doubt a woman like you knows anyone like her."

The woman let out a breathy chuckle. "Does not the ugly thorn bush produce the rose?"

"How much?" the man beside them asked.

"Two silver coins."

The man growled under his breath. "Too expensive for me."

The crone turned to Lev. "I can see from your clothes . . . your bearing . . . you are a man of importance . . . come. Come and see my beautiful one."

The dancer's filmy costume lifted away from her as she spun to the music's quickening tempo, treating those around her to a glimpse of the dark, smooth skin of her stomach. Lev's pulse sped up. "She is like this one?"

"Skin as dark and soft as the queen's finest horse. Eyes the color of emeralds."

The music stopped and the dancing girl fell to her knees while the crowd applauded. Some threw coins. Lev's pulse continued to race.

"She had better be everything you say, old woman, or neither of you will see a coin from me."

"Follow." The stooped figure made her way through the market. "See for yourself."

Lev shadowed the woman as she veered onto a street off the square. After another turn, she stopped in front of a wooden door, scarred with gouges and stained with time. She rapped her ancient knuckles on it before pushing it open. "Nasrin, my rose, come and meet our guest."

Lev stepped into a dimly lit room. Only the embers from a cooking hearth provided any light. His stomach growled as the scent of garlic and onions reached him.

The old woman chuckled. "Perhaps you are too hungry to satisfy yourself with something other than food?"

Lev ignored her. "I do not see anyone else here." He put his palm over the hilt of the knife at his belt. "This had better not be some trick, grandmother." He stepped backward toward the door.

"Never, my lord. Nasrin is only sleeping." The woman hurried over to a curtained doorway, then whispered harshly to someone inside. She gestured for Lev to come closer.

He shook his head. "I will not pay for something I cannot see. You promised a woman as beautiful as the one in the square. Have her step out into the light."

After another harshly whispered exchange, the crone stuck her hand past the threshold and pulled out another woman.

No, not a woman, a young girl. The tiny figure could be no more than thirteen or fourteen. A shawl covered her slender shoulders. Lev's heart sank. He had no desire to take a frightened child to bed. "You promised me a woman."

The crone spoke rapidly in a different language at the girl before pushing her toward him. "My granddaughter is a woman, my lord. Small, as are all the women in my family. But more lovely than a diamond. Nasrin, greet our guest."

The girl lifted her eyes to him and Lev's knees weakened. He had never seen eyes so large or so green. They flashed against her dark skin even in the dim light of the room. Accustomed to the prostitutes in Jerusalem who painted their faces with kohl and rouge, he was unnerved to see her beauty came naturally. She was young, but no younger than Sarai had been when he had taken her to his bed. But this girl, unlike his wife, was not afraid of him.

As if drawn by an unseen power, his fingers touched her cheek. *Smooth, like silk.* His fingertips tingled as he traced down to her jaw. Her lips, full and pink, did not smile at him. Rather, they parted gently, as if inviting him to kiss her. When he drew the shawl from her shoulders and let it drop to the floor, he felt her tremble.

"Show me your two coins," the old woman insisted as she came between them. "Then you may take Nasrin to bed."

Lev kept his eyes on the girl as he loosened the tie on his pouch and pulled out two silver coins. He would have paid all he had to spend an hour with the exquisite girl in front of him.

The old woman took his money then pushed them behind the curtain. "Enjoy yourself, my lord."

Lev reluctantly left Nasrin's side a few hours later. The girl sat in the corner of the alcove and watched him as he put on his outer belt and robe. He had kept his tunic on, concerned even now that the letters strapped to his stomach might find their way back to Aristobulus.

Nasrin had said nothing during their time together, but she had seemed eager enough to do all Lev asked of her. Her eyes followed him with interest even now. Bright and curious, he realized how much those eyes reminded him of Anna's. Anna's were not this glorious green, but they had sparkled with the same intensity and life. Lev knelt down in front of the girl. He drew her to him and kissed her again, her full lips soft against his. She smelled of lavender and lemon and he breathed in deeply so he would not forget it.

The wrinkled woman sat on the floor beside the hearth, stirring a cooking pot. She did not look up as he left the alcove.

"Grandmother," he called. "How much to keep her for me until tonight?" He did not mind sharing the prostitutes of Jerusalem, but Nasrin . . . he loathed the thought of any man but him enjoying her.

"Four silver coins." She continued stirring her stew. "Before you leave."

The price was steep, but when he looked back at Nasrin, her lips rose in the first smile he had seen on her face. Her white teeth shone like pearls in the dark alcove. The curve of her breasts made his heart beat hard in his chest. "Two now and if, when I return, the girl assures me she has not been touched again, I will you give you the others."

Nasrin's eyelashes fluttered as her smile softened. When he turned to her grandmother, he found her holding out her palm. He dropped the coins in her hand.

"She is yours." The crone's ancient fingers closed around the silver. "Until tonight."

Lev hurried from the house before his desire for Nasrin drew him back into the alcove. As much as he hated now to think of it, preparations needed to be made for his journey back to Jerusalem. Nasrin's scent still haunted him. He could not stop thinking of her skin . . . her eyes . . . her body. Every moment away from her would be torture.

He stopped by the barracks to speak with his soldiers. He left them coins to take to the market to buy the provisions then set off for the palace. He would dine on whatever the queen left for him tonight then return to Nasrin for the evening.

Lev approached the nervous-looking guard outside his room. "You have news?"

The man nodded, his brow knitted with worry.

"Spit it out, man. What has happened?"

"My lord, it is the prince. He is—"

The door swung open behind him, nearly knocking him off his feet. Aristobulus stood in the threshold, eyes glistening with manic intensity. His hair looked as if the prince had tried to pull locks of it from his head. He strode forward, grabbed Lev's robe, dragged him into the room, and tossed him across the floor.

Lev stumbled, tried to right himself against the wall, but slid to his knees.

Ari marched over and yanked him to his feet. "Where is it?"

"Where is what, my lord?"

Spittle showered Lev's cheek as the prince screamed, "You know what. You stole it."

Lev remained calm even as he looked at the disarray around him. The prince had upturned every inch of the room. "I swear to you, I do not know what—"

Aristobulus lowered his voice to a whisper. "What have you done with the letter from Ptolemy? Give it to me now, or you will die."

"You are too late. I sent it to Antipater this morning."

"Fool!" The prince let him go with a thrust. "Tell me why I should not throttle you here and now?"

Lev straightened his robe and tunic, taking his time to formulate his thoughts. "Because I know the route my messenger takes. The safe places he will stay for the night. I can easily retrieve the letter again, if I desire."

The prince stalked over to him. "And is your life worth that?"

Lev raise his hands to his sides, palms out, to demonstrate his lack of resistance. "Kill me now. But you know as well as I that there are hundreds of places a messenger may stay along the road. You will never find him before he reaches Jerusalem. And Antipater. And once my master has that letter in hand he will take it to Salome." Lev walked over to the upturned chair and righted it. He turned over the table as well. "What do you think you mother would do should she learn of your deceit?"

Ari scowled. "What is your price? Name it."

He had planned his first demand last night when he took the document, but a second entered his mind. He offered the chair to the prince. "Two things, my lord."

Once Ari sat, Lev spoke, "I want your assurance that when you take the throne from your brother, as we both know you will, you will not kill me or my family. I may work for Antipater, but I will be loyal to you, even as I do your brother's bidding."

"And the second?"

Lev swallowed. He would not have believed he could be so entranced in such a short time but the truth was in the need that propelled him to ask, "You will give me a talent of gold."

Ari's cheeks reddened in anger. His limbs quaked with rage. "You think too much of that letter's worth."

"Do I? I suppose we shall see what your mother thinks of your betrayal." Lev spun away to pick up the half-eaten loaf of bread the prince had tossed earlier. He placed it on the table. "My messenger will arrive in Jerusalem in three days. You have until tomorrow night to change your mind. After that, I will not be able to reach him in time."

Aristobulus seethed, pushing the chair over as he stood. "Half a talent. That is all. I will give it upon receipt of the letter."

Lev shook his head. "I want half the sum before I make the journey. The other when I give you the letter."

Ari's lips twitched as he struggled for control. "I will send a man with the money tomorrow at sundown. After the Sabbath."

"And once I have it, I will send one of my soldiers to intercept the letter." Lev bowed as Ari stormed toward the door. "A pleasure doing business with you, my lord."

Chapter 24

The Same Day

As Anna wove the indigo fabric for Helena's new robe, her mind wandered in many directions. One moment, she found herself deep in prayer about Caleb, and about her father's desire to have her betrothed to someone else. She pleaded with Adonai to at least let her see Caleb before a deal was sealed between Phanuel and some man she did not know.

Then, as her heart wearied with sorrow, her mind strained toward the strange premonition she had felt in Ashkelon. Something stirred in the air. A change. Whenever she thought of it, her skin prickled as if chilled by a cold wind.

"Come now." Tamar stood in the doorway. "Even you must stop for the Sabbath."

Anna ran her fingers across the fabric she wove. For once, she dreaded the thought of going home to her father. Perhaps this would be the night he decided her future.

Together they walked out of the palace. Anna sighed heavily as she watched the parade of people making their way from the temple. Some smiled, seeming to relish the coming Sabbath and the peace it would bring. Others hurried past with furrowed brows as if, like her, they worried what would come with the new day.

Tamar muttered a curse.

"What is wrong?"

"Is that not your father and brother on the hill there?"

Anna spied her father and Daniel. "Yes."

"That man beside them . . . do you know him?"

Shorter than her father, the man seemed to be about thirty. "I have never seen him before."

"He is a rabbi. He tried to make a match with my widowed neighbor, but her kinsman took her back to their home in Ephraim." Tamar pulled Anna into a hard embrace. "I will go to Caleb now. Perhaps I can convince him he cannot wait to talk with your father."

"Tell him I have never stopped loving him." Anna pushed her friend away. "Please, hurry."

Tamar ran down the hill and disappeared within the crowd. Anna turned her attention back to the men approaching.

Phanuel's smile brightened his face. "Daughter. Peace be with you." He took her arm and positioned her next to the stranger. "This is Nathanel. He is a rabbi in the Temple."

It took a moment for Anna to swallow, it seemed as if her sorrow had lodged in her throat. "*Shalom*."

"*Shalom*, Anna." Nathanel's deep voice easily carried over the din of the people in the street. "Your father tells me you have studied God's word with the rabbis in Egypt." He did not wait for her to comment. "I look forward to hearing what you may have retained from your studies."

His words pricked her pride. *As if I would forget what I have learned?* "Rabbi Chaim insisted we memorize all of the books of Moses, and I found I love David's songs. I meditate on what I learned throughout much of the day as I work." She stared at him through the gauze of her veil. "I assure you, I remember Adonai's words and His teachings very well."

Daniel growled. Phanuel's arm tightened around hers. Nathanel lifted a brow. "Your father said I might find you spirited."

She bit her lip rather than answer him with the "spirited" retort she longed to give him. She would not embarrass her father by letting her anger get the best of her, but she resented the rabbi talking about her as if she were a horse to be sold.

"Nathanel will come to dinner tomorrow, after the Sabbath," Phanuel informed her. "I am sure we will all have a spirited discussion about the scriptures then."

"I look forward to it." Nathanel bowed toward her. "With much anticipation."

Anna wished she felt the same. They parted ways when she and her family turned down the next street toward their home. The men called "*Shalom*" to each other, but she kept silent.

"I thought, perhaps, a learned man would be agreeable to you," Phanuel whispered as soon as they left Nathanel behind. "He is a wealthy man. His family have been respected rabbis for many generations."

Anna's heart pounded. "Have you already made a contract with him?"

"No. I wanted you to meet with him first. You have told me nothing of what you desire in a husband."

Daniel stiffened and turned to Phanuel. "He has a fine house, two floors and a courtyard! She would have servants and entertain some of the most learned rabbis and Pharisees in Jerusalem. What more could she want?"

Anna waited until they were behind closed doors before she answered him. "I want a man who will treat me as his help-mate, not some unique object to parade out to entertain his friends with her ability to recite scripture." She hugged herself as she sat down on the bench by the table. "I want a kind man. A good man."

Phanuel sat next to her. "I know Nathanel to be an honest man. He is generous to his servants and to the poor of the temple." He drew the veil from her face. "Is it that he is in his third decade? A younger man may be more attractive to the eye, but their hearts are not always as steadfast."

"It is not his age." She tried to imagine her father's reaction if she told him of her love for Caleb, a man even older than the rabbi.

Phanuel rested his hand on her knee as Tova placed the *challah* bread on the table, its buttery scent filling the room. "Then do not worry yourself tonight. Meet with him tomorrow. Perhaps, after the Sabbath, God will soften your heart toward him."

Around her, the family scurried to make ready for dinner. Tova served up a hearty bowl of stew for each of them, Daniel played with Isaac, and Phanuel washed his hands. Anna sat, calling out silently to Adonai that she might see Caleb one last time before her father set her betrothal.

A loud rap on the door made Isaac cry out. Daniel jumped to open it. There, as if God had made him appear, stood Caleb. His eyes sought and found Anna. She could not breathe for the fear she saw in them.

Daniel surveyed him. "May I help you?"

Caleb had not changed in the three years since Anna last saw him. His shoulders were still broad and strong. His hair and beard showed little gray. Only around the eyes, where the creases appeared a little deeper, had he aged at all. She willed him to speak.

"I have come to speak to Anna's father."

Phanuel rose. "I am he."

Caleb kept his gaze on Anna. When she nodded, he stepped past Daniel to face Phanuel. "Sir, I wish to make my desire known. I seek a betrothal to Anna."

"You?" Her father's brows furrowed, then relaxed. "You mean for your son?"

Caleb's gaze remained firm. "No, sir. I mean for myself." He cleared his throat in the silence that fell over the room. "My name is Caleb bar Reuben. I am—"

"We have met before." Phanuel's eyes narrowed, as if he sought to recall the meeting. "You brought Anna home from the palace. The night she fell ill."

Caleb nodded. "I have a fine job within the queen's household and have lived frugally over the years. I can offer Anna a house of her own. Food, clothing, whatever she would need." He took a moment to swallow. "I know I am much older than any suitor you would normally consider, but think of it not as age, but as wisdom. I have waited long for a wife, fearing God would not grant me the privilege of being a husband. The time Anna and I have spent together gave me hope again. You may ask the queen herself about my reputation. My honesty. My work."

Anna walked over to stand by the man she loved. "Father, you asked me what kind of man I would consider for my husband? There is no finer man than Caleb."

Caleb's strong features did not wither under the pinched scrutiny of Phanuel's face, or Daniel's heated stare. "God has gifted me with many trials over the years. I have been through the fire, literally, and persevered." He cleared his throat. "I believe He brought Anna into my life as a gift. And that is how I would treat her. As a precious gift to be cherished, honored, and protected every day that I live."

Her father's brow softened, but he did not speak. Daniel motioned to the door. "The Sabbath is almost here. You should go."

Caleb's eyes rested on Anna's face. "Whatever happens, know I have loved you, and will continue to love you, until my last breath."

"And I you."

Daniel shut the door then turned to glare at Anna. "He is almost our father's age!"

"He little older than Nathanel. And what do I care about his age? He is the kindest, gentlest, most decent man I have ever known." She pointed her finger at him. "You, of all people, should know how careful I have been with my heart since Lev."

Phanuel lowered himself to the bench. "He is crippled."

"He was not born that way. He was injured in the army." She sat opposite him. "You told me you would pray that God would send me a good man. I believe Caleb to be that man."

"His deformity—"

"It is not a deformity, it is an injury. I do not care about that. His appearance, his age, mean nothing to me. He is the man I love."

Phanuel shook his head. "You do not know what love is."

"How can you say that, when you taught me so much?" She held her father's gaze. "It is sitting beside a person when they are in pain, wishing you could take their pain into yourself. It is being content in your time with them, not having to speak, but enjoying their presence." She grinned as she thought about all the things that made her love Caleb. "It is drawing strength from them when you have none of your own." She squeezed her father's hand. "It is knowing, without a doubt, that he would give his life for mine, because he has already proven his faithfulness to me."

Phanuel stared, his forehead creased in concentration. "You are certain of him?"

"I am."

His eyes followed Tova as she lit the Sabbath candles. "There is not time to rescind our invitation to Nathanel." He scratched his beard. "We will honor our guest tomorrow with a fine meal and conversation. We will not inform him of this . . . other suitor, until I have prayed and found Adonai's will."

Lev did not trust Aristobulus to keep his word and so kept four soldiers with him when he set out to see Nasrin in the evening. He did not put it past the prince to hire some bandit to slit his throat in an alley. After all, Ari had all but admitted he did the same to Anna's betrothed those many years ago.

Lev's blood roiled with the excitement of the forbidden. Here, in Damascus, he was not bound to follow the rules of the Sabbath. Here, no one was required to stop living for a day, to rest and do nothing but study or pray. All around him men talked, laughed, drank, and carried on with their lives, free from the burden the Hebrew God put on his people.

He stopped at several stalls in the market to buy wine, bread and cheese from the vendors. Torchlight flickered around him, casting strange shadows on the limestone walls. It took him a moment more to get his bearings in the dark and remember which street led to Nasrin's home. The way, which had been fairly unoccupied that afternoon, now revealed the seedier underbelly of the city. Women dressed in cheap, colorful fabrics stood in dimly lit doorways, beckoning to any man passing by. The heady scent of incense fought to cover the smell of alcohol, sweat and urine. But the filth, which usually turned his stomach, could not deter him from spending the night with Nasrin. The hair on his arms prickled at the thought of her bright green eyes, wide and round like a lamb's. Her skin just as soft.

He led the guards down the next alley and found the familiar door. "Two of you, wait here." He gave coins to another of the soldiers. "Take turns with the watch. Enjoy yourselves, but make sure I am not disturbed until the morning."

He left the men to decide who would stand guard first, pausing to knock only a second before opening the door and entering the house. Nasrin and her grandmother looked up from the table. A bowl of couscous sat in front of each of them.

The old woman stood. "You have the other coins?"

Lev nodded, but his eyes never left Nasrin. He laid his purchases on the table and placed the rest of his payment into her gnarled hand.

"Good, good." The crone clutched the silver to her chest. "Sit and eat, my lord. Before you enjoy the night." She greedily pulled the wine toward her. "I will get cups."

Lev sat down on the bench across from the girl. She had stopped eating when he entered and seemed unsure whether to continue. He ripped off a piece of bread and passed it to her as her grandmother handed him a small pottery bowl of wine.

"I am sorry I cannot offer you something better." The old woman poured wine into another clay bowl.

He drained his drink. "What you have here is worth more than any silver chalice." Nasrin nibbled the bread he had given her. He dipped a piece of bread into the bowl the girl's grandmother had given him. "What does your name mean? Nasrin?"

Her lips rose in a shy smile but she did not answer. Instead, she looked toward her grandmother.

"She only speaks Persian, my lord, although she can understand a few words of Arabic." The woman whispered harshly to Nasrin. "Her name means 'wild rose.' And she is as pretty as the flower, is she not?"

Lev nodded, glad to know the girl's earlier silence had not been timidity, but a lack of understanding. "Her parents? Where are they?"

"Dead, my lord." Her wrinkled fingers stabbed a piece of bread into her stew. "My son was a soldier, killed in battle. Her mother died soon after the child was born."

A lightness filled his spirit as he poured himself another cup of wine. The lack of relatives meant fewer complications to the plans forming in his mind. "A sad tale. And you? What brought you here, to Damascus?"

She jutted her chin toward Nasrin. "I would not let such a jewel go to waste in our tiny province. Only in the city could we find men rich enough to pay what she is worth."

Lev's stomach churned. He loathed the thought of Nasrin being sold as a common harlot, becoming one of the painted ladies who had called out to him on his way there.

"You are offended?" asked the old woman. "Did you think you were the only one?"

"Of course not," he barked. "But you speak of her as if she were nothing more than a tunic to be tried on by every man who can afford to buy her."

"Her beauty will last no more than a year or two." She lifted her cup toward him. "We must do what we can to survive."

Tension crept up his neck. "How long have you been in the city?"

The cup trembled as she sipped her wine. "Only a few months. Our village . . . it was overrun by the beast of Armenia and his army."

"Tigranes, you mean?"

"Curse his name!" She spat on the floor. "I put Nasrin down the well to hide her. Keep her from soldiers. I prayed to the gods for protection. They answered me." She struggled to catch her breath. "The soldiers . . . they took everything . . . and so we came here." Her haunted, but determined eyes bore into Lev's. "Do not think ill of me, my lord. If I could have sold my own body to keep us alive, I would have. Nasrin knows she must do this to survive."

Lev poured another bowl of wine to the brim. He would not speak yet of his plan until he had taken the girl to bed again. He had to be sure she was worth the price he knew he would have to pay. He gestured toward the alcove. Nasrin lowered her eyes as she stood and made her way to her pallet. She did not wait for him to follow her.

"My men guard your door, to assure we will not be disturbed. I have paid handsomely for this night, and I expect you not to disturb us as well."

The old woman's eyes flashed. "You will not harm her."

"Never. But I do intend to get all that I paid for."

She pulled the empty dishes toward her. "I will sleep by the hearth, my lord."

He nodded as he strode toward the alcove. Nasrin had already removed her outer robe and sat in the corner. Lev paused and took one of the oil lamps from the table. He set it and his wine down on the floor, then pulled the curtain shut. He removed his outer robe, folded it then put it on the floor as well. He carried the wine and lamp over to the girl's pallet and sat across from her.

"Here." He passed her the wine. She took a sip. He picked up the oil lamp and held it near her face, using the light to search for flaws. He found none. Her skin was perfect. Smooth and unblemished as the finest silk. Rich and brown in color, like honey warmed over the fire.

She put down the wine when he lowered the oil lamp. He drew her to him and breathed in the scent of her, reveling in the mixture of spices and citrus. His lips explored her neck and shoulders before he slipped the linen tunic over her head. At the sight of her naked body, Lev knew there was no price too high to possess this girl as his own.

Chapter 25

The Following Day

Anna spent the daylight hours of the Sabbath playing with Isaac so Tova could rest. At least her nephew occupied her mind so that she did not dwell on Nathanel's looming visit. She tried, without success, not to let worry twist her stomach into a knot. She dared not offend her father's guest, but she did not want to impress the rabbi either. If Nathanel did not like her, maybe he would not make a formal offer to her father. But she could not bear it if her behavior caused any stain on her father's reputation. He was a man of honor, and she must uphold that position no matter what the cost.

Once the sun set, the family went about readying the house for their guest. Anna stirred the mixture of goat, cumin and onions Tova had left over the embers the night before. The savory aroma filled the house as she poked the fire to set it simmering again. Tova unwrapped another loaf of challah bread that she had saved. Daniel and Phanuel rolled up the texts they had studied during the day and placed them on shelves above the hearth.

Anna had just finished sweeping the floor when Nathanel's knock came. Although anticipated, everyone seemed to hesitate, as if surprised at the interruption.

"I expect you to represent this family well," Phanuel reminded Anna as he crossed to the entrance. He took a deep breath and swung the door open. "*Shalom*, Nathanel. Welcome to my home."

"*Shalom*, Phanuel. I have been anxiously awaiting this evening throughout the Sabbath." Their guest came in and surveyed the house with a cursory glance until he saw Anna.

She lowered her eyes at his frank perusal. She had looked at him long enough to take note again of his thick, graying eyebrows and full beard.

"My, my, my," Nathanel nodded toward her father. "You said she was a comely girl but you misspoke." Anna's cheeks grew warm. She heard her father's sharp intake of breath, as if he too, was surprised at the insult.

The rabbi let out a loud laugh. "Oh, my friend! I only meant that she is not a girl at all! She is a woman!"

Phanuel chuckled nervously. "She is past the age most girls are betrothed because of the time she spent in Egypt."

Nathanel continued to study her. "Understandable. She was there how long?"

"Four years, my lord." Anna answered him. "I studied with the rabbis in the afternoons and learned about weaving, spinning and embroidery in the mornings and evenings."

"A full day for any student." He nodded with what seemed to be approval. "And what is your day like now that you are back in Jerusalem?" He took the stool Phanuel offered him.

Anna sat at the opposite end of the table. "I am weaving cloth for Helena, Prince Aristobulus's wife. I also help make the tunics for the priests." She pressed on before anyone could interrupt her. "In a few weeks, when Queen Salome opens her school, I will go once a week to help instruct the girls."

Phanuel sat next to his guest. "You did not mention this before." He glanced over at the rabbi as if to judge the man's reaction. "Why?"

"Queen Salome spoke with me upon my return to the palace. As I have not yet started teaching, I had not thought to mention it."

"I am not sure I agree with the queen's desire to teach women." Nathanel shook his head. "It is a man's place to learn the scripture. He should then instruct his family."

Daniel came behind Anna and gripped her shoulder, willing her to bite her tongue. She pushed her anger down before she spoke. "I am sure that you, being a wise and generous man like my father, would instruct your family well. But what of those less fortunate?"

The rabbi's eyebrows drew together, like two caterpillars butting heads. "How do you mean?"

She kept her voice level. "What of those whose fathers are not learned men? Or an orphan? Would you leave them to suffer the wrath of our God simply because they do not know His Law?"

"Of course not. But anyone can go to the temple or the synagogue in their village and hear the law taught. They do not need to go to school."

Tova hastily set out the bowls of stew while Anna continued with her argument. "True, they can hear it, but it is in the discussion of the Law that true understanding comes."

Nathanel turned to Phanuel. "Your daughter has learned to debate well. Your doing?"

Her father shrugged. "She has always had a curious mind and a strong opinion." He lifted his hands. "Let us say the blessing before our meal."

Anna bowed her head, thanking the Lord for helping her to curb her temper. Before she could take a mouthful of stew, Nathanel resumed their conversation.

"While I might be persuaded that all boys should be allowed to attend school, I am still not sure women would be able to understand the complexities of the Law." He quickly lifted a hand. "I mean no disrespect to you, Anna. You are obviously an exceptional woman, but I fear most females are too simple. The stress of such learning could lead to . . . well, mental, even spiritual, distress."

Both Phanuel and Daniel coughed as if something had caught in their throat. Tova's eyes flashed as her lips puckered in a tight frown. Anna prayed for wisdom before speaking. "May I ask, sir, what you think of our queen?"

"Excuse me?"

"Salome has ruled now for almost five years. Have we not had a time of peace and unprecedented prosperity?"

Nathanel nodded as he swallowed his stew. "Again, there are exceptions to every rule. I fear the average girl would be overwhelmed."

Her father's eyes willed her to answer civilly. "I suppose, being a rabbi, you have not had the opportunity to speak with many women like myself, my lord. I can assure you, I attended class with many other women who had no difficulty understanding Adonai's law and His love for our people."

The rabbi wiped his hand across his mouth. A gesture that only succeeded in smearing broth into his beard. "I have not studied the effects of learning on the women of Egypt, but I know their culture is much more . . . liberal . . . than our own. I fear you may have been led astray by some of your teachers."

A sharp gasp escaped her throat, but she stopped herself from laughing outright at the rabbi. "Then what have you to say about Miriam, my lord? Was not Moses's sister considered a prophet? And Deborah, who led our people into freedom from the Canaanites? Were they not women whom God used to His glory?"

"Exceptions again. As you are, my dear."

Anna's ire crept up her throat like bile. He spoke to her as a father chastises a toddler. "Perhaps we are exceptions because we are the only women blessed to have been taught well." Her shoulders tensed with the effort it took to keep her voice civil. "Maybe more of my sex would have had the opportunity to serve Adonai if they only knew of His ways."

Nathanel snorted. "Although I appreciate your argument, it does not convince me. I fear the teaching you received in Egypt has resulted in this error of ideology."

"The queen's counselor, Shimeon bar Shetach, did not find fault with my instruction. We spoke at length on our journey from Ashkelon."

"Those witches, they hung there," Daniel interrupted. "Shimeon was brave to take on such evil."

"Indeed," Phanuel said, relief at the sudden change of topic evident across his face. "Like the prophet Samuel of old, ridding the land of sorcery."

"A righteous man," Daniel continued, keeping the discussion steered toward something other than that of women and schooling.

"I saw the gallows." Anna shivered at the memory. "When I arrived from Egypt, the city still teemed with people who came to see them die."

"Sorcery is in affront to the Lord," Nathanel snatched the last piece of bread from the basket. "The people were right to witness His judgment."

Phanuel frowned. "Although it may cost Shimeon dearly."

"How do you mean?" Nathanel asked.

"I heard a rumor that the witches' families are vowing revenge against him. They have brought charges against his son, Eliezer."

"Eliezer?" Crumbs scattered on the table as the rabbi waved his hand. "What do they accuse him of?"

"Murder."

"That's preposterous!" Nathanel wiped the bread around his bowl. "A son of Shimeon's would never shed blood."

"But eighty witches were hung. If their families band together to supply false testimony, it would be enough to convict him."

"But it would be false." Broth flew off the rabbi's bread, plopping near the center of the table. "Surely the Sanhedrin would see through their ploy."

Anna sipped her wine. "But the Law says only that two witnesses must agree in their testimony to convict. If they practice their stories so that they concur on all points against him, Eliezer will be executed." She felt the eyes of those around the table on her. "Is that not true?"

Phanuel waited for Nathanel to speak, but the rabbi only stared, as if unable to comprehend Anna's logic. "Unfortunately," Phanuel continued, "you are correct, Daughter. Should they make their testimony compelling enough, Shimeon's son will die."

A heaviness settled in Anna's chest. "It is sad that the Law, which Adonai gave us for our protection, can be twisted by men into a tool of revenge."

"Indeed," Nathanel whispered.

An idea of such clarity shot through her that she spoke without censoring the thought, "Perhaps the Law is not enough. Perhaps it was given only to show us how short we fall from Adonai's perfection." Even though she sensed the rabbi's disapproval, she kept speaking, "I believe God will bring us a new Law soon. A new teaching to bring us closer to Him."

Nathanel licked his lips with a slurping sound. He folded his hands on the table. "This is heresy from Egypt. Exactly what I worried about."

Phanuel groaned softly.

Anna placed her fists on either side of her bowl. "Are we not to be looking for the prophet foretold by Moses? A man who will speak God's words?"

"The Messiah," Daniel whispered. "The one who will usher in God's Kingdom."

"Exactly," Anna said.

Isaac broke the tension with a shriek. His pudgy hands reached across the table as Tova moved her stew away from his curious fingers. Her chin dipped in humility. "I am sorry. He wants to eat what he cannot yet have."

The rabbi chuckled, but it was without warmth. "And why should he not? It is delicious."

"Would you like more?" Phanuel asked, seemingly desperate for another distraction.

"If there is any to spare."

Her father tilted his head toward Anna. She rose and took the pot from the hearth. She brought it to Nathanel's side. This close to him, she could see the lines in his face. The pits and crevices in his cheeks. She knew him to be younger than Caleb, but he appeared older. He smelled stale, not like Caleb's musky scent. His eyes studied her as she ladled the stew into his bowl, and she knew the moment his thoughts turned to making her his wife.

His face flushed and he focused on his meal. "Thank you. I have enough."

Anna served Phanuel and her brother the rest of the stew before returning to her own, barely touched, bowl.

The rest of the meal passed in a blur as the men discussed the latest news of the temple and the city. When Isaac began to fuss again, Nathanel rubbed his stomach. "I think that signals the time has come for my departure." The rest of the family stood as he did. Isaac's whines turned to cries. The rabbi bowed toward Phanuel. "I thank you, my friend, for your hospitality."

Anna's father returned the bow. "Thank you, for gracing our house with your presence."

The rabbi did not move from the table but let his gaze wander toward Anna. He nodded as he surveyed her. "My offer for your daughter still stands, Phanuel. I think she would make me a fine wife, once I correct the errors in her education."

Anna's jaw clenched so tight she could feel it in her temples, but she did not speak the retort that danced around her lips. Instead, she stared at a splotch of stew on the table the rabbi had left behind.

Her father escorted their guest to the door. "I am pleased, my friend. I will let you know what I decide after I bring it to God in prayer."

Nathanel's brows furrowed. "There are other suitors?"

Phanuel kept his expression neutral. "It would be imprudent for me to discuss this in front of my daughter. You will know my answer soon."

The rabbi gave them a quick nod before leaving.

Tova took the now squalling Isaac to her pallet to nurse him as Daniel stood. "I do not understand how you can even consider a tailor when there is a man like Nathanel interested."

"Because I know Caleb." The bread Anna held in her hands crumbled into pieces. "And I know nothing of this Nathanel."

Her brother's eyes bore into hers. "I was not speaking to you. How can our father consider such a match?"

Phanuel let out a breath more growl than sigh. "Do you not remember what the prophet Samuel said? God looks at the heart of a man to determine his worth, not his outward appearance."

"But surely Nathanel's wealth is evidence of God's blessing?" Daniel threw up his arms. "What can the tailor offer?"

"Love," Anna pleaded before her father could answer. "Caleb loves me."

"Love," Daniel spat. "Lev claimed to love you and you saw how long that lasted."

Anna hid the pain her brother's barb caused her. "Caleb is steadfast. Content in his position," she argued. "Lev was not such a man. Power and wealth mattered more than his feelings for me."

"And yet," Phanuel sat by her side. He rested his hand over hers. "You claimed to have loved him as well. How can you be so sure of your feelings now?"

After a momentary flash of uncertainty, Anna's spirit calmed her. "I know because since I left for Egypt I have prayed daily for God's guidance and wisdom. I have been taught God's word and now have a deeper understanding of His will for my life. Before, when walking up to the temple was the farthest I journeyed from home, was it any wonder I saw Lev as something exotic to be desired? But now?" She chuckled to herself. "I do not mean to boast, but I do so only as a reminder of the great things God has done for me. I have seen stone pyramids, so high they seem to touch the sky! And I have spoken with queens from two different countries."

Daniel's fist pounded the table. "That is why you need a man like the rabbi. He, too, has seen and done great things!"

"But do not you understand?" Anna's voice broke. "A man like Nathanel would want me as a possession, something to wear in the city like one of the ornamental robes I embroider. While Caleb," she could barely swallow from the fear lodged in her throat. The despair that her brother would sway their father's opinion. "Caleb would delight in discussing all I have seen and learned. We share a common talent. He has much he could teach me while I can share my knowledge with him as well. It is all that, Brother," she choked back a sob. "For all those reasons, as well as for the love I know God has given me for him, that is why I believe Caleb is the man God has chosen to be my husband."

Daniel frowned. "And what of Nathanel?"

That he still argued for the rabbi sparked Anna's anger. She pulled her hand from Phanuel to point at her brother. "Perhaps you are not so concerned with my well-being, as with your own."

"What do you mean?"

"What would being related to a man like Nathanel do for your own position in the city? Would you sell my happiness to see yourself lifted up among those that rule?"

"Anna!" Tova called from the corner where she nursed Isaac. She softened her tone when the baby fussed at her breast. "You know that is not true. Daniel's only concern is for you. Your future."

Her father stood. "We will speak no more about this matter until I have prayed to Adonai."

Anna's hands shook as she cleared the bowls from the table. She fought against the tears welling in her eyes. The thought of being that man's wife instead of Caleb's . . . to know that every day she would have to hold her tongue, suppress her curiosity, and force herself to accept all that he said without question made her want to scream in fury.

She took the bowls out to the courtyard to wash them with water from the cistern. To sleep with such a man . . . she knew what the marriage bed required of her, and for the first time she feared it. Caleb, she believed, would be gentle and kind. She knew he would never hurt her. But Nathanel. He would not mean to be cruel, but he would not consider her pain because it was her duty to lie with him and give him sons.

One of the clay bowls dropped to the ground, shattering into pieces. *Oh, Adonai! I beg of you! Do not let my heart be so shattered. Let my father accept Caleb's suit. Let him be my husband.*

"Take it," Aristobulus threw two leather pouches onto the wooden table in Lev's room. They landed with a solid thunk. "Take it and bring me that letter."

Lev picked up a sack, surprised and secretly pleased at its weight. "I will send my man immediately. You will have it within the next two days." He hefted the money between his hands. "After I receive the second half, of course."

The prince did not attempt to hide his hatred. "When I have it in my hand, then you shall get your gold. May it bring you nothing but misery."

"I do not seek to do you harm, my lord. Antipater pays me well to be his scribe and informant. He would have rewarded me generously for that letter." He lifted his arms in a supplicant gesture. "You must see how I need to be compensated for my work."

Ari sniffed in disgust. "And will you betray me if that half-Jew offers you more money?"

"The letter will be in your hands. I swear to you, I have made no copies."

The prince paced the small room with his long strides. "I have not made my mind up about you, Lev bar Malachi."

"How so, my lord?"

"I cannot tell what it is you want." Ari spun to face him. "Therefore, I have not decided if I can trust you. Are you only interested in gaining wealth? Or is power also your desire?"

Lev tied the pouch to his belt. "I want both, my lord. Al-though of the two, I think I prefer the latter."

The prince raised an eyebrow. "Why?"

"Because in the coming war between you and your brother, I think you will bleed Israel dry of her wealth, and only those of us who have information, or know how to get it, will be of any use to you."

"You assume John and I will battle."

Lev shrugged. "I know you want the throne."

"My brother is too weak," Ari chuckled as he spoke. "He will not fight for it."

"You are right about him being weak." Lev fixed his eyes on the prince. "But Antipater is not. Do not underestimate my master. He can be very persuasive."

"And if war comes? With whom will you side?"

"Must I choose, my lord? The battle is between you and John." Lev shrugged. "I know you will eventually win, but I would prefer not to distance myself from Antipater while you two fight for control."

Ari straightened his shoulders "What could the half-Jew give you that I could not?"

Lev studied the prince. Aristobulus looked the part of a future king. Broad shouldered and fit. His hair and beard cut short in the Greek fashion. His brown eyes fierce with the desire to rule kingdoms. But he lacked one thing. Patience. Something Antipater had in abundance.

The prince continued to stare. "Well?"

"I think you are a fool to alienate my master. Antipater has friends in many different countries, which gives him the ability to look outside of Israel to a larger future."

"Does not the letter you stole prove that I am seeking outside alliances?"

Lev coughed in an attempt to disguise a disdainful laugh. "With other kings with whom you can make treaties. What you lack are people like me who can gain knowledge those in charge do not want you to have. There is no one better at gathering information and using it for his own benefit than Antipater. And with that information, he will be able to bribe his way into the council chambers of whoever wins the throne of Israel."

Ari growled under his breath as he waved his arm. "All this will not matter if you do not stop your courier. Go now, and send your man to fetch him back. I will come tomorrow night to get what is mine."

"Very well, my lord." Lev walked out to the hallway with the prince, but motioned for his guard to attend him. As soon as they were out Ari's hearing, Lev paused. He passed the man several silver coins. "Make yourself scarce until tomorrow afternoon. You cannot be seen in the palace or the guard house, understand?"

The man nodded.

"If anyone asks you later where you have been, you will say that you went to bring back a courier I sent to Jerusalem."

"Yes, sir."

"Good, man. Come with me now. After we find the other soldiers, disappear until tomorrow."

Once he had acquired his guards, Lev made his way through the city to Nasrin's home. He found he had a weightlessness in his soul he had not experienced since Anna had been lost to him. Like a burden had been lifted from his back. The young Persian woman had renewed a fire within him that had lain dormant since his wedding to Sarai. Before, he had found a kind of release from buying a night with the prostitutes back in Jerusalem, but never contentment. Nasrin gave him that. Her sweetness, combined with her willingness to do anything he asked of her, made him almost giddy.

If all went according to his plan, he would convince Nasrin and her grandmother to come back with him to Jerusalem. He would use the money gained from his trade with Aristobulus to rent them a house in the city, a place where he could spend his evenings away from work and his wife. He chuckled to himself as he turned down the alley toward her house. He had gained power through his association with Antipater and John Hyrcanus. He had gained wealth through his dealings with Aristobulus. Now, he would finally enjoy the passion that had been missing since Malachi forced his marriage to Sarai. After years of disappointment, his life was finally beginning to play out as he had always planned.

Tamar scurried into the weaving room and shut the door behind her. "Well? What did your father say?"

Anna kept her eyes on the loom in front of her. "Nothing."

Tamar squatted next to her. "What do you mean, nothing? Surely he must have given you some indication of his thoughts?"

Anna wove the next thread of wool through those hanging from the top bar of the loom. Concentrating on the task in front of her had been the only thing to keep her sane throughout the morning, but now Tamar's questions threatened to bring her to tears again. "He says he must pray for the will of Adonai."

Her friend grumbled beside her. "For how long? About what? Either my brother is acceptable or he is not." When Anna did not answer, Tamar took her by the shoulders, twisting her so they were face-to-face. "Did he already choose the rabbi?" She shook her. "Tell me! Have you already agreed to marry for position and wealth?"

"No!" The tears she had fought against all morning welled in Anna's eyes. "I have pleaded your brother's case before both Daniel and my father. They know my heart is set on Caleb. But I must marry whomever Phanuel chooses." She took hold of her friend's hands. "Tell Caleb that I will fast and pray that God will move my father's heart toward him. Tell him . . . tell him . . . oh Tamar," her voice broke as she crumpled against Tamar's chest. "My life will be empty of joy if my father does not choose Caleb."

"My brother has suffered too many losses in his life. Surely Adonai would grant him this one request." Tamar rubbed Anna's back. "I will fast as well. I'll send my daughter, Ruth, to make a sacrifice on Caleb's behalf. We will make such a ruckus in the heavens that the Lord will have to let you and my brother marry." She kissed Anna's forehead. "Come. Leave this solitary work for today and sit with us in the sewing room."

Anna sniffed back her tears as she nodded. "If I do not have any distractions, I will go mad with worry."

Her friend pulled her to her feet. "You need to listen to Bilah tell one of her stories. That will cheer you up."

Anna spent the afternoon with her friends, but it did little to ease her distress. By the time it came to quit their work for the evening, her melancholy mood had spread to the others. Bilah tossed her sewing with a grunt. "I am useless today. My stitches are as sloppy as a child's."

Mary sighed. "Mine, too." She folded her linen with care then turned to Anna. "Are you ready to go?"

She ran her hand along the robe she worked on. "I want to finish this before I stop for the night."

"Shall I wait for you?"

Anna shook her head. "I will be along shortly."

Tamar put away her needle and thread. "I should get on to my own family." She placed a hand on Anna's shoulder. "Do not fret, my friend. God will answer our prayers."

Anna concentrated on her stitches. *But what if His answer is no?* She raised her head when Tamar let out a gasp of surprise. Caleb stood beside her.

Tamar stepped into the hallway to give them privacy, while still providing supervision. Anna rose from her stool, but did not approach him.

Caleb's eyes drank her in, as if he tried to memorize everything about her.

"What is wrong?" Fear pounded in her chest. "Has something happened?"

"No." His arm trembled as he reached out to brace himself against the doorframe. "Your father has invited me to dine at his house two nights from now . . . what do you think it means?"

As much as she wanted to run and embrace him, Anna rooted her feet to the floor. To be seen touching so intimately could bring scandal to her reputation, something she dared not do while her father searched for her husband. "I think he wishes to know what kind of man you are before he agrees to our betrothal."

"Do you really think he will consider me?"

Anna smiled. "I know he will. My father is a good man, and I told him that you are the husband I desire."

Caleb's fingers picked at the limestone threshold. "I have spoken to princes and kings and yet I am as nervous as a schoolboy when I think of meeting with your father."

"You have no reason to be." Anna's voice grew firm. "You must be sure of yourself. My father must know how brave you are; how strong." She dared to move toward him. "You must fight for me, Caleb, if you truly wish to marry me."

Determination flashed in his eyes. "Do you have any doubt?"

"No, but my father may. Convince him of your worth and of your desire to care for me, and I know he will be swayed to grant your request."

Caleb stepped into the room so that he stood only a foot from her. The air between them sparked, as if waiting for lightning to strike. They did not touch each other, but each seemed ready to burst with the energy required to deny themselves.

"I would cross any sea, fight any army, wrestle with the Lord Himself, if it meant that I could have you have as my wife."

"You need not do any of that, my love, you only need to pray that God sways my father's heart to accept you."

"I will not cease praying until that happens."

They stood together, but apart, for several minutes until Caleb finally turned toward the door. Stopping in the threshold, he looked back over his shoulder. "No matter what, I will love you until I die."

Anna was deep in prayer at the loom the following afternoon when Ziva called from the doorway, "Pack your things."

Anna dropped her spindle, the blue thread unraveling into her lap. Her friend stepped into the weaving room and, with a wave of her hand, commanded again, "Pack your things."

Anna's hands shook as she wound the thread back around the rod. "What have I done wrong?"

"Queen Salome travels to Ashkelon tomorrow to attend the trial of her most trusted servant's son. You will attend her."

"But . . . but . . ." Anna fought to think clearly. "Why does she want me in Ashkelon?"

Ziva put her hands on her hips. "In truth? She wants another woman to talk to about the law."

"Shimeon and the other rabbis know far more than me."

Ziva shook her head. "Shimeon is distraught. Salome does not wish to add to his burden, and she is tired of talking to learned men. She hopes your schooling in Egypt may have taught you something the old men have forgotten."

Anna's stomach sank. "When must I leave?"

"Tomorrow morning."

Caleb would be dining with her father tomorrow night. She might finally have an answer to her prayers, but now she would have to wait until she returned from Ashkelon.

"What is the matter, child? You look ill." Ziva paused before clucking softly. "Do not worry. If he is convicted, Salome would not require you to watch the execution."

Anna lowered her eyes. A man's life was at stake and she was more concerned with her possible marriage. Whatever her father decided, she knew he sought God's answer before accepting any man's offer for her. God's will would be done whether she prayed here or in Ashkelon. She would pray for patience to wait another week to learn her fate. "I need to send a message to my father, so he does not expect me home for the Sabbath."

"Of course." Ziva nodded before leaving the room.

Anna hurried to the sewing room to see Tamar. Her friends sat around the center table, bent over their sewing.

Bilah looked up as Anna entered. "Ah, look who graces us again today with her presence. I hope you are in a better mood than yesterday."

"Seeing you always brightens my day, Bilah."

The rotund woman chortled. "You see how she lies? You cannot trust her! Why yesterday, nothing would make her smile."

Anna slipped onto the bench next to Mary. "I am sorry for my melancholy yesterday, but today you must all help me."

Bilah threw up her hands in mock exasperation. "Help her! As if we do not all have our own work to do. Now we should do yours as well?"

Tamar let out an exaggerated sigh. "Can you be quiet for a moment, Bilah, and let the girl explain?"

Anna glanced around the table. "I only need your advice, I promise. No extra work."

Bilah placed her sewing down with a flourish. "Why did not you say so? I am full of advice."

"Not all of it good," Mary muttered.

Anna's gaze sought Tamar's. "I am to journey to Ashkelon. I will serve the queen while she attends the trial of Shimeon bar Shetach's son, Eliezer."

The mood around the room grew solemn. Even Bilah's teasing stopped. She frowned. "Again you seek to darken our day."

"Shush," Tamar scolded. "What advice do you need from us?"

"I am not sure what clothes to bring. My instinct is to wear solemn colors, but then, should I bring something more elegant?"

Mary reached over and touched her arm. "I believe darker colors would be best. This will not be a time to show opulence but rather sobriety."

"That is what I thought, too." Anna nodded as she stole a second look toward Tamar. She did not want the others to know of Caleb's suit so as not to cause him embarrassment if her father chose Nathanel. Tamar would tell Caleb about her trip. "I leave tomorrow for Ashkelon."

Tamar's bright brown eyes flashed with understanding. "Do you know when you will return?"

Anna shook her head. "It may not be until the Sabbath after next."

Tamar nodded. "We will miss you, all of us, while you are gone."

Chapter 26

Two Weeks Later

Lev returned to Jerusalem in secret. He wished to set Nasrin and her grandmother up in a house before he announced his presence to Antipater. Or Sarai. He doubted his mentor would have anything negative to say about his new arrangement. Al-though happily married, Lev knew the older man enjoyed a dalliance with a prostitute every now and then.

Sarai and his parents would be another matter. Lev had no delusions. Ordinary Jews were supposed to take only one wife and stay faithful to her. Well, he would keep the letter of the law, if not its heart. Grandmother Masha, for he had finally learned the old woman's name, had not insisted he marry Nasrin before they moved with him to Jerusalem. Her only stipulation had been that the house be purchased with her and Nasrin's names on the deed.

"Then you may not throw us out on the street," she had said, "if you should ever tire of her."

He had given them the illusion of ownership. Their names were indeed printed on the deed . . . of rental. The property belonged to Lev. He loved Nasrin, but he did not trust the grandmother.

The deal had gone smoothly, as if Adonai himself had granted Lev permission to take Nasrin as his concubine. They moved their meager possessions into three rooms near the first city wall. By keeping them away from the Temple Mount, they had less opportunity to mingle with anyone he knew. The quarter around them housed more immigrants than Jews, so the two would blend in with the others.

On the morning of his third day home from Damascus, Lev strolled through the bustling streets of Jerusalem to Antipater's home. The servant at the gate led him to the library where his mentor sat at a large wooden table. Piles of papers and scrolls were stacked neatly along one side, while the area in front of Antipater held only an open parchment which the old man studied.

Lev bowed as he entered. "Master, I have news."

Antipater groaned softly as he stood, as if the movement caused him some pain. "I am glad to have you back. Much has happened in the weeks you were gone." He crossed in front of the table to embrace Lev. "But first, your news. What did you find out?"

Lev relayed Queen Selene's desire for help from Israel. He also spoke of Aristobulus's letter to Ptolemy.

Antipater stroked his thick black beard as he returned to his chair. "Do you have proof of his treachery?"

"Nothing physical. But I saw the letter Ptolemy wrote to him." The past few weeks had made Lev more confident in his machinations. Was it his successful negotiations with Aristobulus, or his relationship with Nasrin? All he knew was he had a newfound confidence in his ability to play the game of politics. His lie came easily. "I followed Ari out to Ptolemy's camp. He is working out a plan to turn Damascus over to the Ituraean. Even as he promises to honor Israel's treaty with Selene."

"If only you had that letter. Then we might have convinced the queen. Without it . . ." Antipater's deep voice drifted off. "Did you discover anything else?"

Lev pulled the second letter from his tunic and placed it on the table. "I managed to slip this from his desk."

The Idumaean scanned the parchment. His lips curled up in a smile. "So Zacharias bar Judah is interested in rebellion, is he? This could be useful."

"Surely it would convince the queen of Ari's duplicity?"

Antipater's eyes glinted. "Even she could not deny it. Perhaps this will be enough to sway her to make John her co-heir while she still lives. The more power he has before she dies, the harder it will be for Aristobulus to oust him when she is gone." He stood, tapping the letter against his palm. "I wish she were not in Ashkelon at present."

"What brought her there?"

His mentor's black robe shimmered as he passed by the sunlight streaming in through a window. "The trial, of course."

"Trial?"

"You have not heard?" Antipater stopped pacing. "Shimeon's son is being tried for murder. There is little doubt he is innocent, but four witnesses have stepped forward to confirm his guilt. The Sanhedrin must convict him based on their testimony alone."

"Is there nothing that can be done?"

A breathy chuckle escaped Antipater's throat. "Shimeon bar Shetach is a Pharisee through and through. He will not bend the law, not even for an innocent man. Not even for his son. Eliezer's fate will be sealed any day now. No doubt they will order his execution after the Sabbath."

Lev played out several scenarios in his head, trying to think of the best course of action. "She will be angry when she   returns. We should present the letter as soon as possible."

"Although she agrees with the Pharisees in principle, she wishes she had the power to supersede the law and grant leniency. It may make her prone to give Zacharias mercy he does not deserve."

Lev snorted. He should have thought of that outcome. "Her school will open soon as well. Will that not also distract her?"

"Yes, but it will also remind her of the differences between the Sadducees and the Pharisees. Her desire for girls to learn is not a popular one with Zacharias and the other Sadducees." Antipater resumed tapping the letter against his palm. "Let us wait until after the school opens. Once the initial thrill has worn off, she may begin to sense the resentment her enemies hold. We add this letter to that anger, and we may finally get her to react in the way we need."

"You think she would openly give John power now?"

"Why not?" Antipater lowered himself into his cushioned chair. "Her husband declared her co-ruler while he went off to war. It is how she assumed the role seamlessly after his death."

"But we are not at war." Lev sat on the wooden chair opposite him. "Will she risk sharing her throne during a time of peace?"

Antipater waved the parchment. "With this and your news about Ari's meeting with Ptolemy, we may finally convince her that war is inevitable." The old man's face softened as he studied Lev. "You have done well. I am proud of you, my son."

Lev had expected to feel some twinge of remorse for conspiring with Aristobulus, but instead, his heart beat with excitement. He had done it. Won the confidence of both sides in the coming conflict. Whatever the outcome, he would be safe. Not only alive, but in the position to continue to rise in power and influence.

Antipater stood. "John is expecting me this afternoon. He wishes to travel to Jericho to visit the new palace his mother has built for him." He put his hand around Lev's shoulders. "I would like you to accompany us."

"I've only just returned from Damascus, my lord." Lev thought of Nasrin. His hands gripped the arms of the chair at the thought of leaving her bed for a month or more. "My wife will be delivering our child soon."

His mentor's eyes narrowed. "The child is not due for several months."

"Yes, but—"

"But what?"

Lev hesitated. The confidence he had only a moment ago fled from him.

Antipater drew his arm back. "Perhaps there is another reason you do not wish to journey with us?"

"I have . . . purchased a woman, my lord. A concubine." Lev tried to gauge his mentor's reaction but his mentor's face was blank as the slate tiles on the floor. "I wish to see her settled before I travel again."

"I see." Antipater stroked his beard.

"I was going to tell you tonight, once our business was done, as I will be spending most nights with her."

The older man's sharp gaze studied him. Apparently satisfied with what he saw, Antipater nodded. "I do not begrudge you, my son. I know you have needs your wife cannot satisfy." He picked up several scrolls from the table. "I trust you to keep your work with me to yourself. You will not discuss it with this woman."

Lev chuckled. "She is Persian, my lord. She does not speak Hebrew and only a little Aramaic."

Antipater joined him in laughing. "So her witty tongue was not what attracted you?" He tucked the scrolls under his arm before patting Lev on the back. "I hope she brings you contentment. But let me caution you, as one who has been in this position before: do not neglect your wife. We are not yet like the nobles we serve. Our only heirs will come through the women we have married, not those who serve our passions."

Anna knelt in the corner of Queen Salome's tent as the wind howled mournfully outside. She lifted up yet another prayer of comfort for Shimeon bar Shetach. The tent walls, made of goatskin and dyed a deep maroon, undulated with the rare spring storm. A crash of thunder seemed to express even Adonai's displeasure at the events of the past week. Eliezer bar Shimeon would be executed come morning, even though he was innocent.

Six men had come forward and testified in the days before the Sabbath. All six told the same story. The same lie. Eliezer had been drinking when an argument arose with another man in the town square, a man with whom he had disagreed before. None of the witnesses could say what the argument had been about, only that Eliezer struck first, punching the man in the stomach. The victim slapped Eliezer across the face. Eliezer then picked up a stone and cracked open the other man's head. Anna shuddered as she recalled the details the witnesses described. Eliezer kneeling over the man's body and continuing to pound the rock into his skull. Blood spattering and covering Eliezer.

It did not matter that no bloody clothes had been found in Eliezer's possession. Nor that he denied arguing with any man in the square.

The victim's head had been so badly beaten, no one could identify him. None of Eliezer's friends remembered him holding a grudge against any man. None of this mattered. All the court judged was the testimony of the six witnesses, each verifying the others' word about the events of that night.

It did not even matter that after the guilty verdict had been pronounced, two of the men approached Shimeon bar Shetach and confessed that they had lied under oath. Eliezer was never in the square. The victim was a drunkard who had fallen and cracked his head while trying to lift a jug of water from a well. The other injuries had come later.

Anna wondered why the liars had come forward. Was it to give some kind of comfort to Shimeon, to console him that his son was truly innocent of breaking one of Adonai's most sacred commandments? Or did the men tell him the truth knowing that nothing could be done to spare his son? Did they only want to add to the poor man's pain? Whatever their reason, they had fled Ashkelon after admitting their sin, with enough gold in their pockets for their story, Anna guessed, to stay hidden for good.

In the end, nothing could be done to save Eliezer from the court's decision. He would be executed when the sun rose and the rain ceased falling long enough for the men of the city to gather in judgement. Eliezer would hang for a murder he did not commit.

Why, Lord? Why do you allow men to twist Your laws? You are a God of mercy. Of justice. Surely, this is not what You intended.

The tent walls shook as another rain-filled gust pelted the fabric. Anna trembled. She could not tell whether it was cold or fear that caused her shivering. *Probably both.* Queen Salome had left the tent, with Ziva accompanying her, as soon as the sun set, heralding the end of the Sabbath. They had gone to Eliezer's house, to sit with his soon-to-be widow as she kept vigil the night before her husband's death. Anna had been ordered to stay behind to keep the fire in the tent burning so that the queen would find it warm when she returned after the execution.

In the center of the tent, embers from the fire ring glowed orange. Anna gathered her shawl around her shoulders before walking over to stoke them back to life. It was impossible to tell how much time remained until dawn, but it seemed to Anna that she had been praying for hours. She had not dozed off, as far as she could tell, but her mind had wandered.

She could not help wondering what she would find when she returned to Jerusalem. A life with Caleb, working in the palace by his side and sharing their thoughts; or one with Nathanel, trapped in his house like an ornamental vase? Shuddering, she poked at the embers with a rod until they burned bright then added a handful of straw to create more flame. Once the straw caught alight, she threw in several pieces of dried dung. She would save the remaining branches until the queen returned.

She held her fingers over the flame, hoping some of the heat might warm her chilled body. Her eyes strayed to the wooden table next to her. Several scrolls sat rolled up on the corner. Another lay open across it.

Queen Salome had left orders that Anna should keep the fire and pray during the night, both of which she had done. There had been no warnings about what she should *not* do while alone in the tent. Although the scrolls, table and seat were the queen's possessions, nothing had been said about them being touched only by Salome.

Anna inched closer to the open scroll. The queen had been furiously studying the ancient texts for the past week, trying to find some detail in the law that Shimeon had overlooked. Something allowing a ruling monarch to overturn the courts. But Adonai had not wanted any one man, or woman, to hold that kind of power. A king's favor could be bought. The judgement of the Sanhedrin could not.

Salome had last been reading in the Law of Moses. Anna pushed an oil lamp closer to the scroll. Although the rabbis in Egypt had not taught her to read, she had gleaned some understanding of letters from years of looking over her father's shoulder as he taught Daniel. Her eyes scanned the text. Yes, here it was written by the scribes, ". . . on the evidence of two or three men shall a testimony be confirmed." Unfortunately, by the laws of the Pharisees, once the verdict had been given, it could not be changed, even if the witnesses lied.

Anna sighed at the injustice. Her hand unknowingly touched the rolled end of the scroll so it opened to an earlier portion of the text. She blinked as the words on the parchment seemed to lift off the page.

"The Lord your God will raise up for you a prophet like me from among you, from your fellow Israelites. You must listen to him."

"When, Lord," Anna whispered. "When will this prophet come?"

Soon

She gasped at the voice echoing in her head. Her heart hammered within her chest. She waited for the voice to speak again but only the storm outside made noise. *Perhaps she had imagined it?* The prophetic words sat dry and dull on the parchment once again.

Anna's fingers lingered over the stack of scrolls. Would Salome be angry if she unrolled another so she could read it for herself?

"Adonai," she whispered. "Please forgive me if this is wrong." She lifted a scroll from the pile. "But I desire to know you more. I want to know more about the prophet to come. Teach me." She unrolled the parchment carefully, as if it might crumble in her hands. "Show me, Lord."

The scroll contained the words of Moses that he wrote down concerning Jacob and his son, Joseph. Although the story was one that never ceased to thrill her, Anna almost put the writing aside as she knew it so well. What could she find about the Messiah in these passages? Her eyes skimmed over the yellowed page, picking out the words she understood from sitting at her father's side for so many years. She recognized the name Joseph and remembered how he had been sold into slavery in Egypt then wrongfully jailed. How he had interpreted Pharaoh's dreams and risen to be the second greatest ruler in the land.

Anna sighed as she began to close the scroll. As she rolled it up from one end, the other uncurled further. She paused as she came to the newly opened text. It revealed the final blessings of Jacob to his sons. His words to Judah appeared darker than the others. "Your brothers will praise you . . ." The rest of the text sprung from her memory: *The scepter will not depart from Judah . . . until he to whom it belongs comes . . . the obedience of the nations shall be his.*

A strange fluttering stirred in her chest, as if a thousand butterflies took flight. *Would the Messiah come from the tribe of Judah?* Surely, she was not the first person to read this passage and ask that question. She longed to speak with Shimeon again and hear his thoughts.

Shimeon. Stricken with guilt, Anna hurried to close the scroll and set it back with the rest. This was no time to indulge in her private hope for the Messiah. Shimeon, Eliezer, and even the queen needed her prayers. Perhaps Adonai could yet be moved to spare Eliezer's life. She stirred the fire one more time before settling back into the corner of the tent to resume her prayers. But now as she prayed for Eliezer's salvation and his family's peace, Anna added her desire to see the Lord's Messiah. Moses had written the scrolls hundreds of years in the past. Surely, the time had come for the prophet he spoke of to appear.

Queen Salome returned to the tent several hours later, her dark mood settling inside as cold as the rain still falling outside. She tossed her cloak and ornamental robe to the floor while Ziva scurried to unpack a thicker woolen robe from her trunk. Anna placed a new log on the fire as Salome paced the packed earth covered with woolen rugs.

"I cannot fathom why God has allowed such a travesty." Salome paused as Ziva helped to put on her robe. As soon as it was in place, she continued to walk the length of the tent. She waved her hand toward the scrolls. "All the wisdom of God Himself, and still men find ways to corrupt the truth. What is the point? Where is the justice?"

The fire cast the tent in a crimson glow as the flames reflected off the red walls, giving color to the queen's anger. Anna crept back to her pallet behind a curtain in the corner to keep out of her mistress's way. Ziva put a pot of water on to boil then joined Anna.

"She held her fury while she was with Eliezer's family." Ziva whispered, "I do not know how. She offered the only comfort she could, that his widow would receive a pension for as long as she lived, or until she took another husband." Ziva blew on her fingertips to warm them. "After that, the queen sat in silent prayer for the whole night."

Anna pulled her blanket from the floor and wrapped it around her friend's shoulders. "And did they hold the execution? Even in this rain?"

"Nothing could stop them. They made the preparations before the Sabbath. Had the gallows built before sundown so they would be ready as soon as the sun rose . . . or the rain ceased for a moment." Ziva gathered the blanket around her as if to shield herself from the memory. "I suppose, in a way, it was a blessing. At least now it is finished. There is nothing left for anyone to do but bury the poor man's body."

They sat in silence and watched Salome rant to the air until Ziva rose and poured the now boiling water into a pot of herbs to steep. Once the tea had brewed, she gave them each a cup. "This will warm us all and, God willing, ease our pains."

Anna breathed in the scent of chamomile, lemon, and jasmine, letting the aroma relax her tense muscles.

Salome sighed as she swallowed a mouthful. "We will leave this accursed city tomorrow, whether the rain stops or not."

"Should I begin packing now, Mistress?" Ziva asked.

"No." The queen paused as she took another sip. "Rest this morning. It is has been a long night for all of us. You can begin packing later."

After the tea, Anna settled onto her pallet to rest, but her thoughts spun. If they left tomorrow, they might be back in Jerusalem before the next Sabbath. Perhaps Caleb would tell his sister about his meeting with Phanuel. If Tamar knew, she would not keep it from Anna.

Unless Caleb did not tell her.

But surely, Tamar would ask, would demand to know what had happened. She would not let him keep the news to himself.

Unless it was bad news. Then he might keep to himself again. Hide in his home and refuse to see anyone as he had done before.

Anna groaned as she tossed on her pallet.

Ziva grunted on the floor next to her. "If I was not so exhausted, I would hit you. Stop your thrashing! You are like a bird in a cage."

"Sorry." She tried to keep still, to silence the warring within her head, but she could not. She rolled onto her back and stared up at the ceiling.

"What has upset you? Is it the trial?"

"I cannot get my thoughts to quiet. It is the trial, yes. But I also think about what my life will be like when we return."

Ziva settled onto her side. "Are you worried about teaching at the school?"

Anna faced her. "A little. My father is seeking a betrothal for me. There is one man he is considering whom I do not believe will allow me to teach."

Ziva yawned. "Even if the queen commanded it?"

Anna shrugged. "He is a rabbi and a Pharisee. I am sure he would twist some law so that he could deny Salome without it being treason."

"What of Caleb?" Ziva yawned again. "Your father came to speak to Salome about him and—"

Anna's heart jumped in her chest. "He did? When?"

"As if my mind could sift through the past week to come up with that answer? It was before we left Jerusalem, how about that?"

Anna tried to still her excitement. "What did she say?"

"The queen did not ask my opinion on the matter. I only know your father came to speak to her and Caleb's name was mentioned." Ziva drew her blankets up under her chin. "It was brief, I remember, as we were preparing to come here. I assumed he came to verify the tailor's character. And he would only do that if he were considering him for your husband." She glared at Anna. "Now, I beg you, quiet yourself and let me get some sleep."

Anna smiled to herself as Ziva rolled away from her. A good report from Salome would go a long way to make Caleb worthy in her father's eyes. She snuggled into her blankets, contenting herself with thoughts of making a home with the one man she loved.

Chapter 27

A Week Later

Lev rested with his head against Nasrin's breast, listening to her heartbeat. His fingers wove through her hair. "Are you happy here, my rose?"

The girl smiled at him, but he knew she did not comprehend question. He had hoped she would learn Aramaic now that she lived in Jerusalem, but she seemed as unreachable as ever. Her inability, or unwillingness, to communicate with him proved to be a thorn in his side. Physically, she was as beautiful to him as she had been the first moment he had seen her. However, it had been almost a month since he brought her home, and still she would not speak to him directly. They communicated through Grandmother Masha, and the crone was getting tiresome in her demands. It was not enough he provided them with a house and food. Always the woman wanted new clothes for her granddaughter, fine scarves and jewels.

The girl stirred underneath him, her eyes asking the only question she seemed capable of: was he ready to sleep or would he take her again this night?

Annoyed, Lev rolled on top of her. He paid enough for her body, he may as well use it. The girl sighed as she adjusted herself beneath him.

A sudden pounding on the door startled them both. Grandmother Masha grumbled as she stirred from her pallet by the hearth. "Who disturbs us so late?"

Lev stared down at Nasrin. "Who knocks?" His cheeks grew warm with rage. "Are you seeing other men?"

The girl's brows furrowed, sensing his anger if not the cause.

"I come in the name of Prince Aristobulus." A man's voice broke through the night. "For the scribe, Lev bar Malachi."

Lev slipped his tunic over his head before opening the curtain separating Nasrin's bed from the rest of the room. One of the palace guards stood by the door. He took off his helmet, his dark eyes taking in Lev's appearance with obvious amusement.

Lev straightened his shoulders. "What does the prince want?"

The man's weathered face appeared tired. Or perhaps he was bored. "The prince does not confide in me. He only commanded I fetch you."

Fetch? The hair on back of Lev's neck rose in defiance. *I am not his servant.* Yet, even as he rebelled, he knew Aristobulus may not pay him, but everyone served the nobility. "Give me a moment."

He returned to pick up his clothes from Nasrin's floor. Once dressed, he followed the guard through the narrow streets of the lower city and the gates of the second wall. Here, the roads widened as the houses were bigger and more opulent.

The night was not yet half over. A bright, silver moon hung high overhead as they turned the corner into the courtyard of the Hasmonean palace. The guards, armed with spears, moved aside to let Lev and his escort pass through the entrance.

Lev stopped as they approached the end of the hallway. "I know the way to the prince's rooms."

The soldier snorted. "The prince is not in his rooms."

"Then where is he?"

The man tilted his head down the opposite hall. "He is sitting in the throne room."

"Where is the queen?"

The soldier sniffed again. "Not yet back from Ashkelon." He gestured with his arm. "If you know the way, I will leave you to find him and return to my post."

Lev nodded to dismiss the man, but waited until he was out of sight before he made his way to Aristobulus. He approached the throne room with caution, but the guard outside the door seemed to be expecting him and opened the door without Lev announcing his identity.

The massive room, with its tall marble columns lining the way toward the marble dais, never ceased to stir a sense of awe in his soul, even though it did not have the opulence of Selene's palace in Damascus. The light from dozens of torches reflected off the polished stone walls. At the end of the room, Aristobulus lounged on the throne, watching Lev approach as one watches a spider crawl along a wall.

Lev straightened his shoulders and did not lower his eyes as he neared the steps to the throne. He bowed, but did not speak. Aristobulus was a prince, not yet a king. Lev would give the man respect, but he would not fear him.

Neither man spoke. Lev sensed the prince's frustration. Ari wanted him to speak first. To beg to ask why he had been brought to the palace in the middle of the night. Lev would not give him the satisfaction. He knew too much about Ari's plans to let the man intimidate him.

Finally, Aristobulus stretched his arms out wide. "What do you think, Lev bar Malachi? Does the throne suit me?"

"It does, my lord. But is it not a little early to be declaring yourself king while your mother still lives?"

The prince's brown eyes darkened. "I am declaring nothing."

Lev shrugged. "She may not see it that way if she found you here."

"No worries about that." He grunted. "She sent word she would be arriving back the day after tomorrow."

"Before the Sabbath?"

Aristobulus fidgeted on the throne. "Of course. Her precious school opens next week. She would not miss that."

"It is obvious you do not approve. Do you not want girls to learn?"

"I have no problem with educating noble females. My own wife, Helena, is a brilliant tactician."

"Then what do you dislike?"

The prince glared. "It is the poor I do not want educated. We have enough trouble with the Pharisees and scribes, we do not need the poor to add their voices to the others, all demanding justice and equality." He leaned back. "I did not call you here to discuss the merits of my mother's foolhardy plans."

Now we come to it. Lev could feel the irritation radiating from the prince, but still he refused again to take the bait and beg the prince for more information. He would wait until Ari gave it up willingly.

The prince scowled. "You annoy me, Lev bar Malachi, but I respect your stubborn streak."

Lev bowed his head in humble acceptance of the comment.

"My mother is not young. She will not sit on this throne for much longer. I will have it when she dies."

"And what of John?"

Ari opened his hands wide so they rested on the arms of the throne. "That is where I could use you, my friend."

"And why should I help you?"

The prince's lips curled up into a half-smile. "You promised me some time ago. Do you not remember?"

His skin prickled as if chafed by sand. "I remember. I told you then I would not commit treason."

Ari chuckled. "Nor would I ask you to. But when the time comes, whether this year or several years from now, I want your help removing my brother from Jerusalem."

"To kill him would be treason."

"I do not want to kill him, as much as I loathe him. He may be a weak idiot, but he is my brother."

Lev took a deep breath to quiet his nerves. "Then what?"

Aristobulus leaned forward. "Convince your master that it would be in John's best interest to get him out of the city." He waved his arm, as if conjuring a spell in the air. "Let him retire to his palace in Jericho. I will allow him back for the Festivals to parade around as a prince."

"And what makes you think I can convince him to leave?"

The prince grunted. "Your job is convince Antipater to persuade John."

Lev considered the prince's request. "Does it have to be Jericho?"

Ari's hands slapped the arms of the throne. "Take him to Egypt. Take him to the moon. Just get him out of Jerusalem and away from the Pharisees who want him to be king even more than my mother does."

"When the time comes, my lord. I will do this for you."

The prince's brown eyes narrowed as he scrutinized Lev. "Do you think you can convince Antipater?"

Lev bowed toward him. "I am sure I can."

Chapter 28

Two Days Later

They crested the last hill on the road into Jerusalem as the sun sat crimson on the horizon. Anna stared down at the streets below as she walked behind the queen's litter. She longed to be home with her father so she could learn of her fate, but Salome requested that she spend the Sabbath in the palace. The queen retired to bed as soon as they arrived, exhausted from the four day journey from Ashkelon and the emotional stress of the trial and execution. But by the following afternoon she summoned Anna to discuss what her duties would be at the school when it opened the following week.

"It will be a challenge for you at first, to engage the girls," Salome said as she reclined on an upholstered couch. "They have never been encouraged to think about the scriptures for themselves. Or to ask questions. You must prod them. Lead them."

"Yes, Your Majesty."

The queen pressed a gnarled finger against her graying temple. "The rabbis will start in the beginning, with Genesis. You have studied this book with the rabbis in Egypt?"

"Of course."

Salome closed her eyes.

"Are you well?"

"Just trying to clear my thoughts from the horrors of last week. It is difficult to concentrate with such images burned into my memory." A servant girl hurried over carrying a goblet, but the queen waved her away. "No wine. I do not wish to erase the pain. It is best to remember such things and grow from them."

"What good can come from an innocent man dying?" Anna whispered. "I cannot fathom it."

Salome let out a long sigh. "Neither can I. But God does not think as man does. The psalmist wrote that His ways are higher than ours."

"What good can come from any death? What is there beyond Sheol?"

"Indeed." The queen's eyes focused on something within. "What can a human do once she has passed from this world? There is only this time, and what Adonai purposes for us to do." She blinked, as if waking from a dream. "That is why the school is so important to me. How can we know God's purpose for us if we do not know Him? And how can a child know Him if they do not know His word?"

Anna remembered how she had tried to explain the same thing to Nathanel.

"What are you thinking?"

"Why do men think Adonai does not want women to know Him?"

A soft smile lightened Salome's face. "Only some believe that."

"But does He ever command such a thing?" Anna's brows furrowed. "Nowhere in His word do I remember seeing it."

The queen's smile now touched her eyes, causing them to sparkle. "But some men fear giving us such power."

"Power?"

Wisps of graying hair floated around Salome's face as she nodded. "We are partly to blame. Men can be easily swayed by the beliefs of a pretty woman. Remember how Balaam brought in the temple prostitutes to lead the Israelites astray in the wilderness? And did not Solomon's wives draw him away from the true faith?"

"But then . . ." Anna thought hard to voice her opinion correctly. "Should not our knowing God's Word be a good thing? If our influence is so great, we would at least be influencing our husbands for good."

"One would hope they would think the way you do," Salome said. "But they argue that since it was the women who seduced the Israelites away from Adonai in the past, including our forefather Adam, we cannot be trusted with God's word. We will distort the truth and lead men astray once again."

A servant girl stood in the threshold. "Your Majesty, the Sabbath is over. Will you break your fast this evening?"

"Yes."

"Also, a message arrived for the seamstress before you returned to the palace, but I did not have time to deliver it before the Sabbath began."

The queen arched an eyebrow. "What is it?"

The young woman paused, recalling the encounter. "Her   father, Phanuel, requests that his daughter be allowed to come to his house upon her return from Ashkelon. If possible, a   messenger should be sent so he can prepare for her visit."

Salome grunted softly before turning her attention back to Anna. "I suppose it was inevitable."

Anna's heart beat like that of a rabbit's caught in a snare. Her voice cracked when she asked, "What was?"

"Your betrothal. I assume that is why he wishes to see you." Salome watched her closely. "Has he given you any idea whom he has chosen?"

Anna's chest constricted so tightly she could not take a breath. She shook her head.

"By all accounts, both Nathanel and Caleb are honest and good. Either should provide well for you. I told Phanuel as much when he came to speak with me."

"You spoke well of Nathanel?"

"I had no reason not to."

"He will take me away from the palace." Anna's voice came out on a choked sob. "I would not be able to teach."

"Still, Phanuel asked only about each man's character and circumstance." Sympathy flooded the queen's eyes. "I would not presume to come between a father and his concern for his daughter. He will make the choice he feels is best for you."

The servant coughed in the doorway. "Should I send a messenger, Your Majesty?"

"Yes. Anna will spend the night in her father's house tonight." The queen stood. "Come, child." Salome reached out to cup Anna's chin. "At the very least, I believe even Nathanel could be persuaded to allow you to keep your position here until the wedding ceremony took place." Her mischievous grin melted years from her face.

Anna tried to smile in return, but her fear of losing Caleb caused her lips to tremble.

Salome called to one of the soldiers standing guard at the door. "Escort this young lady to her father's house." She glanced at Anna. "I would not have you roaming the dark streets alone. Come back tomorrow with the news of your father's decision."

Anna bowed then left the room, pausing to instruct the soldier to wait for her at the palace gate. "I wish to retrieve my cloak before going out."

She made her way through the halls to the servants' quarters, relieved to find the room she shared with Mary and the other servants empty, as she had no desire to explain to anyone where she going. Grabbing her mantle, she hurried back to the main hallway and met the guard at the gate. He walked a few paces behind her as she made her way down the Temple Mount. The stars shone bright across the heavens, like a river of jewels flowing across the sky. It seemed too much to hope that her father had chosen Caleb. Even taking her time, Anna made the turn down the last road to her father's house more quickly than she liked. She slowed her steps further as she approached the door.

"Is something wrong?" the soldier asked from behind her.

Fear weighed her down. She could not even lift her arm to knock and announce her arrival.

"Are you lost?" he asked.

"Not yet," she whispered. "But I may be once I go inside."

"I hope that is not the case," a deeper voice spoke.

Anna whirled to find Caleb standing beside the soldier. Her brother, Daniel, next to them. Her heart leapt. "He chose you?"

The tailor nodded. "Does that please you?"

The relief broke over her like a crashing wave. Tears flooded her eyes.

Daniel stepped toward her. "Why are you crying?"

She threw her arms around him. "Because, you great fool, I am so happy!"

Daniel grunted as he nudged her toward Caleb. "You had better be." He opened the door and golden light from the oil lamps spilled out onto the street. "Come inside. Father has prepared the contract."

Anna stared up at Caleb as the soldier headed back to the palace and they were left alone. Caleb took her face in his scarred hands, wiping the tears from her cheeks with his thumbs. "You are sure you want me? Old and wounded as I am?"

Anna turned to kiss the fingers that had been burned together. "I have never been more certain of anything."

"Come, Daughter," Phanuel called. "Let us make your betrothal official."

She clasped her hand with Caleb's. Together, they entered the house.

Phanuel, Daniel, and Tova all wore the fine robes she had brought them from Egypt. The long wooden table had been cleaned and Anna could smell the linseed oil used to freshen the wood and keep it from drying out. A goblet she had never seen before sat in its center. *Purchased just for this occasion?*

Anna's heart quickened as Phanuel's eyes glistened with tears. She dropped Caleb's hand to embrace her father. "Oh, Abba. Thank you. You have made me so happy."

"As you have made me, from the moment I first held you in my arms." He took a shuddering breath then kissed her cheek. "Now let me go, so that everything is made official."

Anna stepped away and into Tova's arms. She longed to squeal with excitement, but contented herself with a fervent hug before turning to watch Caleb approach the table.

Two oil lamps flickered next to a piece of parchment, their golden flames illuminating the words her father had printed in his exact handwriting. Never had it seemed as beautiful to Anna as now. The gentle swoops and lines of the Hebrew letters spelled out the fulfillment of her deepest desires.

As Caleb and her father discussed the details of the contract—how many gold coins would Caleb provide for her bride price? What gifts would Phanuel give as her dowry—Anna's mind thought on how good Adonai had been to her. How God's ways were so much better than her own. If Lev had defied his father, she would be living far from Jerusalem. He would probably be working as a scribe for a rabbi, hating every moment because it lacked the thrill of politics in the city. She might have had a child by now, and would be trying to steal some time each night before sleeping to embroider a piece to sell at the local market. Never would she be working on the fine robes she made now. If she had married Lev all those years ago, she would not have gone to Egypt. She would never have the power of God's word living inside her, constantly giving her strength to face each day, each challenge.

Anna's gaze fell on Caleb's face as he bent over the betrothal contract. Her body filled with warmth as love for him pulsed through her. *How different he is from Lev.* Although she had definitely felt Caleb's desire for her, it was not the violent passion she had sensed in Lev. Instead, Caleb looked on her as something to be treasured and protected. He honored her and longed to share his life with her, not possess her. And because he seemed to want nothing more than to please her, it filled her with the same desire. She wanted to spend every moment with him, whether it be working at the palace or alone in their own home. To bless him with a son, a boy to carry on his family name. A daughter he could shower with love. She blinked back the tears of joy, hoping the men would not see them and think she regretted her decision.

Her father's voice broke through her thoughts. "You shall be my son-in-law." He clapped one hand on Caleb's shoulder then picked up the goblet of wine. "Now you both must drink from this cup to signify you are forsaking all others and will remain faithful until death."

Caleb took the cup first, his eyes finding hers before lifting it to his mouth and sealing their covenant. He passed it to her. "If you are certain you want this, then drink."

"I am certain." As she swallowed the sweet liquid, she thought she had never been so happy.

Phanuel took the cup from her hand. "Then, in the eyes of God and in the way of the Law, you are husband and wife."

Anna wished she could walk back with Caleb to his tiny yet well-kept house and start her life with him, but she knew she must wait for the formal wedding ceremony. "Father, as Caleb already has a home for us, must we wait a year to be married?"

Her father scratched his long beard. "It is the usual betrothal."

She grinned as a soft blush rose in Caleb's face. He coughed nervously. "I have spoken with the family who owns the home next to mine. It has been empty since the father died and the widow went to live with her son. They are willing to sell it to me so that I might enlarge our home." He nodded toward her. "To make it ready for our family."

"See there?" Her father gestured toward Caleb. "He has work to do to make the house ready for you."

"Only a few weeks' worth," Caleb argued. "No more than a month at most."

Phanuel sighed. "You will wait a year. For tradition's sake, if nothing else." His face hardened. "You are not a young man. I will not cast judgement on any past indiscretions you may have had, but I expect you to be faithful to my daughter alone from now on."

Caleb's face flushed again. "I would never do anything to dishonor her or your family."

Anna slipped her hand again into Caleb's. "I will use this time to make a gown to wear for our wedding. And linens for our home."

He tilted his head down toward her. "I need only you, my love. Nothing more."

"Then it is settled." Phanuel gestured to Tova. "Bring out the honey cakes and wine. Let us celebrate."

Sarai's brown hair lay tangled around her head. She sat hunched on the upholstered bench in her bedroom. Arms wrapped around her swollen stomach as if willing the child she carried to stay inside her belly.

From the doorway, Lev looked at her with disdain. "What is wrong with her?"

His mother, Judith, stood next to his wife. She glared back at him. "She has always been frail of heart."

"Is it the child she carries?" He kept his distance, refusing to step past the doorway. "Has it caused her to lose her senses?"

"No!" Judith crossed the space between them in two broad strides. Her hand flashed out and struck his cheek.

Shocked at his mother's violence and the sting of her anger, Lev stepped back into the hallway. "What have I done? I have not come near her since I came home from Damascus."

Judith followed him out of the room then waved toward the servant girl coming up the steps. "Leave us." She spoke in a harsh whisper. "Did you think you could keep your whore a secret? Jerusalem is a city of gossips who love to spread unhappy news."

He had always loved his mother, but Judith's rebuke made his stomach tighten into a hard fist. "Sarai has never wanted me in her bed. She tolerated it only so I could give her my seed. I would think her glad I found someone else."

"You have bought this whore a house. Given her the deed to it! How—"

Lev hit the wall with the side of his fist. "She is not a whore. She is my concubine—"

"Concubine?" Judith scoffed, her voice rose in volume. "Who do you think you are? King David? Or perhaps Solomon the wise?" She waved an accusing finger at him. "You are Lev bar Malachi, a humble scribe. You do not have concubines. You have a prostitute who sleeps with you because you pay her."

His fingers stayed curled at his side. He punched them against his thighs. "You know nothing of my relationship with Nasrin."

His mother let out a harsh laugh. "I may not know her name, but even I know she is playing you for a fool, and you are too blind to see it."

His hand rose, seemingly of its own accord, reaching out to grasp his mother's neck.

Her eyes widened as she swatted it away. "You would do me violence for telling you the truth?"

"I love Nasrin." Lev tried not to shout. His voice came out as a harsh whisper. "She would never betray me."

Judith's ire softened as she studied him. "Oh, my son. What has happened to you? That you would turn so far from Adonai and seek love from a Gentile harlot instead of from your own family? From God?"

"My family?" Lev snorted in disgust. "You mean her?" He pointed at Sarai. "She was never my wife. She was the woman my father chose for me because it suited him financially. She has been afraid of me since the day we drank from the betrothal cup."

"You never forgave her for not being Anna."

Lev staggered back as if she had struck him again.

"Malachi was a fool to think you would ever forget her." A tear dropped from Judith's lower eyelash. "She would have kept you in Adonai's will."

The knot in his stomach tightened even further. "But that choice was not given to me, was it?"

His mother squared her shoulders. "You had a choice. Do not blame anyone but yourself for the path you decided to take."

"I could not have asked Anna to leave Jerusalem to live in poverty with me in a foreign city."

"She would have followed you anywhere." Her voice stabbed through him, piercing him with its truth. She placed her hand on his chest. "In your heart, you know that to be true. You cannot blame your unhappiness on anyone but yourself."

"I am happy now that I have Nasrin. I have everything my father tried to take from me—power, wealth and a woman who loves me."

"And what of your daughter?" Judith pointed behind her toward the bedroom. "What of this shell of a woman who may be carrying your son? I called you here to help her. Would you leave her like this?"

"What can I do for her? She loathes me."

She grabbed hold of the front of his robe, clutching it in her fists, pulling him toward the room. "She fears you because she knows you do not love her. If you could find it in your heart to show her some affection. To spend more than a night with her to make a child. You would find she is worthy of the effort."

Lev looked over her shoulder toward his wife. Sarai's expressionless eyes looked at nothing. He peeled his mother's hands from his chest. "Send for the doctor. She is beyond my help."

Judith's anger softened. "Do not do this, my son. Please. Do not turn away from everything I tried to teach you."

His mother seemed to have aged a decade over the course of their argument. Lev sighed. "Perhaps I have too much of my father in me after all, as much as I tried to fight him."

"It is not too late."

Her pleading tone scraped against his nerves. He had enough of doing what others asked him to do. Antipater . . . Grandmother Masha . . . Aristobulus . . . God . . . always someone demanded something from him. His time. His skills. His money. His obedience. Only with Nasrin was he free to take and not give. With her, he did only what he wanted. Whatever he desired.

"Please, Lev. Please, come back to us."

He pulled her into an embrace then kissed the top of her head. "I love you, Mother. I always have."

"I love you, too, my son."

He rested his chin against her hair and felt her body relaxing in his arms. "But I will not give up Nasrin. I will not return to this house until the babe is born."

"Will you stay then?" She raised her face to look at him.

"Only if she gives me a son."

Stricken, she pushed him away. "God forgive you for saying such a thing."

"If He truly exists, I doubt very much He has time to worry about what I choose to do in my bed." He hurried on before she could interrupt him. "I am done with your God and His rules. I am done believing there is more to this life than what I can see and touch. Goodbye, Mother."

Chapter 29

Autumn, 71 B.C.

Lev wiped the sweat from his forehead. Even though fall harvest had passed, it seemed that summer held on to Israel, baking the land in dust and heat. Even here, in Antipater's upper study, he could smell the stench from the city below, as if the streets themselves perspired. He glanced up from the letter he read as Antipater entered the room, grinning. His satisfaction was contagious and Lev could not help smiling. "She signed the order?"

Antipater clapped his hands together. "She signed the order. John Hyrcanus is now joint ruler with her"

"And Aristobulus?"

"Has no recourse." Antipater strode to the open window. A light breeze blew in, cooling the stuffy air in the room. "All my work . . . all these years . . . I can finally see the pieces coming together as I planned." He gazed outside as if looking over his own kingdom. He may have started his career as an outsider to Israel, but he had embraced the country and its people as his own. At least in how he could use them to fulfill his dreams.

Lev wondered at his mentor's confidence. "Master, I do not think we have heard the last of Ari."

"Hmm?" Antipater stroked his narrow beard. He did not look at Lev, but kept his focus on the city outside.

Although three months had passed since he had met with Ari, Lev knew the queen's youngest son still craved her throne. Aristobulus might lead her army now and obey all her commands, but Lev knew the prince would never accept John Hyrcanus's rule. "Aristobulus is still not to be trusted."

"Nonsense." Antipater shooed away a fly that buzzed about his head. "He would not dare to go against the queen now that she has officially made John her joint ruler."

"Salome's journey to Ashkelon weakened her. She is healthy enough now, but each illness is harder to shake off. She knows this. That is why she signed your decree."

Antipater still faced the window but shifted his gaze toward Lev. "When she dies, John will be king. It has been ratified."

"When she dies, Aristobulus will gather the army he has commanded in her name and storm Jerusalem. The Sadducees will raise more soldiers to follow behind him." Lev's fingers fisted in frustration. "Surely, you must know that."

Antipater's lips drew into a hard line as he weighed Lev's accusations before speaking.

Lev pointed toward a map with the evidence of Aristobulus's ambition. He had spent the afternoon pouring over the latest correspondence from their allies throughout Israel. "This is the last of the fortresses loyal to the queen. The rest have been given to the Sadducees for refuge. If Salome should die—"

"Then within weeks, he would have an army ready to wage war against John." Antipater yanked the map from the table and began to roll it up.

"Is there no way to convince John to act before it is too late?"

Antipater shook his head. "He will not go against his mother's wishes. You would think he were a child, not a grown man destined to be king."

"I am sorry, Master, to bring such news to your attention when you thought you had achieved your goal." Lev scratched the back of his neck. He knew what he wanted to suggest to his mentor would not be taken well, but thought it best to broach the subject. "I wonder . . . should we reach out to Ari?"

"No," Antipater snapped. "To give in to that madman, it is not worth the price." His nose wrinkled up as if smelling dung. "He is overly confident. Arrogant."

Lev laughed to himself. *The same words could be applied to you, my friend.*

"When the time comes, I am sure I will be able to convince John to wage war against his brother. I only hate waiting to take action until then. It would be much simpler with Salome still on the throne." Antipater let his breath out in a long, slow sigh. "It is a game of strategy. We must see beyond the immediate moves Ari will take and outmaneuver him." He sat in a chair, folded his hands together then brought the index fingers to his lips. "Not only Ari, but the Romans as well. They have taken Cyzicus and are looking toward Armenia. If they are not stopped, they will march on Israel." His eyes took on a familiar gleam, and Lev knew his mentor's mind worked hard to unravel this puzzle. "How can we move all the pieces to our best advantage?"

"I think we must prepare to get John to safety should   Salome die suddenly."

"We must not let Ari take the throne. To do so would spell John's death."

"We may not have another option, Master."

"King Aretas. In Petra." A smile spread across Antipater's thin lips. "My family served the Nabateans in the past. They, too, suffered defeat under Israel's last king. If we can convince them that we can control John, while Aristobulus is as tyrannical as his father, surely Aretas would give John protection. Help him keep the throne." He glanced up. "I will write letters of introduction for you."

"Me?"

Antipater stood. "I cannot go. It would arouse too much suspicion within the court. Ari's spies would have me stopped. But you . . . you could move freely." He paced the room with excitement. "We will ask Aretas to prepare a place of refuge for John if Ari revolts before Salome's death. When she is gone, and he no longer has his mother's protection, John will be forced to act. And we will be there to guide his every decision." Antipater clapped his hands together. "You should make the necessary preparations to leave after the Sabbath."

"At once, my lord." Lev gave his mentor a slight bow. "Is there anything else you need from me today?"

Antipater waved him away. "In the morning we can discuss your trip in detail."

This trip to Petra would be Lev's first to the Nabatean stronghold. Located in the south, near the trade routes to Egypt, Petra was rumored to be a spectacular sight within an otherwise barren region. The Nabateans had managed to harness what little water could be found and used it to create an oasis in the desert. Great buildings, carved from the limestone caves surrounding the area, were said to tower over the inhabitants. Lev brushed the sweat threatening to drip into his eyes. The smells of sweat, dung, and garbage hung in the air at this time of year, overpowering the aroma of incense and spice that normally masked them. To be out of Jerusalem was a blessing in itself, to visit such a marvel would only sweeten the journey.

Lev made his way to the Baris Fortress and spoke with the commander on duty. He arranged for a small detail of soldiers to accompany him to Petra. The roads in the south were often populated with thieves hoping to steal from honest travelers such as himself.

Once he had the commander's assurance that his men would be ready to leave after the Sabbath, Lev wove his way through the crowds on the Temple Mount and walked down to the marketplace. Heat radiated from the road like coals left on a fire. He squinted at the glare from the bleached stones in the buildings around him. The breeze that had cooled Antipater's study did not blow down below on the streets. Instead, the air lay still, like a cloak, stifling everything so that the people around him seemed unable to move. Even the animals were sluggish. Donkeys brayed stubbornly at their masters, refusing to carry their loads another step. A camel lowered itself in the middle of street, causing angry outbursts from the crowd, but no one had the energy to escalate their outrage to a brawl.

Lev maneuvered through the throng to make arrangements with various merchants to supply provisions for his journey. After several hours, he sighed to himself. He supposed he should see Nasrin before he left for Petra, but the thought did not satisfy him as much as it had in the past. She was still beautiful, but not in the intoxicating way she had been when he had first brought her to Jerusalem. Her body was as familiar to him now as his own. He knew every curve. Every flaw. For she had many.

Her eyes, which he had loved for their deep green color, were too close together. It had not bothered him before but now it irked him. The good food he provided for her had rounded her stomach, thighs and arms. Some men preferred their women soft, but not him.

And, most irritating of all, the woman still had not learned enough Aramaic to hold a conversation with him. Three months and she could only greet him, talk about the weather or ask him to buy her a new piece of clothing or jewelry. Now that her bloom had withered, he understood something about himself: the admiration of others sustained him more than physical pleasures. No woman could satisfy him as did political power.

He paused in the street, deciding against spending the rest of the afternoon with Nasrin and her grandmother. He spun around and walked back up the hill. It had a month since he had been to his own house on the event of his second daughter's birth. Sarai had named her Salome, after the queen. It would be wise for him to check on his household before he left for Petra.

Anna hunched over the dress for Princess Helena, her nimble fingers dancing through the fabric, finishing the intricate pattern along the hem. Although she worked in front of the open window for light, no air moved within the room. Around her, the other women sat silent as their fingers pushed their needles through the fabric with the tiniest of movements. Not even Bilah spoke, as if knowing it would only add to the oppressive heat.

"Which one of you is the embroiderer?"

Anna lifted her head to the girl in doorway. "I am."

"Queen Salome wants to see you in her sitting room." With that, the young girl left.

Anna sighed, knotted the thread to keep it from unraveling, and set the garment down.

"Would you like one of us to accompany you?" Tamar asked, wiping the sweat from her brow.

"She only wants to discuss the school, I am sure." Anna tutored the girls twice each week. Since its opening, Salome had requested regular meetings with her to learn how the girls were adapting. Anna grabbed her mantle, which she had removed because of the heat, and draped it over her head before venturing out into the hallway. Although deeper inside the palace, the air was cooler here away from the sun, until she started up the stone stairway to the next floor. With each step the temperature rose. A baking heat, not wet with moisture, but dry, searing and painful. She rested her hand on the marble wall at the top of the stairs, hoping to cool herself, with no success.

Ziva spotted her as Anna peered into the queen's sitting room. "Come in, child. Come in." Ziva waved her inside, her forehead glistening with perspiration.

Queen Salome reclined on the couch. Two young women stood behind her, waving palm branches over her head. Whatever breeze they created did not reach Anna, and seemed to do little to cool the queen. A wide band of sweat beaded across Salome's pale brow, but the queen's eyes sparked to life when she caught sight of Anna.

"Sit." Salome gestured to the chair opposite her. "Tell me how your students did this week."

"We were discussing the life of Abraham. Specifically the covenant God made with him."

They talked over the week's lesson as a servant brought them watered wine and dates. After an hour or so, the queen sat back on her couch. "I am pleased with the reports I hear from the rabbis. The girls are progressing well."

"I only wish we could convince a more learned rabbi to teach them."

"Do not belittle your contribution. It is true, a rabbi might have more knowledge, but you and the other women give the girls something unique."

"What is that?"

"An example." Salome's brown eyes held hers. "They have not known women of their own station to have studied as you and the others have. To have travelled, as you have. You let them see what has already been done, so that they may dream of doing something more."

Anna's heart warmed at the thought. "Thank you, Your Majesty, for having such faith in us."

"It is faith well earned." Salome's eyelids fluttered. "This heat tires me." She lifted her hand to cover a yawn. "I am traveling to Tyre tomorrow. Perhaps the sea will provide an ample breeze to keep me cool."

"I will pray for your safety while you are away."

"Thank you, child." She gave a brief wave. "You may go."

Anna bowed, even though the queen had settled even further back on her couch and closed her eyes. After most of her talks with the queen, Anna stayed to speak with Ziva, but her friend had already left to attend some errand or duty. She nodded toward the guards at the doorway before walking down the otherwise empty hallway. She turned the corner to head toward the servants' stairs.

"Wait."

Her heart missed a beat. *Aristobulus.*

The prince's fine linen robes made no sound as he approached her. Anna glanced around, suddenly aware of how alone they were in the dimly lit hall. She stepped back.

Aristobulus slowed. "Hold, little seamstress. I wish to speak with you."

Despite the heat, the hairs on the back of Anna's neck prickled. She took another step backward, but found she was now against the wall. She calculated how fast she could run to the stairs, but doubted she could reach them before the prince. She gathered her courage and lifted her chin. "What do you want?"

The corner of his mouth lifted. "So cold to your prince?"

Anna shivered, recognizing the look on his face. She had seen the same on cats in the streets as they stalked their prey. Her eyes darted again toward the stairwell.

The prince grabbed her arm. She tried to pull away, but he tightened his grip. "Do not run from me."

Her voice cracked. "Let me go."

"I let you go, and I will not get what I came for." With his other hand he pushed her against the wall.

Anna's body froze in fear as the prince pressed his body onto to hers. Even in the months since their betrothal, Caleb had done nothing more than hold her hand. Aristobulus lowered his head to hers but she turned away so his lips only brushed her cheek. She took in a breath to scream, but before the sound left her, he slapped his hand across her mouth with such force she bit her tongue.

"Scream, and I will do more than kiss you." He thrust her head back against the stone, sending a wave of pain down her back. Her mouth filled with the tang of blood. "If you fight me, I will drag you down this hallway to my private study. Do you understand?"

It took effort to move against the prince's hand, but she managed to nod.

"You are not the one I want to hurt. But I will if I have to." He kept his hand on her mouth, but let the other travel up her arm to her neck. His fingertips ran lightly from her collarbone to her chin. "At first I could not see what your friend Lev saw in you." A soft moan escaped his throat. "But now? This close to you, I think I understand." He pulled her mantle from her head, letting it slip to the floor as he fumbled to loosen her braid. "Was he ever this close to you?" His fingers grasped her hair. "Did you let him touch you like this?"

She struggled to shake her head even as tears rolled down her cheeks.

He pressed closer still, so that she could feel his breath against her ear, his chest touching hers. "Lev took something very valuable to me. And you, seamstress, are the only thing I know he wants, but cannot have. I have waited months for this opportunity." His free hand moved down her body to cup her breast. "The next time I see him, I will tell him how wonderfully soft your skin felt against mine. And how sweet you tasted on my tongue."

He removed his hand, covering her mouth with his before she could scream. Frozen with shock, she winced as his lips bruised hers. His tongue invaded her mouth. *This is because of Lev? Because I was once foolish enough to think I loved him?* Anger flooded her body, filling her with strength. She reached out, took hold of the prince's face, and pushed him away. Her fingers dug into the soft flesh of his cheeks. His eyes widened but he tempered his surprise with a grin.

"Enough." She did not scream and her voice did not waver. "You have taken what you said you wanted. Leave me be."

"Indeed. And I am nothing if not a man of my word." He pulled her hands from his face, but then brought one to his lips. "Perhaps, when I am king, you will consider becoming one of my concubines?"

She slapped him with her free hand before fleeing down the servants' stairwell toward the safety of the sewing room. His laughter echoed after her. She brushed her hair from her eyes, realizing with horror that she had left her mantle behind. What would she tell the others? She could not admit what had happened. What if Caleb found out? What would he do?

With legs of lead, she turned back. She prayed that Aristobulus would be gone as she crept up the stairs. She paused to listen near the last step. All was quiet. She peeked around the corner.

The prince was gone, as was her mantle.

Now he had proof he had been alone with her. Touched her. Would he show it just to Lev? Or would he use it to ruin her before the queen? Before Caleb?

Her stomach lurched. She made it down the stairs and out into the courtyard before retching into a bush.

Shadows crept across the courtyard as Anna hid herself in an alcove. Caleb would be arriving at the sewing room, as he did every evening, to say goodnight. She must face him. Tell him what happened. But how?

Her hands trembled as she fought to re-braid her hair. Perhaps, if she did not look so disheveled, she might conceal all the prince had done. She wiped her face with the hem of her tunic then pinched her cheeks to give them color. She stepped into the fading light and shivered, though the air still hung hot. *No. I am no longer a child.* Under the law, Caleb was her husband, though the wedding had not yet taken place. He must be told what happened. To keep it from him would mean their marriage would be built on hidden truths. Lies. Something she could not bear.

With determined steps, she made her way to the sewing room. Most of the women had left for their homes, but Tamar and Mary stood in the corner, folding a newly made tunic between them.

"There is my sister!" Tamar rested her hands on her hips. "Spent the day being fanned with—" she stopped. "What has happened?"

Anna clenched her jaw, willing her tears not to fall again. She could not find her voice.

Mary's forehead was lined with worry. "Where is your mantle?"

Reaching out for the table, Anna steadied her shaking legs before lowering herself to a stool.

"Is it the heat?" Mary asked as she hurried over.

Tamar knelt in front of her. "Did something happen?" Anna longed to answer, but her lips seemed to have sewn themselves together. Tamar took her hand. "Sister, tell me."

Anna gathered her courage. She would speak of this only once. "Send for Caleb."

Tamar did not hesitate. While she was gone, Mary brought her a cup of watered wine. Anna sipped it, praying as she did that the wine, and the Lord, would give her strength. Tamar's voice sounded from the hallway.

"She left hours ago to attend the queen. She would not say what happened."

Caleb's shadow fell over Anna as he entered the room. The cup of wine rattled against the table when she set it down.

Caleb pushed another stool next to her and sat. "What is wrong?"

She looked up into his eyes. She could read his concern as her heart sank with the fear that he might reject her. "Whatever you think of me after this, know that I love you."

"And I love you." His brow furrowed as he waited for her to speak.

"Oh Caleb," her voice cracked. "I have been so careful. Always when I attend the princes or their wives, I ask someone to go with me." She looked to Tamar and Mary. "You know I speak the truth."

Tamar stood behind her brother. "It is true."

"But I never thought to be so cautious with the queen. I was foolish."

"The queen harmed you?" Caleb leaned forward and lifted her chin so he could see her face.

"No! Not her . . . But when I left her sitting room . . . Aristobulus . . ." she tried to turn her head away but Caleb's fingers held her firm. Choking out the words, she told him all that had happened in the hall. "I swear to you Caleb, he did no more than that, but I fear he will claim he did since he kept my mantle." She clutched his hands. "I am no harlot. I am still a maid. Please, believe me."

He pulled her to his chest. "I know you tell the truth." He held her as she sobbed against his shoulder. "You are not to blame." His arms stiffened even as the heat of his anger radiated off his skin. "But as your betrothed, I forbid you to live in the palace." He gently lifted her chin so he could see her face. "I will take you to your father's house tonight." The room spun around her, but Caleb would not let her collapse. "You are safe now. And I will see to it that no one harms you again."

Lev strode through the courtyard and swung open the door to his house. A servant he did not recognize ran toward him. "May I help you?"

"Who are you?"

The man straightened his shoulders. "I am Shem."

Lev took notice of the servant's muscled arms and broad back. "And what, exactly, are your duties?"

Shem's brow furrowed as he surveyed Lev. "Who asks?"

Lev would have pounded the insolent servant had the heat and his endless walking not exhausted him. "I am the master of this house." He shoved Shem out of the way. "Where is my wife?"

The man, now pale, sputtered, "I am sorry, Master. I am new and your arrival was not expected." He bowed at the waist as he scurried alongside him. "The mistress is in the courtyard with the children. Can I get you anything?"

"Wine." Lev strode through the threshold leading to the garden. He paused, struck by the scene before him. His three-year-old daughter, Tirzah, sat at her mother's feet, tossing leaves of the almond tree into the air so they fell around her head like raindrops. Sarai, who had just months before looked haggard and lost, now smiled and laughed like a young girl herself. The babe, Salome, suckled at her breast.

His heart softened for a moment, before a seed of jealousy sprouted in his thoughts. *What has caused this change? Has she found someone to replace me? Perhaps this Shem does more than protect the door?*

"Abba!" Tirzah jumped up, her brown eyes wide with happiness. Her dark brown curls flew behind her as she ran to him. She held her arms out to be picked up.

Although still prickled by the change in Sarai, his daughter's joy diverted his anger. He grinned as he lifted her. "You have grown so tall! You will be taller than me soon."

She kissed his cheek. "Mama says that you went away. Are you home now? Will you stay?"

He nuzzled his nose into her soft mane of hair. "Just for a few days."

She frowned as she thrust his head away. "You never stay." She pushed her lower lip out into an impressive pout. "You go too much."

He smiled, recognizing his own stubborn streak in his daughter. If only she were a son, he could groom her to work with him. "This time, I am going far away. But I promise to bring you back a gift." He set her down. "What would you like? A new dress? A fine doll?"

Her brows furrowed as she thought very hard. "A stylus and a wax tablet."

"Why would you want something like that?"

"So I can be like you."

His chest warmed with her words. Even with his long absences, she still loved him. Wanted to be like him. He glanced over to Sarai. She may not have been the wife of his choosing, but she had not reviled him to his daughter. For that, he should be grateful.

The gentle laughter fled from Sarai's face as he approached. Her eyes turned cold and gray. "You sent no message, my lord. I would have had the cook prepare something besides fish for dinner."

He stared at her a moment longer. Whatever backbone she had mustered withered under his scrutiny. She turned her gaze to the baby and the warmth returned to her smile. *She has found solace in the child, not a lover.* "You seem well."

Sarai lifted Salome to her shoulder, her cheeks blushing as she readjusted her shawl to cover her breast. "Our daughters bring me much pleasure."

Tirzah tugged on his arm. "Abba, come see! I can write like you." She pulled him over to an almond tree, pointing to the dirt underneath. "See! That is my name!"

Lev grinned at the crude lines scratched in the mud. "Not quite, but it is a very good attempt."

"I want to go to school, *Abba*. Like Miriam and Leah."

"And who are they?"

"Mama's maids."

"They came with me when we married, my lord." Sarai shifted the baby on her lap. "Miriam asked to attend the school that the queen opened, and I allowed it. She and Leah both. They go every other day so one is always here to help."

He nodded, remembering. The school opened soon after he had brought Nasrin to Jerusalem. He shook off the irritation the whore's name sent through him. "At what age can they attend?"

"I am not certain, but I believe it to be around their eighth or ninth year."

He tousled Tirzah's curls. "Well, now, you will have to wait a few years."

She batted his hand away. "You teach me."

"Perhaps I will. If Antipater and the High Priest do not keep me too busy." Shem approached and Lev took the cup of wine he offered. Tirzah ran back to scratch more letters into the dirt with a stick, and he turned his focus back to Sarai. Her hair was in intricate braids that wound around her head. Her cheeks were full and pink. The babe had probably rounded her stomach as well, but no matter. He had thought her too thin before, bedding her had been like sleeping with a skeleton. A little weight would not affect her body as it had Nasrin's.

"Is something wrong?" Sarai's brown eyes darted back to Salome's face.

"No." He watched as she stroked the baby's chin. "You are well now, since the child's birth?"

"Yes." Her cheeks blushed. "I am sorry for . . . my mind is at peace."

"And what brought on this change?"

She breathed in deeply. "Our daughters need me to be strong. And I have learned much from your mother."

Lev's heart quickened at the mention of Judith. "What has she taught you?"

Sarai would not meet his stare. "That if a woman is to survive, she must find the strength within herself to live. She cannot look to others to help her. Only herself. And God." She glanced up. "That is not to say I would not welcome your help." Just as quickly, she turned her gaze to the baby. "But I am learning to trust my instincts when it comes to running the household and raising our daughters."

"I am glad to hear it." He forced himself to smile. Now that he was out from under Nasrin's spell, he could see how abominably he had treated Sarai. Perhaps, if she could give him a son, he might be persuaded to return more often to their home.

"Do you need more wine? Or your feet washed?" She called a servant girl over and gave her the baby. "Fetch a bowl of water and some oil for the master's feet."

He tried not to be bothered by her frenetic desire to please him. "I need only the wine. Thank you."

Sarai's hands twitched in her lap as she sat, echoing the tenseness between them.

Lev lowered his head. Perhaps he had made the wrong decision in coming here. But at least Sarai would not ask him about Nasrin. That was a blessing.

"I have made you unhappy." Sarai's voice caught in her throat. "I am sorry."

"I am only tired." He lifted his eyes to hers. "My visit is long overdue." He did not enjoy the pangs of guilt throbbing in his chest. He may not love Sarai, but at least, once her initial despondency over Nasrin had passed, she had not sought to bring her father or his parents in to force him back home. She had taken care of his house and his children. He was not sure how much of a relationship he wanted with her, even now, but she was still his wife. If he was to have a legal heir, it would be through her.

He made short work of the wine in his goblet, swallowing it in three gulps. His months with Nasrin had taught him that a beautiful body and enthusiastic lovemaking did not keep him content. He needed something more. He held the goblet out and waited for Shem to refill it. He leaned toward his wife, keeping his voice low so Tirzah would not hear. "I would like, very much, to take you to bed tonight."

Sarai's cheeks flushed.

"I need a son."

Chapter 30

Spring, 70 B.C.

The journey to Petra, along with the endless bowing and supplications he had to make to King Aretas, left Lev weary and agitated. Months of political machinations, while exciting, left him mentally exhausted as well. His body ached. Every muscle was tight and sore as he rode his horse the final miles toward home.

Once he and the soldiers passed through the gate to lower Jerusalem, he dismounted and sent all but one guard back to the Baris Fortress. The streets in the lower quarter were too narrow to ride through easily. To the remaining soldier he gave a message to deliver to Antipater. "Tell him I will return to him first thing in the morning. But I seek to rest first and make myself presentable."

Lev walked mindlessly toward the lower quarter. He would let Nasrin wash the dirt of travel from his skin and ease his tired muscles. He had not often come down before sunset except on the Sabbath, so he was startled to see the evidence of everyday life in the streets. Children ran about kicking a leather ball. Women sat together in groups, gossiping while they mashed chickpeas or kneaded dough. The aroma of garlic tickled his nose and caused his stomach to rumble.

As he turned toward Nasrin's house, the women on the corner stopped talking to stare at him. One bent down to speak into another's ear, and soon all five chattered together like tiny birds in a tree at sunset. He shook off the strange sense of foreboding but glanced back and saw them watching as he lifted his hand to knock on Nasrin's door. He stopped before his knuckles hit the wood. Their faces told him what waited inside. He kicked open the door.

Grandmother Masha screamed and dropped the bowl she stirred. Yellow couscous splattered as the bowl rolled across the floor. The curtain to Nasrin's pallet was drawn closed.

"You did not tell us you were coming, my lord!" The old woman rushed to greet him.

Lev knew the sounds of a rutting man when he heard them. The grunting of one too far into the act to stop, no matter what the interruption.

"My granddaughter is not home!" She tried to steer him to the door. "Come back later. I will fetch—"

He flung her away, surprised at how light she was under his grasp, how far she flew across the room. She hit the stone wall, collapsing to the floor in a heap.

The moans in Nasrin's alcove stopped.

Lev ripped the curtain from the doorway, revealing the truth he already knew. Nasrin lay naked beneath a fat man with his tunic drawn up to his waist. The man's piggy eyes stared at him, rounded with shock.

"I paid two silver pieces for her." The stranger gestured to the other room. "The old woman said that was the girl's price."

Lev took hold of the man's tunic and pulled him off Nasrin.

"I paid for her!" the man cried. He thrashed a fist toward Lev. "I want my money back!"

"So do I," Lev muttered as he dragged the man across the front room and pushed him out to the street. He slammed the door then turned back to deal with Nasrin.

"At least give me my robe!" the stranger shouted from outside. He pounded on the door. "And my purse!"

Lev strode over to Nasrin's pallet, grabbed the man's possessions from the floor then flung them outside. "If you ever come here again, I will kill you."

The man scurried to pick his things off the ground before stumbling up the street. The clutch of women still stood at the corner, watching. Lev growled as he stepped back into the house.

Nasrin sat in the corner of her room. She pulled a blanket up to her chin to cover her nakedness, reminding him of Eve in the Garden. But her face did not show embarrassment or remorse as it should.

Grandmother Masha called out something in Persian.

Nasrin stirred at the words, her face finally reflecting the fear Lev knew she should feel. He grinned with satisfaction as her eyes darted about the room, seeking some kind of escape. He easily caught her arm when she tried to dash past him and shoved her against the table. Lev's blood boiled under his skin, but he refused to let it dictate his actions. He had learned much studying how Aristobulus and Antipater dealt with anger. Seldom did they show it. His focus turned to Masha when she moaned on the floor by the hearth. A small pool of blood puddled by her head. He had lost control once this evening. He would not do it again.

"Whore," he made sure his voice was gentle, even as he thrust his finger in her face. "Whatever spell you and your grandmother put on me has been broken. I will no longer play the fool for you."

"P-p-please, my lord," Nasrin stuttered. "I feared you would not return."

"That is the most coherent thought you have ever spoken to me," Lev sneered. "But your fear now should be what I will do now that I am back."

"Please." Tears streaked with kohl made black rivers on her cheeks. "Help my grandmother."

"You help her." He backed away from her.

Nasrin watched him with wide eyes as she slowly stood up. She paused, as if waiting to see if he would grab her again, then scurried over to the hearth.

Lev strode over to a niche in the wall and took out an elaborately carved wooden box. Setting the box on the table, he paused. "I will tell you what will happen now."

He withdrew a piece of paper, the lease he had negotiated for their house. The one that proved his ownership of the property. It was time the harlot pay him back for all he had given her.

Anna dried herself with the towel Tova held out for her. "I worry about wearing my wedding gown. What if I ruin it?"

Bilah let out a hearty laugh. "Do not fear. Caleb will be more than willing to make the celebration a quick one if you tell him that!"

Around the room, the other women joined in the merriment. Tamar and her eldest daughter Ruth, along with Mary and Tova, attended Anna as her companions on this, her wedding day. After much pleading, her father had compromised on the length of their betrothal, allowing them to marry after only nine months. The time had passed slowly, like honey poured on a hot summer evening. Now that the day was here, however, it seemed to Anna like she had only blinked the months away.

Tamar and Bilah anointed her skin with fragrant oils, specially purchased for this night. The aroma of jasmine and roses wafted through the tiny house. Once she had been properly perfumed, Ruth and Mary helped Anna slip on the first of her garments, a linen tunic.

Ruth sighed as she touched the embroidery along the tunic's neckline. Woven with gold and silver thread, the intricate pattern of lines resembled grape vines tangled on a hillside. "It is a shame no one will see your handiwork. It is so beautiful."

Again, Bilah chuckled. "I do not think Caleb will even notice it tonight."

Anna blushed. Her married friends had all told her what to expect in the marriage bed, but each had a different tale. Anna suspected Caleb had been with other women—after all, he was much older and had been away at war. She knew men often took women as their reward for a well fought battle. But would this make him more, or less, forceful in bed? She shivered, even in the oppressive heat.

Tamar took her hand to lead her to a stool, whispering in Anna's ear as she did, "Do not worry. My brother has the tenderest heart of any man I have ever known. He will be gentle."

Relief spread though Anna's muscles as Mary brushed her hair. Ruth rubbed oil onto Anna's feet as the other women spread out the precious stones that would be woven into her hair. Anna had bought pearl and jade beads herself. The others who had been married brought their own treasures for her to borrow. Beads of amethyst and onyx, garnet and silver, gold and lapis spilled over the table. In the afternoon light, the jewels sparkled and gleamed.

The women took turns braiding the stones into Anna's hair, the process taking several hours. Oil lamps were lit as the sun set and evening drew close. Anna's heart began to beat faster. Once night came, her bridegroom could arrive at any time to take her to his home. She must be ready, once he knocked, to leave. What if he came now? Before she had put on her gown?

Anna fidgeted on the stool. "Are you finished yet?"

"Patience." Tamar yanked on yet another strand of hair. "As excited as my brother is to take you as his wife, I warned him not to come too early."

After what seemed like an eternity, the women stood back to admire their handiwork. Anna suspected she looked beautiful by their sighs and nods, but all the beads made her hair feel like it weighed ten pounds. She hoped she could keep her head upright throughout the festivities.

Bilah and Tova held out the formal tunic for Anna to wear. She stepped into the linen fabric that she had woven herself with Egyptian flax and gold thread. It shimmered in the flickering flames of the oil lamps. Mary tied the ribbons at Anna's neck to keep the gown in place. Tamar and Tova then placed the heavier wool robe over her shoulders. Anna slipped her arms into its sleeves. The robe's deep russet color and gold threads made her feel as beautiful as any queen. The women came forward to place so many rings and bracelets on her that Anna wondered if she would be able to walk to Caleb's house or whether they would have to find a wagon to carry her there.

Once they were satisfied they could not put another piece of jewelry on her, the women again stepped away to look at her. Tova picked up the last item on the table. A pearl and garnet headdress. Phanuel and Daniel had bought it as a special gift. Tears filled Anna's eyes. How she wished her mother could see this day.

Tova shook her head. "No tears. The kohl around your eyes will streak." She carried the headdress over and positioned it over Anna's lavishly braided hair. "I'll go next door to let Phanuel and Daniel know you are ready, so they can wait for Caleb in the street."

Tamar fastened the veil of Egyptian gauze and gold thread onto the headdress so that Anna's face would be hidden until her father removed it at Caleb's house. "Now, Sister, you are ready for your groom."

The women all cheered. Bilah poured a cup of wine and passed it to Anna. "Quiet your nerves, take a few sips."

Anna slid the cup under her veil and lifted it to her lips, surprised her hands did not shake. Instead, a sense of peace filled her. Adonai had answered her prayers.

Her friends shared another cup of wine. Their laughter sang throughout the crowded room, but Anna heard none of their jokes, so focused was she on what this night signified.

The moment she left her father's home, she would cease to be who she had been all her life. This humble room would no longer be her home. She would be Caleb's wife. His home would be hers. And, God willing, it would be the home where they would raise their children. Her heart soared at the thought.

Three knocks thundered through the room, silencing the other women's chatter.

Phanuel's voice echoed in the silence. "Who comes to the door of my house? What is your purpose?"

Anna's heart fluttered as Caleb answered, "I, Caleb bar Reuben, come to your house to seek my beloved. My bride."

Tova glanced at Anna. "Are you ready?"

Anna could not breathe to answer so she nodded instead.

The others stood in lines on either side of the door, whispering words of love, touching her arm or shoulder as Anna walked between them. Tova opened the door.

Caleb's gasp at seeing her matched her own at his appearance. A myriad of torches blazed around him, reflecting off the gold threads of the robe she had embroidered for him. The linen, cream with a russet yolk and shoulder panels, decorated with colorful flowers and gold stripes, shimmered. He wore a golden cap, adorned with pearls and crystal stones. No king could have been dressed as fine. His eyes filled with tears. The people around him inhaled as one as they waited for Caleb to speak.

"Beloved," his voice cracked. He swallowed before trying again. "My beloved, will you come home with me and be my bride?"

Anna's heart threatened to burst within her chest. "I will."

The crowd, which had been silent in expectancy, roared with a great shout. Several shook timbrels, their metallic cymbals jingling in celebration. Another struck up a lively tune on a wooden flute as Caleb took hold of Anna's hand and led her out into the night. Everything around her; the flames of the torches and oil lamps that accompanied them through the dark streets, the shouts of joy from those assembled, the colors of the tunics around her; all seemed brighter, louder, and more beautiful than anything she had seen before. She concentrated on Caleb, gripping his hand tightly so as to ground herself in the moment and not let her mind get overwhelmed as she turned the corner to begin the walk up the hill to his house.

Lev wandered for hours through the dimly lit streets of the lower city with no purpose and no destination. Antipater would ask too many questions about why he was not visiting the whore since traveling to Petra, and that was a conversation he did not want to have.

He pushed away any more thoughts about that afternoon as he passed through the gate leading into the upper city. His mother had been right. The girl was only a common harlot. He had been a fool to pay what he had for her.

"Mind your step!"

Lev had not expected the road to be crowded at this time of night, but a mass of people blocked his way. The torches and music indicated a celebration of some kind. He surveyed his surroundings as he had no idea where he had walked. Even with the oil lamps and torches, it was difficult to get a clear look at the buildings around him.

A flash of light caught his attention. From one of the side streets came a man and a woman, both bejeweled and robed as royalty. *A wedding.* Poor souls, to think that marriage could bring them happiness.

As the people let out loud ululations of joy, something about the groom's walk piqued Lev's brain. The man favored one leg, his gait off balance. Lev's stomach knotted. He pushed his way through the crowd to get a closer look at the couple before they turned away from him.

The crippled tailor. It has to be him. Although the man's rich robes and handsome face almost confused Lev, there could be no doubt. Lev turned his gaze to the bride. A veil covered her face and hair, hiding her identity, but Lev knew.

"Anna," he whispered. His heart rose to his throat, making it almost impossible for him to breathe. He scanned the crowd around the couple and found his proof. Daniel and Phanuel strode behind them.

The mob engulfed him, forcing him to walk up the hill amid their dancing and singing. His feet moved without thought, his eyes glued to Anna. She held the tailor's hand. She did not seem to mind his listing walk. Occasionally, her head turned toward the cripple, and he smiled down at her. Lev could see the man's lips moving, *speaking what to her?* Was she forced into this unholy marriage? Was the cripple reminding her of whatever bargain he had made with Phanuel? Lev turned his heated gaze to her father. How could he allow this monstrosity to wed Anna?

They walked uphill and wound through several more streets until they reached a road with rows of houses on either side. A canopy had been set up outside one of the doorways and the couple stopped underneath. Phanuel stepped forward and drew the veil from his daughter's face.

Lev stared in disbelief as the rest of the crowd went silent. Anna's beauty overwhelmed them all. She had not painted herself with rouge, but her eyes sparkled in the torchlight as she looked on her groom. Her long, brown hair had been braided with gemstones so radiant as to create a halo around her head.

Phanuel spoke words and placed Anna's veil around the tailor's shoulders, but Lev could hear nothing save the pounding of the blood in his ears. *This could have been me. I could have had her as my bride.* She looked on the cripple as she had once looked at him. Even now, he sensed her passion. *She loves him? Could it be true? Could she love the cripple?* She lifted her face toward him, her smile so pure, her face full of joy, even as the tailor lowered his head toward her to place a gentle kiss on her lips.

Wanting to run away, but unable to stop watching, Lev stumbled back as the people around him cheered.

"I thought I would find you here." His father's voice spoke into his ear. "Still panting after the scribe's daughter? After all this time?"

Malachi stood at Lev's side, his mouth set in a sneer. Lev spun on his heels, desperate to get away from him, away from this celebration, and find somewhere quiet where he could sit alone with a full sack of wine and forget this day ever happened.

His father grabbed his arm. "We must talk."

Lev looked over his shoulder in time to see the tailor lead Anna into his house. His muscles numbed, as if he had fallen into a freezing river. *The cripple will take her to his bed. He will touch her as I never could.*

Malachi dragged him down the street. "You are acting like a school boy, not a grown man. Enough of this." His father muttered nonsensical words as Lev faltered alongside him, the numbness of his body filling his brain. He had accomplished so much in his life, but now, all he wanted was Anna. Nothing else mattered.

They arrived at his father's house and Malachi shoved him through the gate, then dragged him into the library. Lev collapsed onto one of the wooden stools.

"Act like the powerful man you brag you have become." His father slapped his cheek.

The sharp sting cut through Lev's fog. He started to push himself up, but Malachi shoved him back. "I have suffered your behavior long enough. Your refusal to come to dinner, to speak with me. I am still your father, and you are bound to honor me."

"Honor you?" Bile churned in Lev's belly. "For what? All that I have gained I did on my own. Without you. The one thing that would have made my life perfect, you stole from me."

"Perfect?" Malachi spat the word. "No life is perfect. Nor is any woman, you fool. You have a wife who can give you everything you need."

Lev barked out a harsh laugh as he compared Sarai to Anna. "That shivering leaf of a girl gives me nothing. She is useless."

"At least she can bear children."

"Daughters." Lev shook his head. "What use are girls to me?"

"Then bed her until she gives you a son." Malachi's cheeks reddened. "It is your duty to this family."

"I owe you nothing."

"It is God's law—"

"Your God, not mine." Lev's shoulders rounded as he finally gave into his body's exhaustion. "Believe in Adonai if you must, but I know it is all superstitions and ritual, designed to make some richer and more powerful than others."

Malachi's eyes narrowed. "You betray your faith? Your heritage?" He pointed a finger into Lev's face. "It is that heathen you serve. He has done this!"

Lev snorted. "No, it was you who showed me the truth."

Malachi was speechless. His mouth hung open as he stared at his son.

"All my life I watched you speak the word of God for your own benefit. You prospered as you manipulated it to say what you wanted." Lev rested his elbows on his knees and leaned forward. "And when someone stood in your way, blocked your purposes, you used money and power to knock them down. Religion is your tool and your livelihood." He choked on the sour vomit his stomach longed to spew. "At least I am honest about my desire for power. I do not prey on the weak and gullible. I have the courage to throw my lot in with those already in control and seek to move them to my will."

Malachi grabbed the front of Lev's tunic and drew him up. "Do not think you are better than me. You are nothing but a slave in your master's house, living off the crumbs he deigns to give you."

"I am no man's slave." Lev pried his father's hands away. "When this city falls, I alone will be in a position to save you. And on that day, I will remember the night you told me you would ruin me if I insisted on taking Anna as my wife." Lev took a step back and hoped his face portrayed the dismissiveness he felt. "On that day, when you come crawling to me for help, I will turn you away as you were so willing to turn me away. As this city goes up in flames, you will burn. You, and all you have held on to so tightly, will disappear in the ashes, and I will think of you no more."

Lev smiled at the lightness in his chest. If only he had gathered his courage to stand up to Malachi years before. He took one more look at his father's pale face. "Until that day, I will not see you again."

BOOK THREE

Circa 68 B.C. — 67 B.C.

A time for war

Chapter 31

Summer, 68 B.C.

Anna sat in the courtyard of the school with her back against the trunk of a sycamore tree. Its shade provided little relief from the oppressive summer heat. Around her sat the young girls she taught two afternoons a week. Her charges were bright and eager, although today most were sluggish from the weather.

"Come now," she scolded them gently. "Surely you must have questions. You cannot understand everything about the Feasts after one lesson."

A loud yawn escaped from thin Susannah before she clapped her hand over her mouth. "I am sorry. It is just so hot."

Bayla piped up, her thick golden curls lying flat against her head. "What does God mean when He says the Feasts are signs?"

Anna shifted to accommodate her rounding belly. "What do you think He means?"

Bayla's eyes narrowed as she thought hard. "Is it a sign for us? Like a reminder of something?"

Anna nodded, tracing her fingers over her stomach, hoping she might feel the child she carried move under her hand. "But a reminder of what? Is it of something in the past? Or something to come?"

"If it is something to come, then does that mean He will one day celebrate the festivals Himself?"

Now it was Anna's turn to think hard. "I had never thought of that, but the text certainly implies that, does it not?"

One of the youngest girls, Adine, yanked up blades of grass. She often seemed distracted, but Anna had learned she was actually listening very closely to everything being said. "Has he not already performed the Passover Feast? In Egypt?"

Susannah stifled another yawn before she spoke. "But God did not sacrifice the lamb, our fathers did."

Adine looked up from the grass. "Do you think He will come down and kill a lamb? Is that what will happen?"

In the two years that Anna had been teaching, none of the girls had ever pondered this question. She had often wondered at the significance of the Feasts, but had never been able to articulate it like these students.

"Anna?" Adine wiped her hands on her tunic. "What do you think?"

She smiled at the youngster. "I am not sure. God does not always explain Himself, does He?"

"But why make us celebrate them?" Bayla asked. "If not to prepare us for something?"

Susannah's eyes brightened, no longer dulled by the heat. "They are to remind us of all He has done and continues to do for us."

"Very good," Anna said. "And how do they do that?"

The girls spent the next hour listing the different Festivals and how each celebrated an aspect of Adonai and His provision, grace and salvation. Caleb strode out to the courtyard as they finished discussing the Feast of the Tabernacles. Little Adine squealed and ran to meet him. He patted her on the head and greeted the others.

"I did not mean to disturb your discussion. The palace grew too warm to work. I thought to stop here on my way home to see if you were done for the day."

Anna lifted her arm to him. "I think we have exhausted ourselves on the topic of the Festivals. At least for the moment."

Caleb helped her to her feet, kissing her hand as the girls stood and called their goodbyes. "How are you feeling, my love?"

She rested her cheek against his chest, enjoying the sound of his heart beating so strongly within. "I am well, but tired."

"Shall we go home now so you can rest?" As she nodded, his rough tunic rubbed her skin. He wrapped his arms around her, cocooning her in his strength. "Do you know what I am today?"

"What are you today?" she asked, although she knew his answer. He asked her this every night, whether they walked home together from the palace or from the school.

"I am so very happy," his breath caressed her head.

"Why are you so very happy?" she whispered in response.

"Because God has blessed me with you, my love." He shifted his hand to her stomach. "And He has blessed your womb with our child."

She snuggled closer to him. "I pray He continues to bless it so that this baby will be strong enough to keep growing within me."

"Do not fret. God will allow this child to live."

A chill ran through her, even in the afternoon's warmth. "What if—"

"Hush now," Caleb soothed. "Enjoy this moment. This day. Do not look for worries."

She breathed in deeply, taking in the comforting smell of him, sweat and wool, and incense from the temple.

"Now, talk with me about your lesson today," Caleb said as he slipped his arm around her shoulder. "So that I may be as wise as you."

They walked arm-in-arm to their home, the same house Caleb had lived in before they wed. He had expanded it to include the room next door so that now a half-wall separated their bed from the dining table and cooking hearth. They shared a courtyard in the back with several neighbors and, in exchange for their skills with the needle, their neighbor Mava made them a loaf of bread each day.

The aroma of garlic from the lentil soup Anna had left simmering over the embers in the morning greeted them when they opened the door. Mava's loaf sat in the middle of their table, along with a small date cake.

Caleb lit a wick with the embers and used it to light the oil lamps. "She is already spoiling our child. The poor thing will be fat as an ox if she keeps bringing it cakes to eat."

Anna gave him a playful smack. "Are you suggesting I am as large as a cow?"

"Not yet." He smirked. "But soon."

She took their wooden bowls down from the niche in the wall. "If this baby is large, it will be *your* fault. My family are all small in stature."

Caleb embraced her from behind as she spooned up the soup. His hands caressed her stomach. "I do not care if this child is as big as a horse or as small as a rabbit. I am just so thankful that God has blessed us with a baby."

Although his words brought her joy, a shiver ran down her spine. "I pray every day He will let me carry this one to life."

"You are already further along than the last two." Caleb bent down to kiss her neck. "Do not dwell on the past. This one will live. I know it."

Anna broke free from his hug to set the bowls on the table. "Should I bring water in or will you wash with me outside?"

"I will wash with you."

Together they went out to the courtyard and used the water from the communal cistern to wash their hands before the meal. Back in the house, Caleb said the blessing and broke off a piece of bread for them both.

Anna dipped her bread in her bowl to gather some soup. "Tell me about your day. Is there any news from the palace?"

"Helena and Joanna would both like to see us tomorrow."

"New robes for Tabernacles again?"

He spooned up a mouthful of stew. "That would be my guess. Helena has loved the last two you made for her. Joanna is sure to have heard of your skill now that she has moved here to Jerusalem."

Anna lowered her hand to her lap, hoping Caleb would not notice how it trembled.

He watched her closely as he swallowed. "I will be with you."

Her cheeks flamed with heat, even now, at her humiliation in the hands of Aristobulus. Adonai had blessed her with a merciful husband. Another man, like Nathanel, could have had her brought up on charges before the Sanhedrin. After all, she had not screamed.

Caleb came to her side, drew her up, and embraced her. "You were not to blame. And I will keep you safe now."

They finished their simple meal in conversation. Caleb insisted on washing their bowls out in the courtyard for her. "You need to rest. Keep your strength."

If she were not so tired she would argue with him, but her ankles were swollen and a sharp pain radiated across her back. She undid her sandals, took off her outer tunic, and then settled down on their pallet. Caleb hummed while he worked. She recognized the tune as one of King David's songs. He stopped when he returned.

Anna shifted on the floor. "What is wrong?"

"Nothing." He continued to stare down at her. "You are just so beautiful. I had to tell Adonai again how grateful I am for you." He put away the bowls and snuffed out the lamps. He crawled in next to her.

Anna slid over so her head rested on his chest. "Sing me a song of thankfulness to lull me to sleep."

His deep voice resonated through the night, easing the pain in her back and the worry on her heart.

A shaft of bright light sliced through Anna's dreams. She blinked, trying to make sense of the intrusion. She rolled to her side to reach for Caleb, but found his spot empty. Voices muttered and she fought to clear her head.

"Go back to sleep, my love," Caleb whispered. "Never mind us."

Anna forced her eyelids open. Caleb knelt by the bed, and the willowy form of his niece, Ruth, came into view. "Is something wrong?"

He brushed her hair off her face. "Nothing at all. I asked Ruth to come fetch the water from the well for you." Anna started to lift herself up but Caleb laid his hand on her shoulder. "Tamar does not need her now, and you could do with the help."

"I can do it myself." Anna pushed against him to no avail.

"I know you can, but why not let Ruth help so that you may have some more rest?" He left off trying to hold her back and instead, cupped her face. "You work so much . . . at the palace, at the school . . . let us do this for you."

The concern in his eyes convinced her to accept his pampering. At least for this one morning. She would need all her strength and wits to deal with the two princesses today.

It seemed like only seconds later, Caleb knelt by her side and stroked her hair. "My love, it is time now."

Anna moaned. "Time for what?"

He chuckled. "To go to the palace."

"Already?"

His fingertips trailed underneath her chin, tickling gently. She squirmed at his touch, but it energized her enough to open her eyes.

"There you are." His brows knit together with worry as he stared down at her "Do you feel well enough to walk to the palace today? Or should I tell the princesses you are too tired?"

Anna caressed his arm. "I am well enough to attend to them. I only need a moment to wake up properly."

He brought her hand to his lips and kissed it. "Should I wait for you?"

A yawn escaped as she answered, "No. You go on ahead."

"Come to the tailors' room when you arrive, and I will send a messenger to Joanna and Helena that we can attend them at their pleasure." He leaned over to kiss her lips. "Take your time."

Once Caleb and Ruth had left her, Anna rose from her bed and stretched, taking measure of how her body felt this morning. She had rested well in the night, but her back still ached. After washing herself and putting on a new tunic, she sat at the table to enjoy a piece of bread and cheese. She bowed her head first, praying, "Hear, O Israel, the Lord your God, the Lord is one. I thank you, Adonai, for your many blessings. For my husband and for this child. Lord, bless them and keep them well. Help me through this day to be ever mindful of your presence. Help me to obey your commands." She ate her simple meal and made her way up to the palace, letting Caleb know of her arrival before settling in to make the priests' robes with the other seamstresses.

Caleb came for her several hours later. "Helena is ready to see us now."

Anna secured her needle in the material before standing up, wincing as a sharp pain spread across her back. She caught her balance on the table.

Caleb hurried over to her side. "Are you well?"

The pain passed as she breathed deeply. "I must have stood too quickly." She smiled up at him. "Do not worry."

His sister, Tamar, clucked, "Men think we are so weak, and yet we are the ones Adonai chose to carry their children." She glared over at her brother. "Relax."

Anna took Caleb's arm. "Come. Let us see what the princess wants this time." For the past two years, she and Caleb had made Helena a new robe for the Feast of Tabernacles. Joanna, John Hyrcanus's wife, was a bit more frugal. They had only made one new robe for her, but Anna knew Joanna had clothes made in Jericho, as well.

As they entered the wing of the palace reserved for the noble's private rooms, two young boys raced down the hallway. The taller one appeared to be about twelve-years-old. His dark hair fell in curls down to his shoulders. Another boy, maybe seven, chased after him. Caleb pulled Anna toward the wall as the boys barreled past them and around the corner. A haggard looking man peered out of a doorway ahead.

"Did you see which way they went?"

"Down that way." Caleb pointed.

The man scratched his graying head. "I suppose they will be back. It is no use chasing them." He surveyed Caleb. "I do not suppose you are the princes' new tutor of Greek?"

"Sorry," Caleb shook his head. "I am a tailor."

The man let out a long sigh as he returned to his room. "Ah, well . . . ."

Caleb glanced down at Anna. "Our child will be better behaved than the two princes, I promise you that."

"You will train him up well."

They entered Helena's favorite room. At least Anna presumed it was her favorite, as it was where she usually found Aristobulus's wife. Their feet whispered as they crossed the marble floor. Helena sat along the edge of the giant reflecting pool in the middle of the room, dangling her hand in the water.

"It is oppressive." Helena brought her fingers to her throat and let the water trickle down her bare neck. "This heat. How I wish we could go to Joppa, where the sea air cools the land." She sat up as Anna and Caleb approached, surveying them. "No one told me you were with child. Will you be able to finish my robe before the babe comes?"

"I believe so." Anna bowed her head. "With my husband's help."

"I want something in blue this time. Can you find the proper dyes?"

"Of course. What shade would you prefer?" Anna felt Caleb stiffen next to her as they waited for Helena to answer. Queen Salome usually wore a deep violet for public appearances. To wear something similar might be seen as an act of defiance.

"Something dark and rich. Like the night sky." Her mouth curled up in a smile as she watched them. "You may place a stripe or two of a lighter shade, so no one mistakes me for Ari's mother."

Anna removed her measuring string from its pouch at her waist. "And the style?"

They spent the next hour discussing the robe's cut and embroidery before they took their leave and made their way down the hall to Joanna's private room.

Like her husband, Joanna seemed happiest being out of public display. She sat watching her daughter, Alexandra, struggle to play a tune on the lute. A balding man leaned over to position the young girl's fingers on the instrument's strings.

"Again, Your Highness."

The girl, about thirteen-years-old, furrowed her brows in concentration and strummed the lute. A harsh, discordant note echoed throughout the room. Anna tried not to cringe as Alexandra looked up in horror at the intrusion.

"Who are you?"

Caleb and Anna bowed as he answered, "We are the tailor and seamstress your mother sent for."

"Ah, yes." Joanna stood. "Alexandra, you will stay here and practice with your tutor." She gestured to Anna and Caleb with her ringed hand. "Follow me. We can use the family sitting room for our work."

They followed the slender woman into a sedate room decorated with plush couches and thick, colorful rugs. The windows were open, but no breeze blew. The afternoon sun provided the only light. "Will this be bright enough?" Joanna asked. "I do so hate to light torches and lamps. Even a little flame seems to add to the heat." She lowered herself to one of the couches and gestured Anna and Caleb toward one opposite. She pulled a lock of her light brown hair off her neck. "I heard Aristobulus's wife has also requested your services. Is that true?"

Anna used Caleb's hand to steady herself as she sat. "Yes, your highness."

"I suppose she wants something in dark blue again." Joanna's voice was soft, but Anna could hear the edge in it. "Always she tries to make herself look like the queen."

"There is only one queen," Caleb said as he lowered himself next to Anna. "We will make that apparent."

"I do not need to be in blue or purple. I know I will be the next queen. It has already been decreed." She spoke with quiet dignity. "I have always found I look best in more russet and golden hues."

Anna leaned forward as they discussed Joanna's gown in more detail. They had settled on the style and cut of the robe when the door swung open.

"I do not want to hear it, Antipater." John Hyrcanus strode into the room. His hair had thinned even more since Anna had last seen him, and his stomach was almost as round as hers. "My brother will not betray our mother."

The tall Idumaean followed behind the prince, his dark skin glistening with perspiration. "Do not ignore the rumor I have heard, Your Highness. Let me at least send Lev to investigate."

John and Antipater continued their argument but Anna's concentration was on Lev's entrance. He did not notice her, his gaze focused exclusively on his master and the prince. She had seen him, from a distance, only a few times since her marriage. Caleb reached for her hand and clutched it tightly. She tried to reassure him with a squeeze of her fingers. Although Lev was still a handsome man with broad shoulders and thick, dark curls of hair, he no longer had any hold over her emotions. She noticed a hardness in his features now.

For a moment, it seemed as if a shadow obscured them. Anna blinked, sure that the dim light had played a trick on her sight.

Joanna stood, surprising the men. "Husband, I am sorry. I did not know you would be using the sitting room today."

John smiled when he saw his wife. "Nonsense." He opened his arms wide and embraced her lightly. "You are a welcome distraction." He stepped back, taking notice of Anna and Caleb, his brow furrowing as if he tried to recall if he should know them.

Joanna bowed her head. "I am having a new robe made for the Feast of Tabernacles this year. Do you mind?"

"Of course not! Perhaps I will have something new made as well." He motioned toward Caleb. "What say you, tailor?"

Anna kept her gaze on the prince, but could feel Lev's eyes on her as she and Caleb stood to bow. Caleb and John walked to another couch while Anna and Joanna sat to discuss her choices. As Joanna had much simpler tastes than either Helena or John Hyrcanus, she described her thoughts concisely and left Anna while she went to sit with her husband and Caleb.

Anna knew without looking up when Lev approached.

He whispered from behind her. "You married the cripple."

She did not turn around. "I married Caleb, tailor to the nobility of Israel and the finest man I know."

When he did not comment right away, she thought perhaps he had left her, but a glance over her shoulder proved her wrong.

The lines in his face softened as he looked at her. "Are you happy?"

A rush of joy filled her as she thought about the life she shared with Caleb. "I am very happy." The hardness returned to his eyes, and her joy turned to sadness. "Are you?"

Before he could answer, a guard called from the doorway, "My lord, the queen requests you attend her in her sitting room. Your advisors as well."

John gave his wife a quick kiss on her cheek. "My mother calls. I will dine with you tonight and tell you all her news."

Lev nodded toward Anna. "Please send my greetings to your father and Daniel."

Anna folded her hands across her stomach. Her heart ached, not because she grieved the life she might have had with Lev, but for the despair that emanated from his soul. He may be far richer and have more power than she and Caleb would ever know, but she sensed it had not brought him the contentment he had longed for in his youth.

Joanna seemed surprised that Anna and Caleb remained. She waved her hand toward them. "You may leave me now."

Caleb helped Anna to her feet. He waited to speak until they were alone in the hallway. "You seem . . . distracted."

The crease between his brows indicated his concern. She tried to smile, but felt her lips falter. "I am worried for Lev. There is some shadow that hangs over him."

Caleb's brows drew even closer together. "You care for him still?"

She stopped walking. "Only as one cares for an old friend."

Caleb snorted his disgust. "He is not a good man. If you had heard the rumors I have heard, you would not worry. You would forget him."

"I have heard the gossip." She stepped up and placed her hand on his shoulder. "Husband, you know I love you, and you alone. But Lev was once my brother's best friend. And his mother was kind to mine, providing her with herbs to ease her headaches. I know it must pain Judith to have her son so far from the Lord." She leaned against his chest. "Perhaps, on our way home tonight, we might stop and see Daniel and Tova? Maybe my brother could be persuaded to talk to his old friend and bring him to repentance."

Caleb kissed the top of her head. "You are too good for me, my love. Your heart cares too deeply, even for those who have hurt you."

She lifted her eyes to his. "But when I met you, all those hurts were forgotten. You have healed every last one."

Queen Salome Alexandra had aged. Lev had heard vague rumors about her health. He considered them false when she rallied herself to journey to Damascus and broker a peace with the Armenian, Tigranes. Even Antipater had been impressed with her political maneuverings, how she had effectively ransomed Israel, ensuring her country's safety while Tigranes went on to conquer Damascus and behead Queen Selene.

But observing her now, Lev suspected Salome was as ill as the gossips whispered. The queen's thick silver hair was now thin and white. Dark circles nested under her eyes. The robe she wore dripped off her body like melted candle wax, pooling on the floor at her feet. She shuffled when she walked. Even still, with these new impediments, her voice carried strength and authority. She glared at John Hyrcanus with fury. "What have you done?"

"They needed to be banished." The High Priest surveyed the room for support. Antipater looked away. The prince's gaze landed on Shimeon. John thrusted his arm out in the Pharisee's direction. "He said they were plotting against you."

Salome turned her ire toward her advisor. "What proof did you have? Was there a trial?"

"Sister," Shimeon's voice was low and condescending. "The Sadducees have always been your enemy—"

She gripped the back of a chair for support as she took a step toward him. "There is a difference between disgruntled talk behind closed doors and actual treasonous plots." Her breath rattled loudly, like the crackling of dead leaves. She paused to cough, thick and wet with mucus. "But to exile so many . . . without a trial . . . ." Her chest heaved with exertion. "You have given them a reason to actually make good on their threats to revolt."

John puffed out his chest. "They would not dare."

Lev avoided rolling his eyes, not wanting to show any sign of disrespect. But in truth, he had no respect for John Hyrcanus. The man had no idea what it took to lead a nation, even though he had been playing at the role for over a year.

The queen glared at her son. "Then where is your brother now?"

John's brows furrowed. "I . . . he . . . is he not here? In Jerusalem?"

Salome shook her head slowly. "That is what he wanted us to believe. His scheming wife even sent messengers making excuses to me on his behalf when I requested he attend me." The wracking cough roared up again. A servant brought her a bowl to spit in. Her lip curled in disgust but she spewed the wad of mucus from her throat. "He has been gone for almost two weeks and not one of us knew." Another servant brought her a piece of linen.

Antipater waited until the queen had used the cloth to wipe her mouth before he spoke. "Do you know where he has gone?"

Her cheeks flushed with rage. "To Ptolemy. Aristobulus and the Ituraean have sent word to all twenty-two of my fortresses to rally their soldiers against me."

"Then we must organize our army!" John pounded his fist in the air. "We will meet him in battle to defend your crown."

For the first time Lev could remember, Salome looked at her son with disdain. "We will do no such thing."

"But . . . surely . . . ." John sputtered.

Shimeon and Antipater both stepped forward, but it was Antipater who argued first. "Your Majesty, Aristobulus cannot be allowed to overthrow your rule."

"Of course not. But I will not be drawn into a war with my own son." She coughed again into the linen. "I have sent soldiers to imprison Helena and his children in the Baris Fortress and sent word to my son of their captivity. If he so much as moves one soldier toward Jerusalem, I will have his wife strung up from the highest gallows I can build so that her body will be seen above the walls. If he brings an army this way, I will slaughter his children."

Lev had never considered the queen to be a strong monarch. Until now. He could sense her determination from across the room. This was no bluff. She would murder her own grandchildren if it kept Aristobulus from coming against her in battle.

Shimeon approached her. "Are you certain of this course of action?"

No trace of weakness could be heard in her voice. "I have never been more certain of anything in my life." She surveyed the men in the room. "I may be old. I may be ill. And I am most definitely a woman. But I am not stupid and I am not, yet, dead. I want this matter settled before Adonai ushers me into Sheol."

"Do not even speak of such things." John's eyes filled with tears.

Again, she glared at him. "My constant prayer since you and your brother were born was that you would have the humility, strength and courage needed to rule Israel. Adonai, in his infinite wisdom, gave you the heart and the humility. But he gave Aristobulus the strength and the courage. If only He had seen fit to give you one speck of your brother's drive." She lifted her gaze toward heaven as if she talked privately with God. "In the end, I decided it would be better for Israel to be led quietly by you rather than to be manipulated and crushed by Aristobulus. Do not make me regret my decision any more than I do. Become the leader I have been praying for you to be. Be strong!"

John lowered his head as if her rebuke weighed him down.

Salome looked to her brother. "Shimeon, reach out to the Sadducees and see if some reparations can be made so they will withdraw their support from Aristobulus."

The old Pharisee bowed to her. "Of course."

Lev waited patiently, knowing she must have something to say to his master. She spoke to him last. "Antipater." Her mouth chewed on his name, as if it were difficult for her to say it. "My second husband trusted your father enough to bring him into the palace to be his counselor, and he served my husband well. You have stepped seamlessly into your father's position, gaining the ear of my son." Her eyes surveyed him from the top of his head to his sandaled feet, then back up again. "This land and its people have given you everything you have. You would be nothing without us. Do not betray Israel. Do not betray John."

Antipater bowed. "I, and my sons after me, will serve this nation with all our hearts, souls and our minds until our last breath."

She exhaled loudly. "Leave me now, all of you." She sank onto an upholstered couch. "I am tired."

The men bowed and exited the room together, but Shimeon parted from their company as soon as he reached the hallway. John Hyrcanus's feet pounded on the marble floor as he stomped toward his private apartments. Lev and Antipater followed close behind.

Lev leaned toward his master. "Do you think her threat will work?" he whispered. "Or is Ari so heartless that he would sacrifice his family for the throne?"

"Helena, perhaps . . . although she is almost as shrewd and calculating as the prince himself. He could not have gotten this far in his deception without her help." Antipater grunted as he tried to keep pace with John. "But he will not risk the lives of Alexander and Antigonus. His sons are his legacy."

The pains came on sharp and hard in the middle of the night. Anna knew immediately what it meant and she let out a wail of heartbreak, waking Caleb from his sleep.

"What is it?" He reached for her in the dark. He pulled her next to his chest. "What is wrong?"

She could only cry out again in sorrow as she felt the child pass through her loins.

Caleb felt it, too. "No! No, Adonai, please! Not the child." He clutched her closer. "Not again."

Guilt consumed her. She could not give to her husband the one thing he asked of her, a child. Her womb was weak. She was cursed. But why? What had she done?

When her sobbing eased, Caleb rose and lit an oil lamp. Blood covered the bottom of his tunic.

Anna shuddered, then turned to look down on the pallet. The child was no bigger than her hand. She could see its legs . . . its tiny fingers fisted by its face. Even in death, the child appeared perfectly formed. Anna's grief rose up again as she stared down at her baby. "Why? What have I done wrong?"

"Nothing, my love. You are blameless."

She lifted the baby into her hand. So small . . . so wanted . . . so loved . . . even now. "Adonai, please, take our child into your care. Please . . . please . . . ."

Caleb knelt and took the child from her. His tears fell, washing the tiny body with his grief.

"I do not understand," Anna sobbed as her husband cradled the stillborn baby. "Why am I not worthy?"

Caleb's chest shuddered as he drew in a deep breath. "You are worthy. Adonai is preparing us. Strengthening us. So that, in His time, when He blesses us with a child, we will be able to face anything."

She wondered at his faith. Perhaps this was why she had not been able to carry the child to life, because she had doubted she could after the loss of their first two babies.

"No, my love," Caleb's voice called her out of her dark thoughts. "I know what you are thinking. God did not punish you for your worry."

"But . . . ."

"No. He is too merciful. He does not punish those who earnestly seek Him, as we both have. No, we are being prepared for something, and we will praise Him through this trial." He stared down at his child's face. "We will name her Miriam. After your mother."

Chapter 32

Three Weeks Later

"But *Abba*!" Tirzah's brows narrowed to a point over her nose as she frowned. "You only just came home!"

Lev picked his daughter up and sat her on his lap. "The prince needs me, little one. And I must obey."

Tomorrow he must leave for the Nabatean kingdom to   confirm King Aretas's willingness to defend John Hyrcanus.   Antipater worried Queen Salome was sicker than her counselors let on. Time was running short and alliances needed to be solidified before she died. Lev tapped Tirzah's nose with his finger. "What would you like me to bring you this time from Petra?"

His daughter bit her bottom lip as she considered her answer. "A horse!"

He squeezed her to his chest. "A horse? What would you do with a horse?"

Her brown eyes glinted with determination. "I would learn to ride it so I could go with you!" She slipped her arms around his waist. "Do not leave again. Please, *Abba*."

"It will be a shorter trip this time, I promise. There and back in little over a month. I will return in time for the Feast of Tabernacles." Lev kissed the top of her head. "Now, off you go. It is time for bed."

"But—"

He unwrapped her arms from his body. "No more. If you are brave enough to want to ride a horse, then you are strong enough not to cry about me leaving for a few weeks."

She slipped down from his lap. "Yes, Abba." Although a tear tracked down her cheek, she lifted her chin in a gesture of determination. "I am as brave as a son. You will see."

Lev clenched his jaw. No doubt Tirzah had heard him and her mother arguing over the past few months about his desire for a male heir. He laid his hands on Tirzah's shoulders. "I know you are." He kissed her forehead. "Now off to bed."

A servant stepped forward and took his daughter's hand to lead her away. Lev lowered his head with a sigh. As a rule, he did not agree with women going to school, but he did wish more for Tirzah than the life of wife and mother. He would try and find her a husband to match her strong will and honor her innate intelligence, not snuff it out. Perhaps a wealthy merchant, a man who would be willing to let her travel with him. She would be a shrewd negotiator in any business deal. He groaned as he stood. That still did not solve his present problem. He needed a son.

He had convinced Sarai to give the baby to a wet nurse to feed, hoping it would make her again fertile. He had tried to encourage his wife to enjoy the marriage bed, to teach her some of the ways he had learned to pleasure a woman during his travels to Petra and his time with Nasrin. Sarai remained an unenthusiastic lover.

"Master?"

Lev looked up to find the manservant, Shem, standing in the doorway. "What is it?"

"There is a gentleman to see you."

Lev frowned. He was expecting no one. "Did he give a name?"

"Daniel bar Phanuel."

The name called up echoes from his past. "Did he say what he wanted?"

"No, my lord. What shall I tell him?"

Lev blinked and tried to focus his thoughts. "I will meet with him in the library. And bring us some wine."

Lev hurried down the hallway to the small room in which he did work. He removed the papyrus scrolls that covered two stools and shoved them onto the shelves.

"Master, Daniel bar Phanuel is here."

Lev whirled around. Although he had seen his friend walking behind Anna in her wedding procession, he had not been close enough to notice the subtle differences the years had made. His beard grew thick, now reaching well down his neck. Daniel's hair still curled tightly but he kept it shorter than when they were students together. His dark brown eyes did not hold the same anger they had when last they spoke, but his gaze was intent. Focused. As if he feared to look around the room.

Lev spread his arms wide. "I would embrace you, as is the custom for old friends, but something tells me you have not forgiven me."

Daniel shrugged. "I spoke out of anger in the past. Out of ignorance. Now I know it is the Lord who guides our path."

Lev bit his tongue, holding back the sarcastic comment he longed to make.

Daniel narrowed his eyes. "I can see you wish to argue with me, but I am not sure about what."

"You have not traveled as I have. Seen the things I've seen." He motioned for his friend to sit as he did. "There are many gods in this world. All claim to influence our lives in one way or another."

"I know there are many that claim to be gods. But there is only one true God." Daniel's gaze searched his face. "You used to believe that as I do."

Lev sniffed. "But now I work with men who have the ability to change the course of history." He glanced toward the doorway as Shem entered with a jug and two goblets.

Daniel took a sip of wine but waited until the servant left before he spoke. "Who do you think gave those men their power, if not the Lord?"

Lev sighed. "I think smart men manipulate those around them to achieve their goals. There is no mystical being directing our path." His friend let out a sharp laugh but made no comment. "You do not agree?"

Daniel watched him from over the rim of his goblet. "Anna was right."

Lev's stomach lurched at the sound of her name. "Anna spoke of me?" He swallowed some wine. "What did she say?"

"She is worried for you."

"Worried? Why?"

Daniel took another sip of wine. "Since she came back from Egypt, she is different. I cannot explain how, but her thoughts are deeper. As if they come from outside herself."

Lev leaned forward. "She thinks of me? Even after . . . even though she is married to the cripple?"

Daniel stiffened. "This is why I know God directs our path. Because when I was young and foolish I thought, as Anna did, that you were the man she should marry. But now I see that Caleb was Adonai's chosen for her. He is everything you are not."

Bile rose from his stomach, but Lev swallowed it down. "Yes. He is poor. Old. Crippled and insignificant."

Daniel's face reddened. "He gives Anna a good home. Everything she needs—"

"Does she live in a house like this?" He swept his arm to encompass the room. "Can he give her jewelry? Silk gowns? Servants?" He slammed his goblet down on the table as he stood.

Instead of arguing, Daniel shook his head. "You never understood that Anna did not desire any of those things. She wanted a man to love and a husband who would serve her out love. She and Caleb seek the will of God. Together."

"Did Anna send you here to tell me how happy she is with the tailor? Was that your message?" Lev breathed heavily through his nose, trying to control his temper. "If so, you can go now. Your job is done."

Daniel finished the wine in his cup and placed it on the table next to Lev's before standing to face him. "She worries about the choices you have made. She had hoped I might convince you to repent and return to God's path."

Lev snorted. "As I told my father, you believe in Adonai if it brings you comfort. But I will trust on my own strength to succeed."

His friend's face softened. "And then what?"

"What do you mean?"

Daniel shrugged. "When this life is over? What is there to hope for?"

"I will leave a legacy to my son."

"You have had a son? I had not heard that news." A warm smile lit his face. "Congratulations."

Lev clenched his jaw. "Sarai has not given me an heir yet. But it is only a matter of time."

Daniel's grin faded. "And if she does not? What then?"

"A son is the only immortality a man can have."

"But what of Adonai? Of his promise of Sheol for those who keep his Law?"

"There is this life alone. There is no other."

Daniel stared at him a moment longer. "If that is what you truly believe, then I will not try to persuade you any longer."

A sadness swept over Lev as Daniel turned to leave. "You are welcome any time. I have missed our arguments."

Daniel stopped in the doorway. "I have missed my old friend. I miss him still." He glanced over his shoulder. "You have become a different man. And this man I will not miss."

Daniel's footsteps sounded down the hallway as Lev stood alone. The silence of the house unsettled him. He swept his arm out and knocked the empty goblets off the table, listening to them rattle along the stone floor as they rolled.

Shem ran in. "Is everything well, Master?"

Lev stared at the man, wanting to strike him and not knowing why. He steadied his breath. "Everything is fine. I am going to bed. Wake me at first light." He trudged up the stone staircase toward his wife's bedroom. He had one more night before he left for Petra. One more night to try and conceive a son.

Anna walked beside Esther as they made their way to the queen's private sitting room. Although it had been eight years since they had met while Anna embroidered the High Priest's ephod, the time had passed quickly. "I thought you served   Helena now, the prince's wife."

Although younger than Anna, the girl's face seemed older. "I-I was . . . but . . . she . . . asked the queen to find another position for me."

The color drained from Esther's cheeks, Anna feared she might faint. "Are you unwell?"

Esther's step quickened as they approached the staircase. "I am grateful to serve Salome. She is a kind woman."

"She is, indeed." Anna also picked up her pace. Her sandal caught on a stair, and she reached out to steady herself on Esther's arm.

The girl flinched at Anna's touch.

Anna saw the emotions flash behind the girl's eyes before she turned away. Fear and shame. The same things she herself had experienced after Aristobulus had accosted her. She suspected he had done the same, and probably more, to Esther. "I am glad you are away from the prince and now under the queen's protection."

Esther's pace slowed. "As am I."

Anna paused behind her. The stairwell offered them more privacy than any of the hallways in the palace, as soldiers did not stand guard at the top, but she did not know what words would bring comfort to the girl. "Did he hurt you?"

Esther braced her hand against the wall as her shoulders sagged. "Did he . . . ever . . . ." her voice trembled into silence.

"He tried."

A soft sob escaped the girl's throat. "There was no one to help me."

"Then you are not to blame."

Esther hiccupped as she tried to breathe. "I can never go back to my father's house. But Salome has promised I would be allowed to stay in her service. She will not cast me out when my father's debt is paid."

Anna's heart ached. This might have been her fate if Caleb had not been merciful. "I am sorry." The only reason he did not accompany her now to the queen's room was because Aristobulus had not returned to Jerusalem, even though his wife and children remained prisoners in the Baris Fortress.

Esther lifted her head then walked up the last few steps. "The queen is waiting for you."

Anna knew by Esther's tone she did not want to talk any more about the prince. "Do you know what Salome wants?"

"No," Esther said. "She only said to bring you to her. She has been quite ill."

"There were rumors throughout the servants' quarters. No one has seen her for many days."

"She is better now, but weak." Anna had hoped Esther would give her more of an answer, but the young girl did not speak again until they reached the doorway. "Go in quietly, she may be sleeping."

"Should I wake her?"

Esther stepped aside. "If you do not, you may be here for many hours."

Anna crept silently around the corner. Queen Salome reclined on the one couch in the room, asleep. The heavy tapestries had been taken down from the windows, allowing a gentle breeze to move the air.

Anna sat on the wooden stool across from the queen. Sorrow filled her as she noticed the near transparency of Salome's skin. *She is dying. Adonai, please . . . please bless her. Help her to rally her strength yet again to rule. Her reign has proven to be a blessing to Israel in so many ways—plentiful rain, good harvests, and peace—She has been a good and wise leader. Let us enjoy many more years under her authority.*

Salome's breathing stuttered for a moment as her eyes opened. She blinked a few times before setting her gaze on Anna. "How long have you been here?"

"I only just arrived, Your Majesty."

The queen sniffed. "Staring at the dying woman, were you?"

"I was praying for the Lord to bless you and keep you in good health."

Salome sat up. "Do not pray for that. I am ready to die."

Anna's heart thudded in her chest. "Do not say such things, Your Majesty! Israel needs you!"

"Israel needs more than me, I am afraid." She seemed to drift off again, although her eyes stayed open. "Adonai has been so long silent, I think even the priests have forgotten that we are His people. I fear God has abandoned us to our own machinations. And left on our own . . . I fear we will destroy each other."

The queen's sorrow lay heavily on Anna, like a yoke of wood pressing against her shoulders. "Surely that is not the case."

Salome blinked as she focused again on Anna. "What did you say?"

"Our God will not forget His covenant with us, surely. His promises to King David and Moses. He will always be our God, though our people are not always faithful to Him."

"I hope you are right." Salome paused to cough. A servant brought her wine to drink. "I was surprised to learn you were still sewing here in the palace. I thought you would have been home with your child."

Anna clasped her hands together in her lap. "I lost the baby."

"I am sorry for your loss. Still . . . you are young. You may have another."

The seed of despair that had taken root in Anna's soul sprouted another limb. It stretched its dark sadness throughout her body. Anna clenched her teeth together to keep her tears from falling.

"Do not despair, child. Many women lose a child before they can carry one to birth."

"I have lost three." Her words came out with a sob. "I cannot bear to lose another."

"And the tailor . . . your husband . . . what does he say?"

A tear dropped onto Anna's fists. "He is patient."

"Let that be a blessing to you. Some men are not so kind."

Another tear fell. Anna wished Caleb would rail against her. She wanted him to shout, be angry, even hit her. Then she could be justified in her desire to be left alone. She could not stand his touch anymore. If she should lose another child, she would lose her mind. She felt pressure on her shoulder. Surprised, she looked up to see Salome standing over her.

"Do not despair. I have a sense about such things." The queen cupped her face as a mother would her own daughter's. "You are strong and God is wise. He has given you this sorrow to refine you. To strengthen you. But He will reward you if you stay faithful to Him."

Anna breathed in deeply. Salome spoke the same words Caleb had the night of baby Miriam's passing, as if God were confirming His truth through the queen. "I will stay faithful to Adonai. I will put my trust in Him."

"Good." Salome smiled. "Now, I want you to work on a new gown for me. A very special one. I want it to be woven with gold thread. And spare no expense with the linen!"

Anna grinned at the queen's enthusiasm. "When do you want it finished?"

"Take your time. I will not need it for . . . six months, I think. Maybe a year."

"What is the occasion?"

The queen clapped her hands together. "My funeral." She shook her head. "Do not look at me like that. It *will* happen. There is no denying it." She sat down as she cleared her throat. "Despite what it looks like, I have no intention of dying anytime soon. But I would like to be prepared when it comes."

Anna wiped the tears from her cheeks. "I will make you the most beautiful gown any queen has ever worn, even the queen of Sheba."

Salome's eyes sparkled. "Wonderful!"

They discussed the garment for several more minutes before the queen yawned. She seemed to struggle to keep her eyelids from closing. Sighing quietly, she reclined along the back of the couch. "Leave me now. We will discuss more about the decoration after you have made the gown."

Anna rose.

A gentle cooing sound escaped the queen's throat as she closed her eyes. "You have offered the proper sacrifices for cleansing after your miscarriages?"

"Yes." Anna's heart skipped a beat. Salome seemed to be speaking from a dream.

The corner of Salome's lips rose in a small smile, though her eyes remained shut. "When the Festival of Tabernacles is celebrated . . . as you remember Adonai's provision in the wilderness . . . and rejoice in

His present blessings . . . then do not fear to lie with your husband . . . you will have a child."

Anna waited, hoping to hear something more, but the queen began to snore softly. She walked back toward the sewing room feeling strangely elated. As if her feet floated over the marble floor. Her heart fluttered inside her chest, causing her to lose her breath. She paused at the bottom of the stairway. She could not contain her excitement. If she went back to work with Tamar and the others, they would see something different about her. The depression that had hung on her every limb was gone. She did not want to try and explain how she knew Salome's words were true, she just did. And she would not let anyone take her newfound hope away.

Instead of turning down the hall to the sewing room, Anna found herself running toward the nearest door leading outside. It seemed that even the weather offered her hope. The sun shone brightly against a clear blue sky. She dodged through the priests, scribes and pilgrims meandering outside the Temple walls until she found herself in the courtyard itself.

The marble columns rose up from the ground like giant trees. White-robed priests stood on the Temple steps or around the bronze altar blazing in the center. Off to the right knelt a group of women. Anna took a place to the rear and lifted her prayers to God.

Adonai, may the words Salome spoke be true. I ask not for myself, but for Caleb. He has suffered so much in his life, allow him to have a son, Lord. I know you to be good and merciful. I trust You will grant Caleb's desire. I trust You, Lord.

Chapter 33

Fall, 68 B.C.

The road home to Jerusalem hummed with people. They scurried up the hill toward the first gate like ants. Many carried bundles of willow and myrtle branches, along with palm fronds and citrons, all required by Adonai for *Sukkot*, the Feast of Tabernacles. Lev had never bothered celebrating the festival with Sarai and his children before and would not have bothered returning for it this year, except that he had promised Tirzah. He growled under his breath as his horse balked at trying to maneuver through the ever-increasing crowd. He managed to guide the beast to the side of the road so he could dismount.

He turned to the soldiers who followed behind him. "Avram, come with me. Bring my saddlebags." He pulled his cloak tighter around his neck to fend off the brisk wind. "The rest of you, return to the Baris Fortress. Take the animal with you."

The temporary shelters of branches and fronds set up outside the houses made the already teeming streets even narrower. The travelers next to him, peasants from the north by their accents and threadbare tunics, shouted with joy then pushed through the mass of people to make their way toward a smiling family. All around him, greetings and celebrations took place. The stench of the thousands of pilgrims that now infested the city, in addition to the thousands that lived there, overwhelmed him. It was bad enough the population swelled ten times above average, but that they lived outside in shelters for the week added to smell. Lev muttered with frustration as he plodded his way toward his house. By the time he approached the second gate, near the Temple Mount, he could move more freely.

Along his street, larger and more formal *sukkot* had been built, most on rooftops or in courtyards behind gated walls. Lev's wealthy neighbors might adhere to the letter of the law, but they would certainly not feel obligated to share their lives with their neighbors for the week. He sighed with relief as he approached his own home. Someone had built a shelter on his roof so he would not have to bother.

Tirzah stood just inside the gate. "Abba! You came!"

"I promised you I would, did I not?"

She hugged him as he stepped inside the courtyard. "I thought you might forget again."

"Avram," he called over his shoulder. "You can leave my bags in the house, then tell Antipater I have returned. Inform him I will attend him first thing in the morning."

Tirzah grabbed his hand. "Come see the *sukkah* Shem made! It is even bigger than last year's! We have room for a table and blankets and pillows. Mama even had a special bed of straw made for you to sleep on!" Tirzah babbled as she pulled him through the dimly lit hallway then out to the courtyard. "Mama said Salome will sleep with us but she cries too much. You will tell her to take the baby away, yes?"

"If she cries, yes. I need to sleep before I start work again in the morning." Lev trudged up the stairs along the courtyard wall.

"But you will stay tonight? And sleep with me under the stars?"

He nodded as they stepped onto the roof. Shem had built an impressive shelter of sturdy branches and palm fronds. Sarai sat inside it, but stood when she caught sight of him.

"I am glad you are home. Safe." She clapped her hands. "Hannah, bring my lord water and oil to wash his feet. Shem, some wine." Her arm swept toward a low wooden table in the middle surrounded by plush pillows striped with cream silk. "Come. Sit and rest after your journey."

Tirzah tugged him inside. She flitted around the *sukkah* like a moth, pointing out the mattress where he would sleep, then dancing over to the other side of structure where the servants would sleep. A young woman sat in the corner, an older baby suckling at her breast. It took Lev a moment to recognize her as the wet nurse he had hired in hope that Sarai would soon be able to bear another child. His blood stirred when the woman lifted her deep brown eyes toward him. She resembled one of the priestesses he had slept with while in Petra. He had partaken in a ritual seeking the favor of Allat, the Nabatean goddess of fertility. A tingling sensation ran down his spine as he recalled the smell of incense and the priestess's sensual touch.

"Mama." Tirzah's whine broke him out of the memory. "Abba said he did not want the baby to sleep with us."

Lev dragged his gaze away from the wet nurse's face to look at his daughter. "Only if she cries."

Tirzah scowled, but then she pointed to an assortment of branches just outside of the shelter. "Make a *luvlav* with me!"

Sarai knelt and fluffed a pillow. "Sit here, my lord." She turned to Tirzah. "Let your father refresh himself from his journey. We will make our *luvlav* after we eat."

Tirzah sat among the branches of palm, myrtle and willow, picking them up and waving them about in the air. Lev skirted around her so that he could sit down. He watched her play while a female servant removed his sandals to wash the dirt from his feet and Shem brought him a glass of wine. As he sipped, he observed the wet nurse bare her breast as she removed his sleeping daughter. His mind again wandered back to his experience in the Nabatean temple. The images were hazy, as he had been given a powerful drink before presenting himself to the priestess, but he could remember how the woman's fingers seemed to burn his skin as she caressed him. She assured him, after they had come together, that his virility had pleased the goddess. Allat was sure to bless him with a son.

Sarai stepped in front of the wet nurse to pick up her daughter. Lev blinked several times, trying to shake off the intense memory. He ate well as Tirzah recited the events of the past month while he had been away. He found it easier to listen to her after the wet nurse left the shelter.

"And then *Sabba* gave me a new tunic. It is blue with pearls and shiny stones that sparkle in the sun. But Mama says I cannot wear it when you are home. Why?"

Lev glared at his wife. Her cheeks paled under his scrutiny. He turned his attention to Tirzah. "Who gave you the tunic?"

"*Sabba* Malachi. He came to visit and—"

Lev's fist pounded the table. Goblets rattled. The oil lamps shook, their flames dancing wildly. "You allowed him into my house? After I forbade it?"

Sarai took a shaky breath. "You said only that you did not want to see him. You did not say he could not visit his grandchildren."

"I should think you would be smart enough to understand what was implied."

"I am sorry, my lord. It will not happen again."

"Abba, why—"

"Quiet, Tirzah." Sarai placed her hand on her daughter's arm. "Let your father eat in peace."

An undercurrent of hostility hung throughout the rest of their meal. Only Tirzah's childlike enthusiasm for the festival could break the mood in the shelter. She darted over to the assortment of branches as soon as she had finished eating.

"Abba! Please help me make my *luvlav*."

Lev wanted only to drink another cup of wine and go to sleep, but he could not disappoint his daughter as she pleaded with her wide eyes and pouting lips. "It has been many years since I made one. I may not remember how."

"I know you can, Abba. You can do anything!" Tirzah plopped herself down on the ground.

Lev sat beside her. He picked up a palm branch. A wave of melancholy washed over him as he remembered creating the bundle of required plants as a boy with his mother. He lifted the palm toward Tirzah. "Do you know what the palm branch represents?"

She shook her head.

"It is the spine of the man who loves Adonai. Straight and true." Lev studied the branch. Once, long ago, he had wanted to be that kind of man. But now? Now he no longer believed in an invisible God. And he wanted too much in this life to waste his time with all the superstitious rituals the Law, and the Pharisees, demanded. Still . . . an ache settled in his chest as he thought about the comfort he used to feel reciting the ancient prayers and performing the rites.

"What next?" Tirzah shook her own palm branch in front of his face.

Lev wrapped the bottom of the palm branches with strips of gauze. "Next, we take three myrtle branches. Their leaves are shaped like eyes." He picked up the branches. "To symbolize Adonai's vision." He secured them to the right of the palm and then fixed Tirzah's together. "Finally, we need two willow branches."

Tirzah handed them to him.

"These represent man's lips. That they should praise God." He tied the willow branches to the left of the palm then gave it a shake. "There now. You have a *luvlav* to wave at the festival tomorrow."

Tirzah thrusted her group of branches toward him. "That one is yours. This one is mine."

He dutifully tied her bundle together.

"Now make one for Mama!"

Lev's chest tightened, but he did as his daughter insisted. Once finished, Tirzah used it and her own to dance around the shelter. Lev smiled at her enthusiasm, but his eyes soon grew heavy. The trip from Petra had been long and he still felt the ache in his bones from the constant dry air. He wished he could excuse himself and go to his own quiet room, but he knew Tirzah wanted him to sleep under the stars with her, as God ordained, during the week-long celebration.

When the sun finally set, Sarai settled Tirzah onto the straw mattress. "Time to go to bed now." She kissed her daughter's forehead.

Tirzah yawned. "Abba, will you come lie beside me?"

Lev stretched out on the pallet, lifting his arm so she could rest her head on his chest. "Look at them all," she whispered as they looked up to the sky. "How many stars are there?"

"Count them and you will know."

"One, two, three, four, five . . ." Lev's muscles relaxed as his daughter kept counting, her voice growing weaker the higher she went, "ten, eleven, twelve . . . ."

He had no idea how high she counted as he fell asleep soon after she reached twenty.

Young Isaac tottered about on his pudgy legs. Anna's heart ached to see Caleb's delight every time her nephew brought him another wooden block.

"Shall we make a tower?" her husband asked, placing one block atop the other on the bench.

Isaac grinned, then toppled the tower with a smack of his hand. Nephew and uncle let out a loud belly laugh, followed by Daniel and Phanuel. Anna's chest tightened.

Tova leaned over to whisper, "Your time will come."

Anna shut her eyes rather than look at Tova's round belly. She would give Daniel another child by Passover. *When Lord? When will it be my turn?* She opened her eyes when the men all laughed again. Caleb had swept Isaac up into his arms and was rubbing his beard across the boy's stomach. The child screeched with delight. Even Anna smiled at his joy.

A brisk wind blew through the cracks in the shelter Daniel had built for his family on the roof of their new home. Her brother had finally convinced their father to move closer to the Temple Mount so they would not have to walk far to their work. Between their two wages, Daniel and Phanuel no longer worried about providing for their family, although her father still spent most of his income on scrolls and giving to the poor. This new house boasted an upper floor with two bedrooms, one for Daniel, Tova and Isaac, one for Phanuel. The bottom floor had twice the space of Anna's childhood home and included a separate room in which the men could study and a large courtyard they shared with only one neighbor.

Anna pulled her cloak around her shoulders as she looked out over Jerusalem. People danced in the streets to the tune of wooden flutes and the beat of timbrels. The wind carried the sound of others singing, although she could not make out the words. Firelight flickered in the streets and on rooftops as families gathered in their temporary shelters to celebrate the final fruit harvest of the year and remember how Adonai had guided them through the wilderness for forty years before leading them into their promised land. Her heart lightened as she watched the revelries below. She took a deep breath. *I will wait upon Adonai. For He is good and his mercy endures forever. He will give us a child.*

Caleb caught her eye and nodded, as if he had read her thoughts. He carried Isaac over to Daniel. "Here. Take your wild beast back!"

Her brother lifted his brows and let out an exaggerated sigh while Isaac wriggled and kicked to be free. "Must I?"

Caleb stretched out his hand to Anna. "Are you ready to head home, my love?"

Anna nodded as he lifted her to her feet. "We will see you tomorrow, yes?"

Phanuel stood. "We will stop at your house on our way to the temple for the procession." He clasped Caleb's hand. *"Shalom."*

"Shalom, Father," Caleb answered then exchanged the blessing of peace with Daniel before placing his arm around Anna. "I am tired, wife. You may have to carry me home."

She leaned into him. "I wish I could."

They walked slowly together down the hill, weaving their way between the dancers and musicians. Turning the corner to their own street, they called out greetings to their neighbors who had set up their *sukkot* along the front of their houses. Caleb had built theirs in the courtyard, away from the crowds. Although friendly with their neighbors, Anna knew he preferred his privacy to carousing until late into the evening. They paused inside their house to grab an extra blanket and an oil lamp before making their way to the shelter outside.

"Shalom, Caleb. *Shalom,* Anna," called their neighbor, Mava. The older woman stooped in the threshold of her hut, barely illuminated by the lamp she carried. "I wish you a peaceful night." With that, she pulled a thin curtain loose and stepped inside the shelter Caleb had helped her build earlier in the day. Her silhouette flickered against the fabric as she sat down, but then disappeared when she snuffed out her lamp.

Anna followed her husband into their own modest shelter of branches. They had only furnished it with blankets and a few pillows to sleep on. Caleb used the flame of their lamp to light the kindling he had set inside a stone ring. "This should keep out the worst of the chill tonight."

Anna slipped under the blankets while he got the fire to catch. She stared up at the swath of stars overhead. Caressing her stomach, she thought of the patriarch, Abraham, to whom God promised as many descendants as there are stars.

Caleb groaned as he lowered himself to his knees and then crawled under the covers next to her. "I feel old today."

She rested her head on his chest. "You built two shelters. And helped with Daniel's. Of course you are tired."

His fingers played with a curl in her hair. "What were you thinking of, before I interrupted you?"

She breathed in deeply, enjoying the scent of the branches that mingled with his sweat and the smoky fire. "I was thinking of Abraham."

Caleb's soft chuckle made her head bounce. "I hope Adonai does not make me wait until I am a hundred years old to have a child."

"Why do you think He made Abraham and Sarah wait so long?"

"I do not know." His breath blew warm over her brow as he spoke. "But His timing is perfect, so there must have been a reason."

Anna snuggled closer to him, her hand moving to find the beat of his heart. "And why do you think Adonai asked Abraham to sacrifice Isaac?"

"Perhaps to prove his faith? Remember, Abraham was the first man God called to separate himself from the tribes around him. The first of our faith."

Anna nodded, her cheek rubbing against his tunic. "That is what Rabbi Chaim said, too. But I wondered what you thought."

He kissed her forehead. "Do you think I am as wise as the learned rabbi?"

She rolled so her arms rested against his chest and she could see his face in the moonlight. He smiled as she looked down on him. "You are one of the wisest men I know." He reached up to brush her hair back, and she felt his heartbeat quicken.

They had joined together twice since Salome's prediction. Both times, Anna had initiated the intimacy. Caleb had been cautious. As if afraid he might overwhelm her with his desire. Tonight, she sensed a difference. It was as if their talk about Abraham, together with the time spent with their nephew, created an urgency within them both.

Caleb's breathing grew more rapid. He took hold of her hair and brought her lips down to his. This was not a gentle kiss, but one of passion. And need. After a moment, he pushed her away. "Is this what you want, my love? Tell me to stop now, and I will." His muscles trembled beneath her, but she knew if she asked, he would stop. This man she loved would do anything to make her happy.

Her blood grew warm even as a cold breeze blew through the gaps in the branches. She sat up to slip off her tunic. "I do not want you to stop."

A soft moan escaped Caleb's throat as he drew her down to kiss her again.

Chapter 34

Six Months Later

Anna pulled the loaf of bread from the hearth then stirred the pot of curried goat stew that hung over the flame.

"I should be doing that." Her niece, Ruth, gently pushed her toward a stool. "You rest."

Anna's swelling stomach made it difficult to sit down, but she reveled in her new awkwardness. Tamar's daughter, Ruth, went to the well for Anna each morning and stayed until Caleb came home. She was tall for a girl of almost twelve, with a servant's heart and a quiet laugh. She cooked and cleaned and pampered Anna so that she felt spoiled. *"Not spoiled,"* Caleb had assured her. *"Loved."*

Anna's fingertips ran over her belly, and the babe inside answered her touch with a kick. She giggled. None of her other pregnancies had come so far. It never ceased to amaze her. She caressed her child as she watched her niece work.

Ruth puttered about the small house, making preparations for the dinner she would serve in a few hours. The curls of her hair refused to stay bound in the braid down her back. They sprung out about her head like a lion's mane.

The door swung open.

Anna was chuckling to herself as she turned to greet Caleb, but her happiness evaporated with one look at his somber expression. His shoulders were slumped and his skin pale. She took a hesitant step toward him. "What has happened?"

"The queen is dead."

Ruth sank to her knees on the floor. Anna clutched her hands protectively around her belly.

Caleb let the door slam shut behind him. "John is beside himself with grief. He has locked himself in his rooms."

Dread filled Anna's body, making her limbs cold and leaden. "Where is Aristobulus?"

He drew her into an embrace. "I do not know."

The baby within her squirmed but Anna did not remove herself from her husband's strong arms. "Will he return for her funeral?"

Caleb's chin rested on the top of her head. "Not without an army behind him."

"Surely he will not fight his own brother for the throne."

Caleb kissed the crown of her head before letting her go. His eyes met hers. "You, of all people, know Aristobulus has no restraint. He takes what he wants, no matter if it is his or not."

The memory of the prince's cruel advances caused her to shiver. "We must pray he does not succeed."

Caleb held out a hand to help lift Ruth off the floor. "Before John locked himself away he sent out one request."

"What was that?" Anna asked.

"He asks that you return to the palace to finish Salome's shroud."

"Me? But what of the baby?" When she had known she carried another child, she stopped walking to the palace. Caleb brought work home for her, but they had not been allowed to remove the precious funeral garment from the palace.

"It is the king's command, my love. We cannot refuse." Caleb sat down beside her. "And you have said again and again that you are sure this child will be healthy."

Anna's mind raced. She trusted Adonai, but yet, to do such an important job in the time allowed . . . .

Caleb took her hand in his. "I will help as well. The work will go quickly."

Ruth sat down across from them. "I cannot believe she is dead."

Anna remembered well the strange emotions she had experienced when Alexander Jannai had died. It was as if Jerusalem was no longer tethered to the ground without the king, at least until the funeral was over and Salome assumed the throne. Ruth, undoubtedly had similar feelings, as Salome was the only ruler the girl had ever known.

They ate their meal in weighted silence. Anna could not know what the others thought, but for herself, she worried about the coming months. Queen Salome's rule had been one of unprecedented peace and prosperity. Adonai himself seemed to bless everything she put her hand to. Or perhaps it was the queen who sought to do His will, and so was successful. But what of John Hyrcanus? He shared his mother's love of knowledge and the Law, but Anna sensed he lacked her confidence and strength. What would happen to Jerusalem if, as Caleb suspected, Aristobulus sought to wrench the throne from his brother? Surely God would side with John and protect his throne? But Adonai's ways were not always the ways of men. She could not fathom a purpose for allowing Aristobulus to rule Israel, but that did not mean God did not have one.

Caleb rested his hand over hers. "Do not fear, my love. Adonai will keep us safe."

"Amen." Anna forced a smile, even as her heart grew heavy with worry.

"Your Majesty," Antipater pushed the tray of food toward the king. "You must keep your strength."

King John Hyrcanus II sniffed as if the smell of bread offended him. Although his hairline had receded over his years as High Priest, his beard had grown long and full. He ran his fingers along the length of it. "To eat before my mother is buried? I cannot."

"There is much work to be done before she can be interred. You must have the strength to give her a proper burial."

John waved the food away. "A little wine. That is all I will have."

Lev rubbed his temple, hoping to lessen the headache he had developed since stepping into John's room. Although he would grieve

Judith's passing, he would not dishonor his mother by acting like a spoiled child. He wondered again why Salome had chosen this weakling to be her successor.

Antipater waited until the king had sipped some wine before he spoke again. "Sire, please. You must consider what I have told you. Aristobulus has not been idle these past two years. While you have been attending to your duties as High Priest, he has been amassing an army of embittered Sadducees."

"Mother gave me the crown." John jumped to his feet. "He would not disobey her last wish."

"Salome understood the danger. It is why your brother's wife and children remain prisoners." Antipater tilted his head toward the king. "If you would only listen to the—"

John grasped the edge of a table. "Please, Antipater. Next week . . . after she is entombed . . . then I will listen to all that you advise."

Lev had been with Antipater long enough to recognize the frustration behind his master's eyes, but the older man did not voice his displeasure. Instead, he came to stand by the king's side. "Of course, my friend. Is there anything I can do to help with the preparations?"

John let out a stuttering breath. "Can you oversee all the plans? The procession? The mourners?"

"Leave everything to me, my lord." He placed a hand on the king's shoulder. "Rest now. I will take care of it all." With that, he signaled the servant to bring more wine then strode toward the door.

Lev followed. "Can he afford to wait until Ari makes a move against him?"

"Of course not. But I fear he'll collapse if we push him to act before Salome is in her tomb." Antipater hurried down the hallway. "We can send word to those generals still loyal to John. Have them prepare for battle. Look for new recruits." He motioned for Lev to catch up to him. "Write a letter this afternoon in my name. Find couriers to deliver it to the generals here and in Jericho."

Lev blinked in the harsh sunlight as they stepped out into a courtyard. "What else do you need?"

"Time. I need more time to convince John of the danger he is in."

Lev surveyed the courtyard, taking in the silence around him. No servants bustled about, attending to the queen. John Hyrcanus wanted no interruptions and his family held vigil in their rooms, fasting until Salome Alexandra lay in her tomb. Still, even with the abnormal stillness, Lev knew not to say anything here in the palace. There may still be someone lurking in the alcoves.

As he followed Antipater out to the street, Lev's mind spun with thoughts of how to keep his long ago promise to Ari to get John away from the city. And what words he should use to convince Antipater of his plan.

Once they passed through the gates to Antipater's house, he began calling out orders. "Did you bring your stylus and tablet? We have much work to do."

Lev kept his voice low as they entered the library. "Do you want me to send any letter to Ari?"

The older man's brown eyes appeared murky, like the water of a still, deep pond. "What kind of letter?"

"Perhaps something to effect that though we seem loyal to John, we would be his allies as well."

"To what point? Ari must not wrest the crown from John's head. He is too—"

"I understand, Master." Lev struggled to keep his voice controlled. "But whether we desire it or not, the chance is real that Ari will defeat John in open battle. John does not inspire the soldiers' confidence." Antipater hung his head and mumbled unintelligibly. Lev continued, "I think we must offer our services to Ari now, before he comes to power. Otherwise, should he take the crown, his first act will be to root out and destroy all who are loyal to his brother."

His mentor stopped muttering.

Lev continued on. "We promise Ari our loyalty, then take our time building up support for John behind the scenes. Ari will not expect his brother to fight back."

Antipater stared at Lev as if seeing him for the first time. "We give Aristobulus the throne, then make our move?"

"Once Ari has power, we know he will abuse it. The Sadducees will want retribution for their loss of authority. The Pharisees will rally behind John's cause so that they can keep their new positions.

We already have the Nabateans' promise of refuge and an army if and when Ari overthrows the king."

"You negotiated for their soldiers as well as John's refuge when you were with them?"

A slow smile crept across Lev's mouth. "I thought it prudent."

"How much do they want?"

Lev opened his hands out in a gesture suggesting the price would be small. "Only what was once theirs to begin with."

Antipater grunted. "The land John's pig of a father took from them, no doubt."

"Twelve border towns for thousands of soldiers fighting for their own land. I thought the trade a good one."

His mentor threw his arm around Lev's shoulders. "I have taught you well. I could not be prouder of you if you were my own son."

Lev grinned. *I did nothing for you. All I did was to preserve my own life when John goes down in flames.*

Two weeks later, the sky hung gray and heavy with storm clouds, as if Adonai Himself joined with the crowds in the streets to weep over the death of Queen Salome Alexandra. Around Anna, the people craned their necks to get a glimpse the queen's body as horses drew her funeral bier down the street. Anna did not look. She did not want to remember the queen this way. Cold. Lifeless.

She clutched Caleb's hand, grounding herself in his touch, drawing from his strength. Salome had been more than a monarch to Anna. She had inspired her to achieve more than she had ever dreamed possible. And now she was gone.

"It seems like ages ago," Tova spoke near Anna's ear, "that we watched King Alexander Jannai's funeral procession. And yet, it has been less than ten years."

Anna's eyes misted. "We were children then."

Tova glanced down at her son, Isaac, then to the baby girl swaddled across her chest. "Now we have children of our own."

Anna caressed her belly. "Soon."

The shriek of mourners echoed through the air, making it impossible to hear anything else until they passed. Fat, round raindrops fell as the procession continued up the hill.

Daniel leaned over to speak to Caleb, "Come to our home while it rains. You'll be soaked through if you try and make it back to yours."

Caleb pulled his cloak free of his belt so he could draw the loose fabric over Anna's head. "Thank you, Brother."

Daniel covered Tova, while Phanuel took Isaac's hand and ran ahead. Anna and Caleb stumbled into the porch area behind the others as the steady drops turned into a torrent. Tova ushered them into the main room. She stoked the fire in the brazier until its embers caught light.

"Come and warm yourselves."

Isaac giggled with glee as he played with the water dripping from Phanuel's beard. His laughter seemed out of place after such a solemn occasion, but Anna welcomed the distraction. So much uncertainty loomed for their futures now that Salome had died, and it all centered on which of her sons would take the throne.

Tova gave her baby to Anna to hold, then picked up her son who shrieked in anger at being taken from his grandfather. "Come, little man, we must dry you off." She carried him, kicking and screaming, up the stairs to the bedrooms.

Caleb took his cloak from Anna's shoulders and laid it by the fire to dry. Then he pulled aside the curtain that led to the private courtyard. The rain now fell in heavy sheets and lightning flashed across the sky. "It is late in the year for a storm such as this."

Daniel joined him in the threshold. "It is an omen of what is to come."

Anna held the baby close, drawing warmth from her niece's tiny body, even as a chill ran through her. "You feel it, too?"

Phanuel drew a stool up to the fire. "Anyone who seeks the Lord can feel it. It will be a time of turmoil. Aristobulus is too much like his father. Hungry for power and devoted to the Sadducees because of the money they can give him."

Anna had no doubt Aristobulus would be capable of the same brutality as Alexander Jannai. The king's need for vengeance had caused the most powerful Pharisees to flee to Egypt rather than face possible crucifixion at his whim. If Aristobulus gained the crown, there would be no peaceful transition of power between the Pharisees and the Sadducees.

Her father glanced over at Daniel. The lines in his face seemed to deepen. A shadow clouded his eyes. "If you are sure in your decision, you should ask Caleb now, before it is too late."

Daniel's gaze darted toward the staircase, to make sure Tova and Isaac were still out of sight. He braced his hand against the wall. "Brother, the king has demanded that all men of less than thirty years join his army."

Anna caught her breath as her stomach dropped.

"Once the official week of mourning has ended, he plans to gather the new troops to ready themselves to face Aristobulus."

Caleb whispered, "Surely, as you have a family and have never been trained, they would not expect you to go to war."

Daniel shook his head. "Every man between seventeen and thirty years must fight." He straightened his shoulders. "And I want to do this. John Hyrcanus must keep the throne. His brother will take away all we Pharisees have gained these past ten years." He placed his hand on Caleb's shoulder. "If I do not come back, do I have your promise you will take care of Tova and my children?"

Caleb's face paled as he nodded.

Daniel shook him. "Will you swear it?"

Caleb took hold of Daniel's shoulder. "I swear it. But you will live to see your children grown. Do not doubt that."

Daniel gave him a weak smile. "None of us knows what the day will bring. I will trust in the Lord."

Both Phanuel and Caleb uttered, "Amen," but Anna stared into the fire, her heart heavy. She had been too young to   remember the wars of Alexander Jannai, and Salome had been able to keep the peace without calling for extra soldiers. Anna doubted the battle would be fought in Jerusalem, but wondered where Aristobulus would make his stand. And what would be the cost for his defiance for the people of Israel. And for her family.

Chapter 35

Six Weeks Later

Sleeping on a cot in the wilderness surrounding Jericho wreaked havoc on Lev's muscles. He stretched his arms over his head to try and loosen the knot in his back then groaned as he shuffled toward the entrance to his tent. The sun barely crested the horizon, the first rays illuminating the hills to the west with a pale gray hue, but the valley still sat in darkness.

The camp lay still around him. Only the sound of gentle snores carried on the breeze. Beneath the peace, Lev sensed a trembling. A stirring. The fate of Israel would be decided within the next few days, perhaps this day, and he wondered if all his planning would come to fruition. He hated that he had so little control over what would happen next. John Hyrcanus II and Aristobulus II would decide the next move.

Ari had mobilized the soldiers garrisoned in the fortresses throughout Israel and sent word to his brother that he planned to march on Jerusalem and take the throne. John marched twenty miles with his army, down the rugged hills of Jerusalem, to the plains outside of Jericho. Ari's army had gathered in the north, but now camped at the base of the eastern mountains. Although almost evenly matched in number, Ari's soldiers were the better trained. The ranks of John's soldiers were fortified with newer men, not seasoned in battle or the discomforts of war. His only real hope was to convince Ari of his legal right to succeed their mother on the throne.

Lev did not hold out much chance of that.

"Master?"

Lev scratched his beard as he turned toward his servant. "Fetch me water and bread."

The man nodded as he stepped back into the tent, returning a moment later with a skin. "Would you like to finish this first? Or wait until I pull fresh water from the spring?"

"Give it to me." The warm liquid eased the dryness in his mouth, but his throat remained parched. He tossed the skin back to his servant. "Bring me cold." As the man turned away, Lev grabbed his arm. "Wait."

"Yes, Master?"

Lev surveyed the camp again. He had one possible move left to keep himself safe from Ari's wrath should John's army fail. "There is a soldier in our army, under the command of Dagan." He pointed toward where Dagan's division slept, some three hundred yards to the west. "Go to Dagan and tell him Lev, scribe of Antipater and John Hyrcanus, wishes to see Daniel, son of Phanuel. He is to mention it to no one else. You will guide this man here. Do you understand?"

"Yes, Master."

"Go, before the rest awaken."

With a nod, the servant scurried through the sleeping men, his feet stirring up small clouds of dust. Lev watched until the man faded into the gray of dawn then went back into his tent.

He folded the blanket from his cot, then straightened the papyrus, maps and ink on the table. He paced to the tent opening. A glance toward the horizon told him others might soon be awake, but the wind blew low clouds from the west. Lev hoped they would come in quickly to cover the sun, perhaps giving him a few more minutes to convince Daniel of his plan before the camp woke.

Lev picked up a stylus, but set it down again. It would be safer to deliver his message orally. Any parchment could be intercepted and interpreted as treason by either side.

He stood again, heart racing almost as fast as his thoughts. So many things could go wrong. But if he did nothing at all, if he allowed things to play out without at least trying to defend his position, he could lose everything. He paced the width of the tent, reviewing all his options, trying to see if he had missed any moves the princes might make.

Another glance outside lifted his spirits. The clouds blocked the sun, extending the coming of dawn by a blessed few minutes. The scattered fires were mostly embers, left burning overnight in an attempt to keep off the night's chill. He spied one fire burning bright, a soldier's shadow bringing the flames back to life but, as it was at the far eastern side of the camp, Lev hoped it would not wake too many others. A quick scan toward Dagan's soldiers showed no movement.

Lev went back in, prioritizing his thoughts as he circled the tent. It seemed to him he had walked miles before his servant finally returned.

"Daniel bar Phanuel is here, my lord."

Lev nodded. "Bring him in, then fetch us fresh water."

Daniel ducked inside the tent as the servant left. His hair lay flat against the right side of his head, while the left stuck out at an odd angle. His eyelids still held the puffiness of a restless night of sleep.

Lev smiled. "I am glad you came."

"When the servant of the king speaks an order to my commander, do I have a choice?"

Lev put his hands on Daniel's shoulders. "Do not think of it as an order. I hope you see this as an opportunity."

Daniel's brows furrowed. "For what?"

Lev guided him over to the table. "Sit." He pushed a half-eaten loaf of bread toward him. "Eat. Listen to my offer."

Daniel remained standing. "I will wait and eat with the others in my division."

"Will you at least sit?"

He paused for a moment, the lines in his face deepening as if he thought hard about what he should do. Finally, he lowered himself to the stool.

Lev chuckled as he sat across from him. "You look like you have many questions."

"How did you know where to find me? Why have you called me here?" A look of fear crossed his face. "Has something happened in Jerusalem? Have you news of my family?"

Lev leaned over to place his hand on Daniel's arm. "I looked for your name among those that had recently enlisted." He gave his friend a gentle squeeze. "And your family is fine. For now."

Daniel pulled away. "For now?"

Lev had considered the many ways he could approach Daniel. He sifted through them again before he spoke. He made his voice measured and calm. "Have you thought about what will happen if Aristobulus takes the throne?"

"Of course."

"What do you foresee?"

Daniel swallowed. "The Sadducees will again have the king's ear. They will demand he return the power Salome gave to the Pharisees in the courts. And they will want retribution for their persecution and exile."

"And what happens to you, my friend, should you survive a battle here in Jericho? Will you be safe in Jerusalem now that you have aligned yourself with Eli, a leading Pharisee and member of the Sanhedrin?"

Daniel clenched his jaw so that his mouth barely moved as he spoke. "Aristobulus must be defeated."

Lev sighed. "But you know, in your heart, he will not be. The retribution you spoke of will come. If you are fortunate, you may only lose your home and money. The streets of Jerusalem could run with rivers of blood from those Aristobulus and the Sadducees kill."

Daniel bristled but Lev continued before he could interrupt. "As much as I, too, want John Hyrcanus to remain king, it simply will not happen at this time." He let his voice rise in passion but not volume. "I have wandered about the camp, listened to the men. The veterans will not fight against Aristobulus's soldiers, men with whom they have fought side-by-side with in previous battles."

"But John is their king."

"Because a woman deemed it so." Lev shook his head. "The army wants someone who understands war and what it means to go to battle. Someone strong."

Daniel's eyes narrowed. "I will not betray John."

Lev folded his hands together. "I do not ask you to."

"Then what do you want?"

"I need two things from you. Errands, if you will. Nothing more." Lev leaned forward. "First, go now, before the camp wakes, to Aristobulus."

"I will not betray—"

"There is no betrayal in simply delivering a message." Lev waved a hand to dismiss any more argument.

Daniel's eyes held his gaze. "If there is no betrayal, why not deliver it yourself?"

Lev smiled. "If I were seen leaving the king's camp, it might cause suspicion. But who would notice a soldier leaving camp to deliver a message for his king? No one need know you are going to Aristobulus."

"What is your message?"

"Tell him Lev has kept his promise. Aristobulus needs only to call John's soldiers to his side, and they will abandon the king."

Daniel's face reddened. "You promised that monster your help?"

Moments flashed through Lev's mind. The death of Anna's first betrothed. The stolen letters in Damascus. The promise to help Ari get John out of Jerusalem. Everything Lev had planned for the last nine years hung in the balance. "I made a promise only to get us to this moment. So there need be no battle. No blood shed."

"Surely John will still fight with those of us who remain loyal to him?"

"Antipater will convince him otherwise."

"You will allow that foreigner to decide who leads Israel?"

Lev's fist pounded the table. "That brilliant man will save John's life. If he fights now, do not doubt Ari will slaughter him on these plains and set his head on a pike outside the walls of Jerusalem. John must give up the throne for now, if he is to retake it later."

Daniel sat back. "How will he do that? Without an army?"

The side of Lev's mouth curled up in a smile. "Because, Antipater and I have an army waiting for him in Nabatea. King Aretas has already offered John refuge. Once he is under Aretas' protection, the

Nabateans will rally behind him. A well-trained, well-paid army of seasoned soldiers will then storm Aristobulus in Jerusalem."

Daniel's eyes now sparkled with excitement. "You are sure of this?"

Lev nodded. "Antipater foresaw this conflict long ago, and we have been in negotiations with Aretas for years. All you need do is convince Aristobulus I have done as I promised. He need not fight his brother here. Tell him, even if John retreats back to Jerusalem, Antipater will convince him to give up the throne and leave the city. Before winter comes, Aristobulus will be king and John will be gone."

"What else must I do?" Daniel sat up straighter. "You said there was another errand."

Lev paused. "Perhaps I misspoke. Not an errand so much as an opportunity."

Daniel watched him, but did not speak.

Lev picked up a piece of rolled papyrus sealed with wax. "This is a letter to your commanding officer, releasing you from service to the army so that you can serve Antipater."

His friend looked as if he walked past a dung pile. "I will not serve a Gentile. I cannot."

"Then serve me, instead. You would be working under me."

"You do not serve the Lord's purposes—"

"How do you know? Throughout the Torah there are stories of how Adonai used foreigners to serve him. Cyrus the Great. Nebuchadnezzar. Perhaps he uses Antipater for his purpose as well. If you truly believe John Hyrcanus should be king, then know that Antipater is the only man who can make that happen."

Daniel's face took on a sickly yellow color. With the back of his hand he wiped off the beads of sweat along his brow. "I do not know . . . what is right?"

Lev held the scroll out to him. "If not for John Hyrcanus, then for your family, you must agree."

"Why?" Daniel lifted his head. His voice tinged with anger. "What will you do?"

"Me? Nothing. But you said yourself, Aristobulus will let the Sadducees have their way in Jerusalem. The Pharisees' time is over. Your master, and those who serve him, will be imprisoned, if you are lucky. Exiled or hung more likely." Again, he waved the papyrus in front of his friend. "If you work in my household, I can make sure you and your family come with us when we escape to Nabatea. You will be out of Jerusalem and whatever retribution the Sadducees bring."

Daniel's face mirrored his thoughts. Lev could read the confusion, contemplation, and worry before Daniel spoke again. "What of my father?"

"Phanuel may come, too. Of course."

"Malachi will never allow it."

Lev snorted. "I leave my father to face judgement in Jerusalem."

Daniel's eyes widened. "You cannot be serious."

Lev lifted his chin. "My father decided long ago to put his needs above his family's. I will let him suffer the consequences of that choice now."

His friend studied him, as if trying to peer into Lev's soul and decipher all of his thoughts. "Why do you choose me? After all that has come between us?"

A warmth filled Lev's spirit. A lightness that only came when he thought of Daniel. "Because, you are the only true friend I have. I could not bear the thought of a man like Aristobulus causing your death. Not when I have it within my power to save you."

A smile spread slowly over Daniel's lips. "Perhaps Adonai is not done with you, after all. Perhaps this is His way of bringing you back to His path."

Lev barked a laugh. "If that thought allows you to take my offer, than dream on, my friend." He extended the papyrus one last time. "If you agree to serve me, take this to Dagan, then deliver my message to Aristobulus. If not, I will say goodbye to you now and we will never see each other again."

Daniel closed his eyes and muttered a prayer. Lev held his breath, his lungs beginning to burn before his friend finally looked up. "I'll accept your offer on one condition."

"What is that?"

Daniel grinned, a smile reminiscent of their younger days together. "You will not make me call you Master."

Lev thrust the scroll into Daniel's hand. "Agreed, my friend. Agreed."

Before the sun reached its zenith, Aristobulus called for a summit between himself and John Hyrcanus, along with their counselors. Lev sat on a horse next to Antipater. John's army stood in wait behind them. All eyes watched the brothers ride out to meet each other on the plains outside of Jericho. The wind from the west blew steadily, whipping the standards of each army to attention. It did little to lessen the heat emanating from the dry ground. It seemed nature abhorred the coming violence as much as Lev did, and so did her best to quell the rising tension before it exploded by using the heat to leech the energy from the soldiers. They had stirred little during the morning until now. The armies did not know the outcome of the battle as the kings met on the field.

But Lev did.

Daniel had delivered Lev's message to Aristobulus and returned with the prince's answer. "He says he will call the soldiers of Jerusalem to him before he leads a charge. If they come, and John surrenders, he will not kill the king here in Jericho." Daniel had paused a moment, as if getting the courage to continue. "The prince says, if his brother does not leave Jerusalem and the throne by the Feast of Trumpets in three months' time, he will kill John, and all who serve him."

A sharp laugh from Aristobulus broke Lev from his thoughts. The brothers stood fifty yards away, but the wind easily carried Ari's strong voice. At first, no words could be deciphered, but the mocking tone was evident.

John Hyrcanus slumped back from his brother's verbal attack, but then he pulled himself up in his saddle and answered back, "I have ruled Israel by our mother's side for the last three years. She, Queen Salome Alexandra, declared that I would succeed her on the throne. You are a traitor to the rightful king of Israel!"

Ari laughed again, as if he had no cares. As if the fate of Israel did not stand on the outcome of this meeting. The soldiers behind Lev began to grumble. Several commanders called out orders to "Hold! Stand firm!"

Ari pulled on his mount's reins so that the horse stepped backward. Then, with a kick of his heels, he spurred the animal forward, galloping past the king so he now rode in front of John's army. His hair had grown longer, but he still kept his beard shorter than his brother's. While John's purple tunic with gold border announced his claim to the throne, Ari chose to look like a military leader. Leather straps laced around his legs and protected his shins. A leather breastplate covered his chest. Only with his cape, which was a deep indigo color, did he reflect his desire to rule.

"My fellow soldiers," Aristobulus called out to the army of Jerusalem. "Let us not fight as enemies when we have stood together on many occasions as friends!" The wind carried his voice. "Show my brother, this weak, untrained, undisciplined fool, who a real soldier follows! Come to me, my friends! Come join your brother soldiers. We need not fight each other. We need only show my brother that you have no desire to fight for such a feeble king. Follow me! And we will make Israel the greatest nation the world has ever known!"

Behind him, Lev sensed the restlessness of the army transform into a powerful sea of rebellion. Almost as one, the seasoned veterans roared their approval of Aristobulus's call. They surged forward, abandoning their ranks, leaving the novices behind. The new recruits drew their swords in a valiant attempt to stop the betrayal, but they were taken down like rabbits in a lion's mouth. Ari laughed with pleasure as the elite of his brother's army defected to serve him while John Hyrcanus watched with eyes wide with horror at the slaughter.

Lev followed as Antipater rode to John's side. "My lord, you must retreat. Your soldiers have betrayed you."

John shook his head. "Some remain loyal. They fight for me."

Antipater grabbed the reins of the king's horse. "They fight each other, my lord. When your brother unleashes his men, they will seek you out and kill you. Come."

John shook his head. "No. The Lord will surely fight for me."

"Surely He does not want this bloodshed between brothers. Go back to Jerusalem while you still have the crown." He paused to survey the plains. "You cannot negotiate if you are dead."

John's face reddened. His cheeks trembled as his army betrayed him. Before the soldiers could reach him, he galloped away from the camp. The soldiers roared in anger and heaved forward as if they would chase him down on foot.

"Hold, Brothers!" Aristobulus commanded. "Hold fast! We have no need to shed any more blood today! The king knows he has lost. The throne is mine! We will march to Jerusalem and take it without force, so that all will see, though I am strong, I choose to be merciful."

The soldiers shouted their approval. A thunderous sound that vibrated within Lev's chest as he followed John and Antipater toward Jerusalem. He knew he must act quickly if he, and his family, were going to survive more than a few months of Aristobulus's rule.

Chapter 36

Three Weeks Later

Lev scrutinized the ledger one more time. Monies had been poured into his father-in-law's estate so he could oversee the maintaining of Lev's property while they lived in Petra.

Benjamin refused to go "into exile" again, as he called it, choosing to remain in Jerusalem even under Aristobulus's rule. "I am too old for him to bother with. I am content to live alone and read my scrolls. I will make no trouble for the new king."

It eased Lev's mind to know Sarai's father would take care of their finances in Jerusalem. Benjamin would ensure his daughter's future stayed intact.

The next column in the ledger showed the money Lev would use to establish a household in Nabatea. Sarai and the children would have to make do with a smaller home and fewer servants, but at least they would be far from Aristobulus's reach.

The numbers in another column represented the money paid out for provisions for the journey. Although most of these would be bought by John Hyrcanus, Lev had given a substantial amount to Daniel, so his friend could find shelter for his family along the way.

The real money came not from John, but from Antipater. The Idumaean had been reluctant to add another scribe to his own payroll, until Lev convinced him Daniel would be a useful courier and spy once they reached Nabatea. He did not tell Daniel of the arrangement. His friend would balk at accepting any wage from Antipater, whom he saw as a Gentile. Antipater's generosity however, ended with paying Daniel's small salary. Any provision for Daniel's travel expenses must come out of Lev's pocket.

He sat back from the ledger, content. The plans he and Antipater had worked on for years were finally coming to fruition. It would take another year or two before John could recapture the throne, but Lev had no doubt it would happen. He was grateful to have learned patience from Antipater. He was no longer impulsive, as when he had wasted a small fortune to buy Nasrin. He had learned the value of stepping away from a problem to examine it from all sides.

His fingers tapped against the table as he thought of the Nasrin. The whore had been a mistake. One of the few choices he regretted in his life. Befriending Daniel was not been one of them. They may not share the same faith anymore but he knew, beyond a doubt, Daniel would never betray him.

Lev roamed his study, packing the last of the scrolls, ink, and papyrus. He could have had one of his servants do the work, but he found solace in doing the preparations himself. He wiped ink off his stylus, then carefully wrapped it in cloth to protect the tip.

Had he remembered the scroll Antipater requested? He glanced at the open chest on the table. Yes, it lay with the rest. He recognized it by the purple ribbon. Had Shem remembered to find Tirzah's doll? Sarai had sent a messenger from Jericho, where they waited for him. His daughter had left the treasured toy under her bed, not understanding she would not be returning home in the evening. He would make sure to check with the servant before he left Jerusalem.

Lev looked up as Shem's voice echoed down the hall, "The master has forbid you to enter!"

"I am his father, damn you!" Malachi's voice stormed closer. "I will not tolerate this disrespect."

Lev smiled. Although his skin tingled with apprehension at the coming encounter, his chest warmed with it. He had long dreamed of this day. "Let him in, Shem. I will see him."

A series of grunts and footsteps sounded before Malachi appeared in the doorway. He had gained more weight in the two years since their last encounter. A sizeable double chin now rolled down his neck. He took a moment to survey the room, taking in the crates of packed scrolls. "So it is true, what I heard."

"What was that?"

Malachi stepped in the room. "You are leaving Jerusalem."

Lev nodded.

His father trailed a finger along one of the now empty shelves. "When were you going to tell your mother and me?" He rubbed his fingers together to free them of the imagined dirt he had collected.

"I informed Mother last week." Malachi's face paled and Lev felt his own warm with satisfaction. "I see she neglected to mention I offered to take her with us to Petra."

His father sputtered, unable to form words.

Lev leaned against the long wooden table in the center of the room. "I told you this day would come, and so it has."

"You would leave us?" Malachi's white cheeks reddened. "Your mother and I? You would leave us to suffer under Aristobulus?"

"I planned only to leave you. But Mother would not come without you. Do not worry. My spies will tell me when she becomes a widow. I will see that she is well taken care of."

"You . . . you . . ."

Lev smiled at his father's obvious distress. "You should be proud. I learned to be just like you."

"You are nothing like me!" Malachi's red cheeks quaked. Sweat glistened along his forehead.

"You taught me to hold on to an unreasonable hatred. I watched you with Phanuel." Lev shook his head. "I never understood how one could hold so much hate inside, until you denied me Anna." He stood face-to-face with his father. "The night you told me to choose between Anna and my work with Antipater. Did you feel this triumphant?"

"Lev, I must speak with you—" Daniel froze in the threshold.

Malachi turned, hatred pouring from his eyes. "What is he doing here?"

Lev could not believe his good luck. That the son of his father's enemy would appear at this exact moment so he could revel in the final blow to Malachi's ego. "Daniel works for me now. He, and his family, will be coming with me."

Malachi's fist went to his chest, grasping at the neck of his tunic as if he could not breathe. "Phanuel?"

"Is coming, too."

His father made a wheezing sound as he stumbled back. Daniel reached out to support him, but Malachi knocked his hand away. "Damn you! Damn you all!" He lurched out into the hallway and disappeared from view.

Lev clapped his hands together. "That was even more gratifying than I dreamed it would be."

"Go to him. Offer to help him escape."

Lev emphasized his answer with slow, methodical shakes of his head. "Even if your god demanded it of me, I would offer that man nothing but my disdain."

Daniel's eyes widened. His mouth opened, but he did not speak.

Lev put a hand on his friend's shoulder to usher him further into the study. "You came here for something. What was it?"

Daniel pulled away but still remained quiet.

"I will not debate this with you." Lev swept his arm toward the boxes. "As you can see, I have things I need to settle here. If you will not talk, leave."

"I-I must know. Before I say anything more. What are your feelings toward my sister?"

Lev felt the familiar pain that rose in his gut whenever he thought of Anna. Regret. Anger. Sadness.

"You love her still?"

"Why ask this now?"

Daniel shifted his weight. "What of her husband?"

Lev's stomach churned. "What of him?"

"What do you think of him?"

"I prefer not to think of your sister with such a man. She deserved a better husband."

Daniel clasped his hands together. "But if I assured you that she loved him? That she is happy with him?"

"What matter is it to me?"

"If they came with us to Petra, would you leave them be? Or would you try and remove him from Anna?"

Lev growled. He did not want to admit the thought had occurred to him in the past. "Of course not." He shook off Daniel's concerns with a wave of his hand. "Besides, he is so old he will probably die soon anyway."

Daniel's brows, which had been furrowed, softened. "She loves Caleb. Even if she is widowed, she will never take another husband."

Bile churned in Lev's stomach. Burning acid he struggled not to vomit. If he had only defied his father all those years ago, he might have known such devotion.

He feigned interest in a scroll that lay on top of one of the crates. "What reason would they have to flee Jerusalem?"

"My father worries how the new king will rule. He fears we will not return to Jerusalem, and he is loath to leave her here."

Lev unrolled the scroll. "A tailor and a seamstress matter little to Aristobulus. And you can tell Phanuel that he will return to the city within two years. Three at the most. When Antipater has restored John Hyrcanus to the throne."

"Can I have your assurance? You will keep away from Anna, if I can convince them to come to Petra?"

Lev tried to focus on the parchment in his hands, but he did not see the words. "If they can pay their own way, it matters not to me whether they come."

Anna sat on the rooftop of her brother's house while below, Tova settled her children down to bed. A swath of stars illuminated the early summer sky, and she pulled a shawl tightly around her shoulders. Although the air had been warm that afternoon, the temperature had cooled some with sunset.

"Praise to you again, Adonai," she whispered her thanks. "For Daniel's safe return from Jericho."

She had not heard much about the battle, or lack thereof, between Aristobulus and John Hyrcanus. Since finishing Queen Salome's burial shroud, she spent most of her days inside her house. Caleb brought her little news from the palace along with tunics to sew for the priests. She did not even hear the gossip from the well, as Ruth was the one to daily fetch the water.

Voices rose from the men below, and Anna walked over to the stairwell, hoping to hear some of the conversation.

Instead, Tova appeared, carrying her baby across her body in a sling. "Let's stay up here a moment longer."

Anna moved back. "You could not get little Mary to sleep?"

"She wants to be with me always." Tova groaned as she sat along the roof's edge.

Anna struggled to balance her weight as she sat down next to her friend. "So, dear sister, what is it my brother and husband argue about?"

"They are probably discussing the battle." Tova's gaze shifted to her daughter's face. "I am sure it is nothing important."

Anna's skin prickled, but there was no breeze. "You know something. What is it?"

Her friend remained silent.

"We have never kept secrets before. What are you hiding?" Anna waited, knowing her friend could never stand silence for long. Gentle laughter carried across from the rooftop next door where a small family had gathered. Insects chirped ancient melodies to each other. Anna wrapped her arms across her chest, trying to quell her nervousness. "Please tell me what is wrong."

Tova glanced over at her, then quickly turned her focus back to her child. She let out a deep sigh. "Daniel has accepted a new position. One that requires us to move away."

"Leave Jerusalem?" Anna pressed her palm against the stone, trying to balance herself as the world seemed to spin around her. "Where will you go?"

Tova swallowed. "Petra."

"So far?" Anna's voice came out strangled. "But why?"

"I cannot believe my own ears." Caleb's voice exploded from below. "You cannot be serious."

Anna shivered at his outburst. Full of anger she had never before heard. She could not make out Daniel's muffled voice, but could clearly hear Caleb's reply: "Why would you choose to work for Lev?"

Anna could not comprehend how a discussion of Daniel's new job could lead to Lev. Again, Caleb's voice rose up. "You have aligned yourself with that . . . that . . . ."

"He is my employer. I do not have to agree with him on his past choices. Only those he makes now."

"Lev broke faith with you. With your sister."

Anna pushed herself up. "Daniel is working for Lev?"

"Please do not be upset." Tova reached out to grab Anna's arm.

The ground still rocked under her feet. The world shifted into a kind of dream. A nightmare. "Does Lev still work for Antipater?"

"And John Hyrcanus." Tova stood. "Lev has sworn he will help John reclaim the throne."

Anna ignored Tova's cries and hurried to the stairs. Her heart pounded as she made her way down into the house. Her father sat on a stool next to the table. Caleb stood by the courtyard door, his back to the room.

Daniel stood at the far end. "Brother, hear me out. It is the only way to assure my family's safety in the coming war."

Caleb turned around as his hands sliced at the air. "What war? John Hyrcanus returned with his tail between his legs. He practically threw the crown at his brother."

"Anna," Daniel caught sight of her at the bottom of the stairs. "You should go back to the roof."

Caleb pointed at her, his face crimson. "If you knew what that swine did to her . . . you would never consider this folly."

Anna froze, her mind racing to the past. Caleb had been present the night Lev and Aristobulus humiliated her so many years ago, but she had never told her family. Even now, the thought of her father knowing their abuse caused her chest to tighten. She had grown so much, but that memory made her feel small and insignificant. Although she stayed silent, she pleaded with her husband to keep her shame secret.

Daniel glanced between them, as if trying to decipher the unspoken tension. "What are you saying?"

She forced herself to remember her courage. "It is of no importance, Brother. Something that happened long ago which made it clear Lev was not the man I should marry."

Tova stepped down from the stairs and came to Anna's side. A quiet tension filled the room as they all waited to see what Caleb would say.

"There will be no war," Caleb said softly. "Aristobulus is king. All that remains is to install him as the High Priest."

"And what will happen to us under this madman's rule?" Daniel walked over to Phanuel. "I have been a scribe for one of the leading Pharisees in the Sanhedrin. A man who voted to remove several leading Sadducees from their positions. They will return and demand Aristobulus seek revenge." He put his hands on Phanuel's shoulders. "My father is a Pharisee. One who has supported John Hyrcanus. No doubt he will be seen as an enemy as well."

Caleb's breathing slowed, but his fists stayed clenched at his sides. "Then leave Jerusalem, if you must. But do not align yourself with a man like Lev."

"He has been misguided in the past. Too full of ambition. But perhaps my father and I can turn his heart back to God." Daniel took a step toward Caleb. "You could, too, if you came with us to Petra."

Anna lowered her head. Leaving Jerusalem would mean leaving her work. But should Caleb demand they stay, would she ever see her family again?

"There is more, Brother." Daniel explained Antipater's plan to return with the Nabatean army and help John retake the throne. "Lev assures me that it will be done."

"Lev is a pig." Caleb spat. "No better than the Gentile master he serves."

Although Phanuel's voice was quiet, its passion filled the room. "Do not forget the great prophet Daniel, for whom my own son is named, served a Gentile king. A brutal king. Some would say a madman, too."

Anna gazed at her father. The years had aged him, yet beneath his gray hair and weathered skin, she could still the see the man whose strong arms had comforted her when she was afraid. She could not imagine him living away from Jerusalem. Away from the Temple.

"I have prayed to Adonai for His guidance and I believe we are to go to Petra." Phanuel pushed himself from the table. "Do not be so quick to dismiss this course of action, Caleb. Pray about it. Seek God's will."

Daniel nodded. "We must leave soon to travel with Lev's family and to find a place for ourselves in Nabatea."

"I will pray," Caleb promised. "But it would take the voice of God Himself for me to trust Lev."

Phanuel clapped his hands together as he caught Anna's gaze. "If that is what it will take to allow my new grandchild to go with us, then that is what I will pray for."

The baby kicked hard in Anna's stomach. She caught her breath then chuckled. "I think he knows you are speaking about him, Father."

"Ha!" Phanuel laughed. "So you know it is to be a boy? How can you be so sure?"

She sat down on a stool then reached behind her to take Caleb's arm. She pulled him to her side. "I know it is. My husband has been so faithful these past two years. Never once did he show me any anger at my failure to carry a child."

"You are blessing enough for me, my love." Caleb lifted her hand and kissed it.

Anna rested her head against him. "God will give you a son to carry on your family name, I know it."

Tova's eyes glistened in the lamp light. "I hope to be at your side when your time arrives. But more, I hope we can raise our children together, as we dreamed of in our youth."

The baby kicked again. "God will tell us what we are to do."

They left a short time later and walked in silence, Anna wrapped snugly under Caleb's arm. Many people enjoyed the pleasant night. Young men laughed as they strolled together. Several older men gathered in a circle, their voices rising and falling with emotion as they debated the fate of Israel under the rule of Aristobulus. Conversations drifted down from rooftops as families told stories or prayed together after their evening meals. Caleb let out a heavy sigh as he opened the door to their home. "I will pray, but I do not believe Adonai wants you anywhere near Lev."

She lowered her gaze from his intense stare.

He dropped his head so their foreheads touched. "Say what you want to say, my love. I will listen and not be angry."

Anna's stomach churned and her baby gave another solid kick. "You know I have no feelings for Lev. That I love you alone."

"I know. But if he was capable of such cruelty in the past, what would he be capable of now?"

She struggled not to show her fear. "What of Aristobulus? What is he capable of? Now that he is king?"

Caleb drew her into an embrace. "What will he have to do with you, if Lev is gone to Petra? I believe Aristobulus will forget all about his earlier threats once he rules in Jerusalem. Besides . . . ." He rested his chin on the top of her head. "You need not return to the palace after our child is born. You would be safe."

Safe. Anna breathed the word in deeply, but wondered if it was true.

Chapter 37

One Week Later

Anna sat on the floor of her house, her back pressed against the wall as sunlight streamed in through the west-facing window and dust floated in lazy circles, undisturbed by any breeze. Tova sat next to her, their shoulders touching. Little Mary nursed hungrily at Tova's breast while Isaac slept with his head on Anna's thigh.

She stroked his fine brown curls, as untamed as his mother's. "He is so handsome."

Tova chuckled, "Handsome, yes. But stubborn and wild. I do not know where his temper comes from."

Anna wrapped a soft lock of her nephew's hair around her finger. What would her own son be like?

As if reading her mind, Tova asked, "You are still certain you carry a boy?"

"Certain? No. But I hope so. For Caleb's sake."

"Your husband is not like most men. He will be pleased with a daughter as well as a son."

"True." Anna continued to stroke her nephew's hair. "But a son would carry on his family line. His brother has had only girls. It is for myself also, that I pray for a son." Her fingers rested in the nest of curls. "Caleb is older than most fathers . . . and now that my own family is leaving for another country . . . I will need a son to care for me . . . if I am widowed."

"Oh, Anna," Tova gasped. "You must not think of such things. Daniel has promised we will return in a year. Two at the most. You will have many years yet with Caleb. And many more children as well."

Anna forced back tears. "You are right. I am just tired. This baby keeps me up all night. Kicking and punching to free himself."

Tova leaned her head against Anna's shoulder. "And what if he is a girl? Then what?"

Anna looked down at her rounded stomach, remembering how her mother had sat patiently and taught her how to hold a needle and work the thread into intricate patterns. "I will teach her to embroider and weave. Imagine if Adonai grants her my skill along with Caleb's patience and eye for color? She would be able to demand any price for her garments!"

Memories of all she had learned from Miriam continued to come to her mind. Even when sickness plagued her, Miriam spoke her mind to Phanuel, wanting Anna to be able to serve at the palace. "I would teach my daughter to be strong. And all about the Law as well. She would be as wise as Abigail and Deborah. A woman who knows how to calm a man's anger. And how to lead men into to battle against the Lord's enemies."

"Like you," Tova whispered.

"I am not that wise." Anna shivered as she thought of her dealings with Aristobulus. "Or that brave."

"You are the smartest woman I know. You have achieved so much more than any woman I know."

Anna nudged her friend with her shoulder. "But remember, all those years ago, you were the one who told me to go to the palace. You said that Adonai might have a special purpose for me there."

"And He did. He sent you to Egypt to learn so many things. And do not forget all the girls you have taught."

Although Anna knew she would still be able to work as a seamstress, she doubted she would return to teaching. She could always sew at home, but a toddler would be too much of a distraction at the school. A warm glow of satisfaction pushed away the sadness of that thought. She missed her discussions with the students from the school but knew they had learned not only God's Law from her, but that their lives had worth. They could achieve whatever they dreamed of, as she had.

She caught her breath as the muscles across her abdomen tightened. "You are certain it is normal for my stomach to harden like a rock?"

Tova lifted Mary to her shoulder. "For several weeks. It is God's plan."

"His plan to what? Worry us to death?"

Tova laughed. "No, to make us ready to endure any pain to have our bodies back again. I am sorry to say, it only gets worse until the babe comes."

Anna shifted her weight, trying to ease the ache now radiating to her back. After another minute she found she could breathe again. Mary fussed and squawked as Tova patted her. Isaac woke with a start then he, too, began to cry.

"It is like this every afternoon at this time. The two of them start a choir of suffering, as if I have not seen to their needs all day." Tova stood and bounced Mary while Isaac sat up and tugged on her robe.

"Come here, Isaac." Anna pulled him away. "I will give you a crust off the bread Ruth left for us. But only if you stop crying."

Tears as big as raindrops fell from the boy's lashes, but his shrieks softened into hiccups. He let Anna guide him to the table and give him the promised treat. He stuffed the bread into his mouth then ran back to his mother.

"We should go." Tova patted her son's head. "Daniel and Phanuel will be coming home soon."

"Will they be angry you came to visit me again?"

"Of course not." Tova took Isaac by the hand. "They know I want to spend every moment I can with you before we leave."

Anna leaned against the table as another cramp tightened across her stomach. It took a moment before she could catch her breath. "Has Daniel decided when you will go?"

"It will be soon. That is all I know." Tova paused in the doorway. "Should I fetch Ruth to sit with you?"

"Caleb will be home any moment. I will be fine."

"Until tomorrow, then."

Once the door shut, Anna shuffled to her pallet to lie down again. She had to use the wall to ease herself to the ground. The heady scent of garlic turned her stomach. Ruth had left a stew simmering over the hearth. Although grateful Caleb would have a decent dinner, Anna could not stand the smell. She covered her nose with her arm and hoped she might get some rest before her husband arrived. Sleep had been a rare occurrence the past few weeks. Not only because her swollen stomach kept her from finding a comfortable position, but because her thoughts strayed to Daniel's decision to leave Jerusalem. Would the city still feel like home without her family?

She turned to her side and watched with fascination as the baby rolled within her, stretching and pushing so hard even the fabric of her tunic moved. "I know, little one. I will be so busy with you there will not be time to miss my family."

She let out a gasp as another cramp dug into her abdomen. This time, the ache increased in intensity, and was not just a tightening of her muscles, but a knife-like stabbing. Long and hard. She cried out in agony and in fear. Her forehead beaded with sweat. She pushed herself to her knees and waited for the pain to ease again.

When it did, she tried to get to her feet but found the baby had shifted within her so that she struggled to find her balance. Something was wrong. She knew it. She could not catch her breath. Could barely think.

She crawled to the door, hoping Tova might still be on the street. Her arm trembled as she tried to reach the latch. Too high. She could not reach it without standing. She cried out in frustration, a guttural sound made of no words. Bracing her hands on the door, she pulled herself up and tried again.

A push from the other side made her collapse to the ground, blocking the door from opening.

Caleb's laugh barely reached her ears. "What are you hiding, my love?"

The door pressed against her back.

"Anna? Why will you not let me in?"

Her fingers dug into the earthen floor. She struggled to drag herself far enough away that he could come inside. He would know how to stop this pain. He had to know how to stop it.

The door opened a few inches. "Anna?"

A moment later, her body heaved to the side as he thrust himself into the house. He let out a strangled cry and dropped to his knees. "What do I do, my love? What do I do?" He cradled her head in his lap. "I will get Tamar."

He carried her to the pallet and settled her down on the blankets. "I will be back as soon as I can."

As much as she had prayed for this moment, now that it was upon her, she cried in fear. The intense pain lessened, but not the memory of it. Sweat drenched her forehead and back. She clutched at the blanket covering her. *I am afraid, Lord. Please make the pain stop.*

It came again. Worse still. Anna clawed the floor, her fingers digging grooves into the hard-packed dirt. By the time the pain had passed, she found Caleb back at her side. He held her hand as Tamar scurried about, making preparations.

"You should go, Brother. Go to my house. Or Daniel's."

Anna breathed heavily through her nose, praying the suffering would not return. Perhaps the Lord had heard and stopped her travail? But no. It came again. Hard. Fast. Excruciating.

"You are doing well." Tamar wiped Anna's forehead with a cool cloth.

"Caleb?" Anna cried out again.

"I am here."

Anna squeezed Caleb's hand. "I have loved you. Remember that."

His face paled. "And you will continue to love me. And our child."

Waves of pain swept through Anna's body. She arched her back to try and ease it. "Love our child. Promise me." Her fingernails dug into the flesh of his palm. "Promise to love it no matter what happens."

"Hush, now." Tamar pushed Caleb away. "Every woman thinks she will die, but you will not. I forbid it." She turned to her brother. "The midwife should be here soon. Go. Fetch Tova to help us."

From somewhere outside herself, Anna heard voices. Knew her husband had left her. Gripped with fear, she screamed his name. "Caleb!"

Instead of her husband, an old woman lowered herself down. Dark brown eyes studied Anna. "My name is Miriam. I am here to help."

Anna smiled weakly. "That was my mother's name."

The woman's thin white hair and deep-set wrinkles gave Anna confidence. "You have helped many children into the world."

"I will help your child as well." Miriam placed the birthing stool in the far corner of the room, near the fire but away from the table. She hung a thick rope over a beam in the ceiling as Tamar helped Anna over.

"There's time yet," she said to Tamar. "Bring dirt from the courtyard to catch the blood." Miriam removed Anna's sash. "Arms up, girl. You do not want to ruin your dress."

Miriam continued to order Tamar as Anna undressed down to her linen tunic then lowered herself to the stool. She cried out as pain struck her again.

"Grab onto the rope," Miriam barked. "Hold on tight."

Rational thought left Anna's mind as the babe within her fought to be born. She screamed as her body pulled and stretched her muscles so that she thought they would snap.

Time had no meaning. She wove in and out of consciousness, knowing only pain and her fear. She thought Tova held her hand. Pressed a cool cloth to her brow. Had Tamar tried to give her a sip of wine? Maybe, or maybe she imagined her thirst had been quenched for a moment. When she could no longer feel her muscles, no longer acknowledge the agony, when she was convinced she had died, at that moment, a shout of celebration reached her ears.

"It is a boy!" Miriam cried.

Tamar whispered in her ear, "You have given Caleb a son. Just as you said."

Miriam helped Anna slip down to the floor, then placed the child on Anna's belly. It took every last bit of energy for her to stay awake. She glanced down.

Love consumed her the instant she stared into his light brown eyes. A fierce fire within her chest. She would protect him with everything she had. She would see that he was fed and clothed and loved until the day she died. She stroked his cheek, still red from crying and dried his tears. She kissed the black hair that crowned his head, marveling at its silky softness. She counted his toes and his fingers. Ten of each, perfectly formed. And two beautiful ears. "Praise Adonai."

Anna cried out when Tamar took him from her, but her sister-in-law scolded, "He must be cleaned and swaddled."

Once the midwife had finished tending to her, she left Anna in the care of her family. The women fussed about, sweeping up the dirt and blood. Tova placed a shawl over Anna's shoulders to keep her warm. Tamar sent a neighbor to fetch her brother then gave the baby back to his mother.

Caleb arrived a few minutes later, his face pale and worn. He hesitated in the doorway, staring down at Anna. "You are well?"

"I am wonderful."

Tova pulled him inside. "It is over now. You may come in."

He glanced toward his sister "She will live?"

"It was a difficult birth, but yes, she will live."

Anna sighed contentedly. "Come, meet your son."

He limped to the pallet, gazing at the bundle resting in her arms. "A boy?"

Anna nodded.

"My son," he whispered with reverence.

"Do not look at him like he will break," Tamar scolded. "Pick him up."

A look of terror flashed across Caleb's face.

Anna chuckled as his sister picked up the baby and held him toward her brother. "Here, you old fool."

Caleb took the child as if his son was made of fragile pottery. His tears flowed freely. "My heart is so full."

Anna's lips curled into a smile even as exhaustion took her body and she fell into a deep sleep.

The following week brought the full force of late summer weather. The air hung heavy and stagnant over Jerusalem. The heat struck Lev's skin like a brazier as soon as he stepped out onto the street.

Daniel slapped Lev's back. "Do not look so . . ."

"So what?" Since Lev did not know how he felt, he hoped someone else could discern his mood and explain it to him.

"I cannot tell. But you do not seem well."

"I was up all night with Antipater, finalizing the plans for our journey. It is not yet noon and the heat is already unbearable. You've insisted I come with you to your nephew's *bris*, and yet I know I will not be welcome." Lev cast a sideways glance at Daniel. "Have I forgotten anything?"

His friend grinned as they strode down the road. "The most important thing. You must convince Caleb to come to Nabatea with us."

"And yet, you have not told me how I am to do that. There is no love between us. Why would he listen to me if he will not take your advice? Or Phanuel's?"

"He holds something against you." Daniel put up his hand to stop Lev from commenting. "I do not want to know what it is. All I know is that for my father's sake, I want you to try and work it out."

Lev's conscience prickled at the reminder of how he had treated Anna in the past, *was it eight years ago?* He had watched Aristobulus torment the poor girl. The prince, now king, had touched her. Kissed her cheeks. Who knows what else might he have done if the tailor had not arrived?

Lev wiped his brow. Ari had only toyed with Anna for his benefit. To prove there was nothing Lev wanted that Ari could not have. Would he be any different now that he was king? Or would his hunger for power only increase?

Lev and Daniel passed through the gate separating the upper city and Temple Mount from the more crowded city below. Dust rose from the street, drying his throat and making his nose itch. He dreaded the trip they would soon take to Petra. The desert would be even more unforgiving than Jerusalem.

That thought stirred another, and he turned to Daniel. "Where is your family?"

"My wife and children went to Anna's house early today to help prepare."

"And are they ready for the journey? You'll want to make sure you have enough water."

"We are prepared."

"Antipater wants to leave at first light tomorrow."

Daniel grinned. "I am grateful that Adonai caused the delay so I could see this day."

"I do not think your god had anything to do with it." Lev scratched his nose, hoping to stifle a sneeze. "Antipater needed to make arrangements in Jericho in order to throw Aristobulus from our true destination."

"Believe that if you must," Daniel wiped the sweat from his forehead. "I think it was meant that I see my nephew become one of God's chosen people."

Turning down another street, they stopped in front of one of the modest, limestone houses. A low murmur of conversation could be heard from inside, punctuated by laughter.

Daniel paused with his palm on the dark wooden door. "Are you ready, my friend?"

Lev swallowed before nodding. He could not remember the last time he had felt so ill at ease. He had more wealth and position than anyone within this house and yet his heart pounded. Why?

"I hope you do not mind," Daniel announced to those inside as he pushed open the door. "I brought someone who wished to give his blessing to your son."

The general conversation continued as they stepped inside, but the smile dissolved from Caleb's face. Phanuel moved over and whispered something in his ear. The tailor thrust his shoulders back, straightening to his full height. The heated anger in his eyes softened.

"Welcome, Brother." He hesitated only a moment before continuing, "And Lev. Welcome to my home."

Lev bowed his head. A quick glance proved that although not poor, Caleb and Anna did not live in the splendor he did. And yet the home was spacious enough to hold Caleb's extended family. Uncles, aunts and cousins bustled about the room. The furnishings were simple, but well-made. A glimpse through the back doorway proved they had a courtyard where a number of younger children played. The house had something his did not: a sense of family and peace.

"Come." Daniel's hand gently guided Lev inside. "You are welcome."

A sudden movement in the corner of the room caught Lev's eye and Lev's heart sped. Anna stood. The same glow that had illuminated Sarai's face at the birth of their daughters now radiated from her.

"It is good to see you again," she swayed with the baby in her arms. "How is your family? Daniel never brings us news."

"Well, thank you." He coughed to clear the emotion from his throat. "My wife and children are in Jericho now . . . waiting for me."

"And your mother? How is she?"

"Fine." He let out another cough. The truth was he had not seen Judith since refusing to take Malachi to Petra.

Anna seemed to sense his discomfort. She glanced toward her husband. "Now that Daniel has arrived, I think we can begin."

Several women called to the children outside and soon Lev stood shoulder to shoulder with Anna's family. Parents held onto their babies and toddlers as they circled the table at the center of the room. A thick piece of cloth had been laid down to protect the wood and comfort the baby. Younger children hovered as close as they could, although some of the older boys turned away as Caleb placed his son on the cloth.

The child whimpered when his father unswaddled him. Phanuel stepped forward and unwrapped a leather bundle to reveal a small knife. A nervous chuckle rose from the men.

Phanuel lifted the knife over the baby. "What is the child's name?"

Caleb put his arm around Anna. "His name will be Reuben, in honor of my father."

"Then, in fulfillment of the commandment the Lord gave to our forefather Abraham, and again to the prophet Moses, I welcome you, Reuben, into God's chosen people."

Reuben let out a shriek as Phanuel performed the circumcision. Anna turned her face into Caleb's shoulder. The men congratulated him while the children ran back outside. Reuben's wound was covered with a healing salve, and he was swaddled and given to his mother to comfort him.

Within another few minutes the cloth had been removed and the table cleaned. The women laid out trays of bread and cheese, and bowls of dates, raisins, and almonds. Daniel helped Caleb pass out cups of wine.

Lev stood in the shadows, watching the celebration with a tinge of jealousy. He had yet to have a son. Even though his faith had grown lax over the last few years, he would relish the opportunity to observe this tradition. Whether or not circumcision marked him as a child of God, it made a son part of these people. A part of Israel. And Lev longed to leave a legacy behind in this place.

"Wine?"

Lev blinked up at Caleb. "What?"

"Would you like wine?" He held out a small wooden cup.

"Thank you." Lev took the drink. "Caleb, is there somewhere we could talk?"

The older man lifted a brow. "Why?"

Lev shifted his weight under the Caleb's stare. "Please. Before I leave Jerusalem, there are things I wish to put right."

Caleb studied him for a moment more before tilting his head toward the courtyard. Lev followed him outside and up a narrow flight of stairs. Caleb shooed several boys down to the courtyard so they could have some privacy. Sitting down on the low wall surrounding the roof, he scratched his graying beard but did not speak.

Lev paced across the rooftop. Daniel had brought him here for one reason, but everything about this day reminded him of the past. Something spoke to his heart, urging him to make amends.

"Stop." Caleb held out his arm. "You know I have never liked you, so you need not worry you will offend me."

Surprised, Lev barked out a laugh. "That is true." He sat down, several feet away from the tailor, but he looked out over the rooftop, his mind seeing the past. "I thought, when I was younger, that power was the one thing that would make me happy. Power to change the government, rule over people. Have their respect."

Caleb snorted softly as he took a drink.

"I have learned, too late perhaps, that power is not enough. Not that I want a life without it, mind you, but maybe other things can give satisfaction. Happiness, even." He turned to face Caleb. "You have found a peace I will probably never know. And you have given it to Anna." He took a moment to swallow. "She deserves that. Especially after the way I treated her. The way I allowed Aristobulus to treat her."

Lev leaned in. "I want you to know that I would not hurt her again. Or let any other harm her. She will always have my protection, if I am able to give it, as payment for the pain I caused her in the past."

Caleb's forehead creased, but he remained silent.

"Once John leaves with us for Petra, I have no idea what Aristobulus will do. Now that he is king, he may be content just to reign over Israel. Or seek battles on foreign lands." He stood. "You and Anna are probably safe here. Especially once I leave. But I know her father wants her to come to Petra with us. With him. If you wanted to join us there, be assured, I would not seek to do you, or her, any harm."

Caleb's brows furrowed, his gaze so intent it seemed as if he wished to look inside Lev's mind to glean the truth. Lev did not flinch. He meant his promise.

A child's giggle floated up from the courtyard. The hot sun beat down on him, but still Lev did not move.

"The heat is brutal. Let us go back inside." Caleb thrust out his hand.

Lev took it and helped him up. Face-to-face, they stood.

"I have no desire to leave Jerusalem . . . but I know Anna will miss her family." Caleb squeezed Lev's hand. "I will consider all you have said. Perhaps we will join you in Petra."

Lev pressed his hand on Caleb's neck. "Either way, I promise to protect her family as best I can. Please let her know."

"I will."

EPILOGUE

32 Days Later

Reuben squalled and squirmed within the sling across Anna's chest, clearly not satisfied with her attempt to calm him with her free hand. He was hungry, but being jostled among the hundreds of other people swarming the outer courtyard of the temple meant Anna could not feed him just yet.

"Not much longer." Caleb limped forward, struggling to hold a tiny lamb in his arms. The animal bleated as its large black eyes darted around in fear.

Dread filled Anna's heart as they approached the priests waiting at the base of the brazen altar. They would take the lamb Caleb carried, and the turtledove from the cage she held, and deliver them up the stone ramp to be sacrificed to Adonai. Their bodies placed on the fire and burned. It was the price paid to purify her after childbirth. To cleanse her from any sin.

She understood that God was holy, and as such demanded that those who desired to follow Him make themselves free of sin. Only blood could cover their transgressions. But the smell of the burning sacrifice rising from the altar turned her stomach. There would never be enough blood to cover her sins. Every day she fought to trust

Adonai. She worried about the health of her son and husband, of her family in Petra, about her country.

And yet, the God of the Hebrews was merciful. The sacrifices He required were limited to those of cleansing, thanksgiving and atonement, unlike the gods of the nations that surrounded   Israel. They wanted offerings for rains and good harvests. For fertility. For success in battle. Their gods wanted more than grains and animals. They often required parents to sacrifice their children. To put their own sons into the fires. Or give their daughters to the temples to be used in sexual rites to   satisfy their gods. She leaned down to kiss Reuben. Adonai was merciful. He found such practices abhorrent. But still, sin must be atoned for and she would obey. With Caleb at her side, she stepped before the white-robed priests.

Caleb presented the lamb to a priest with dark black hair. "These are the sacrifices required for my wife's purification."

The bearded man eyed Anna and Reuben. "Was he your firstborn?"

"Yes." Caleb wrapped his arm around Anna's shoulders. "And we have paid the five shekels to redeem him."

The priest gave a token nod before he and his partner turned up the ramp and another pair of priests came to take their place. Caleb led Anna away from the altar. "It is done."

Although no breeze moved the still summer air, Anna felt a wind caress her skin. She paused in the courtyard. From this spot on the Temple Mount, she could see Jerusalem spread out below, its people moving through its streets like ants in the sand. She wondered if this was how Adonai saw them from His throne in heaven, but knew, as the air again chilled her, that He longed for more of a relationship with His people. More than their sacrifices, He desired their very hearts. Tears welled in her eyes as the certainty of God's love for her . . . for her family . . . filled her spirit. That the God of the universe wanted to know her and be known by her. She stopped walking, wanting instead to sing out in praise and thanksgiving.

"Are you unwell?"

Anna wiped her eyes. "Can you not feel Him?" She laughed as she stood on her toes to kiss her husband. "Oh Caleb, I feel Adonai all around me here. I never want to leave this place."

Caleb brushed a strand of hair from her forehead. "You have made your decision, then?"

She glanced once again over the city. She thought of all that had happened since that day, long ago, when she walked up the hill to the Hasmonean palace to serve Queen Salome Alexandra. Her skill with the needle had been used to create the ephod worn by the High Priest. Never could she have believed she would have such an honor. Then she had been allowed to learn and study God's Law and even teach it to other young women. Something else she never would have thought possible. And now she had a husband who loved her and their son to raise. If they travelled to Petra, what would Reuben's life be like, growing up in a foreign land, so far away from the Temple? The words from one of the songs of the sons of Korah came to her mind: *"Better a day in Your courts than a thousand anywhere else. I would rather be at the door of the house of my God than to live in the tents of wicked people."*

She lifted her eyes to Caleb's. "Our place is here. In the sight of the temple. In Jerusalem." She took one more look over her shoulder at the temple then grasped her husband's hand. "Let us bring our son home."

ACKNOWLEDGMENTS

Although the initial stories are usually written alone in front of computer with copious amounts of chocolate, coffee and tea readily available; they are fine-tuned and nurtured with the help of many wonderful people. I'd like to acknowledge a few of them here.

Margaret Lukas, author of the soon to be released, *River People*, I can't thank you enough for reading this novel through, chapter-by-chapter and line-by-line; tweaking the story and encouraging me along the way. And then you blessed me by reading it one more time, with your trusty #2 in hand, to help me polish and shine the final manuscript. You are an awesome woman and I am so thankful to have you in my life.

Anna Weir, story and copyeditor extraordinaire. Thank you for helping me flesh out these characters to make them more dynamic and interesting; for your encouraging texts as you read the first manuscript, and your ability to talk me back to reality when I fell into the abyss of author self-loathing. I adore you!

Michael Weir, for your talent in creating the maps and your patience in dealing with me, I am so grateful!

Kayleen Meckle, Beta reader and proofreading master! You totally rock! Thanks for rechecking it all and finding those commas and ellipses that slipped through the cracks. I am so blessed to call you friend!

To Shannon Smiley and the awesome authors at Coffee Klatch: Rhonda, Patti and Ann. Thanks for helping me work through a lot of the first draft. Your input helped me to focus my ideas and plough through to the finish line.

Then there are those who I know I can call for prayers and encouragement. Their support means the world to me. Rebecca H., Janet & Steve P., Cher P., Laura H., Linda D., Linda & Bryan H., Kerri S., Sonja V., Cathy T. and Julie S.

Saving the best for last, I thank all my family, but especially John. Sorry ladies, God gave me the perfect husband. Thank you for your patience when I'm ranting; or when you're trying to talk to me and

I'm staring into space thinking about the next plot twist. Thank you for working so hard so I can live my dream of writing. I love you tons.

All praise and honor belong to God the Father, Son and Holy Spirit. He has done great things for me!

ABOUT THE AUTHOR

Kim and her husband live in Nebraska with three fur babies, lots of books, and a variety of stringed instruments that only her husband knows how to play.

Visit Kim's website to learn about upcoming performances and signings: www.kimstokely.com
Follow her on Facebook
www.facebook.com/kimstokelyauthor
or on Twitter: @KStokelyWrites

Check out these books by the author on Amazon
Biblical Fiction
Woman of Flames
Contemporary Christian Fiction
Winter Trees
Spring Rains
Young Adult
A Shattered Moon
Where Shadows Lie

Made in the USA
Las Vegas, NV
17 January 2022

41627900R00222